Praise for

GONE TONIGHT

"Jaw-dropping. Layered. Triumphant."   —*The New York Times*

"Sarah Pekkanen's startling, breathtaking tale of a mother and daughter will plunge you into a plot layered by lies and trauma but still infused with love. Through deft writing and thoughtful character development, she's created a fast-paced thriller in *Gone Tonight,* daring to ask deep questions about love versus fear and control versus protection."

—*Reader's Digest*

"*Gone Tonight* is all the best of Pekkanen's last few collaborations. . . . Easily the best thriller I've read all year. In an oversaturated market where even the best authors seem to be phoning it in, Pekkanen is here to remind her readers that thrills can still be shocking, twists can still be unexpected, and reading can still keep you up way past your bedtime. This is the thriller I've been waiting for."   —*Bookreporter*

"Filled with buried secrets and jaw-dropping deception, Sarah Pekkanen's *Gone Tonight* is a page-turning thriller about a mother-daughter you won't soon forget. What would make a teenage girl vanish into the night and live a life on the run for two decades? Read *Gone Tonight.* It's a wild ride."

—Harlan Coben, #1 *New York Times* bestselling author

"*Gone Tonight* is an intense, harrowing story about long-buried secrets and the trauma they inflict. The mother-daughter relationship is both thrilling and heartbreaking, with characters you won't soon forget. Captivating from beginning to end."

—Samantha Downing, international bestselling author of *My Lovely Wife*

"With prose that cuts like a knife—full of both emotion and twists—
Gone Tonight proves why Sarah Pekkanen is one of the finest thriller
writers working today. Just when you think Pekkanen couldn't
possibly outdo herself, she delivers with what will undoubtedly be
crowned one of the year's best novels. Fresh, inventive, and with a
gut punch you won't see coming, *Gone Tonight* is this decade's *Gone
Girl*. Believe the hype." —Alex Finlay, author of *The Night Shift*

"Readers are in for a wild cat-and-mouse game as this tight duo
(boundaries, what are they?) faces terrible odds when Catherine delves
into her mother's past and Ruth hides the pair from an encroaching
threat. Overall, it's an eye-opening look at how 'our minds . . . talk
us out of things we don't want to know.'" —*First Clue*

"Prepare to stay up until the wee hours devouring *Gone Tonight* by
Sarah Pekkanen." —*Real Simple*

"Your heart will race until the final page." —*Westport Magazine*

GONE TONIGHT

SARAH PEKKANEN

ST. MARTIN'S GRIFFIN
NEW YORK

Published in the United States by St. Martin's Griffin,
an imprint of St. Martin's Publishing Group

GONE TONIGHT. Copyright © 2023 by Sarah Pekkanen. All rights reserved.
Printed in the United States of America. For information, address St. Martin's
Publishing Group, 120 Broadway, New York, NY 10271.

www.stmartins.com

Designed by Steven Seighman

The Library of Congress has cataloged the hardcover edition as follows:

Names: Pekkanen, Sarah, author.
Title: Gone tonight / Sarah Pekkanen.
Description: First Edition. | New York : St. Martin's Press, 2023.
Identifiers: LCCN 2022058086 | ISBN 9781250283979 (hardcover) |
    ISBN 9781250289179 (international, sold outside the U.S., subject to rights
    availability) | ISBN 9781250283986 (ebook)
Classification: LCC PS3616.E358 G66 2023 | DDC 813/.6—dc23/eng/20221208
LC record available at https://lccn.loc.gov/2022058086

ISBN 978-1-250-33616-3 (trade paperback)

Our books may be purchased in bulk for promotional, educational, or
business use. Please contact your local bookseller or the Macmillan Corporate and
Premium Sales Department at 1-800-221-7945, extension 5442, or by email at
MacmillanSpecialMarkets@macmillan.com.

First St. Martin's Griffin Edition: 2024

10 9 8 7 6 5 4 3 2 1

For Margaret Riley King

Find a part of yourself hidden in the twilight.

—Fennel Hudson

ACT
ONE

CHAPTER ONE

CATHERINE

My mother walks through our tiny living room, her eyes sweeping over our old blue couch and coffee table, before she briefly disappears into the galley kitchen.

"I just had them in my hand." Her voice is tinged with something darker than frustration as she begins another lap.

I should jump up from the couch and help her look for her keys so she isn't late for her shift at the diner.

But I don't want her to notice I've begun to tremble.

"Check your purse again?" I suggest.

She frowns and reaches into her shoulder bag.

My mother is organized. Methodical. Detail oriented. Her purse isn't a jumble of crumpled receipts and loose change. Sunglasses in a case, small bills facing the same way in her wallet, cherry ChapStick and hand lotion zipped into her makeup bag—it's containers within a container.

She shakes her head and walks to the raincoat hanging on a hook by our front door, searching through its pockets.

Maybe her father is absentminded. Perhaps her cousins grew distracted when they approached middle age. It could be something our relatives tease each other about when they gather for holidays.

I don't know. I've never met them.

When I had to create a family tree in the fourth grade, I was able to fill out only two names on a single branch. My mother's and mine.

My stomach tightens as I watch her bend down and check around the mat by the front door where we put our shoes. She looks even thinner than usual in her uniform of black slacks and matching polo shirt with a red waitressing apron tied around her waist.

She hasn't been able to eat for the past few days. At night I hear her restless movements through the thin wall that separates our bedrooms.

Tomorrow she has an appointment with a neurologist.

Everyone loses their keys, I tell myself. The neurologist will have a simple explanation for my mother's strange new symptoms. He'll prescribe medication and advise her to get more sleep and send us on our way.

But my pulse is accelerating.

I force myself to inhale slow, even breaths. The worst thing I can do is fall apart. My nursing classes taught me about the power the body wields over the mind, and vice versa. Right now I need a steady physiology to assert control.

It works. After a minute, I feel able to stand. I walk over to my mom, thinking hard, then dip my hand into the big pocket of her apron.

Relief crashes over her face as I pull out her keys.

"I'm losing my mi-"

"Could you grab another box if the diner has any?"

I don't really need more moving boxes. I just couldn't bear to hear her complete that sentence.

I already have a half-dozen cardboard boxes I pulled out of a recycling bin behind a liquor store. I don't own many possessions and I pack quickly. I've had plenty of practice.

When families move out of houses in the suburbs, neighbors throw going-away parties and the moms get weepy after a few glasses of wine.

People like us, we move on to a new apartment and no one notices.

I'd planned to sort through my books and clothes this morning. But until we see the specialist, everything feels suspended in midair.

My mom rises to her tiptoes to kiss my cheek, then opens the door and is gone, her footsteps growing fainter.

I wait for silence. Then I reach for my phone and call up the list I'm secretly compiling.

Misplacing her keys might not be another piece of evidence. Still, I document it along with today's date.

Then my eyes roam over the dozen other incidents I've recorded of all the things my mother has lost—a twenty-dollar bill, her train of thought, her way home from the drugstore that's just a mile away.

All happened within the past month.

CHAPTER TWO

RUTH

I'm good at disappearing. We women do it all the time.

We vanish in the eyes of men when we hit our forties. We dive into roles like motherhood and our identities slip away. We disappear at the hands of predators. We're conditioned to shrink, to drop weight, to take up less physical space in the world.

"Hi, I'm Ruth, and I'll be your server."

I spoke that line at least twenty times during my shift today. It's a safe bet none of the customers I greeted could repeat my name five seconds later.

That's a good thing. Being inconspicuous suits me.

No one takes notice of me as I walk down the path parallel to the Susquehanna River, watching its surface gently ripple as the current draws it beneath the South Street Bridge. The air feels swollen with moisture and clouds blot the brightness from the day, but I keep on my dark sunglasses.

My feet ache from fetching sunny-side-up platters and club sandwiches and bottomless coffee refills, but I push myself to move faster.

I didn't tell Catherine I was running an errand on the way home. She may worry if I'm late, especially since I set my phone to airplane mode when I left work so she can't see my destination.

I climb the curving, split staircase that leads to the library entrance. I push open the front door and follow my routine: I make sure no one I recognize is nearby, then choose the most secluded computer.

The old wooden chair creaks as I settle into it and use my library card to gain access to the internet.

It would be easier if I could borrow Catherine's MacBook to do my checking—like I used to until I learned about search histories. Who knew computers keep tabs on you even after you shut them down? It's creepy.

Now I don't even use my iPhone to google anyone from my past since Catherine and I share a phone plan and I might unknowingly be leaving electronic bread crumbs.

Catherine thinks I don't miss anyone I left behind. I encourage her to believe this because it means fewer questions. But I ache for my dad and brother. Even if they've washed their hands of me. Even if the thought of me conjures disgust in their minds.

After all these years, it's still hard to breathe as I begin my search.

I look in on my little brother first, connecting with him in the only way I can. Timmy has a Facebook page, but it's set to private so what I can see is limited. His profile picture shows his two-year-old twins. His daughter has a smile that looks like mischief brewing. His son is a near replica of Timmy when he was young, and I wonder if he'll live for baseball and ice cream, too.

I stare at Tim—he must've shed his childhood nickname—wondering how he met his wife and what he tells her about me. If he mentions me at all.

I search for my father next. There's nothing new, just a few grainy photos I've seen countless times, and in those it's hard to make out his face clearly.

Still, I soak him in, trying to conjure the sound of his voice—husky yet tender—when he tucked me in at night, and the way he would rest his cool palm on my forehead when I had a fever as if he could pull the sickness out of me.

What I would give to feel his arms wrap around me one more time and inhale the warm, woodsy scent of the Old Spice he wore.

When I left my parents' house as a teenager with nothing but a few changes of clothes, a little money, and a gold watch, I knew they would be relieved I was gone and would never try to find me.

One thing kept me from collapsing and giving up: the baby growing inside me.

I may no longer be a daughter or a sister, but I am—and will *always* be—a mother.

Catherine and I have each other. We've never needed anyone else.

The final person I check on is my old boyfriend, James Bates.

There's nothing new on James either. He never married, which I have mixed feelings about.

There aren't any recent photos of James, so I've constructed an age progression image in my mind: his sandy-colored hair is close-cropped now, graying at the temples. The lean frame he had at nineteen is thicker, and lines bracket his mouth. All this only adds to his appeal.

Late at night is when I think about James the most. When I can't sleep, even though the time my shift will start is drawing closer. I try to imagine what James is doing at that exact same moment, nearly a hundred miles away.

I always come to the same conclusion: He's lying in bed in the darkness, just like me.

I wonder if he's thinking about me, too.

A heavy crack erupts beside me, the noise exploding through the air. I leap to my feet, twisting toward the sound.

"Sorry." The teenager who dropped a stack of hardback books onto the table next to me shrugs.

"You need to be more careful!" My voice is loud and harsh. Heads swivel in my direction.

I'm no longer invisible.

Which means I need to leave the library as fast as I can.

CHAPTER THREE

CATHERINE

The doctor rises from a chair behind his desk as we enter his office. I'm not sure what I expected, but it isn't this: a small, sterile room with mud-dull carpet and a schoolhouse-style clock hung on the beige wall. But the diplomas displayed on his bookshelf are from good schools, and I've checked him out. He's the best neurologist around.

He walks around his desk, not avoiding our eyes but not smiling either. I can't read a verdict in his expression. He's good at navigating this fraught moment, but then he must have a lot of practice.

"I'm Alan Chen," he introduces himself.

"Nice to meet you," my mother replies. "I'm Ruth Sterling, and this"—she touches my shoulder—"is my daughter, Catherine."

I step forward to shake his hand as his eyes widen in surprise behind his glasses.

Now our roles have shifted and I'm the one who has had practice navigating this uncomfortable moment. Dr. Chen urges us to sit down and offers us water, but all the while I can see him doing the mental math.

My mother has a few silver strands glittering like tinsel in her chocolate-brown hair and slightly crimped skin around her big hazel eyes. She looks her age—forty-two. I look older than my twenty-four years, and I'm told I act it, too. That's probably because smiling isn't a reflex for me the way it's expected to be for young women.

Dr. Chen recovers quicker than most. By the time he is back in his chair, opening the chart on his desk, his expression is inscrutable again.

He jumps right in: "Ruth, can you tell me about some of the symptoms you're experiencing?"

I'm certain that information is already documented in his folder in the pages of paperwork my mother filled out, along with the results of the blood test from her primary physician that ruled out possibilities like a vitamin B12 deficiency and Lyme disease.

"At first it was little things." The material of my mother's slacks rustles as she crosses her legs. "Dumb stuff that happens to everyone. It just started happening more often to me. Like I couldn't remember the word I wanted. Forgot to unplug the iron. That kind of thing."

"And you noticed an increase in these sorts of events how long ago?" Dr. Chen prompts.

The silence stretches out. A red button on the doctor's desk phone begins to flash, but he ignores it. A strange current is humming through the air. It feels electric.

I'm about to break in with the answer—a month ago—when my mom opens her mouth and beats me to it.

"Maybe four months ago." Her voice is almost a whisper.

I suck in a quick breath and whip my head to the side to look at her. Her expression is calm, but her hands are restless. She's toying with the delicate topaz ring she always wears, spinning it in circles around her finger.

Dr. Chen jots a note on one of the papers in his file. "And it's getting worse?"

My mother nods.

I pull my iPhone out of my purse and call up my list.

5/07: Put sunglasses in kitchen drawer.
5/10: Called ice cubes "water squares."
5/12: Forgot what month it was.

Dr. Chen asks my mom a few more questions, then closes his folder. "There are some tests we can run. . . ."

My throat is so tight I have to clear it before I can speak. "Cognitive tests, or do we go straight to brain imaging?"

My mother leans forward and even now—standing alone in the path of what must feel like a great onrushing cement wall—pride fills her voice. "Catherine's going to be a nurse. She just graduated cum laude and she's about to start work at Johns Hopkins Hospital. She's moving to Baltimore in two weeks."

"Congratulations," Dr. Chen tells me. "Hopkins is an impressive place. What's your specialty?"

"Geriatrics. I work part-time at a nursing home." I watch as the irony hits him. He may be the expert in neurology, but when it comes to my mother's presenting symptoms, I'm no novice.

I'm assigned to the Memory Wing, the section of our facility where people with dementia or Alzheimer's or traumatic brain injuries reside. I see symptoms like the ones my mother is describing nearly every single day.

I refuse to assume the worst, though. I know my job could be shaping my fears, and there might be a simple reason for my mother's confusion and memory lapses.

My mom is petite, but there's nothing soft or weak about her.

She's a fighter. Indestructible. She has to be.

We talk with Dr. Chen about various testing options, but my mom resists scheduling a CT scan. I assume it's because of the expense. We've got a bare-bones health care plan, and after the cost of this appointment our savings account will be one car breakdown away from being demolished. Then something happens that makes me feel as if I've plunged into ice water.

My mom stands up and paces between her chair and the wall. My stomach coils tighter with every step. The longer her pacing, the worse the news. It's as pure a formula as a mathematical proof.

My mom paced when I was in the tenth grade, shortly after I began dating my first boyfriend and was enjoying the best school year of my life—right before she announced she'd lost her job, we were being evicted, and we were moving from Lancaster to Harrisburg, Pennsylvania.

She paced at Christmastime, when I was four, and then she told me Santa's workshop had had a fire and I wouldn't be getting any presents.

She paced just before she told me why her conservative, religious family had cut her off, why I'd never met any grandparents or aunts or cousins and never would: She got pregnant in high school, her boyfriend denied I was his, and they threw her away—every single one of them did. But she didn't care because I was worth all of them put together.

The wall clock's needle-thin red hand sweeps in relentless circles. It strikes me as unbearably cruel that, as they sit in his office, Dr. Chen's patients are forced to confront the dwindling of the very thing they desire most.

My mother reaches the wall and turns for another lap.

The swelling pressure closes in on me, and my voice sounds as high and panicky as it did when I was a child and awoke from a nightmare: "Mom!"

She stops pacing. She meets my eyes for the first time since we entered the office.

The news she delivers isn't bad.

It's catastrophic.

"There's one thing I didn't put down on the forms. Maybe I just couldn't deal with having to write the words. . . . My mother and I were estranged, but she passed away right before she turned fifty. An old friend tracked me down years ago to let me know."

This is the first I've heard of *any* of this.

I'm still reeling as my mom continues, "She died from early-onset Alzheimer's."

CHAPTER FOUR

RUTH

It turns out there's yet another way to disappear. Your mind can begin to erase itself.

Catherine is driving us home, one hand gripping the steering wheel, the other tucked in mine. I know the look on her face, the set of her jaw. She's holding back tears.

I'm sorry, baby.

I don't say the words because they will send her over the edge, and I'm just barely keeping it together myself.

So I reach for the radio with my free hand. "Thunder Road"—the best version, the haunting, acoustic one from Brisbane—comes on and I exhale, feeling some of the rigidity leave my body.

"What kind of monster doesn't like Springsteen?" I ask.

Catherine doesn't immediately recite her usual comeback and I hold my breath. Then: "A monster with taste."

I leave it there, not replying with my usual: "I should've given you up for adoption."

A thin line can separate laughter and tears, and I don't want to push her in the wrong direction.

Catherine turns onto the highway, heading toward home, and I give her hand a squeeze, then let go. She needs both on the steering wheel. Catherine drives too fast. What's more, she expects everyone on the road to be as quick and decisive as she is, and she isn't grateful for my helpful tips, even though I've been driving a lot longer.

I'm not one of those mothers who deludes myself her kid is an angel—or who flutters around, gushing that I don't know what I did to deserve a daughter like Catherine.

Of course I deserve her. I've devoted my life to raising her well.

Catherine is a competent cook—probably out of necessity—and she's smarter than me, except for her taste in music.

She's a hard worker. She got that from me.

She's not a shouter. She didn't get that from me.

My daughter is tall and fine-boned and graceful, with delicate features that bely her grit and determination. It's like someone waved a magic wand when she was born, gifting her with her grandmother's thick, wheat-colored hair with the slight widow's peak, her grandfather's golden skin, and her father's blue eyes.

Sometimes when I look at my girl, I'm awed that I created something so beautiful.

And sometimes I wonder how different my life would be if I hadn't.

I lower my window a few inches, closing my eyes as fresh, cool air sweeps across my face.

I expect the whole drive home to be silent because Catherine always gets quiet when she hears bad news. It's her pattern. When I tell her something she doesn't like, she slips away, hiding inside herself. You can be right there in the same car, close enough to smell the sweet traces of the shampoo she used this morning, and have absolutely no idea what's going on in her mind. The worse the news, the longer her silence.

I've asked her to tell me, more than once: *You've got plenty of words, can you use some of them?*

I'm just thinking, Mom!

Funny how you can't get your kid to be quiet sometimes, but when you actually want to hear what's going on, they act like you've barged in on them while they're in the bathroom.

The quiet between us isn't so bad right now, though. It's actually a relief.

This appointment was every bit as horrible as I expected—I don't think I'll ever get over watching Catherine's eyes shatter—but now that it's behind us, I know exactly what I want and don't want.

I'm not going to get a CT scan, or a lumbar puncture, or any of the other tests Dr. Chen and Catherine talked about.

I'm not going to see another expert.

I'm going to keep waitressing at the diner and living in our apartment.

And maybe this seems selfish, or narcissistic, or whatever term is in fashion these days, but what I want more than anything is for Catherine to put off her dream of moving to Baltimore and working at Hopkins.

I need my daughter to stay close to me.

CHAPTER FIVE

CATHERINE

I see my mother every single day, which is to say I don't truly see her at all.

She has always been a touch distracted, but I missed the demarcation line she crossed when she slipped past ordinary forgetfulness into something infinitely darker.

I don't know if I'll ever forgive myself, even though it isn't like she has cancer. Early detection won't make a difference in how this turns out.

The thought is a live wire. I yank my mind away, forcing myself to focus on easing our Bonneville into a tight corner spot in our apartment building's lot.

After we exit our car and push through the heavy side door into the lobby, we discover the elevator is waiting, its arms thrown open to us. It's a minor miracle. With five floors in our building and eight apartments per floor, I usually don't even bother pressing the call button.

As we glide up to the fourth floor, I study my mom, taking her in anew. Trying to see how I could have missed the clues, especially since my job constantly exposes me to tangible evidence of what she will become.

She isn't wearing mismatched shoes or blinking in bewilderment or exhibiting irrational anger, like some of the residents I care for.

If anything, she's too calm. That could be shock.

I catalog the furrow between her brows, her full lips, and the slight sheen to her skin.

"You okay?"

Her question jolts me. I realize the elevator doors have yawned open.

"Sorry." I step onto the diamond-patterned carpet and lead the way down the narrow hall to 406.

When I was a kid, I loved fitting the long nose of a key into a lock. That thrill passed, but our habit stuck. Mom still lets me handle the task.

I wiggle in the metal key and hear the tumblers click, thinking about how she's the only person in the world who knows that bit of my history. She is the co-architect of our existence: I do most of the grocery shopping, she keeps our car filled with gas, and we split the cleaning. She sat beside me on the couch, watching *The Office* reruns and making sure I ate, when my first real love, Ethan, and I broke up last year. Once we slept in our Bonneville for three nights, her in the front seat and me in the back, when a leak from the shower a floor above soaked our apartment and our jerk of a landlord refused to pay for a hotel. Our favorite dinner is something she invented called lasagna pizza, which we make with dough instead of noodles.

How long until I'm the sole memory keeper of our life together?

A sob rises in my throat. It takes everything I have to fight it back.

I set my purse on the narrow hall table as my mother takes off her black flats and puts them on the mat next to her work sneakers.

"I'm going to change." My mom disappears into her bedroom.

I stand there, staring at the empty space she left behind.

Our entire drive home from Dr. Chen's office—it's a sinkhole in my mind. I can't say how many red lights we encountered, or whether any raindrops splattered on the windshield, or if we hit traffic.

How many sinkholes are already swallowing pieces of my mother's brain?

Because I can't think of what to do, I move into our living room and begin to straighten up, refolding the chenille blanket on the back of the couch and collecting my water bottle from the coffee table.

Sometimes our apartment feels cozy. We aren't permitted to paint the walls or use nails to hang pictures, but my mother bought Command strips to affix bright prints—one by Matisse, the others created by me in high school art class. We've cultivated a trio of leafy green plants on the windowsill, and Mom brought in colorful throw pillows from a secondhand store and a big mirror with a whitewashed frame when she was on an HGTV kick.

Other times, this space feels claustrophobic.

More and more lately, I've felt the walls closing in on me.

It's unnaturally quiet in here at 10:20 a.m. on a Tuesday. Most of our neighbors are at work or school, like my mother and I would typically be at this hour on an ordinary day.

I edge closer to her bedroom, listening hard.

I can't hear anything.

If she's crying, her face must be buried in a pillow. I lift my hand to knock, then let my arm drop by my side.

I can't tell her it will be okay. There is no fixing this.

Her door flies open. I take a step back, startled.

My mother stands there in her uniform, her hair swept back in a headband.

"Where are you going?"

"To the bus stop. I still have half a shift left."

Mom moves past me, toward the front door.

"Wait!"

She turns around, avoiding my eyes. "Where did I put my purse?"

A week ago, her words would have been innocuous. Now, they sear me.

"How can you just go to work? We've got to talk—we need to make a plan."

"Honey, there's plenty of time for talking."

"No there isn't! We don't have *time!*" I gasp out the words.

My mother closes her eyes briefly.

"Look, Catherine, I know this is hard. But you need to understand—
I have to keep moving. I can't stop and think or I'm going to lose it,
okay?"

She walks back into her bedroom and retrieves her purse. I follow,
unable to stop the questions spilling from my mouth. "Why didn't
you tell me about your mother?"

"Because she didn't care about us, and I stopped caring about her
a long time ago."

My mom moves to the front door. She leans over to slip on her
right sneaker, pressing her palm against the wall for balance.

"You couldn't even bring up the fact that she *died*?"

"Catherine, don't push me."

I can't put on the brakes. "You've been hiding everything from
me! You told Dr. Chen you've been noticing this for *four months*—
why didn't you say anything? We could have . . ."

My voice trails off.

My mom puts on her other shoe. "Exactly. What could we have
done?"

"There are medicines. . . ."

She shakes her head. "They don't work for everyone. Their effects
wear off and they don't stop the progression of the disease, only some
of the symptoms. There is no cure."

She's reciting things I've told her through the years, facts I've
gleaned from my textbooks and college lectures and evidence I've witnessed firsthand.

She gives me a quick, hard hug. Then she leaves.

I have no idea what to do. I'd expected our routine to shatter.
I was planning to tell my supervisor I had a family emergency and
needed a few days off.

How can my mother be going about her typical day?

My breaths are too quick and shallow, and I know my blood

pressure has risen to a number that would alarm me if I was monitoring a patient.

I look around the apartment. It's still as a tomb.

A vision of the future invades my imagination: Post-it notes stuck everywhere to remind my mother to make sure the stove is turned off and to flush the toilet. A dead bolt on the door with the lock constantly engaged. My mother splayed on the couch, her hair lank and dirty, refusing to shower.

Or worse. It could get so much worse.

It *will* get so much worse.

The walls of the apartment fly toward me.

I run to the front door and grab my purse. I burst into the hallway and head for the stairs, skimming my hand along the metal railing as I spin down four flights and push through the lobby door. Bright sunlight hits my eyes and I squint, searching my surroundings until I spot my mother halfway down the block.

"Wait!" I yell, running toward her.

My mother turns. As I draw closer, I think I see tears shimmering in her eyes, and it pulls me up short. My mother never cries.

I can't leave her here at the bus stop, all alone. I want to be with her as much as I can, for as long as I can. Even if it's just the two of us riding in our old Bonneville with the radio blaring, like we've done thousands of times before.

I know she doesn't want any more questions. So I promise myself this will be the last one I'll ask her right now: "Want a ride to work?"

CHAPTER SIX

RUTH

Tucked in the back of my locker at work is a green spiral notebook. It's so old the once-crisp page edges have turned to velvet.

There's a blank box on the cover for your name.

Instead of mine, I inscribed *For Catherine Sterling.*

I've made sure to put the notebook in a place someone will eventually discover should something happen to me.

The only problem is every page is blank.

I've been carrying it around ever since I left home, intending to write down my story for so long. But every time I try to begin, my pen refuses to move across the page.

Now I have no choice. I only hope I haven't waited too long.

Sam's is fairly quiet at the moment. The electric register beeps as the cashier rings up a man's check, then the bell over the door sounds as he exits. In the kitchen, the cooks are slicing tomatoes and stacking individual leaves of lettuce like playing cards in silver bins, preparing for the next wave of customers.

My shift is over and I've closed out all my checks, but I'm not ready to leave yet.

Catherine is still at work. She told me she's planning to let her supervisor know she isn't going to move to Baltimore, after all. She'll stay by my side. I didn't even have to ask.

I sense eyes on me and look up to catch a guy perched on one of the counter stools staring. Then I feel dampness on my cheeks. I wipe away my tears and whisper, "Allergies."

I turn and walk down the hallway adjacent to the kitchen, heading past the restrooms into the small employee room. The combination to my locker is Catherine's birthday. I take out my notebook and sit down heavily on the lone chair in the room.

I've thought through what I need to tell my daughter countless times. I've replayed certain scenes from my past so often it feels as if I've imprinted them in the grooves of my mind. The details I need to share with Catherine are as familiar to me as if they unspooled just last week instead of nearly twenty-five years ago.

Once I unclip a pen from my apron pocket and finally begin to write, it's as if I've stored the words in a memory cloud, and they're now gently raining down on me. It makes the task I've dreaded for so long as simple as taking dictation.

I've been thinking about where to begin, and I guess I'll start with the day I met your . . . See, I'm already getting tripped up. He isn't your dad. A father changes your diapers and teaches you how to ride a bike and reads you stories. He never did any of that.

James. His name is James.

I met him on the hottest day of the year, in August, right at the start of my junior year of high school.

The main thing you need to know about my high school is that, socially, it was run by a Queen Bee named Brittany. Her mom was the ringleader of the school moms.

Apple from the tree and all that.

Brittany and I were friends up until the ninth grade, when I grew boobs first and got asked to the Homecoming dance before she did. Brittany didn't authorize that turn of events, and next thing I knew, I was uninvited to a group sleepover at her house.

I didn't mind all that much. Being Brittany's friend was a lot of work. There were rules involved. You had to love Madonna but not Whitney Houston. You were required to sit at a certain table in the lunchroom. For some reason, wearing a sweatshirt inside out was a thing. Brittany did it one day, then the next day so did half the girls in our class.

Brittany might have been content to quietly exile me, but there was one other thing she didn't authorize.

I was the best dancer on our school's Poms squad.

You know how some people can hear a song once and play it back on the piano? It's like that with me and dancing. I don't even have to think about it—my body just mimics whatever moves I see and comes up with new ones all its own.

Did I mention Brittany was on the team, too? So were her wannabes. And of course, Brittany's mom, Mrs. Davis, was the parent liaison for the team. Mrs. Davis organized the fundraiser that paid for our trip to the state competitions and sat in the bleachers with her gaggle of hangers-on at practices and games.

On that blistering hot mid-August afternoon, there wasn't a single cloud in the sky, and sweat molded my T-shirt to my body. We had to try out every year, even if we were on the team the previous year. Because our coach was out on maternity leave, Mr. Franklin, who was our school's music teacher, had been pressured by the principal to take over as interim coach. Mr. Franklin didn't seem very happy about it.

Over the summer I'd taught myself to do an aerial—that's a no-handed cartwheel—so I threw one into my performance. A few girls clapped when I did it, then stopped abruptly, like they'd suddenly remembered they weren't supposed to.

When tryouts ended, I went to grab my water bottle from where I'd tossed it onto the edge of the bright-green AstroTurf. My mouth was so dry it hurt.

I uncapped the bottle and tilted my head back, desperate to gulp down some water.

Nothing came out.

I dropped my empty bottle and walked back to rejoin the others, a smile on my face.

I never gave Brittany the satisfaction of a reaction. I didn't do it whenever I found the word slut *written in lipstick across my locker, or got summoned to the principal's office because he'd been told I was selling weed, or overheard Brittany stage-whispering to her lunch table that my mother was a drunk.*

That one was true, by the way. My mom—your grandma—was usually half in the bag by the time she finished her lunchtime wine, which is why I got a used car for my sixteenth birthday. My dad didn't want her driving me or my little brother Timmy when she was under the influence, so I was the one who took us to and from school.

More on that later, though.

I stood at the edge of the pack of girls who'd tried out, dizzy from dehydration in the blazing sun, listening as Coach read out the names of everyone who'd made the varsity team. It was just a formality. Five girls who'd been on the team last year had graduated, and the best five girls from JV were going to move up. There were twelve spots on the varsity squad in total.

Still, every time Coach called out a name, Brittany squealed and threw her arms around the girl like they'd both won the lottery.

Coach went through eight names alphabetically, then got to the spot where my name should have been.

He called someone else's instead.

I took a half step forward, a protest rising in my throat.

Don't react, *my mind commanded.*

It held me back a millisecond before I spoke up. I decided to wait, to let this play out. If Brittany and Mrs. Davis and Coach Franklin—who I was already convinced was half in love with Mrs. Davis, judging from the way he kept sneaking looks at her—were trying to have me cut from the team, I'd find a way to fight it. I couldn't do it here, not when I was so outnumbered.

Coach called the tenth name. The girl next to me turned to stare. I couldn't tell if she was innocent or in on it. She was one of the JV girls who was moving up, which meant Brittany probably hadn't gotten her claws into her yet, but just to be safe, I avoided her eyes and kept my face expressionless.

We were nearing the end of the alphabet.

Coach announced the eleventh name. It wasn't mine.

Brittany's squeal seemed even louder this time.

My cheeks were burning in a way that had nothing to do with the sun. I could hear a few girls murmuring, but I wasn't close enough to understand what they were saying.

Coach banged his clipboard against his leg and told us that anyone who didn't make varsity would be considered for JV. He said if we were on the varsity squad we should stay put. Everyone else could leave.

The girls who didn't make it gathered their things and began to climb the bleachers. Brittany tilted back her neck and sipped from her water bottle, watching me from beneath her eyelashes.

I wasn't going to retreat. If Coach was trying to cut me from the team, he'd have to tell me to go.

One of the girls who was moving up from JV—a seemingly nice one who wore glasses and smiled a lot—spoke up, telling Coach he'd only called eleven names.

Coach tried to look surprised. He was a terrible actor.

He made a production out of checking his clipboard and running his finger down the list. Then he called the names of all twelve teammates— and this time my name was in its rightful spot.

For whatever the reason—maybe Brittany or Mrs. Davis had whispered lies about me to him—Coach was messing with me to let me know the score. He was my enemy, too.

Still, when I tell you my whole body unclenched, it was an understatement. I wasn't a great student—my mild case of dyslexia can make reading a chore—and I couldn't carry a tune or play an instrument or soar over track hurdles. Plus, I'm pretty sure being on Poms was the only thing that kept me from being swept to the bottom rung of the social ladder at school.

And it kept me out of the house every afternoon, which meant less time around my mother, who went from giddy to morose to mean in the hours between lunch and dinner.

Coach announced we were all going to Pizza Piazzo, where Brittany's mom was going to generously treat us all to dinner. Mrs. Davis stood up and waved like she was Miss America when he said that. Then Coach said we'd be electing this year's captain at dinner.

I wanted nothing more than to dash into school and greedily gulp from the water fountain, but I grabbed my backpack and headed to the parking lot along with everyone else. Brittany's mom announced she had room for six girls in her giant SUV that I'm pretty sure fit eight and Coach said he could fit five in his pickup truck.

Magic number eleven again.

I'm sure Brittany thought she'd screwed me over, but I didn't care that I was odd man out. Timmy was waiting for me, and I needed to drop him at home before I went to the restaurant.

I pulled the keys to my Dodge Dart out of the inside pocket of my backpack, then slid behind the steering wheel and drove the half mile to the middle school. Timmy was on the front steps, reading a comic book. When I tooted the horn, he looked up with a big smile.

Timmy never complained about anything. He may have looked more like our mom, but on the inside, he was our dad.

I asked how school was as he climbed into the back seat. Apparently, he'd gotten extra Tater Tots at lunch, which was all it took to make his day a win.

Then I told him I had to go out, but that Dad would be home soon. His smile disappeared. I quickly said he could just hang out in the backyard until Dad got home. He told me he would, and that he'd be really quiet.

I glanced at Timmy's profile in the rearview mirror. In that moment, he seemed to be suspended between a kid who liked cartoons and someone much older.

By the time we got to the house, my dad's car was in the driveway. I breathed out in relief and waved to Timmy as he slipped in through the kitchen door.

I wanted to skip going for pizza, especially since I'd arrive twenty minutes late, but I'd already learned the hard way that any sign of retreat only emboldened Brittany.

When I walked into Pizza Piazzo, the girls were seated around a long rectangular table, with Coach Franklin at the head and Mrs. Davis to his right. Brittany was reigning over it all from a spot in the middle. I heard her laugh spill out as I approached. Brittany had piled her backpack and purse on the lone unoccupied chair. I knew she wouldn't move them until I'd asked at least twice.

I was hot and tired and still so thirsty. The last thing I wanted to do was sit there for the next hour, faking a smile and enduring whatever else Brittany and her mom had cooked up for me. I felt my tears rise and I quickly blinked them away.

Then I heard a low, soft voice asking if he could help me.

I turned and found myself looking at a guy who was a little older than me—maybe nineteen. He was a dead ringer for James Spader, who'd starred in this movie called Sex, Lies, and Videotape I'd seen a while back. Most of the girls in my class were obsessed with James Van Der Beek or Leonardo DiCaprio, but James Spader was my current crush.

My mouth was probably hanging open as I stared at him.

He moved closer, repeating himself a little more loudly as he asked again if he could help me.

And I swear, Catherine, he did.

That night, the waiter with kind eyes did more than help me. He saved me.

CHAPTER SEVEN

CATHERINE

Sunrise Senior Living is divided into three levels: Daily Assisted, Extended Care, and the Memory Wing.

When I began working here right after I graduated high school, I was assigned to the Daily Assisted tier. The people in Daily Assisted are mostly independent, though some use walkers or require help getting dressed. They read large-print books, FaceTime their grandkids, and invite each other over for cocktail hour. A few of them still drive. For those who didn't, I often used the Sunrise van to take them to a nearby strip mall so they could shop or enjoy lunch.

As I gained experience and drew closer to earning my nursing degree, I moved to the next tier, Extended Care. These residents need help transferring in and out of bed and with medication oversight. Most have lost spouses and friends. Their worlds are inexorably shrinking. When I entered their rooms, their faces lit up, even if I was just coming to bring them a glass of Ensure or close their curtains.

I began working in the Memory Wing a year ago.

It's a different universe.

After I drop my mother at Sam's and arrive at Sunrise, I reach for the bag in the back seat that contains two pairs of socks, a set of stackable measuring cups with one missing, a baby doll dressed in a onesie, and—the treasure from my latest Goodwill run—piano compositions by Claude Debussy on an unscratched CD.

I walk through the lobby and greet the front-desk attendant as I flash my ID and use the computer to sign in, then head to the main floor employees' locker room to slip on the extra scrubs I keep there. The locker room is empty, but in the attached kitchen there's a loaf of banana bread on the countertop next to a card with the words *Thank You* written in blue shimmery script.

I've only had coffee today—my stomach was too twisted before my mother's appointment to accept solid food—so even though I'm not hungry, I walk over and peel back the Saran Wrap and cut a slice. If I'm going to work today, I'll need the energy.

The card is from the daughter of a resident, expressing her appreciation for our help in caring for her father.

I finish the banana bread without really tasting it and rewrap the loaf. As I'm trying to think of what to do next, my supervisor, Tin, comes through the door, holding an ice pack to her forehead.

"Oh my gosh, are you okay?"

"Just a little bump." She removes the ice. "How does it look?"

I scan her smooth skin. "No swelling I can see. What happened?"

Tin walks to the cupboard and finds the bottle of Advil, then swallows two. "Mr. Baxter rushed the door and I got a knock in the head trying to block him. I'm fine, I just need to sit down for a few. I'm going to take my lunch break now."

I pour Tin a glass of water as she settles into one of the chairs encircling the round table in the middle of the room. Part of the reason I came in early today was to see Tin, but I don't want to rush her.

Before I can say anything, though, she frowns. "Aren't you supposed to be in later?"

"Yeah . . . I was actually hoping to catch you."

Tin must pick up something in my voice. Her face softens and she gestures for me to sit down.

"I know I gave notice . . . but I was hoping I could withdraw it. I need to keep working here a while longer."

Tin knows all about my plan to move to Baltimore. When I began applying for jobs five months ago, I asked her for a reference. The offer came in quickly from Hopkins, and Tin was the second person I told, after my mother. Tin knows how excited I was to move to a fresh city and construct a whole new life, one that's all my own.

Mercifully, Tin doesn't bring any of that up. She tucks a stray lock of shiny black hair behind one ear. "How long would you want to stay?"

"A couple years. Now that I'm done with school, I was hoping to pick up a few extra shifts."

My mother may not be ready to plan, but one of us needs to. I have to work as much as I can now, because as her memory recedes and her needs grow, I'll have to scale my hours back. And without my mother's waitress income, money will be tighter than ever.

I have no idea how long she'll be able to continue at Sam's. He'll cut her some slack because she's a dependable, hard worker, but he's not going to be happy when she forgets to put in breakfast orders and undercharges customers for things she forgot to add to the bill.

We need to stockpile cash while we can.

"Catherine, are you okay? This is all so sudden. Aren't you supposed to move in, like, ten days?"

I refocus on her. "Yeah. It's my mom . . . she's sick."

"Oh, no. I'm so sorry."

Tin seems to be waiting for me to continue, but I can't.

She finally breaks the silence. "Stay on as long as you want. I can put you on a full-time schedule next month."

I nod vigorously, hoping the gesture conveys my gratitude, then I stand up and busy myself wiping a few crumbs off the counter.

Tin is one of the people I admire most in the world. She's only five years older than me, but she has two master's degrees and oversees a staff of a dozen nurses, assistants, and volunteers. She has a lot of experience comforting distraught family members and works with some of the most challenging cases on the Memory Wing.

If I were going to talk to anyone about what my mother is facing, it would be Tin.

But I can't, not yet.

Not just because the realization of what my mother will become is so overwhelming that I can only comprehend it in short bursts, as if the knowledge is a series of waves breaking over my head and temporarily snuffing out my ability to see, to hear, to breathe.

It's also this: Tin will immediately recognize, as I have, that the incurable disease that has slithered through at least one generation of my family—from my grandmother to my mother—may be waiting to strike again.

It may come for me next.

Tin said I could start work early today, another gesture of kindness. I gather my bag of Goodwill odds and ends and head for the elevator.

The destination for most visitors and employees is floors one through four.

Mine is floor five.

The elevator will take anyone there, but once you step off, you can only walk a few feet before encountering a locked door with a keypad code. Above it, a camera's unblinking red eye signifies it's watching your every move.

From the outside, the entrance is clearly visible, with the door's silver knob contrasting with its beige color.

On the inside, it's a different story.

I input my code and wait for the lock to click. When it does, I push open the door a few inches, check to make sure no one is on the other side, then walk through and wait for it to shut behind me.

I'm in the Memory Wing.

The wall on this side of the door is painted blue and the door is the exact same hue, knob and hinges and all. No signs indicate this is the way out. There's a keypad, but it's also painted blue to blend in. The numbers on the pad are scrambled, with a few positioned upside down.

Unless you know exactly where the exit is and have the ability to decipher a confusing code, it's virtually impossible to leave this floor. Which is the whole point.

As I move down the short hallway, I hear a woman calling, "Can someone please get me a bellboy?"

I round the corner and encounter Mrs. Dennison, who wears a gold-and-black brocade jacket over stretchy slacks. Her silver hair is in an elegant bob—Mrs. Dennison's daughter takes her to the salon every two weeks—and her expression brightens when she sees me.

"Miss, can you help me? I'm looking for a bellboy to carry down our luggage."

"Oh, checkout isn't for another hour," I tell her. "I'll take you to our executive waiting room, where you can enjoy a complimentary beverage and some snacks."

"That sounds lovely, dear. I just need to go tell my husband."

Mrs. Dennison allows me to hold her elbow and guide her toward the community room.

"Frank and I had a lovely stay here. Absolutely lovely."

"I'm glad to hear it."

Mrs. Dennison twists her head around. "Where did Frank go?"

When she first arrived on the Memory Wing and asked for her husband, I watched Mrs. Dennison's daughter explain Frank had died six months earlier. From the pained but weary expression on her daughter's face, it was clearly a conversation they'd had many times before.

But Mrs. Dennison was essentially hearing it for the first time.

"Oh no!" Her face crumpled. "What happened to my Frank?"

She was completely distraught, moaning and shaking. Then her short-term memory wiped itself clean, and it began again: "Where is Frank?"

One of the finest moments of patient care I've witnessed came when Tin stepped in and told Mrs. Dennison's daughter it would be a kindness to let her mother believe Frank was alive.

"But my mother abhors lying!" Mrs. Dennison's daughter protested. "My whole life, she has always demanded I tell her the truth!"

Tin held her ground, and now, as far as Mrs. Dennison is concerned, her beloved Frank is always just a room away.

Mrs. Dennison passes the time waiting to be with her husband by taking art classes and enjoying supervised walks in the garden and listening to music. At night, when she is put to bed, she believes Frank is in the bathroom.

It feels like a bit of grace that her damaged brain permits this hologram of Frank to hover nearby. Alzheimer's has stolen so much from Mrs. Dennison, and it isn't finished pillaging yet. It's a voracious, fiendish disease—so cunning that despite more than three billion dollars a year dedicated to research, no one can find a cure or even a way to slow its progression.

My nursing classes taught me how to trace its path of wreckage. It generally strikes the hippocampus first, the region of the mind that's the Grand Central Station of memory. Its tentacles continue to stretch, wreaking havoc with the intricate, infinitesimally delicate areas governing emotions and movement and the ability to do simple tasks, like use a fork.

In autopsies, even Alzheimer's brain tissue looks confused, like some monstrous hand reached in and swirled everything around.

I settle Mrs. Dennison into a soft chair by the window in the community room with a cup of warm tea by her side—all water taps on this floor are engineered to never go above 110 degrees—then walk over to Mr. Gray, who has a plastic basket on his lap. I take the socks from my bag, separate them, and add them to the dozen or so pairs in his basket.

"So much laundry to do," he mutters.

When Mr. Gray grows agitated, which happens a few times a day, we bring out the sock basket. Matching pairs isn't a tonic for every patient, but working on a concrete task helps center Mr. Gray.

Before he came here, Mr. Gray was an electrical engineer who specialized in the applications of radon. His son once told me that just about everything man sends into space has Mr. Gray's fingerprints on it.

I watch him now, his tongue tucked in the corner of his mouth as he concentrates on trying to find a partner for the tube stock in his hand with pink-and-blue stripes. Then I distribute the rest of my finds, putting the measuring cups in the bin of odds and ends and setting the plastic doll in a toy crib in a far corner.

I'll save the Debussy CD for when darkness falls.

That's when sundowning begins.

I stand in the doorway for a moment, absorbing the scene before me with fresh eyes. The residents in this room are among our easiest. None are shouting expletives or trying to grope or hit me.

It's difficult to predict how the disease will manifest in an individual. There's no way to say which camp my mother will fall into.

My stomach heaves and I run for the nearest bathroom, barely making it to a stall and dropping to my knees before I throw up the banana bread.

I rise to my feet, legs shaking, and walk to the sink. I rinse my mouth with water and wash my hands, wondering how I'm going to make it through the rest of my shift now that every resident I encounter wears the face of my mother.

When Mom needs full-time care, I won't be able to afford a place nearly as nice as Sunrise; it costs more than one hundred thousand dollars a year. I've heard stories about what can happen in some of the bare-bones facilities. Sometimes patients are hit, medicated into oblivion, or left to rot in their beds.

How can I relegate her to that when my mother has devoted her entire life to me? Until I began dating Ethan, my mom and I had never spent even a single night apart—she couldn't afford to send me on any overnight school trips or let me go to the Jersey Shore after graduation, like a lot of the kids from my high school class. But I understood. It's easy to keep perspective when new clothes for us always meant a trip to the thrift store and a bad stretch of tips meant our only food was what she could carry home from the diner. Until I started working full-time, we never had enough money for a landline telephone, let alone cell phones.

All that time together produced an uncommon bond between us. My first word was *Mama*. She knows my every incantation, from the toddler who loved Barney and would eat anything as long as it was covered in ketchup to the moody ninth grader who wore thick black eyeliner and blasted punk rock music. We're the only emergency contacts for each other on the forms we fill out.

I can't lose her, but I'm no match for the disease that has already claimed my grandmother. I'm an ant in the path of an eighteen-wheeler.

I'm spiraling. Dizziness engulfs me, and the shaking in my legs radiates through my entire body.

I close my eyes and grab the cold, hard edge of the sink, fighting to pull my mind away from the abyss.

I can't save my mother, so I have to find a way to keep her at home, where she'll be more comfortable. I'll eventually need someone to watch over her while I work. But the only people who volunteer for tasks like that are family, and we don't have one.

A glimmer of an idea dangles before me. It holds the faintest promise of hope—nothing that will fix or cure the situation but something that could buy a little time.

My mother would try to stop me if she knew about it. So I'm not going to tell her.

She's been keeping secrets from me—about her mom dying from early-onset Alzheimer's, and the fact that her symptoms started four months ago—so I feel entitled to keep one from her.

I'm going to find out everything I can about her dad and brother and friends. And even her ex-boyfriend, the guy I think of as my sperm donor. I've asked my mom for details about her past before, but she has always gotten sad or angry and refused to talk about it. But now everything has changed.

They all expunged my mother from their lives, but that was almost twenty-five years ago. People change. Perhaps her father has softened, especially in the wake of his wife's death.

It's a long shot, but maybe he'll want to apologize and reconcile.

Perhaps he has the money to pay for someone to take care of my mom while I work. Maybe he'll even welcome the chance to do it himself.

The odds aren't good.

But this is all I've got.

CHAPTER EIGHT

RUTH

There's an old adage I keep turning over in my mind: *The eyes are the window to the soul.*

Some people think William Shakespeare came up with the line, while others credit the Bible, or a sixteenth-century French poet. I learned this by reading one of Catherine's high school English papers.

But her paper left out the most important point. Whoever said it was dead wrong. Sometimes eyes don't tell you anything about a person's soul.

Here's my theory: The real window into someone else's soul can only be found inside *your* soul.

It's that little voice, the tingle, the sixth sense—or as I like to think of it, a compass that points to the true north about people. Sometimes the compass arrow gets pulled off course by physical attraction or alcohol or—especially when you're a teenager—by the opinions of friends. More often, though, we convince ourselves we've misread it.

The compass tries to lead us, but it can't make us follow.

Catherine has James's eyes.

They're midway between round and oval. They're the shade of a favorite old pair of jeans. They radiate gentleness and calm.

But I have never once kidded myself that they reveal every facet of her soul.

There's this thing Catherine does when she's sleepy. She rubs her feet together, like they're giving each other a little massage. They move slower and slower as her eyelids droop, then they stop right at the moment she drifts off.

James used to do the exact same thing.

The first time I noticed it in Catherine—she must've been about two or three—my throat felt like it was swelling shut and I had to pretend I needed the bathroom so I could get away for a minute.

I didn't know it was possible to pass down habits to a child you'd never met.

And it makes me wonder: What else did Catherine inherit from James?

It would have been easier to feed Catherine fake details about my family and James through the years. But it pains me to lie to her.

So I've withstood her questions, remaining firm and immobile. Refusing to let any of them penetrate.

If it's the last thing I do, I will keep Catherine and the horrors of my past apart.

I stand up from the bench in the glass shelter as the city bus pulls up, my feet feeling achy and a bit swollen like they always do at the end of my shifts. The bus doors exhale open and I step aboard, flashing my pass.

I pull my focus onto the evening that lies ahead. After I shower and change, I'm going to throw together dinner and pop it in the oven. There's a six-pack of Michelob in the fridge, but I'm not going to drink more than one. I need to keep my mind clear and my mouth from running.

I know exactly what Catherine is up to.

Catherine and I share an Amazon account because all our money goes into one pot. The account is under my name, though, because I set it up.

A few minutes ago, I received an email confirming a new order.

Normally I'd assume Catherine bought socks or pens and carry on with my day.

But nothing is normal right now.

I used my phone to navigate to my account—this investigation wasn't one I needed to hide—and clicked on the recent orders. Catherine's purchase popped right up.

It's a kind of journal—Catherine splurged for the hardcover rather than the paperback—titled *Tell Me Your Life Story, Mom.*

It has a map for a family tree. All you have to do is fill in the names.

It has a page with the headline "My Details and Time Capsule," where you write down things like your place and time of birth, age, and full name.

It has over two hundred questions covering every stage of your life.

I've managed to wiggle out of some pretty dicey situations, but I have no idea how to escape this one.

I'm so lost in thought I almost miss my bus stop.

I step off and walk down the block toward our apartment, passing the store Catherine once compared to a wizard's hat. The tiny, crowded space manages to conjure anything customers want—from lottery tickets to jars of maraschino cherries to organic almond milk.

The owner is out front, sweeping the walkway with crisp, even strokes.

"Afternoon!" he calls out.

I don't answer. My mouth is so dry I can't speak.

Tick-tock, tick-tock, the broom whispers.

Even after I hurry down the street, a phantom echo of the noise chases me. It's a gut-wrenching reminder. No matter how busy I stay or how hard I fight, there's no escaping the fact that my time is slipping away.

CHAPTER NINE

CATHERINE

Here is what I know of my mother's history.

She was born Ruth Mary Sterling on the second of August, forty-two years ago.

She grew up in the Virginia suburbs, not far from Washington, D.C. Her parents were very religious, hence her Biblical first and middle names. When they kicked her out, she moved to Pennsylvania because it was an easy bus ride, plus she'd gone to see the Liberty Bell once on a school field trip and liked the state.

She gave birth to me at eighteen.

The only guy she ever loved was my sperm donor, and he shattered her heart.

The list is so scanty I can hardly believe it.

My mother has never told me the names of her parents—though I've asked many times. She didn't pack any photographs when she was thrown out. She has never pinpointed her hometown for me, or described any of her extended family members, or named the church her family attended.

I can't believe I never got her to open up.

I can't believe it hasn't deeply bothered me before.

But maybe it isn't my fault. My mother has a temper. It doesn't surface often; but when it does, it's a tsunami, rising with almost no warning.

The few times I've pushed past the lines she drew, I've felt her fury gathering force. I usually choose to retreat rather than meet it head-on.

As a child, I learned the consequences of not backing down. I still remember the way she yelled at me and the bruises she left on my arm when I once defied her as we stood by the side of the road.

Now I sit across from her at our table with a folded index card shoved under the wobbly leg, inhaling the delicious aroma of spicy tomato sauce and baked dough.

My mother had music playing when I came through the door after meeting with Tin, and she didn't turn it off when we sat down to dinner. The upbeat pop songs fill the silence between us, disrupting my plans for a free-flowing conversation.

It's as if she senses what I'm up to and is trying to outmaneuver me.

"I'm a little tired." She stretches her arms over her head. "I'm going to turn in early."

My goal for this evening is to extract one new detail about her past. Even a tiny one.

I reach for the knife and cut through the warm, cheesy layers of lasagna pizza, then I serve myself another square.

"Want seconds?" I offer.

My mother shakes her head.

I've planned my approach meticulously. Rather than trying to pierce the armor my mother has erected around her early years, I'm going to look for an opening in her teenage years.

The next song on her playlist provides the inspiration I'm seeking. It's "Everybody" by the Backstreet Boys. They were huge in the nineties, so it probably came out while my mother was in high school.

It's impossible for my mother to sit still when she hears a song she loves. Gentle waves seem to roll through her body in time to the beat.

My mother and I have very different tastes in music. As a teenager, I'd sigh theatrically and try to change the radio station in our

Bonneville when Lynyrd Skynyrd or Boyz II Men played. Sometimes I won control of the dial, sometimes she did.

But here's the odd thing about the way memory works. I know there were dozens, maybe even hundreds of times, we engaged in this mock battle. When I won, I'd flip the dial to Adele or Taylor Swift.

What happened when my mother won?

I assume she swayed to the music, like she's doing now, and maybe sang along under her breath. But I didn't pay attention. I usually opened a book or stared out the window and lost myself in a daydream.

Our brains form memories constantly, from the second we wake until we fall asleep. But if the moment we mentally capture doesn't intersect with our attention, we lose the recollection forever. Emotional significance also helps move our memories into our longer-term stockpiles.

It's why most of us can remember details about our Thanksgiving dinner from one year ago but can't conjure a single recollection about a lunch we had one week ago.

I didn't pay attention when my mother's songs played in the past. Those memories are gone for good.

So I pay close attention now.

Her face looks softer than it did a few minutes ago, and her eyes are remote. She isn't here with me now, absorbing this moment. I'm certain she's trading the memory she could be creating now in order to relive one from the past.

Maybe this song played at one of her homecoming dances. Maybe she wore a pretty dress and wrist corsage and smiled up at the teen-aged boy who opened the car door for her and drove her to the dance. Or maybe she stayed home and cried because no one asked her.

Why won't she let me in?

In another year or so, I won't be able to make any more memories with her. It breaks my heart to know she won't share the ones she has sole ownership over.

I don't realize tears are streaming down my cheeks until my mother's face falls.

"Oh, honey, no."

She hands her paper napkin to me across the table, but within seconds it's soggy and useless. I can't stop sobbing. My shoulders heave and my whole body is engulfed in sadness, like my mother's was just overtaken by music.

She's sitting right across from me, but I already miss her so much I can't bear it. I start to hyperventilate.

She's by my side in an instant, her arm around me, shushing me.

"What can I do?" she asks.

I draw in a shuddering breath. I didn't plan for this to happen, but I grab the opening even though I don't know if I'm seeking clues or simply grasping for a piece of my mother to hold on to.

"Tell me something about yourself. From when you were a teenager."

My mother sighs and returns to her seat. I can see the struggle playing out on her face. She wants to assuage my hurt, but it isn't easy for her.

I wait quietly, not wanting to interrupt whatever mental calculations she is going through.

"Did I ever tell you I was on the Poms squad in high school? We used to dance to this song."

The revelation makes my tears evaporate. They're replaced by a vision of my mother in a uniform, dancing on the football field at halftime. But I need more than that. I need to paint my own mental image of the scene in order to secure a near-replica of her memory inside *my* brain.

"What did your uniform look like? Was your hair long?"

"My hair was almost down to my waist. But I pulled it up in double scrunchies for practices and games. I color-coordinated the scrunchies to my blue-and-gold uniform. It was a short skirt and vest."

It helps. But not enough.

My mother is watching me as carefully now as I was studying her only moment ago. "Want to see my routine?"

I know exactly what she's doing. When I was a kid, I used to beg my mother to dance like J.Lo and the Fly Girls. She was as good as any of them, but the fluid, sexy moves juxtaposed with her waitress uniform or pajamas always made me double over in laughter.

She gets up now, in gray sweatpants and one of my old college T-shirts, and launches into her choreographed dance, high kicking and singing along with the Backstreet Boys.

It's wonderful and ridiculous and magical. I can see her on the football field, shaking her shiny blue-and-gold poms, moving to the music in front of a cheering crowd.

My tears have completely dried up. I'm with the young and the old versions of my mother now, seeing them fit together like shells of a Russian nesting doll.

"You're a terrible singer!" I yell.

She grins and sings louder. Then I notice it.

She doesn't seem to be singing the exact lyrics to the song. Her words have the same tempo, but they're different:

Are we original?
Are we the champions?
Are we the Panthers?

I see the knowledge hit her eyes a second later.

She swishes her imaginary pom-poms once more, then slides back into her seat, even though the song hasn't quite ended.

"I've got to stretch before I ever do that again." She laughs, but it sounds forced. "I probably pulled a hamstring."

She's avoiding my eyes.

"Mom."

"Hey, do you have any laundry? I may throw in a load before bed."

"No, I'm good. But I—"

My mother gasps. I look down to see bright red blood oozing out from her index finger. She's holding the long, sharp knife. I hadn't even noticed she was cutting herself another square.

"Crap!"

"Don't move!" I leap up and run to the roll of paper towels, ripping off a few sheets. I'm back at her side a second later, pressing them into the wound.

"I need to look at it."

She nods and averts her gaze while I briefly pull back the wad of paper towels.

"It's not deep. You don't need a stitch. Hang on, let me get Neosporin and a Band-Aid."

I grab both from the bathroom medicine cabinet and hurry back to her side. Within a few minutes, the bleeding has stopped and her cut is cleaned and covered.

My mom gets up and begins to clear the table.

The Backstreet Boys song has ended.

The moment has passed.

But I've collected two new details about my mother's past, and they're enough to pull my mind away from the question that hit me like a hammer as I bandaged my mother's finger: *Did she actually cut herself to derail the conversation?*

Here's the detail she freely offered up: Her high school colors were blue and gold.

Here's the one she didn't intend for me to know: The mascot was a panther.

CHAPTER TEN

RUTH

I set my alarm for 5 a.m. since I'm the early bird who is opening Sam's tomorrow. By the time the first customer comes through the door, I'll have four pots of coffee brewed—three regular and one decaf—and settled on the warming burners while the cook fries bacon and preps pancake batter.

I'll lose myself in the busyness of the morning.

The words reverberate through my mind: *I'll lose myself.*

I push them away and take a long sip from the second bottle of Michelob I've brought with me into my bedroom.

I let my guard down for a moment tonight. I slipped. But knowing the name of my high school mascot doesn't mean Catherine will come any closer to my family or old friends or James.

I could see it in her eyes, the moment she nabbed that flyaway detail and clutched it like a triumphant baseball outfielder.

She is voraciously hungry for more of my story.

I may have to dole out a few more details, but I need to be more careful than I've ever been before. I really don't want to have to slice open another finger to divert her attention again.

I reach for the bottle of lotion on my nightstand and rub some into my forearm, my fingertips lightly brushing over the old, slightly shiny patch of scar tissue between my left wrist and elbow.

Just as I start to pull down my covers, there's a knock on my door.

For a moment I consider jumping into bed and pretending to be asleep. But Catherine knows I don't sleep much. It was one of the things I taught myself to do without as a single mom. Catherine knocks again and cracks the door. "Mom?"

"Come on in."

"Didn't you say you were going to do laundry tonight?"

"Oops. I forgot."

Those last two words hang heavily between us for a moment.

"I wanted to talk to you about scheduling an MRI and a PET scan."

MRIs can rule out things like brain tumors, and PET scans can help diagnose Alzheimer's. Dr. Chen suggested I get both, but I figured Catherine and I were on the same page: We didn't need more tests.

I take another sip of beer before I answer.

"What good would that do?"

"What if it is something else? Something that can be cured?"

I knew these conversations with Catherine would be the hardest things I've ever done.

"My blood tests were clean. I had a mammogram two months ago and a full checkup two weeks ago. Dr. Chen believes it's Alzheimer's. My family history is diagnosis enough."

"But—"

You know how you can heat water slowly in a pan on the stove, or how there's an instant hot tap in some fancy kitchens?

My temper is of the instant hot variety.

"Do not push me, Catherine Sterling. Those scans will cost us thousands of dollars. Money we don't have! You think I want to battle our insurance company like I did when you were hospitalized with mono, then have to work double shifts for months to pay off the bill?

You think I want more doctors picking at me and telling me there's nothing they can do?"

She's retreating, backing toward the door.

Sometimes anger has its uses.

The thing is, I'm not really angry at Catherine right now. I'm filled with rage at myself.

Rotten genes are programming me. I inherited them from my mother and she from hers. Fury seems to be the legacy passed down to the women in our family.

"I'm sorry." I exhale, long and slow. "It's been a day."

She nods. "Understatement."

"Let's give this a little time before we make any decisions, okay?"

Catherine hesitates, then nods again. "Good night, Mama."

She hasn't called me that in years. I'm glad she closes the door quickly because I can't hold back my tears any longer.

Beer alone isn't going to do it for me tonight. I put down my bottle and walk over to my dresser and pull out the top drawer. The bottle of Xanax with its bitter white pills is lodged in the back. I swallow one, grimacing at the aftertaste.

It will take a little while for the Xanax to relax my muscles enough for sleep to be a possibility.

I return to bed and pull out the green notebook I tucked into my big shoulder bag when I left Sam's. I awakened my muscle memory by performing my old Poms routine, and now my mind is whirling with images from that long-ago time, too. I'm gripped by the need to continue writing my story for Catherine.

Someday, it could save her life.

That night at Pizza Piazzo, James seemed to figure out what was going on with Brittany before I even sat down.

Outsiders are like that. We size up situations quickly because we need to gauge if and when people might turn against us. And we can always recognize each other as allies.

A lot of the guys at my school had this bravado that seemed fake.

They roughhoused and called each other slurs I won't repeat here and swaggered down the hallway while everyone else skittered out of their way. The athletes were the worst, probably because they were treated like gods. They got their lockers decorated by underclassmen before every game, and the theme song from Rocky blasted over the school loud-speaker when they ran onto the field.

James wasn't like any of them. He wasn't like any guy of my generation I'd ever met.

It's hard to pinpoint exactly how he was different, but the closest I can come is to say he wasn't a boy, or even a guy. He was a man.

The first thing I ever said to him was that I would kill for a glass of water.

He laughed and brought me one so quickly that I was still standing behind the chair Brittany had piled her things atop, trying to get her to acknowledge me.

James handed me the water. Our fingers just missed touching as I took it, but it was a close enough call that I felt a delicious swoop low in my belly. He'd put a thin round slice of lemon in it, and just enough ice to make it cold but not so much that there wasn't enough room for a good serving of water. I watched him over the top of the glass while I drained it.

He looked at the chair, then at me, then at Brittany, who was in the middle of a dramatic reenactment of a curling-iron mishap.

James tapped her on the shoulder. She lifted her index finger without glancing at him and continued talking.

James didn't miss a beat. He told her he was just going to move her things, then he scooped up her purse and backpack and put them on a chair at the neighboring table.

That got Brittany's attention. She asked in a loud, huffy voice if he could stop touching her stuff.

James acted like he didn't hear her, which was pretty funny considering that's exactly what Brittany was doing to me. He pulled the chair closer to her, the bottom of its legs making a grating sound against the floor, and told her she could keep an eye on her things and now there was room for everyone in our group to sit down.

Mrs. Davis must've been watching it all because she stood up at the head of the table, her eyes blazing. She snapped at James, saying she wanted to speak to the manager.

I finished my water and slid into the now-empty chair, wishing James hadn't tried to help me.

He walked around to stand face-to-face with Mrs. Davis. He wasn't that much taller than she in her three-inch heels. He flashed a sweet smile, one I would grow to love.

She didn't scare him one little bit, I realized.

I almost lifted my arms and cheered when James told her that he was filling in for the manager, and he'd be happy to hear her complaint.

It took James only a couple of minutes to calm Mrs. Davis down. The free glass of Chardonnay he delivered helped.

The restaurant must have been short-staffed because James was constantly in and out of the dining room, delivering checks and bringing extra napkins when a kid knocked over his soda and refilling water glasses.

He topped mine off twice, without my asking.

Our food arrived right after I did. The restaurant served lasagna pizza, which is how I got the idea to make it for you. I pretended to invent it for reasons you'll understand soon.

I kept my head down and ate while I counted my blessings: I'd made it onto the squad. My dad was home, and he would protect Timmy for the rest of the night. One of the girls who came up from JV—Rosie, the one with glasses who'd pointed out Coach had only called eleven names— might become a friend, or at least someone to talk to during practice. The only thing I knew about Rosie was that her father had died of a heart attack when she was young, and her older sister had dropped out of school last year and almost overdosed. Her home life couldn't be easy either.

I couldn't tune out the barbs Brittany threw my way, but I didn't give her the satisfaction of a reaction. I was pretty sure even James, who was clearing off a table nearby, heard her cackle that she didn't need a second piece because she wasn't a piggy—just as I reached for a third one.

James didn't react either. Not in that moment, anyway.

Coach Franklin stood up and crumpled his greasy, orange-stained *napkin, tossing it onto his plate. He had broad shoulders and shaggy brown hair, and some girls thought he was cute, but I felt like he tried too hard to be hip with his faded Bruce Springsteen T-shirts and the Eric Clapton autographed guitar he kept in a glass case on his office wall.*

Coach told us it was time to elect a captain and Mrs. Davis walked around the table, distributing little pads of paper and pens. The pads all had the logo Davis & Libertelli at the top. Brittany's father was the founding partner of the law firm that was our biggest sponsor.

Subtlety wasn't a strength for the Davis women.

Coach told us to write down the name of the girl we believed deserved to represent us as captain this year, then fold up our papers and pass them down to him.

In the ensuring silence, everyone could hear Brittany stage-whisper to the girl next to her, asking if something smelled kind of rank, while she glanced meaningfully at me. They both laughed in that way only mean girls can—it's an art, really. It combines superiority and malice with a dash of exclusivity.

Strange to think that just a few years ago we were learning how to French braid each other's hair and taking our first-ever sips of vodka from the little airline-sized bottle I'd stolen from my mother's stash, the kind she tucked in her purse when she went out to run errands.

Coach Franklin started piling up the votes in front of him while I looked down at my blank paper.

I'm not sure what prompted me do it. Maybe it was Brittany cupping her hand over her face and making snorting noises. I was well aware I'd put on ten pounds over the summer, and she was making damn sure everyone else was aware of it, too. Or maybe it's because I looked up, saw James's eyes on me, and drew courage from his steady gaze.

I decided to stop trying to be invisible.

I wrote down my own name. I didn't even disguise my handwriting.

I ripped the sheet from my pad and crumpled it up and threw it down the table, then took another long sip of cold, delicious water, finishing my third glass.

When all the papers were in a little pile in front of Coach, he shuffled them around. Mrs. Davis sat with her pen poised over her pad, ready to tally the results.

Coach reached for the first paper and unfolded it. He called Brittany's name.

There were a few excited squeals. Brittany flicked her hair and smiled.

The second vote was for Brittany, of course.

And the third.

But the next two were for me.

I almost dropped my fork.

One vote I knew was coming. But someone else had written down my name? I looked around the table. Brittany and her cronies appeared as shocked as I was.

Coach reached for another slip of folded paper.

He called out a vote for Brittany, her fourth.

Then there was another for me. And another.

With two-thirds of the votes counted, we were dead even at four votes each.

I sensed tension rising around our table like smoke. All the side conversations ceased. Everyone watched Coach intently as he unwrapped the ninth vote. I held my breath.

He called out my name.

Someone gasped. It might even have been me.

Out of twelve votes, I'd gotten five so far and Brittany had four. Was I being set up?

If this was another planned humiliation, Brittany was a few steps ahead of me. I had no idea what she could gain from this. She desperately wanted to be captain. The captain got to lead us on and off the field for the halftime show and stood in front of the squad during certain routines. She would never have willingly given up that spotlight.

There was only one other possibility I could think of: Some of the girls were rebelling against Brittany. They were rising up, trying to unseat the queen. Maybe she'd cut them one too many times with her barbs, or maybe they had grown sick of her rules.

Coach unwrapped the next slip of paper.

He'd stopped smiling.

The tenth vote went to me. One more and I would be captain.

Mrs. Davis leapt to her feet and started to say something, then cut herself off. I glanced across the table and caught a flicker of a smile cross Rosie's face. It looked genuine.

If every JV girl voted for me, and just one of the varsity girls did . . . Even with all the water I'd chugged, my mouth went dry.

Was it actually possible I could be elected captain?

I would work so hard to deserve it. I'd create new routines, the best ones our squad—no, any high school squad—had ever performed. I'd offer one-on-one help on the weekends to any teammate who had trouble learning them.

Coach Franklin was frowning. Mrs. Davis sat back down and tapped her pen against her pad. Her face was a thundercloud.

Coach reached for the next slip of paper, and I could hear the relief pour into his voice as he called Brittany's name.

There was one slip of paper left on the table.

Coach reached for it.

I wasn't sure which I wanted more, for me to win or for Brittany to lose.

The grin that spread across Coach's face told me the vote went to Brittany before he read her name.

But Mrs. Davis still looked furious.

It was a tie, six-six.

I saw Coach lean closer to her and whisper.

James approached them at the head of our table. I heard him offer Mrs. Davis another Chardonnay on the house.

She simpered that she really shouldn't because she was driving.

James promised to make it a small one and she fluttered her eyelashes and told him he'd twisted her arm. Then she asked for an iced tea with extra lemon and two packets of Sweet'N Low on the side.

Even before our town had a Starbucks, Mrs. Davis had perfected the art of high-maintenance beverage ordering.

All around me, girls were murmuring. There had never been a tie for captain before, at least not during the years I'd been on the team.

Coach's booming voice caused everyone to fall silent.

He said that in case of a tie, the coach cast the deciding vote.

My heart plummeted. Of course it had to end this way. Whatever made me believe I'd have a chance?

Then he announced it was pretty clear Brittany Davis was the kind of girl we all wanted to represent us.

Mrs. Davis beamed and steepled her manicured fingertips together as she stared up at Coach. I didn't look Brittany's way. I couldn't bear to see her smug expression.

Coach kept talking, saying our team needed someone who would be comfortable carrying the name Panthers in front of the public. Going to nationals would be an expensive trip, he said, and though we had a good sponsor, some of the girls wouldn't be able to afford hotel rooms.

Like me.

Mrs. Davis beamed at Coach as he wrapped up by saying that our captain needed to speak the same language as the businesspeople we'd have to ask for support.

Every word was a spike in my heart.

He couldn't just say Brittany won.

Coach had to spell out why I could never be captain: My mother was a drunk and my father was a handyman, so I was trash.

Rosie looked down and I thought I saw her blushing. She was embarrassed to witness my humiliation.

I wanted to bolt. No, what I really wanted to do was hurl the heavy pizza pan on our table at Coach's head, then grab Brittany by her Barbie hair and smash her face into the table.

Rage burned within me. A buzzing sound filled my head. They'd gone too far this time—all three of them had. My fists clenched as my breaths came faster.

Then something made me look up.

I saw James carrying the tray with Mrs. Davis's wine and iced tea and a beer for Coach into the room. James's eyes were fixed on me.

I didn't know how much he'd heard of Coach's little speech. But he must have gleaned something.

Because as James held my gaze, he leaned over and spit into Coach's drink. Then he did the same to Mrs. Davis's.

By the time he delivered the beverages to the table, placing them in front of my adult tormentors with a flourish, the hot tears of rage in my eyes were gone.

It wasn't like everything was better, but I'd regained control. Dinner broke up a few minutes later, after Coach and Mrs. Davis had drained their glasses.

James was nowhere to be found when I left, even though I looked behind me a few times on my way out the door.

But the next afternoon, I found a note tucked into the slats of my school locker. It wasn't signed, but it didn't need to be. I knew who wrote the neat, blocky letters.

I watched you today. You should be captain.

CHAPTER ELEVEN

CATHERINE

After a restless night, I wake up and stumble out of my bedroom, hoping Mom made a pot of coffee before she left for work.

But the Mr. Coffee machine is clean and empty in the dark galley kitchen.

I fill the glass pot halfway with water and dump it into the reservoir, then open the cabinet to grab the tin of Maxwell House.

There's a cardboard container of eggs next to the coffee.

I stare at it dumbly for a second, then reach for it and open the tabs. Four white eggs are nestled inside. I touch one of them. It's room temperature.

Mom must've put them away here. They could be a salmonella factory by now.

I drop the eggs into the trash can and the cardboard container into the recycle bin, watching as one of the eggs cracks apart and oozes out of its shell.

My head swims and I grip the edge of the counter.

I haven't decided yet whether I'll undergo genetic testing to see if I've inherited the gene for early-onset Alzheimer's. It's my own decision, one my mother can't deny me. I'll pay for it myself if it comes to that.

Even if the gene is coding my future, it won't necessarily mean an early death sentence for me. Brilliant researchers are constantly working to find a cure. There could be—*will* be—so many advances in the next few decades. And if I turn out to be carrying a mutated gene, I can avoid passing it on if I decide to have kids by undergoing in vitro fertilization. I would have the option of stopping this disease in its tracks, making it end with me.

My palms feel sweaty and my thoughts are racing.

The coffeemaker's gurgling helps pull me into the present moment. I grab a mug and walk over to it. Then I almost drop my mug.

The liquid in the pot is clear.

I forgot to put the grounds into the filter.

My heart feels as if it's exploding, even as my mind searches for an explanation. I was obviously distracted, who wouldn't be? There's no significance to what just happened. My mistake with the coffee isn't an echo of the one my mother made with the eggs.

We all misplace cell phones and lose words and forget items we've made a mental list to pick up at the grocery store, especially when we have a lot on our minds. Those aren't signs of Alzheimer's.

If we forget we even have a cell phone after we've been using it daily for years and get lost on the one-mile drive home from the drugstore even though we've driven the route countless times, like my mother did?

Those can be signs of Alzheimer's.

If I'm carrying the gene, it won't reveal itself for another fifteen to twenty years—longer if I'm lucky.

Still, it takes a minute for my pulse to slow to normal.

I brew some coffee and inhale the rich hazelnut aroma as it drips into the pot. It gives me energy even before I take a sip.

I hurry to my bedroom and grab a yellow legal pad out of my desk drawer. Then I go to the dining table with a mug of black coffee and sit down. I list the few facts I know about my mother and add my two new details to it.

I open my laptop and begin to search for Virginia high schools with panther mascots.

An hour later, my mug is empty and several more pages of my pad are filled with leads, all of which I've crossed out. I've been hopscotching around the internet, searching Facebook pages for different high schools and scrutinizing detailed maps of Virginia and even checking out sports websites that contain high school football team rankings.

If there's a clear answer, it's eluding me.

The urge to take out the trash nags at me. I need to get rid of the broken egg and bloody paper towels and the other pieces of evidence of everything that has transpired in the last twenty-four hours.

I tuck my legal pad into my bookshelf, sandwiching it between two oversized hardbacks, and head out the door. Mom took the car today, so I head for the bus stop.

My mother hates surprises, but I'm going to give her one.

I'm going to visit her at work.

Sam's is a brightly lit diner with shiny chrome-and-red pleather stools and booths, a row of pies under glass domes on the long counter, and oversized laminated menus with pictures of the food offered. Breakfast and pie are served all day.

I once asked my mother who would eat pie early in the morning. "Truckers," she told me. "For some of them, morning is the end of their shift and they like a little dessert before they go to bed."

I sit on the city bus, moving physically forward while looking backward in time.

When I was smaller, the different restaurants where my mother worked seemed like magical places. I'd deliver stiff, shiny menus to tables—more than once a customer tipped me a dollar just for doing that small task—or sit on a stool, watching the cooks move with the speed of professional jugglers as they flipped burgers and decorated them with tomatoes and lettuce, and buttered pieces of toast with one perfect swoop of a knife. Sometimes the cooks would slip me a scoop of chocolate ice cream with a cloud of sweet whipped cream.

When the sugar kicked in, I'd spin around on a stool until I got dizzy or my mother noticed, whichever came first.

As her disease progresses, my mother will stop coming to Sam's. A few months beyond that, she'll forget she was once a waitress.

A few months past that, she'll forget who I am.

I dig my nails into my palms. The burst of pain distracts my mind and pulls me out of the path of the dark, choppy wave.

A few minutes later, the bus stops a few storefronts down from Sam's and I step onto the sidewalk.

I haven't been to my mother's workplace in at least a year, maybe even two.

It looks exactly the same. It's humming with the noise of dozens of conversations, the clanking of silverware against china plates, and soft rock music playing over speakers. All the booths are full, but I find an empty stool at the end of the counter.

My mother doesn't notice me right away. She's taking an order from two women in the opposite corner of the restaurant. She isn't using a pad and pen. My mother never does for parties of four or less.

That needs to change.

My mother steps away from the table and walks to the computer where the waitstaff inputs orders for the cooks. She presses a few buttons, then heads to the serving window and grabs what looks like a BLT and fries from the warming shelves. She delivers the plate to a guy at table six, then checks in on table eight. I can't hear her, but since they've already received their food she's probably asking if they'd like refills of water or hot sauce for their omelets.

My mother appears to be in command of her faculties. No one in the restaurant seems agitated. I can't see any customers trying to get her attention or frowning at their bill.

During the early to mid-stages, some people with Alzheimer's plateau for a while. Others have good days mixed with bad days, and I suspect my mother is having a good memory day now. But even though the progression can branch in different directions, the path always narrows to the same wretched, heartbreaking end.

"Catherine!"

I spin a quarter-circle to my right and come face-to-face with Melanie, another waitress, who is my mother's closest friend.

She leans in and gives me a hug. Melanie smells like my mother always does when she comes home from work. Her skin is perfumed with the scent of the kitchen grill.

I've always liked Melanie. She has a gap between her front teeth that makes her big smile seem even more genuine, and her voice holds the gentle lilt of her Southern roots.

"It's been forever, girl." Melanie pulls back, beaming. "Congrats on graduating. Your mom is so proud."

I thank her, and as we chat an idea floats into my mind. My mother is fiercely private. She won't tell Sam or Melanie about her diagnosis, at least not until she absolutely must. When work gets to be too much for my mom—when she can't find her way to the diner and wanders the streets, or starts a grease fire, or makes so many mistakes customers are in an uproar—she'll get fired.

I'm not going to let things reach that point.

I need eyes on my mom when I'm not around. I'd planned to ask Sam, but he can be a little grumpy. Even though I don't know Melanie terribly well since she lives across town, and she and my mom socialize every month or so at a bar midway between their places, she's my best bet.

I'm about to ask Melanie if I can have her cell phone number so I can call her about a private matter when I feel a hand on my shoulder.

I twist around and see my mom.

Her reaction is the opposite of Melanie's. She's frowning.

"What are you doing here?"

I keep my tone light. "I had a craving for French fries."

Mom's expression tells me that if Melanie weren't witnessing this, we'd be having a different conversation.

"You came all this way for fries?"

"Aww, what a nice daughter," Melanie interjects. "Ruth, I can cover for you if you want to take a few."

"I'm already in the weeds. Thanks, though."

A customer signals for his check and Melanie excuses herself to head to his table.

"Fries and an iced tea?" my mom asks.

A flutter of memory: We're in a restaurant my mom worked at long ago, and she's serving me a tall glass of iced tea with a long silver spoon in it. I must've been about six or seven. It tasted delicious. I didn't know until later that she'd cut it with lemonade.

I still drink my iced tea that way, but now I know to ask for an Arnold Palmer—except when my mom is offering. She knows exactly what I like without my having to specify.

My mom and I share a language that's all our own, one we've constructed through the years. We say *pipple* instead of "apple" because I couldn't pronounce the name of the fruit when I was a toddler, and she decided the term I came up with was better than the original. *Rockamole* is "guacamole" for the same reason. Anyone who's long-winded is a *Darryl,* because we once had a loquacious neighbor by that name.

In a year or two, our shared language, one that's unique to us, will disappear, too.

I give myself a mental shake. If I focus on everything I'm going to lose, I'll also lose the present moment.

And I have a mission to complete today.

My mom swings by with my fries and drink a few minutes later, sliding a bottle of ketchup closer to me because she knows how much I love it.

The fries are golden brown and crispy. But any pleasure I'd normally get from biting into them is muted.

I keep my eyes on Melanie, but she doesn't come near my stool again. I finally seize my chance when my mother goes to take an order from a table of eight. They're probably office mates who work together in one of the buildings on this street. She greets them like they're regulars.

I keep glancing at my mom while simultaneously trying to catch

Melanie's attention. When she finally looks my way, I gesture for her to come over.

"Listen, I can't talk long but I need to tell you something," I whisper. "My mom, she's sick . . ."

My throat constricts. Melanie doesn't flinch or retreat in the face of strong emotion, the way so many people do.

"What is it, honey?"

"Alzheimer's. Early-onset. The doctor is pretty certain."

Melanie's expression doesn't change, but her eyes do.

"She's going to start—"

Melanie puts a hand on my arm. "I know. My boyfriend's grandfather had it. I'm so sorry."

My chin wobbles, but I hold it together. "Has she made any mistakes at work yet? I don't want her to get in trouble."

I see her casting back in her memory, searching for an overlooked clue.

"I haven't noticed a thing," she tells me. "Truly."

That makes me feel a tiny bit better. I'm not the only one who didn't catch the symptoms early on. It also lends credence to my supposition that my mother's disease is still in a very early stage.

"That's good. Just keep me posted, okay?"

"I will, honey. Here." Melanie pulls a pen out of her apron and hands it to me. "Write down your cell number on a napkin. I'll text you later so you have mine."

I do as she instructs, then glance over Melanie's shoulder. My mother is still taking orders at her big table, but she's also sneaking peeks at us. She doesn't like that I'm talking to Melanie. She's probably worried we're having this exact conversation.

"One more thing. When you guys go out for drinks again, could you tell me your plans in advance? My mom and I have location sharing with each other, but if she forgets her phone at home or leaves it at the bar . . ."

"Wow, you still share your location with your mom? Wish I could get my kids to do that with me." Melanie's voice is warm. She's trying to comfort me without saying sympathetic words. "Of course, I'll let you know, hon. But . . ."

A guy at a nearby table gestures to her, making a writing motion in the air to signal he wants the check, but Melanie doesn't acknowledge him.

She's frowning as her eyes grow faraway.

There's something she's remembering. A loose thread, the genesis of an unraveling. Maybe my mother *has* been making mistakes, but they haven't tallied into a pattern in Melanie's mind until now.

I brace myself.

"I wish your mom would take me up on drinks. I've been trying to get her to go out for years. But she always says she's too tired, and you're all the company she needs."

Melanie squeezes my shoulder and hurries off to tend to her table.

Melanie's words were perfectly clear, but I can't make sense of them. Melanie said she and my mother have never gone out for drinks. The blind dates my mother supposedly had—the ones she told me Melanie and her boyfriend arranged—didn't exist. All those girls' nights out when my mother came home late, acting tipsy, were a fabrication.

I don't know how long I sit there, stunned, the fries growing cold on my plate. Finally, something compels me to lift my eyes.

Across the restaurant, my mother is staring at me. She's like a statue in the midst of the swirl of the busy restaurant.

When she catches me looking, she whips around and walks toward the kitchen.

CHAPTER TWELVE

RUTH

Catherine told Melanie. It's obvious.

Melanie doesn't act any differently toward me, but I can sense the shift in her energy. I see her scan my tables, like she's checking to make sure my customers appear happy.

Of all the people Catherine could have told, Melanie is a pretty safe one. I just hope they didn't talk about anything more.

When lunch rush is over, I take a break and check my phone. There's a text from Catherine: Going to catch a movie with a friend tonight. See you when I get home if you're still up.

I pour myself a coffee and lean against the counter and sip it while I ponder her words. Catherine doesn't have a lot of close friends. She's a homebody, like me. And ever since she split up with that loser Ethan, she hasn't been romantically involved with anyone.

I wonder who she's seeing the movie with. I wonder if she's seeing a movie at all.

Still, I'm a little relieved I don't have to face more of her questions tonight. I want to soak my tired feet and try to clear my head.

I finish my shift and slip out the door without saying goodbye to Melanie, just in case she's planning to intercept me with words of sympathy or support.

The Bonneville sputters when I start it. I say a little prayer until the engine catches. We've got nearly 150,000 miles on the car, and I'm hoping to eke out a lot more.

I sit in the parking lot, letting the engine warm up, and watch as a guy driving a red Trans Am rounds the corner and slides into the space next to me. He's a good-looking man, about my age. But it isn't him I'm checking out. It's his car.

I used to love flashy muscle cars. Mustangs, Camaros, Chevelles— and my favorite, the Corvette.

That's the kind of car James drove. He'd gotten it from a guy who'd crashed into a guardrail and whose wife was making him sell it. James knocked out the worst of the dents and touched up the black paint and added a little horsepower.

He drove it to meet me for our first date.

I ease my gearshift into drive and pull out. I plan to swing by the library first to do my checking again, even though I did it only yesterday. Now more than ever, I must remain vigilant.

Only when I'm certain the barriers I've erected around me and Catherine aren't in danger of being breached will I head home.

It almost feels like James is waiting for me there. In a way, I guess he is since I need to sink deeply into another memory of him and write more in my journal.

On the night of my first date with James, my father had to work late.

He said Timmy and I should stop for burgers on the way home from Poms practice, so we did. We spread out our books in the booth and Timmy chewed his pencil eraser as he worked his way through a page of pre-algebra equations. I was of no help since I'd already forgotten everything I'd learned on the subject. I drafted my English essay. The topic was foreshadowing in Shakespeare's play Romeo and Juliet. Usually I dreaded school reading, but something about this slim play spoke to me: teenagers in love destroying their lives.

Trust me, I get the irony.

I expected my dad to be home by the time Timmy and I arrived. But he wasn't.

My dad worked for my mother's family business. It's how they met. My grandparents owned a bunch of houses close to the local college, which they rented out at obscene rates to students who needed to live close to campus and had few other options. Timmy and I sometimes tagged along with my dad when he worked on the places, and I couldn't believe the scam my mother's family ran. They partitioned off rooms to rent what should have been a four-bedroom home as an eight- or nine-bedroom one. The spaces were barely big enough for twin beds and dressers, and the kitchens and bathrooms were a mess, with patched linoleum floors, cracks in the walls, and iffy appliances.

College kids and their parents put up with it because they knew the leases were temporary—those houses were just stepping-stones as they moved toward a better life—plus no one cared if they threw wild parties or let trash bags pile up in the living room. It wasn't like they could do a ton of damage to the places, and if they did, my mother's family simply kept their security deposit. I'm pretty sure they kept most of the deposits even when there wasn't any new damage.

My mother—your grandmother—had a thick streak of evil running through her, as you've probably gleaned by now. She inherited it from her mother, who was a cold, prejudiced, greedy jerk. And that's putting it mildly.

I heard my grandmother refer to my dad as a spic once. I didn't understand what it meant, and I couldn't find the word in the dictionary. From the way the word twisted her lipsticked mouth into an ugly shape, I knew it was an awful one.

Whenever I worry I've got half of my mother's side in me, I remind myself I also have half of my dad's.

A lot of the time when he worked late, he did it off the clock. Like when there was a serial rapist in the area and some of the college girls were getting scared, my father installed locks on each of their bedroom doors. *He paid for those bolts himself, which I knew because I was with him at the hardware store when he bought them.*

His name is Mateo. If you'd turned out to be a boy, that would have been your middle name.

The first night James and I planned to go out, my dad was helping some students deal with a plumbing crisis.

After we finished our burgers and homework and drove home, Timmy and I sat in the driveway for a few minutes, but we couldn't put off going inside for long. Dusk was settling, and I only had thirty minutes before I had to meet James.

The house was dead quiet when I opened the kitchen door, which was unusual. My mother typically fell asleep on the living room couch in front of the TV.

I waited a minute, but couldn't hear a thing, so I motioned for Timmy to get out of the car. We had our routine choreographed as intricately as any of those I'd practiced for Poms. Timmy closed the car door as quietly as possible. I stepped into the kitchen first and looked around quickly. (I'd learned to do that the hard way because my mom once threw her empty wine glass at me when I came in. Luckily, her aim was terrible.) Then I motioned for Timmy to join me.

I couldn't see the living room from my vantage point. But I was pretty sure my mother was splayed out in her usual spot.

Most of the lights were off. I left them that way, even though the house was draped in shadows, as Timmy and I crept upstairs.

The upper level seemed completely still.

I didn't let down my guard, though. I checked Timmy's bedroom and waited until he slipped through his door and closed it behind him.

Across the hall, my parents' bedroom door was ajar. The slice of the room I could see was dark and empty.

I breathed out and went into my room. My mother was probably passed out on the couch and would likely stay that way for the rest of the night.

I moved quickly, no longer worried about being so quiet. I grabbed clean cutoffs and a top and bra and underpants and carried them to the hall bathroom. I slipped out of my sneakers and pulled off my clothes, wrinkling my nose as I raised my arms and caught a whiff of old sweat from Poms practice.

I took the world's fastest shower, then dried off and dressed in rec-ord time. I liked makeup—a lot—but I only had time to apply a few swipes of mascara and cherry-red lip gloss.

I thought I heard a noise, so I cracked open the bathroom door and listened hard for a minute. But nothing had changed. Timmy's door was shut, my parents' door was ajar. The house was quiet.

I had two minutes before I needed to leave.

This next part is so hard to write. . . .

I shut the door and reached for the blow-dryer and turned it on.

You know how you flip your head upside down and aim the dryer at your roots to get more body into your hair?

That's what I was focused on: a little more body in my hair.

The roaring noise of the dryer filled my ears. For one hundred twenty seconds, I couldn't hear anything else.

Then I turned the dryer off.

Kids cry in a lot of different ways. Whether they're angry, sad, in-jured, or tired, it sounds different. I'd heard Timmy cry in all of those ways. I thought I knew all of the ways there were for a boy to cry.

But I didn't.

I can't remember how I got from the bathroom into Timmy's room, but I swear my feet didn't touch the ground. I was in one place, then another, without having consciously moved.

Timmy was flat on his back on his bed, with my mother pinning him down. Her knees were on his elbows, preventing him from moving, as she slapped his face. His nose was bleeding.

I went wild. I flung myself at her, yanking her off my brother and pushing her across the room.

She was bigger than me, but she was also drunk.

She recovered quickly. She grabbed me by my upper arms and slammed me into the wall, cursing me. Calling me a bitch and a whole lot worse.

I could hear Timmy begging her to stop. My sweet little brother, who came to my room when he woke from a bad dream because he knew I'd protect him, had a line of blood trickling from his nose.

Then Timmy's voice faded away and I couldn't hear anything but a roaring in my ears. It sounded a lot like the noise of the hair dryer.

I wanted to kill her. I wanted to claw out her eyes and grab fistfuls of her hair and smash her head against the plaster wall until her face looked like pulp.

If my father hadn't arrived home at that exact moment, maybe I would have.

My dad wrapped his arms around me from behind, trapping my arms at my sides. If you didn't know better, it could almost look like the way a dad would surprise his kid after arriving home from work by coming up behind her and hugging her.

My father ordered me and Timmy to get outside. The noise in my ears receded. I felt like I'd had an out-of-body experience, but I was coming back to myself.

My mother had been slumped on the floor, but her eyes were open and she was already climbing to her feet. She wasn't badly hurt.

She might not even remember what had happened.

I grabbed Timmy's hand and we ran back downstairs, retracing our route through the kitchen. I grabbed a paper napkin from the table as we passed it because my mother always kept nice paper napkins—the kind that almost look and feel like real cloth—in the silver holder.

Appearances were important to my mother. She'd never hit us outside the house, where someone might see. That would be unseemly.

Timmy and I sat on the front steps of the house. I cleaned his nose as best I could, then held him for a long time. To distract him, I talked about all the things he'd do someday. Ride a horse. Fly in an airplane. Go to Italy with me and eat a different flavor of gelato every day.

My father finally came out. He still wore his handyman's coveralls with his name on the left pocket.

He examined Timmy's nose and checked my upper arms. Red dots in the shape of fingertips were already forming, precursors to bruises.

The broken look on my dad's face about killed me. I knew he was trapped. He was a high-school dropout with no resources. My mother's family had some money, plus they employed him. If he left her, they'd fire him and hire a lawyer to help her win full custody of us. It wouldn't be hard since the courts usually favored mothers. I'd heard my mom yell that at my dad before.

Anyway, my dad was raised as a Catholic. He didn't believe in divorce.

I lied and told him we were fine as Timmy nodded.

My dad said he wanted to take Timmy to McDonald's for a cone, and Timmy's face brightened a bit. Dad asked if I was still going out or if I wanted to come with them.

I was so late for my date with James that I doubted he'd still be waiting for me. I didn't have a way of communicating with him, other than through notes tucked in my locker slats. He'd left one asking me out on the date, and I'd written a single word—yes—on a light-purple sticky note, the prettiest slip of paper I had, and put it in the same slat for him to find. I left it there right after practice, and it was gone the next morning when I arrived at school.

I still had no idea how James slipped in and out of school without me noticing. I felt certain that even in a crowd of hundreds, my eyes would be drawn to him.

I said I wasn't sure and that I might catch up with them at McDonald's.

My dad kissed my cheek, then took Timmy's hand and we walked together to the driveway. My father drove a car in even worse condition than mine. He insisted on giving the better one to me because it had air bags. Even when he wasn't with us kids, he tried to protect us.

My mother had tried to defeat him in many ways, like by screeching that he was a loser and a terrible husband, and that she never should've married him. There was plenty my dad could have said back, especially because I'm pretty sure my mother got pregnant with me to trick my dad into marrying her. She was thirty and he was twenty-five when they met, and it's not like she was bringing a lot to the table.

But my dad always accepted her wrath without ever once fighting back or even leaving the room. For the longest time, I couldn't figure out why.

Now I think I know the truth. By absorbing her verbal blows, he hoped he could prevent her physical ones against us kids.

The front of my high school was lit up by tall outdoor lights, but around the back, the parking lot was almost completely dark. There weren't any other cars I could see.

James had given up on me.

I didn't want to go to McDonald's—or back home. I decided to just drive around for a while, listening to the radio. Maybe I'd go by Pizza Piazzo and leave a note for James.

As I swung my car around, my headlights shone on a black Corvette, tucked into the far corner of the lot.

James was leaning against the rear bumper.

He looked so good in his jeans and white T-shirt, even better than he had in his waiter's uniform. The sight of him washed away the ugliness of the previous hour.

I parked and walked toward him. I was a mess—I hadn't even brushed my hair, my mascara was probably smeared, and I wasn't wearing shoes.

But James was smiling by the time I reached him.

He reached out and, with the gentlest of touches, rubbed his fingertip against my cheekbone.

There was a dot of blood on my face, he said.

It wasn't mine. It was Timmy's.

I could have conjured an excuse.

I don't know what made me do it. Maybe it was the way he listened without interrupting once, or the way nothing I said seemed to shock him. I told him everything.

Before I was even halfway through, he reached out and put his arms around me. It was the opposite of the way my father had restrained me. James drew me to him tenderly so that my head was against his chest and his arms were loose around my body.

When I finally finished, his shirt was damp from my tears.

It wasn't exactly the way I'd planned to begin our first date. Any other guy would've run away without looking back.

But James kept holding me. I closed my eyes and listened to his slow, steady heartbeat.

After a few minutes, he led me to the side of the school. The door was unlocked, which made no sense, until James explained that he'd gotten into the school through an open window by jumping up and grabbing the ledge and pulling himself up with his fingertips.

He was stronger than he looked.

He took my hand and electricity tingled all the way up my arm and thrummed through my body.

My school felt different late at night. Like an outline of itself, with the insides scooped out.

Our footsteps echoed down the quiet hallways. James led me to the gym, and we walked past the basketball court toward a small room covered in floor mats. It was where the wrestlers practiced.

He told me not to move, he'd be right back.

James disappeared, and I felt the shadows close in on me.

When James returned, my eyes had adjusted enough to see that he was holding a silver Louisville Slugger baseball bat.

At the sight of him, I felt my pulse quicken. I desperately wanted him to touch me again.

He handed me the bat and told me to let it out.

I didn't get what he meant. He gestured to a rolled-up wrestling mat and said I should pretend it was my mother and give her what she deserved.

I lifted the bat over my head with both hands and slammed it down on the mat.

I looked over at James.

I could tell it wasn't enough for him. It wasn't enough for me, either.

I lifted the bat again. And again.

It all came pouring out of me. All the anger and hurt and helplessness that had accumulated for years. I slammed the bat down for every one of her slaps and threats and scratches and insults.

I slammed the bat down on her for not loving me.

When I finally finished, I was breathing hard and sweating. I probably looked wild.

But I didn't feel helpless any longer. I didn't feel like a victim.

I dropped the bat and turned to face James.

He was staring at me like I'd given him the best gift possible—like I was the gift.

He whispered that he knew I had this inside me the first night he saw me, when I was glaring at Brittany like I wanted to claw her face off after the vote for captain. Then he pulled me against him and kissed me.

I had been kissed before, but never like that. I felt like I couldn't get enough of him. I ran my hands through his hair as the kiss went on and on. At one point he pulled away briefly and looked down at me, then dropped his head to kiss me again, like he couldn't bring himself to stop, either.

After a while, we wandered back outside, holding hands and stopping every few feet to kiss again. We sat on the bleachers, my legs draped over his, and drank a few Bud Lights and shared the chocolate-chip cannoli James had brought from Pizza Piazzo.

When it was time for me to go home, James followed me in his car. He waited until I got into my bedroom and flashed my light, our prearranged signal.

From that night on, James completely consumed me. I was addicted to him. We saw each other whenever we could, and if I wasn't with him, I was thinking about him.

Every time I arrived at school and saw a new note tucked into my locker slats, or whenever I'd look up during Poms practice and see James sitting in the bleachers, it felt like I was glowing, heated from within. It didn't even matter when Brittany left a diet brochure on top of my backpack, or when Coach put me in the back row of every routine, or when my blue-and-gold poms went missing and Coach made me pay for replacements. Nothing could bring me down.

Soon it wasn't enough to only see each other in our free time. When

James had to work weekend shifts, I sat in his section and sipped a Diet Coke and nibbled the cannoli he slipped me. I tried to do my homework but mostly just snuck looks at him.

He told me he suffered from insomnia and often went for drives when he couldn't sleep.

One night, he told me he'd gone by Brittany's house. The way he was smiling—it reminded me of how he'd looked when Mrs. Davis tried to chastise him at the restaurant and he turned the tables on her.

I imagined him letting the air out of Mrs. Davis's tires, or smearing peanut butter into the keyhole of their door.

But when I asked what he'd done, James told me he'd taken their cat from their front yard.

I remembered the sweet little cat—Smokey—from the days when I'd been friends with Brittany. Smokey wore a silver bell on his collar. He liked to sit in your lap and knead his paws against your stomach and purr.

An icicle pierced my chest as I asked James what he'd done with Smokey.

James blinked at me, like he was surprised by the question. Then he said he'd gotten it a can of tuna and would keep it at his place for another day or so before bringing it back.

His words blew away the irrational flicker of fear I'd felt.

He asked me calmly if I thought he'd hurt an animal, and I shook my head. Of course James was only pulling a prank. Why had my mind raced to the assumption that he'd done something terrible to an innocent creature?

Still, I didn't like the thought of Smokey being alone in a strange room, even just for a day or so.

But all of those thoughts evaporated from my mind when James leaned in closer and cupped my face in his warm hands and kissed me again. Then he told me that he also sometimes drove by my house late at night and parked by the curb and stared up at my window.

It felt like he was watching over me, keeping me safe.

I lost my virginity to James a week later, when he took me to a field

in the middle of the woods behind my high school and spread out a blan-
ket under a star-filled sky.

Afterward, he asked me what I was thinking.

I told him the truth. I thought I loved him.

When he whispered it back to me, I felt like I could float right up
to the stars.

One of the things I'd written about in my *Romeo and Juliet* essay
was a quote everyone knows: *"Parting is such sweet sorrow."*

I'd argued that the line just above it is more significant because it
foreshadows the fate of the young couple: *"Yet I should kill thee with*
much cherishing."

I got an A-minus on that essay, and I stuck the paper in my binder
and promptly forgot about it.

Now, though, I find myself thinking about that line quite a lot.

CHAPTER THIRTEEN

CATHERINE

I flip through the book I ordered—*Tell Me Your Life Story, Mom*—realizing how few questions I can answer. I could write down that my mother loves anchovies and hates mustard unless it's the stone-ground kind. She laughs uncontrollably whenever the Amy Schumer movie *Trainwreck* plays, even though she's seen it a dozen times. If she could travel anywhere in the world, it would be to Italy.

But the whole first part of her life—the years that shaped her into the woman she is today—are a mystery to me.

I've never thought of my mother as sneaky or untruthful. Yet in the past two days I've learned how skilled she is at keeping secrets.

My mother led me to believe she had a small social life, that she occasionally dated or went to a bar. Melanie revealed that to be a fiction.

I also believed my mother wanted me to have a social life. Though I don't have a lot of close friends, and it's not like I have extra money to get mani-pedis with the girls or take weekend trips to New York, my mother always seemed happy when I met a classmate for a drink or went out on a date.

Except for this: My mom didn't like Ethan, the only guy I've ever been serious about.

She never said so explicitly. But I sensed it. Ethan did, too.

I broke up with Ethan for a few reasons. The main one was because he drank too much. He worked as a bartender, and though he talked about becoming a photographer, he didn't do anything to advance that career plan beyond buying an expensive camera.

Ethan was charismatic and funny and easygoing, the kind of guy who turned every night into a party. He had sleeve tattoos with red and purple flowers, skulls, a diamondback snake, and the queen of hearts. He wore a woven blue leather bracelet and a single gold hoop earring. He seemed composed of color. He infused it into my life.

The night we broke up—the night he broke my heart—was also our one-year anniversary. He told me to meet him at a French bistro as soon as I got off work. I thought maybe he was going to ask if I wanted to get our own place and live together. He'd been hinting about it. I hadn't decided yet how to answer him.

I arrived a few minutes early and was seated at a table covered by a crisp white cloth. The waiters wore dark suits, and the tables were set with multiple forks and spoons. I ordered a glass of rosé and decided to try oysters for the first time in my life.

For the next thirty minutes, I slowly sipped my wine and discretely checked my cell phone to see if Ethan had replied to my texts and calls.

I've never taken a walk of shame the morning after a hookup, but I sure felt like I was taking one on that endless journey out of the restaurant when it was obvious to everyone around me I'd been stood up.

When I arrived home, Ethan was passed out on our living room couch with the plastic bucket we used to hold cleaning supplies on the floor next to him. It was barely 7:30 p.m.

It wasn't the first time I'd seen Ethan like this. Some nights, he'd forgo alcohol completely—but when he drank, the taste of alcohol overrode the internal shutoff valve most people possess, the one that makes them stop after two or three or four.

My mother told me Ethan had shown up shortly after she'd arrived home from work, saying he'd forgotten his phone here the night before.

When my mom excused herself to go take a shower, he'd helped himself to a drink. Mom and I generally only kept beer in the house, but that night we happened to have a bottle of good Russian vodka. One of my mother's longtime customers, who was from Moscow, had given it to her as a gift before he moved back to Russia.

Ethan liked tequila, bourbon, and beer. I'd even seen him drink a wine spritzer once, when there were no other options. But his favorite was vodka.

He was drunk before I even headed to the restaurant.

It wasn't the first time Ethan had disappointed me. But I vowed it would be the last.

When we broke up, I blocked him. But I never deleted his number from my contacts.

Now I pull out my phone and scroll to his name. A touch of a button is all it takes to unblock someone.

I hesitate, thinking of the empty weeks following our breakup, when it felt like all the sunlight had drained out of my days. I would not have gotten through them if it hadn't been for my mother. She sat beside me on the couch, promising me I'd forget Ethan and find someone even better.

Ethan isn't the kind of guy I want my daughter to end up with, she'd told me, and she'd sounded so certain that it cemented my resolve.

Without my mother's voice in my ear, I probably would have gone back to Ethan and had my heart broken all over again a few more times before I got out for good.

I was so focused on my mother's dislike of Ethan that I never paid much attention to his dislike of her. My mother had my best interests at heart. I took that for granted.

But now I find myself thinking about something Ethan said shortly before we broke up. I hated acknowledging the tension between the two people I cared about most, so I denied it.

She never even gave me a chance, he'd said.

I could stay home tonight and try to talk to my mother again.

But I no longer trust that she's the best source of information about herself.

I press the button to unblock Ethan. All these months later, I'm desperate to know what he meant.

I slowly type out a new text. Hey, it's Catherine. Long time . . . so I have something to ask you. Let me know if you have a few minutes to talk.

I send it before I lose my nerve.

If someone blocks you, your text message to them won't ever be delivered. It'll linger in the ether, in that wispy, gray area of cyberspace between transmission and landing.

My message reaches Ethan. I know because when we were dating, we set our phones to notify each other whenever we'd read the messages we sent.

Ethan never changed that setting. He reads my message about thirty seconds after I send it.

It takes him only a moment to reply.

I'm working tonight if you want to come by.

Ethan has a new tattoo on the inside of his forearm—an intricately etched compass—and his hair is now long enough to draw into a short ponytail.

He looks good.

The bar won't get crowded until 8 or 9 p.m., but a handful of people have arrived for happy hour. I slide onto a stool, watching Ethan laugh and chat with two women while he makes them lemon martinis. He's great with customers. It's one reason why he earns so much in tips.

I've spent a lot of hours perched on a stool here, waiting for Ethan to get off work. This bar has always seemed festive to me, with its strings of milk-glass globe lights running across the ceiling and classic rock playing.

Ever since my mother's diagnosis, though, it's like I'm wearing glasses that reveal the darker underside of the world. Now I notice the grime on the floor; the sour smell of old beer; and the bald guy sitting alone in the corner, frowning at his phone. He's close to my mother's age, and he's rail thin. Maybe his genes have turned against him, too. Maybe his hair loss and lack of body fat are due to chemotherapy.

At the sound of my name, I turn my head.

The wide wooden bar between us saves me from having to offer an awkward hug. Ethan leans down and rests on his elbows, so we're eye to eye. There's nothing but casual warmth in his expression. It's the same face he wears to greet loyal customers. That, more than anything he could say, tells me he has moved on.

I'm the one who broke up with him, yet I feel a tinge of regret. Maybe it's because I haven't met anyone else, and I'm confident Ethan has. Women seem to love him, in part because he's masculine without being the slightest bit domineering.

"You look great," he tells me.

For a moment, I'm grateful I dabbed on lip gloss and outlined my eyes with a coppery brown pencil before I came in.

Then I remind myself I'm here to get information, not flirt with my ex.

Ethan offers me a drink, and I tell him I'll take a Blue Moon on tap. We chat for another few moments, with Ethan breaking away now and then to mix a gin and tonic or uncap a beer.

I'm in no rush. I sent my mother a text telling her I was seeing a movie with a friend, so she won't be expecting me home for dinner.

The question I have for Ethan isn't one I want to casually throw out. I need to study his face while he answers.

But I also want to linger because being around Ethan, back in this old familiar setting, is loosening memories for me. Like this one: When Ethan first met my mom, I thought it went well. He was polite and friendly. He took off his shoes when he came into the apartment without being asked, and he held open the door for me to walk through when we left.

My mother seemed to approve of him. When did that shift?

Ethan and I grew serious quickly. We were opposites in many ways, which made us feel like we fit together well.

Our schedules were opposites, too, and that prevented us from seeing each other more than twice a week or so. But we texted throughout the day and talked on the phone every night, usually when Ethan had a slow moment at work.

My mom asked how I felt about him one morning after I came home from spending the night at his place. She was getting ready for work, and before she walked out the door she paused and asked if Ethan was the kind of guy I could see myself ending up with.

I'd taken it as a sincere inquiry. She wanted to know how much I liked him. My answer was in that spirit, too: *It's too soon to know.*

But now it feels like she stuck a splinter under my skin with that question. It made me more attuned to Ethan's drinking and lack of ambition. It took me out of the present and into the future, when the very qualities I loved in him could turn into liabilities.

My mother had already answered the question for herself. She'd told me so when I broke up with Ethan: *Ethan isn't the kind of guy I want my daughter to end up with.*

I know how she viewed Ethan.

It's finally time for me to glimpse the picture he held of my mother.

A few minutes later, I get my chance. Ethan walks around the bar and slides onto the stool next to mine.

"I know you didn't just come here for a beer."

I nod. I'd practiced how to say this on the way here, arranging and rearranging my words, but they still sound stiff. "This was a long time ago, but you and my mom never really hit it off. . . . I guess I've been wondering why you didn't like her."

Ethan reaches for my beer and takes a sip, twisting the glass around so his lips are in the exact spot mine touched a minute ago. It feels oddly intimate.

Instead of an answer, he replies with a question.

"Did she mess up another relationship for you?"

My surprise quickly recedes as anger rushes in. My mother had nothing to do with Ethan getting drunk and failing to show up for our special anniversary dinner. She was right about him all along. He's still a boy, not a man.

"My mother didn't—"

He interrupts me. "Ever wonder how convenient it was that your mom happened to have a Russian customer who gave her a bottle of Beluga Gold the same day as our anniversary?"

I'm taken aback. It's true that in all the years my mother has worked as a waitress, the only gifts customers have given her are tips. But Ethan's suggestion is ludicrous.

"What are you saying? Are you implying my mother bought the vodka herself so you'd get drunk and I'd break up with you?"

As riled up as I am, I know this to be true: Ethan doesn't hold grudges. He's not petty. And he no longer wants to be in a relationship with me. He must have some other motivation for disparaging my mother. Perhaps it's a simple matter of not wanting to take responsibility for his own role in our destruction.

Coming here was a mistake. I should be at home with my mom, spending one of the limited evenings we have left together.

"She didn't pour the vodka down your throat, Ethan."

I stand up and begin to walk away.

"No," Ethan calls after me. "But she poured me my first drink that night."

I spin around. He is staring at me levelly. There's no malice in his gaze. But I do see pity, and it convinces me of the truth of his words.

What he says next shocks me to my core.

"And I think she might have drugged me."

CHAPTER FOURTEEN

RUTH

Unhealthy patterns echo down family lines. They're bequeathed from generation to generation, like blue-chip stocks or hair color. But there is a silver lining. If we're aware of them, we can edit the script that feels embedded in our genes.

When I left home, I vowed to never repeat my mother's mistakes. I wouldn't deliberately hurt my child. I would protect Catherine with my life.

I knew I wouldn't have a lot of money or a nice house. I'd never graduate from high school or go to Rome.

But I would always have my daughter.

In many ways, my life has unfolded as I envisioned it when I fled nearly a quarter century ago with nothing but a few hundred bucks, a stolen watch, and a duffle bag. My father may have lost all the pride he had in me, but I think he would be pleased with how Catherine turned out: a college-educated nurse with his beautiful golden-brown skin and near obsession with ketchup.

He would love her so much.

Maybe he would still love me a little bit, too.

Catherine is my reason for pushing back against the darkness that has snaked through the line of females in my family, the ugly legacy that has caused so much pain and destruction. She is my fresh start.

I've succeeded in not repeating my mother's mistakes. But I've made new ones that are all my own. Terrible ones that have caused my daughter unnecessary pain.

I settle deeper into the pillows propped on my bed with a sigh. My lower back aches tonight from carrying too many heavy trays, so I added Epsom salts to the hot water when I took my bath. It would be a gift if I could empty my mind and relax, but that's impossible.

I kept seeing James today.

He was one car over at a stoplight this morning. He sat in booth seven this afternoon. He was the shadow in my bedroom that disappeared when I flicked on the light.

He's drawing closer. I can sense it. Soon I'll see a car parked outside my apartment building late at night, its driver watching over me. And then I'll open the door and there he'll be. He'll pull me tightly against him, his strong arms wrapping around me.

He's here with me now, too. The truth is, James has never left me.

I reach for my old notebook again. I need to write down as much of my story as I can, while I still can.

James surprised me by showing up at school one day right after the final bell sounded. I was walking toward the bleachers that encircled the field where Poms practice was held when a cluster of students ahead of me parted and there he was, as if conjured by my thoughts.

I squealed and jumped into his arms. We kissed—a long, deep kiss. Someone hooted, but I didn't care who was watching. The saying "in love" made sense for the first time in my life. Love wasn't just something I felt, like hunger or fatigue. I'd plunged deeply into it. It coursed through every one of my cells.

I lost track of time. I often did when I was with James. We existed in our own universe. Our surroundings never mattered. James lived in a dreary room he'd rented from a widow who needed the income. He'd sneak me in there sometimes, the two of us dissolving into laughter as we tiptoed up the stairs—luckily, the old woman was hard of hearing—and even though stains pocked the walls and the house smelled like dog pee, I didn't care about anything but James. He was tender and sexy and strong, and despite being estranged from his family and having to make his own way in the world, he never once complained.

On that Wednesday afternoon, I finally detached myself from James and started to walk toward the field. He kept ahold of my hand and yanked me back in for one last, lingering kiss.

I protested that I'd see him in three hours since we were going out that night.

James said it was too long to wait.

I laughed. I did that a lot when I was with James. I always felt slightly tipsy around him.

By the time I finally got down to the field, practice had begun. I tossed my backpack and water bottle onto the bleachers—I'd learned to keep my stuff far away from the sidelines—and ran to join the others. The song "Gettin' Jiggy Wit It" by Will Smith was playing from Coach's tape deck, and the eleven other girls were in formation.

But Coach held up his palm to me and told me to take a seat.

At first I thought they were creating a new routine, one that left me out. I wouldn't put it past Coach or Brittany.

Then Coach told me I was being benched because I'd been late three times in the past two weeks.

I started to protest, then fell silent. I didn't think it was true, but James had been surprising me at the end of the school day fairly often lately. But I was only five minutes late, if that. And this was the first I'd heard of Coach tallying up my tardiness—or anyone's, for that matter.

Instead of going to sit on the bleachers, I remained on the sidelines a few feet down from him. Coach was trying to separate me from the team. I couldn't let him.

I expected him to motion me to go in during the first break. But he just told the girls to do it again, this time with more energy.

After another ten minutes, I approached Coach and asked if I could go in.

He didn't even look at me when he replied that I'd go in when he was good and ready.

I swallowed my pride and apologized, promising I wouldn't be late again.

His voice was clipped when he told me that we were not going to have this conversation now.

So I waited. Coach resumed acting like I wasn't there.

When practice was half over, I walked up to Coach again and asked if he was going to make me stand there the whole practice.

He finally turned to me. I couldn't see his eyes behind his shiny aviator sunglasses. I'd disrespected everyone else's time, he sneered, so why did I suddenly think mine was so important?

I'd already apologized. I wasn't going to do it again, not to him. Besides, it wasn't like a football play where no one could practice if I wasn't on the field.

I repeated that I'd only been five minutes late.

Then Coach said I'd had two warnings, and today was my third.

He was bald-faced lying. He'd never given me a single warning. When I tried to say that, he held up his palm again and turned his back on me.

Anger flashed into me.

Before I even knew what I was saying, I blurted out something I shouldn't have. I said I'd appreciate it if he could let me know when I'd be able to join practice—or maybe he needed Brittany and Mrs. Davis to tell him how long my punishment should be.

That was a mistake. Something shifted in his body language.

Coach had been a guy with big dreams once. Those rock star T-shirts, the Eric Clapton guitar behind glass in his office. He probably imagined girls screaming his name while he stood in the spotlight. Maybe he thought he still had power and prestige, even if it was only over a dozen high school girls. My words—loud enough for the whole team to hear—had just torn it away from him.

He shouted that practice was over and ordered me into his office.

Then Coach turned and strode off the field, throwing his clipboard to the grass.

When he was safely out of earshot, Brittany hooted and clapped her hands together. I shot her the finger and followed Coach.

Coach's office was a tiny room off the indoor basketball court. It was windowless and barely big enough to hold a desk, a file cabinet, and two chairs. Next door was the football coach's office, which was four times the size. That probably stung, too.

As I stepped inside, Coach ordered me to close the door.

I obeyed.

Coach took off his Ray-Bans and put them down on his desk. I stood there waiting for my lecture on respect and responsibility.

He moved even closer to me, so near I could smell the mint gum he was chewing. Then he said that I must think pretty highly of myself.

I knew better than to reply. Anything I said would only inflame him. Turns out, not answering didn't help either.

The next thing that happened shocked me to my core. His voice was almost a whisper when he told me he'd seen me strutting around school like I was hot shit.

I flinched because I'd never heard a teacher swear before.

What he did after that was so strange. Coach began to walk in a slow circle around me as my skin prickled.

It felt unnaturally quiet down here. No one was dribbling a basketball on the court. That season wouldn't start for another few months. The football players and coaches were all on the main field. Most of the teachers in the building had left for the day, and the only ones remaining were a floor or two above us.

Coach was behind me now. I couldn't see him at all.

I didn't move. There was nowhere to go in the tiny office. Plus, I knew if I walked out or spoke up, Coach would use it as an excuse to increase whatever punishment he had in mind.

But there was something else holding me in place. Fear.

It made no sense. I was in a public building with a teacher I'd *known for years. Why did I feel as vulnerable and exposed as I did when I was a kid and my mother tore into my bedroom at night and yanked off my covers and began screaming at me for some infraction I wasn't aware I'd committed?*

Coach's breath tickled my ear as he told me he'd seen me grinding against my boyfriend like I couldn't get enough of him.

The building was air-conditioned, and down in the basement, it felt especially cold. I wanted to wrap my arms around myself, but I felt strangely immobilized.

Coach kept walking until I could see him in my peripheral vision. He kept talking in that low, creepy voice, telling me he knew I was a hungry girl, that I was hungry for lots of things.

He slid a hand across my abdomen and I instinctively sucked in. He smiled, and I hated giving him the satisfaction of a reaction.

He let his hand linger around my belly button and told me I was getting a little thick around my middle.

Coach touched all of us girls sometimes. He stretched hamstrings and high-fived us and rubbed out charley horses.

This touch felt different.

Coach's hand moved higher, until it was directly beneath my left breast.

Then he said I was getting a little thick there, too. That I'd been bouncing all over the place at practice.

He skimmed his hand over my breast so quickly it was over before I even knew what was happening. My breasts had felt tender the last few days, and his touch seemed amplified. Like his hand was still there, his palm brushing my nipple, even after he withdrew it.

Tears pricked my eyes.

His voice snaked into my ear as he told me that ten years from now, I was going to be a fat cow, living in a double-wide with a bunch of snotty kids while my husband jacked off to porn because he can't stand looking at me.

I couldn't hold back my tears. They dripped silently down my cheeks. Coach was stripping me raw, just like he'd done the night he made Brittany captain, but this was so much worse.

Then I felt the trail of his fingers sliding down below the elastic waistband of my athletic shorts and underpants and touching between my legs.

I stopped breathing. I couldn't process what was happening.

Coach pulled out his hand and stood in front of me. It felt like he was feasting on my tears.

He reached out in a gesture that might've seemed sympathetic if I hadn't seen the gleam in his eyes. He pulled me close to him, as close as I'd been to James only an hour ago.

He asked if he was being too hard on me.

His arms tightened around me, trapping me, as he rocked his hips forward. He meant the double entendre.

The worst part was, I didn't fight back. I didn't even try to pull away. I just stood there and took it as he ground his pelvis against me, as his breath started coming faster.

It felt like I left my body, but unlike the other night when I'd fought with my mother and went to a place so dark it blinded me, this time I floated up to the ceiling, where I could see everything. I knew what was happening—Coach was getting his rocks off through the thin layers of our clothing—but it didn't feel like it was happening to me.

It was over in what could've been sixty seconds, or ten minutes.

Coach quickly walked around behind his desk and sat down. His face was flushed.

Suddenly his tone was businesslike again. He told me that since I'd refused to give him a formal apology when he'd requested one, he had no choice but to kick me off the team.

I couldn't process his words. It felt like they were coming at me from all directions, as if I was in an echo chamber.

Coach rustled a few papers on his desk, not looking at me, as he said he'd move up someone from JV to take my place, and that he'd email the principal and Mrs. Davis and the team to let them know.

Whatever Coach claimed, Mrs. Davis and Brittany and half of the other girls would back him up. The truth never had a chance.

Just like I never did.

I couldn't say a word. Ice still encased me, but somehow I managed to walk out of his office. I went directly to my car, where Rosie was waiting for me, holding the backpack and water bottle I'd left on the bleachers.

She frowned as she peered at my face and asked if I was okay.

Sure, I replied. I may have even smiled.

I probably didn't look any different than when I'd followed Coach into his office. I was still wearing my shorts and T-shirt and socks and sneakers. My hair was still up in blue-and-gold twisted scrunchies. I wasn't even crying.

But I wasn't the same girl. I wouldn't ever be her again.

I told James everything that night. When he held me, it didn't erase Coach's touch, but it helped thaw me out.

It was hard to keep talking when I got to the part about Coach's fingers sliding down inside my underpants, and what happened afterward. But James didn't react. He kept looking at me gently and steadily, like he was entering into that awful space alongside me so I wouldn't be alone.

When I finished talking, James told me Coach wasn't going to get away with it. James didn't seem angry, despite his words. His voice was calm. He wasn't even frowning.

I was glad he wanted to stick up for me, but I shook my head. Who would believe me? By now Coach's words had settled deep into my brain. Lots of people had seen James and I making out after school. It's not like I had a stellar reputation, which shouldn't matter, but double standards exist. They do.

James had a whole plan mapped out before I even realized where he was taking me in his car.

When we pulled up at my high school, my whole body recoiled. I couldn't imagine ever setting foot inside the halls again. I'd always be scared Coach would call me into his office on a made-up excuse, like to return my uniform, and close the door behind us.

I whispered that I didn't want to be here.

But James asked if I trusted him, and I nodded.

Then he asked if I wanted to make Coach pay.

I did, more than anything.

James opened his car door, then came around to my side and opened mine. He led me to the side door we'd used to enter the school before. He told me to wait and he'd let me in.

He disappeared and I knew he was pulling himself in through the upper-story window, the one that was always cracked open.

He took longer to appear than I'd expected. I began to shiver, even though it wasn't cold out.

Finally, the door opened with a loud squeak. James had turned on the hall light and he was backlit, so he looked almost like a silhouette at first. I instinctively recoiled.

Then my eyes adjusted, and I saw James was holding the silver Louisville Slugger.

I expected him to take me to the wrestling room again, but he veered the other way. He took me to Coach's office.

My whole body was trembling now.

James reached for the door handle. It was locked.

He looked at me and shrugged, and for a second I thought that was it—we were going to turn around and do something else tonight.

Then James began kicking the door with the hard soles of his shoe, again and again, as the cheap, hollow door shuddered. It only took a half-dozen kicks until the wood around the knob began to splinter and the door gave way.

I half expected people to come running at the noise, but of course the building had been empty for hours.

Somehow, breaking in removed the menace from this room. James knew exactly what I needed to offset the sickening helplessness I'd felt in this space.

James flicked on the overhead light. Coach's shiny sunglasses were still on the desk, right where he put them after he'd brought me in here.

James handed me the bat and told me it was all mine.

I lifted it above my head and brought it down on the sunglasses. The impact of the bat against the metal desk jarred my arms all the way down to their sockets. The sunglasses flew off the table, their frames crushed.

Then James pointed to the Clapton guitar.

The words "I can't" died on my lips. Sure I could. Coach had taken something far more valuable from me than a piece of memorabilia.

I stepped forward, holding the bat over my shoulder like I was waiting for a pitch. The room was so small I checked behind me to make sure James wouldn't get hit by my backswing. I took a deep breath, then let loose.

The guitar was completely ruined by my fourth hit, but I whacked it until my arms grew tired.

When I finally handed James the bat, he winked at me and said our work here was almost done.

That was when I heard the distant sound of footsteps coming down the hallway.

Panic shot through me. Coach would probably suspect I was behind the vandalism, but I could create an alibi with James. Our school didn't have any cameras or security guards. No one could prove it was us.

Unless an eyewitness saw me and James.

While all this ran through my head, James was moving around. The destroyed guitar and its case had fallen to the floor behind the desk, so he didn't need to hide them from any passersby. He pushed the door all the way open, so you couldn't immediately tell it was damaged, and he left the lights on. James was still holding the bat, which was evidence of what we'd done.

The sound of shoe soles slapping against the linoleum floor was just down the hall now, drawing closer with every step.

James was so calm he had to have a plan. But he was moving too slowly—there was nowhere to hide. We'd be caught.

My heart felt like it was about to burst.

I wouldn't just be kicked off the Poms squad. I'd probably be kicked out of school. The police would arrive, and everyone would know what I'd done. I might even get arrested.

Right before he came into view, I heard Coach's voice. He called out *the name Donna—that was our vice principal—as if he was expecting to see her.*

It was all over. Coach was coming. We were about to be discovered. I shrank back into the office. But James did the opposite.

He lifted the bat and stepped forward, in perfect timing for the bat to explode in a half circle and meet Coach's stomach as Coach rounded the corner and stepped over the threshold into his office.

Later, I pieced together what had happened. James told me some details when he drove me home that night, and the rest I put together through newspaper articles I researched.

At the beginning of the night, while I was waiting outside the school, wondering what was taking James so long, James broke into the main office and found Coach's phone number on a list of contact information for teachers. He called Coach and identified himself as a police officer who wanted to alert Coach about a break-in at the school and the theft of his signed guitar. He told Coach that the assistant principal—Donna—was already at the scene in Coach's office.

Coach came rushing in. He hadn't surprised us, after all.

It was James who'd surprised him.

The next afternoon, Coach died from his injuries. The papers reported that he'd been hit more than two dozen times with a baseball bat that was found at the scene.

By the time Coach was being removed from machines that had worked to keep his body alive, I was stepping off a bus, arriving in a city a hundred miles away from my hometown. The girl I was before—Ava Morales—was gone.

I had the gold watch James took off Coach's wrist, a little cash, and a duffle bag with a few of my belongings.

James became the lead suspect quickly and I was a suspect, too. They called us the "Oak Hill High teen killers," and a tabloid ran photos of the two of us side by side on the front page.

I knew no one would believe me if I told the truth and said James summoned Coach to the office and swung the bat before I even knew what was happening.

Of all the images of the night of the attack that I keep replaying, there's one I go back to the most: James setting the bat down on the floor, then looking at me as he grabbed Coach's limp arms and dragged Coach deeper into his office, leaving a trail of smeared blood.

James's eyes were as gentle and untroubled as if we'd just finished making love.

His eyes were the most terrifying thing I'd ever seen.

When I saw them, I began to tremble so hard my teeth chattered. I tried to pick up the phone on Coach's desk to call an ambulance, but James pulled me away.

Never leave fingerprints, he told me as he wiped down the bat with his T-shirt. Then he gave me instructions: We'd go home and grab whatever valuables we could—the old lady he boarded with had a safe in her bedroom James wanted to break into—then we'd meet at Pizza Piazzo at midnight. We'd run to a place where no one could ever find us. We'd be gone tonight.

James paused in yanking the gold watch off Coach's wrist and stared at me.

He asked if I was going to come with him.

When I didn't answer immediately, James let Coach's arm drop roughly to the floor and he moved closer to me. I glanced at the baseball bat, still within James's reach.

If I thought I'd been terrified before, now I knew true fear.

I blurted that of course I'd meet him at the restaurant.

James held up the watch close to my face and pointed to the twelve at the top of the circle. I heard the faint sound that would grow to haunt me: tick-tock, tick-tock . . .

James slipped the watch onto my wrist and told me not to lose track of time. He said he'd see me at midnight.

But I ran alone.

You were already growing in my stomach by then, even though I didn't know it yet. I'd probably gotten pregnant that very first time with James, under the stars.

You gave me a new purpose, one that burned through me and kept me going during all the hard, scary times ahead. I knew I had to hide for the rest of my life. It wasn't merely self-preservation. My goal was to keep you safe, too, Catherine.

Everyone would know you were the daughter of the teen killers. You'd be a curiosity, and worse, a pariah. And when James and I were both sent to prison, as we surely would be, my mother and father would probably be given custody of you. For long hours every day, while my father was at work and Timmy at school, you'd be alone with my mother.

I needed to do whatever it took to break the pattern.

Even if it meant that in a way, I would die, too.

CHAPTER FIFTEEN

CATHERINE

Diagnosing Alzheimer's is a slow, methodical process. Symptoms appear gradually. At first, they're typically overlooked or minimized. When they reach the point of undeniability, other potential culprits—brain tumors, strokes, hydrocephalus—are ruled out. In a small number of cases, genetic tests provide certainty, and brain scans can help afford a level of surety. But usually it's a jigsaw method; individual pieces are put together until the picture becomes clear.

I know the exact moment I began to fear my mother might have Alzheimer's. It was three weeks ago, when I called her cell phone to find out why she wasn't home from the drugstore yet. She'd gotten lost. She didn't say so, not exactly, but it was obvious.

After that, I watched her closely. The signs piled up so quickly it seemed impossible I'd missed them before.

Still, I didn't catastrophize. I knew simpler reasons were likely the source of her symptoms.

I insisted she make an appointment with her general practitioner. That was the protocol. When no obvious factor emerged to explain her brain fog, we proceeded to the next level and saw Dr. Chen.

That morning in his office was when the puzzle pieces clicked into place—seamlessly, ruthlessly. The picture was undeniable.

It's past midnight now, and I'm in bed, wide awake. My mother is on the other side of our shared wall.

I walked around for hours after leaving Ethan's bar. I was in such a daze I have no memory of what path I followed, and I didn't notice blisters forming on both of my heels because I was wearing flats instead of my usual sneakers. I only turned toward home when I knew my mother would be asleep.

I can't bear to see her.

I should be exhausted, but I'm as wired as if I just drank a pot of coffee.

I almost can't believe what Ethan revealed, that my mother might have drugged him. That she tried to ruin my relationship with him.

Almost.

Our apartment is as quiet as a graveyard now. I slip out of bed and pull on my robe.

I walk out of my bedroom, my footsteps light, using the flashlight on my cell phone to guide me. I enter the living room and begin to search.

Everyone keeps something from their past—a letter, a memento, a photo. If my mother has a talisman, she must have hidden it well.

Even if she doesn't, some object I've seen a thousand times before could hold new meaning now that I'm seeing my mother in a different light. I want to examine the tangible things that compose our lives.

I begin in one corner of the room and work my way through a kind of search grid. I look under the carpet. I lift up every sofa cushion. I even peek behind the prints on our walls.

There's nothing.

I carry a chair into the kitchen so I can stand on it and peer all the way in the back of the high cupboards. There's nothing unusual there, other than a dusty box of Rice Krispies I wasn't aware we had. I step down and work my way through the lower cabinets. Our usual staples are there: rigatoni, pasta sauce, black beans, brown rice, granola bars, chamomile tea. I'm checking the storage drawer at the bottom of the oven when I hear the creak that means my mother's door is opening.

I turn off my flashlight as goose bumps rise on my skin.

I can't tell if she's coming my way.

There's no reason to feel afraid. I could say I'm getting a glass of water. It's not like she hasn't ever walked in on me in the kitchen and seen me doing just that.

But my mother knows me so well.

I can't shake the sense that if she sees my face, she will instantly know what I'm up to.

I hear the sound of the toilet flush, then, a moment later, my mother's door closes.

I wait a few breaths, then resume my search.

My mother seemed to have materialized at the age of eighteen, when she had me. It's as if we were both born at the same time. She conceals her past well, but nobody moves through the world without leaving a trace.

I can't find one in the kitchen, though. I walk back through the living room and see my mother's purse hanging on the hook by the front door.

I walk toward it and lift it off, then carry it into my bedroom.

I close my door and wait. I think I hear a faint rustling sound on the other side of the wall, but I can't say for sure. There's no way my mother would need something from her purse at this hour, I assure myself.

I check the outer pocket first. All it contains are my mother's keys and the container of Mace she keeps handy when she walks alone at night. Tucked inside the main section is a small makeup pouch that holds a cherry ChapStick, unscented hand lotion, and an emery board. No surprises there. My mother has used cherry ChapStick for as long as I can remember, and she tries to take care of her hands since they get a beating at work.

I take out her wallet and begin pulling items from its folds, placing them on my bedspread. I look at her driver's license first. In the photo, she is unsmiling. She has an ATM card for our joint account, a Visa credit card, and a few coupons. In the slot for cash are a lot of fives and ones. Tip money.

I feel around in the space behind the card slot panel and come across something else. I slide out two crisp fifty-dollar bills, which I guess my mom keeps for emergencies. But there's one more item tucked behind them. It's a different kind of card, one I didn't know she possessed.

A library card.

I turn it over in my hand and recognize her faded, nearly illegible signature on the back: Ruth M. Sterling.

My mother used to take me to the library when I was younger. On my first visit, I got my very own card and felt so proud when the librarian slid that laminated rectangle over the counter to me.

As I grew older, I began visiting the library on my own. My mother never asked to accompany me. She has mild dyslexia and isn't a big reader. She prefers TV and movies and listening to podcasts.

I had no idea she'd gotten her own card. And I can't recall her ever once bringing home a library book. So why does she keep this in her wallet?

I grip it tightly, staring down at my mother's signature, until I notice something about the two folded fifty-dollar bills. Now that they aren't compressed, they've yawned opened, revealing something tucked in the center of the innermost bill: a small slip of paper.

It's a receipt from a book my mother checked out from the library. The title is *Understanding Alzheimer's*.

This makes sense. Even though my mother doesn't want to discuss her disease with me yet, she must be making an effort to learn more about it.

Then I notice the date on the slip.

She checked out the book nearly five months ago.

My heart plummets. Did my mother's symptoms start even sooner than she told Dr. Chen?

I stare at the library slip, not quite comprehending its meaning, until the letters and numbers on it grow blurry.

It's an innocuous piece of paper. Why does it feel imbued with menace?

There's something I'm missing, a series of little clues in these simple objects that add up to something greater than their parts.

A question nibbles at the corners of my mind, slowly forming, before it bursts into my consciousness: If my mother got a library card recently for the sole purpose of reading *Understanding Alzheimer's*, why does her card look so old and worn, with the lamination peeling at one corner, as if she has used it hundreds of times?

Maybe she has secretly checked out other books through the years, keeping the volumes hidden from me.

But that doesn't make sense, either.

Unless her reading history is the talisman I've been searching for. Maybe it's related to her past if she's trying to conceal it from me.

Through the thin wall, I hear my mother's bed creak again. The noise propels me into motion. I stand up and tuck the library card into my sock drawer, then reassemble her wallet and tiptoe into the hallway, holding my breath until I've slid her purse back onto its hook.

I return to my room and climb into bed, pulling up the covers. My feet are icy and my head is beginning to ache. I keep turning over my strange discoveries in my mind, searching for their meaning.

It takes me a long time to fall asleep. When I finally do, my dreams are restless.

The next morning, I wait in bed, listening to my mother quietly go about her routine. Her footsteps pause in front of my door. I close my eyes quickly, prepared to feign sleep, but she doesn't knock or try to come in.

A moment later, she leaves for work.

The second the door closes behind her, I get up and dress, then head to the bathroom to cover my twin blisters with Band-Aids. I force myself to eat a banana to settle my sour stomach.

When the closest library branch opens, I'm the first visitor to walk through its door. I haven't been here in a while—my reading lately has been for school—and I'm relieved the first librarian I see is a middle-aged woman with dreadlocks and a nose ring. I've never seen her before, so hopefully she won't know the name on my card is the wrong one.

I greet her with what I hope is a confident smile.

"Hi, this might sound strange, but I checked out a book a while ago and I wanted to recommend it to a friend, but I can't recall the title."

"Do you recall the topic of the book? Or what the cover looked like?"

I shake my head. "I don't. Sorry."

It sounds implausible. Why would I want to recommend a book I remember absolutely nothing about?

I press on quickly, "Is there any way to look up my borrowing history?"

I hand her my mother's card, but she doesn't reach for it.

"I'm sorry, but we don't keep those records as long as the books are returned on time."

My heart sinks.

"Let's try another way," she suggests. "Have you ever returned a book late—or lost one?"

"I, ah, can't remember."

The librarian's smile is kind. "You would've received a fee."

"Maybe? I'm sorry, I'm not sure. . . . Things have been a little confusing for me lately."

She glances down at my mother's card. "I'll be happy to check." Her fingers click across her computer's keyboard.

She shakes her head. "No, I don't see anything."

I nod and thank her, my heart sinking. I'm about to leave when I impulsively spin back around.

"Do you have a book titled *Understanding Alzheimer's*?"

Her fingers click again, and this time she nods. She comes out from behind the desk and leads me to the correct aisle, pulling the hardcover book off a shelf.

I thank her and walk to a nearby chair, sinking down into it as I open the cover. I don't know what I'm looking for. But I feel compelled to hold the book my mother sought out.

I flip through it, my eyes skimming the pages.

Some of the information is academic, some anecdotal, but it's all wrapped in clear language. One chapter is for caregivers, and it describes the turbulent emotions family members typically undergo when a loved one receives a diagnosis of Alzheimer's. I know this to be true because I see it all the time at work. And I've experienced it myself.

There's a paragraph about a daughter whose father forgot to turn off the gas stove, nearly burning down the house, and another one about a son who says he knew something was wrong when his mother left a carton of eggs in a kitchen cupboard.

I blink and reread that sentence.

My mother did the exact same thing recently.

I lean forward, my posture tightening, scanning the words faster.

Two pages later, there's another eerily familiar anecdote: Family members could no longer deny the knowledge that something was terribly wrong when their beloved grandmother got lost on her way home from the neighborhood drugstore.

My mouth dries up. There's a strange humming in my ears.

It's as if the exact symptoms my mother experienced sprang off these very pages.

I keep reading.

One woman who was diagnosed with Alzheimer's forgot what month it was. A few days later, she called ice cubes "water squares."

I'm hyperventilating.

The book falls out of my hands, landing on the floor, as I leap up and run outside. I'm aware of someone calling after me, asking if I'm okay.

I collapse onto a bench in front of the library, my head in my hands. The world around me is swirling too fast. It's dizzying.

A suspicion is building in my brain, one so bizarre and terrifying I can't yet form the framework to express it.

I no longer know what is real.

This must be what it feels like to lose your mind.

A sob wrenches free from my throat and I begin to shake. My vision blurs. Then I hear someone's voice close by.

"Are you okay?"

I can't catch my breath to answer. I'm crying too hard.

I feel a hand on my shoulder, and for a moment, I think it's my mother, that she has somehow tracked me down. Then I wipe my eyes and look up to see the librarian.

"Can I sit with you a minute?"

I nod and she joins me on the bench. She hands me a tissue, and for a few moments, as I dab my eyes and try to regain control of myself, she doesn't say anything.

"I'm sorry for whatever you're going through," she finally tells me.

I manage to find my voice and thank her.

"If you need any help connecting to resources, we have a lot of information inside. I'll be there if you'd like to talk more." She gives my shoulder a squeeze and stands up before the meaning of her words hits me. I twist around to stare after her, but she has already disappeared into the building.

In a two-minute conversation with the librarian, I pretended to have multiple memory lapses. That, combined with my emotional breakdown, could have easily pointed her toward the wrong conclusion. Does the librarian suspect *I* might be suffering from a medical crisis, one with symptoms of severe memory loss—even early-onset Alzheimer's—because of the way I presented myself to her?

Because of the way I presented myself to her.

Something about those words nags at me.

I dig my nails into my palms and force myself to focus on the facts I've been trying to assemble:

My mother has no social life or close friends, outside of me.

My mother may have tried to destroy my relationship with Ethan.

My mother has not made any noticeable mistakes at work, but she makes them frequently at home.

My mother refuses to undergo any tests that could provide confirmation of her diagnosis.

My mother got a library card and checked out a book about Alzheimer's disease at the same time I began applying for jobs out of state five months ago.

My mother began exhibiting textbook-perfect signs of the disease—as if the book provided a blueprint she followed—right before I planned to move away and begin a new life, one that would push her to the fringes of my world.

My thoughts circle back, retracing themselves: *Diagnosing Alzheimer's is a slow, methodical process. Usually it's a jigsaw method; individual pieces are put together until the picture becomes clear.*

Reversing the diagnosis means moving the pieces into a different formation, testing out combinations until a fresh image clicks into place. The one I'm now creating is a mirror image of the original picture I held. It's a complete perspectival switch.

The idea is monstrous, but I can't dismiss it.

There could be nothing wrong with my mother. Nothing at all.

ACT TWO

CHAPTER SIXTEEN

RUTH

Catherine was five years old when she began to scare me.

Before my daughter, the only child I'd ever been close to was Timmy, who was basically pure sunshine wrapped in the form of a freckle-faced boy.

Catherine was different from the start. She rarely cried, she didn't speak until she was nearly fifteen months old, and she almost never laughed. I wasn't laughing a lot during those early days either—being perpetually exhausted and dead broke tends to dampen one's sense of mirth—so I didn't pay much attention to it.

When Catherine was about a year and a half, I took her to a playground and put her in a bucket swing, the kind with two holes for those chubby baby legs to dangle through. It was a beautiful mid-October morning. The leaves on the trees surrounding the park were brilliant shades of crimson and gold, and the sun gently warmed my skin. At first we had the park all to ourselves, which was nice.

A few minutes after we got there, though, a group of moms arrived. They all had kids around Catherine's age. The moms wore the kind of expensive-looking exercise clothes that typically don't see the inside of a gym, and they carried pretty diaper bags with all sorts of pockets and loops for coordinated accessories like sippy cups and wipes.

One of them had brought along a bottle of bubbles with a wand, and another had a big quilt for all the babies to sit on. The group stayed in a clump most of the time I was there, the moms squealing and snapping pictures with their phones every time one of the babies reached out to try to grab a bubble.

After a while, a mom carried her son over to the swing next to Catherine's. When she gave him a gentle push, her son giggled. They went on like that for a while: The mother pushed, the son giggled, the mother made exaggerated expressions and talked to her boy in a high-pitched voice.

She caught Catherine's attention, too. I watched as Catherine turned her head and studied the mother.

"Well, hello there!" The woman gave Catherine a toothy grin. "Do you like to swing, princess?"

Catherine didn't smile back.

"Look at you, so small and so serious!" The mom began talking in a voice meant to be funny. Catherine wasn't having any of it.

The woman hadn't paid attention to me before, but now I could see her taking me in. I had an old cloth tote bag with a cinnamon raisin bagel wrapped in a paper towel for me and Catherine to share, a spare diaper, and a water bottle to refill at the playground's fountain. It wasn't just my age that separated me from the group of moms with their stackable Tupperware containers of blueberries and rice puffs and their organic apple juice boxes.

I tried to crack a joke. I guess I was pretty lonely, and as I've mentioned, Catherine wasn't the best conversationalist.

"Maybe she can be Wednesday for Halloween. You know, that little girl from *The Addams Family* who never smiles?"

The mom looked shocked. She even stopped swinging her son for a minute, and his smile slipped away, too. Like we were contagious.

The mother's cheer returned quickly, but it seemed a bit forced now. "Is she your little sister?"

I'd gotten that question before. Most people assumed Catherine and I were siblings, or I was her babysitter. "No, she's my daughter."

"Oh! I'm sorry! You're just . . . it's that you're so . . ."

Her little boy's grunts turned into the start of a wail. He wanted to be pushed again. His mom's attention snapped back. "Ooh, I'm so sorry, my little man! Mommy's here! Want to swing up to the sky and grab a cloud?"

The woman didn't talk to us anymore, but I noticed her glancing at Catherine a few more times. Catherine wasn't doing anything unusual. She was just swaying back and forth and looking around. But to this mom, it seemed as if Catherine was a puzzle she couldn't quite figure out.

After a few minutes, I took Catherine out of the swing, and we walked to the bus stop to make our way back to the three-hundred-square-foot room I'd sublet from another single mom who had a two-bedroom apartment. The trip took thirty minutes each way, but the playgrounds around this part of the city were much nicer than the one by me. The only time we'd ever gone to that one, I'd found a used condom next to the slide and broken glass from bottles of booze in the grass.

I tried not to think too much about that other mom's reaction to Catherine, but I guess it stayed lodged somewhere in the back of my mind. When we got back home, I washed Catherine in the kitchen sink because we didn't have a tub. Even when she splashed her hands in the soap bubbles, her expression didn't change. She didn't coo or laugh. She seemed as detached as a scientist.

I tried using the high-pitched voice of the mom at the park: "Ooh, bubbles! Splashy-splash!"

Catherine looked at me like I was a fool, and I guess she wasn't wrong.

I went back to talking like a normal person, and in time Catherine found more words to communicate with me. When she was three, she had a pretty advanced vocabulary, so I guess starting to talk late didn't hurt her one bit.

I wasn't alarmed that Catherine didn't exhibit a wide range of emotions. Truthfully, I'd be even more exhausted if I had to take care of a toddler whose moods ticked like a metronome between angry and joyful and sulky. I liked my quiet daughter exactly as she was.

There was just this one thing.

Shortly after she turned five, we were waiting for the bus to go buy groceries—at times I felt like I spent half my life waiting for or riding buses—and something on the sidewalk behind the glass bus shelter caught her eye. I couldn't exactly see what Catherine was doing, but it looked like she was poking at the ground with a stick. I was distracted and tired. I was working as a telemarketer from home thirty hours a week because it was one of the few jobs I could do that didn't require child care, and I also took whatever babysitting gigs I could get from other parents on my block. Most of them couldn't afford much, and sometimes they couldn't pay me at all, but they always managed to give me a little something, even if it was just a hot meal or hand-me-down clothing and supplies.

By the time I finished rustling in my wallet for my bus pass and walked around behind the shelter to check on Catherine, she was squatting down, staring at something intently.

It was a dead squirrel.

I instinctively recoiled. The squirrel must've been hit by a car and flung through the air before landing in this spot. Its stomach was partially torn open, probably from crows feasting on it. You could see a bit of its pink insides.

Most little kids would've been grossed out or burst into tears—the squirrel still had a fuzzy tail and brown fur and was recognizable as a formerly cute animal—but not Catherine.

She used the stick to gently tap on its limp little paw.

"What are you doing?"

She gazed up at me, then resumed exploring the animal carcass with her stick.

"Stop it!" I almost screamed the command.

Catherine didn't seem to hear me. She leaned even closer to the mutilated creature.

"Normal kids don't do this!" I grabbed her arm, hard, and yanked her away.

Later, I noticed small purple bruises in the shape of my fingerprints marring her upper arm. It was a replica of the injury my mother had inflicted on *my* arm the night I got her off Timmy. You know how parents always say, "This is going to hurt me more than it hurts you," before they spank their child? I swear, it was true. Seeing those marks on her soft little arm gutted me.

But what I couldn't—and still can't—get out of my mind was Catherine's expression when she looked up at me as I interrupted her examination of the dead squirrel. Instead of fear or disgust or sadness—any of the emotions you might expect to see in a little kid who'd just discovered a gory animal carcass—Catherine's faded denim eyes were serene and gentle.

They were James's eyes.

That whole long night, I didn't sleep despite being so exhausted that every inch of me ached.

Even though I'm not scheduled to work at Sam's today, I rise before the sun and quietly move to the kitchen to make coffee. I plan to do what I usually do on my days off: catch up on laundry, clean the kitchen and bathroom, and go to the library to do my checking.

Catherine's door is shut. I've barely seen her in the last twenty-four hours. She didn't come home until late last night, long after I'd gotten into bed.

Her absence feels significant.

I bring a mug of coffee into the living area and sit down on the couch, savoring my first sip. At times like these, when the apartment is quiet and the fresh slate of a new day is before me, it's easier to pretend everything will work out. The mistakes I've made, the choices that may not be the right ones—all will be smoothed out in time. The road ahead will be easier than the bumpy portion I've traveled this far, I try to tell myself.

If 3 a.m. is the darkest hour of the soul, then dawn is the flip side. Few things conjure more hope in me than a sunrise.

On the coffee table in front of me is the journal Catherine bought, its title mocking me: *Tell Me Your Life Story, Mom.*

I pick it up and turn a few pages.

Maybe I can write down a nugget for Catherine and leave the page open for her to see. As a sort of peace offering, even though I'm not sure exactly why I feel the need to extend one.

I just have the feeling she's upset with me.

Catherine doesn't have many friends. All that moving around we did when she was young prevented her from forming enduring ties. Plus, school and work always took up so much of her time and energy she didn't have a lot left over for socializing. It's a little odd that she picked last night to go see a movie, so soon after Dr. Chen told us our days of spending meaningful time together were coming to an end.

I find a page in the journal that has the prompt *Describe when you first knew you were going to be a mom. How did you feel?*

This is both an easy and a hard question to answer.

I find a pen and write the truth. *I felt everything all at once, Catherine. Terrified and happy and sad and determined and awed by the very thought of you. I felt everything. I still feel it all every single day.*

CHAPTER SEVENTEEN

CATHERINE

Sunlight muscles through the cracks in my blinds. I can hear my mother moving around in the kitchen. Every sound has a precise meaning: the gentle bump is the cabinet door above the stove closing; the faint rushing is water flowing from the sink tap; and the gurgle signals the Mr. Coffee machine is doing its job.

I can't keep avoiding her.

The terrible suspicion I felt yesterday hasn't abated, but I'm not ready to share it with anyone yet.

I can barely acknowledge it myself.

I've heard of Munchausen syndrome by proxy, in which a parent— typically the mother—sickens their child with poisons or unnecessary medication. That manifestation of severe mental illness, which is a form of child abuse, gets a fair amount of media attention.

But this reverse Munchausen, or whatever it is, is something I've never heard of before. What kind of mother would go to incredible lengths to fake her *own* disease for the sole purpose of keeping her daughter tied to her?

I rise and throw on cutoffs and a top, then head to the bathroom to wash my face and brush my teeth. I make no effort to keep my movements quiet. There's no reason to avoid warning my mother I'm about to appear.

When I walk into the living room, I see she has poured me a cup of coffee and left it on the table in front of the couch.

I reach for it and take a sip, then sit down next to her. "Thanks."

"Did you have fun last night?"

"It was okay."

"What movie did you see?"

We've done this countless times before, me and mom, sitting side by side on our soft old couch, talking. It never felt unnatural before.

I decide to tell the truth. "I didn't see a movie. I went to see Ethan."

My mother's eyebrows lift above the rim of her mug.

"How is Ethan doing?"

If my mother played a part in the destruction of the only significant romantic relationship I've ever had—if she actually spiked my boyfriend's drink with something like Benadryl to make it appear that he was self-destructing—it isn't apparent from her expression. I see no guilt or remorse, only mild curiosity.

"The same."

She nods. "Still tending bar and talking about how he's going to be a big photographer?"

My mother's doing it again. She's inserting splinters that make me look at Ethan in the worst possible light. My words—*the same*—could stretch to cover a range of possibilities: He's still charming and handsome and fun. He still makes me laugh. He's still in love with me. He still makes me want to be with him.

My mother picked the most disparaging interpretation, the one designed to keep distance between me and my ex.

Anger flashes through me. I bite back the words *Don't try to manipulate me.*

I take a sip of coffee to buy myself a moment to steady my emotions and voice.

Then I look directly into my mother's eyes. "Since neither of us has to work today, I've got a plan."

★ ★ ★

My mother is staring out the window of our Bonneville, looking for the landmarks we once relied on to find our way. "There. Turn right at the Shell station."

We're about an hour from home, but this area was home once, too. We lived in Lancaster for two years, until I was midway through tenth grade, before moving to Harrisburg.

So far today, my mother's memory has been impeccable. She easily recalled the address of our old apartment—I did, too, but I let her be the one to recite it—and she noticed the dry cleaners on the main road leading to our complex has been replaced by a 7-Eleven.

I don't feel like playing along with the banter my mother keeps attempting to ignite. We've taken a lot of road trips before, but this one is different.

We're traveling down memory lane, literally and figuratively.

I take a right off the busy road, and a moment later we pull up in front of our old apartment complex. It looks indistinguishable from thousands of other redbrick buildings in hundreds of cities. The building appears to be solid, but no expense was incurred to give it any design flare. It's a box with windows.

My mother tilts her head up as she gazes at it. "Fifth floor, seventh window from the left."

That was our apartment, a one-bedroom where my mother and I slept in twin beds with a shared nightstand between us. The window didn't open more than a few inches, which my mother told me was a fire hazard. But she couldn't get management to do anything about it, so she bought a fire extinguisher at Home Depot and kept it under my bed and told me that under no circumstances were we ever allowed to light candles.

We were happy here. Eighth grade was painful for me, especially as a new kid joining the school in February, but my life turned around once I made it to high school. My features seemed like they fit my face better, somehow. I suppose I felt a bit more confident in my skin as well. By the end of ninth grade, I'd made a couple of friends, Aliyah and Chelsea, who were studious and shy like me. Once I had someone to sit with at the lunch table, I stopped dreading weekdays.

As for my mom . . . well, she seemed content, too. She was working at a steakhouse and because I was old enough to stay home alone at night, she took on dinner shifts, which were more lucrative. She bought her first car, the Bonneville, because it wasn't safe for her to take the bus home so late at night. We didn't see each other as much because she was usually heading to work by the time I got home from school, but I was fine with that.

It was nice to have a little breathing room for the first time in my life.

That wasn't my only big change.

At the beginning of tenth grade, I met a boy.

Charlie was a sensitive, sweet guy who wrote for the school newspaper and told me that one day he planned to write novels. I believed he'd actually do it, too. He had a smile that started slowly and spread until it took over his entire face, and even though his vision was terrible and he wore thick glasses, he seemed to see everything.

I've learned that our minds skim past slightly garbled written words because we automatically use context to activate the areas of our brains that jump to conclusions about what comes next. That's one reason why it's so hard to catch our own typos. We see what we expect to see.

Charlie's mind didn't work that way. He truly bore witness to the world, cataloging the details everyone else missed. Shortly after we started hanging out together, he told me that our English teacher's handwriting was changing, with the letters becoming tighter and narrower. I didn't believe him, so he made me pull two papers out of my binder—one from the beginning of the year and one more recent. The evidence was there—in blue ballpoint pen.

"At first I thought it was either Parkinson's or a shift in mood," Charlie had told me. "I looked it up and handwriting shifts can be symptoms of either."

"At first?"

He'd nodded. "Now I know it's a change in mood."

I was fascinated. "How can you tell?"

"He stopped wearing his wedding ring a week ago."

Everyone assumed Charlie and I were a couple before we even kissed for the first time. We hadn't been dating all that long before my mother broke the news: We had to move again.

She gave me a single day to return to school and say my goodbyes. When I got home that afternoon, she'd sold or given away our beds and couch and the rest of our furniture to neighbors, and our remaining belongings were packed in the back of the Bonneville.

It was almost like we'd never lived in Lancaster at all.

I glance at my mother now. She's still staring up at the apartment from the passenger's seat. I wonder what memory she is lost in.

If my mother has researched Alzheimer's disease, she would know more recent memories are typically the first to disappear. It would make sense that her recollections from this time in her life would be relatively unmarred.

"Tell me again why we had to leave." It's a struggle to keep my voice from cracking. Charlie, Aliyah, Chelsea . . . we kept in touch for a little while after I left, with promises to call every week and visit, but by eleventh grade we'd drifted apart. They'd moved on while I'd floated backward.

I was alone at a lunch table again.

"One of the waitresses at work accused me of stealing. The owner believed her. Either that, or he just wanted to keep sleeping with her on the side. He told me I could leave on the spot without collecting my last paycheck or he'd call the police."

I already know this story.

"Why didn't you fight back? If you'd let him call the police, maybe she would have gotten fired."

My mom shakes her head. "The world doesn't work that way."

"But why did we have to move so far away? Why did we have to move at all?"

My mother sighs and leans her head back. Then she tells me something I don't know. "I was already a month behind on rent. And remember the Bonneville needed new tires? I was getting hit with a lot of bills. I couldn't keep my head above water. And when I got fired, I knew there was no way I'd ever catch up."

I feel a flash of guilt. I gave her such a hard time back then. While I was discovering the sweet thrill of holding the hand of a boy I liked, my mother was grappling with incredible financial stress. She'd already been slim, but she must've lost another ten pounds during that time, and she has never put them back on.

"So we skipped out?"

She nods. "We had to move far enough away that I wouldn't bump into our old landlord on the street. I still owe him six hundred dollars."

I turn away from her and look out the window again. I can almost see Charlie walking me home that last day and leaning in for a kiss goodbye, then pulling away and using a fingertip to slide his glasses back up his nose. I watched him walk until he turned a corner and vanished.

My heart is breaking all over again.

I'd thought this place could be a portal into understanding my mother better. But this setting yields nothing but sadness.

"Should we keep driving?" she asks.

I nod. When my mom suggests going by my high school or checking to see if one of my old friends is still living in the same house, I tell her I'd rather not.

We end up picking up subs from a deli we used to like, but it's under new ownership now and the food doesn't taste the same.

We eat in the car, and when we're done, Mom gets out to throw away our trash.

I watch her pause as she walks down the sidewalk to give a homeless man the half of her sandwich she didn't eat. Guilt sluices over me. Maybe I've been focusing on the wrong memories.

My mother is the only person in my life who has always been there for me. When I wanted to win our elementary school's spelling bee, she endlessly quizzed me without ever once revealing how boring it must have been for her. She stayed up half the night running up and down the stairs to the laundry machines in our apartment's basement to wash my comforter and sheets when I had the flu and threw up on them. She always made sure I had enough before she ate so I never went hungry, even though I suspect she did, many times.

Given that context, my fears about my mother seem crazy. She never tried to hold me back from going to college—on the contrary, she's the one who sat down with a calculator and crunched numbers until we figured out a way to manage the tuition by me attending classes part-time and living at home. She seemed genuinely excited when I told her about my job offer from Johns Hopkins pending my graduation.

How can I suspect my mother of such a horrific deception?

And yet, I can't shake it loose from my mind.

She returns to the car and opens the passenger-side door, then slides back into her seat.

"Anyplace else you'd like to go?" she asks.

I think for a moment. "Let's drive by your old restaurant."

She instantly shakes her head.

The idea gains momentum in my mind. "C'mon, Mom. We can go in and see if that jerk still owns it. He screwed up both our lives! Don't you want to get a little revenge?"

The more I think about it, the angrier I become. If my mother hadn't been fired, we might've found a way to stay in the apartment. I wouldn't have lost my friends and Charlie.

My mother is staring at me. "What kind of revenge do you have in mind?"

"I don't know, we can start by calling in a complaint to the health department about seeing rodents in the kitchen."

I can't tell from my mother's expression if she likes my idea, so I throw out a few more.

"If we want to get really nasty, we could find out if he's still married and tell his wife about the waitress. Oh—and we can post terrible reviews online. . . ."

My mother interrupts me. "He's probably long gone, Catherine. Even if he isn't, that's all in the past. I'm not going to mount a campaign to punish him for something that happened nearly ten years ago."

"But let's drive by, and we can—"

Just like that, I feel my mother's temper surge. It's a force field that blocks my words and causes me to shrink away from her.

"Knock it off!"

My mother exhales. Then she says, more softly, "I never want to see that place again."

I feel deflated as we drive home. We listen to the radio and make an occasional comment about traffic or the weather, like strangers in a ride share. When we stop at a gas station, my mother buys a couple of Tootsie Pops from the mini-mart inside and hands me a raspberry one, my favorite flavor. But things still don't feel right between us.

My mom takes over the wheel after we get gas, and I rest my head against the window. Fatigue settles over me as the low buzz of the wheels against pavement lulls me into a dreamlike trance.

Then a memory flash jerks me back to full consciousness: The night before we moved from Lancaster, after I'd cried myself to sleep, I awoke abruptly.

It took a moment for my eyes to adjust, but when they did, I saw my mother pacing the length of our tiny apartment, from the living area into our bedroom and back again. She'd already told me the bad news, that we had to leave because of the allegation against her at work. But there must have been something else weighing on her. Something terrible enough to keep her relentlessly pacing through the night.

There was one other thing she did, too. Every time she neared our window, she paused and peered out.

I study her profile now as she briefly maneuvers into the left lane to pass a slower-moving car. My mother is an attractive woman, but she never calls attention to her looks. Hers is a quieter beauty. I used to urge her to grow her hair out from its short bob—it's so lush and shiny—but she never would, and now I'm glad. The simple style suits her. She wears no makeup, beyond an occasional swipe of mascara and her beloved cherry ChapStick, which means I can see every laugh and frown line and freckle on her face.

Her appearance is transparent. But my mother keeps secrets.

For the first time in my life, I'm keeping some from her, too.

I'm beginning to think the trip to our old neighborhood wasn't a waste of time.

My mother refused to drive by the steakhouse. But I remember its name: RJ's. I can still visualize the logo. Those burgundy initials encircled in gold were emblazoned on the plastic bags she occasionally brought home with extra food from the kitchen.

If my goal is to trace my mother's story backward to her roots, maybe RJ's is the first step on the path toward the truth.

Someone she worked with there could recall something my mother once said or did—a clue that could carry me to the next stepping-stone back in time. My mother is extremely careful in what she reveals about herself, but everyone makes mistakes. And perhaps she's less cautious with casual acquaintances, people who are far less interested in her history than me.

My mother turns to me. "What are you thinking about?"

I don't hesitate. "Chocolate."

She laughs. "The candy didn't do it for you?"

"That was just a dessert appetizer."

"Tell you what. Let's pick up a box of mix and make some brownies when we get home."

"Deal."

While the brownies bake, I'll close the door to my room and get out my legal pad and write down every single detail of RJ's I can remember my mother recounting.

CHAPTER EIGHTEEN

RUTH

I stand in front of my closet, surveying my clothes. No chic designer outfit has spontaneously materialized, so I reach for a khaki skirt and a red top with spaghetti straps that I bought at a thrift store several years ago.

Catherine is in the living room, flipping through TV channels. Snippets of different programs fill the air: A man with a British accent declares a pastry filling "disappointing"; a girl pleads with her father to get her a horse; and then the buzzer of a game show blares and a woman cries, "Dolly Parton!" Finally, I hear the familiar dialogue of the movie *Bridesmaids*.

Catherine stays on that channel. It sounds like she's settling in for the evening.

I don't want to leave my daughter, but if I don't get out of the apartment for a few hours I'm going to lose it.

This morning felt surreal. Seeing our former neighborhood unnerved me even more than I anticipated. The apartment next to our old one still had the same silvery wind chimes dangling from the fire escape rail, which means our neighbor hasn't moved.

The woman with the wind chimes made overtures to us while we lived there. I think she was lonely. She brought over muffins when we moved in and let Catherine play with the stray cats she was always taking in. When one of the cats escaped and went missing, she came over and pressed a flyer with the cat's photo into my hands and lingered, clearly yearning for company, until I pretended I had an urgent errand to run.

As I looked up at those wind chimes earlier today, I was gripped with the urge to get out of town as fast as possible.

I didn't like living in that apartment. Even though I kept the place scrupulously clean, I once found a dead mouse under Catherine's bed. Being back in this neighborhood made me feel itchy.

I tried to mask my feelings, but I couldn't help sagging in relief when Catherine agreed to my suggestion that we eat our subs in the Bonneville because the deli was so crowded. It was easy to look out the windshield at approaching pedestrians from my vantage point, and the side mirror let me keep tabs on what was going on behind me. The day was bright, which meant Catherine didn't question the fact that I was wearing my oversized sunglasses.

I couldn't believe my good luck when she wanted to leave after an hour. The only truly dangerous moment came when she suggested stopping by the steakhouse. I deflected her a little too roughly, but after a while the tension between us dissipated.

A Tootsie Pop can be an effective way to bridge the distance between a mother and daughter who share the curse of a sweet tooth.

After I finish changing, I walk into the bathroom and brush my teeth to get rid of any remaining traces of the single small brownie I ate.

I would've loved to have had seconds—just like I craved eating the other half of my sub instead of wrapping it up and giving it to a homeless guy—but being at this weight suits my purposes. I need to look as different as possible from the curvy, long-haired girl I was in high school.

The bones in my face are more prominent now, and my body shape has changed. Still, someone from my past could recognize me if they glimpsed me at the right angle in the right light.

It happened once before, when Catherine was in tenth grade, back when we lived in Lancaster. It's why I felt on the verge of a panic attack the entire time we were there today.

The day I heard someone call my old name, it was gloomy and gray, with the slightest drizzle coming down. If the weather had been different, everything else would have been, too.

I was walking to the drugstore when a woman strolling toward me suddenly stopped in the middle of the sidewalk, her expression as shocked as if she'd seen a ghost.

She must have traded her glasses for contact lenses, but I still recognized her: Rosie, the nice girl from my Poms squad. The last time I'd seen her was when she'd waited for me by my car with my backpack and water bottle on the afternoon Coach ordered me into his office.

I ducked my head and quickly passed her, kicking myself for not having on my sunglasses like I almost always did when I was outdoors. She called out my old name with a question in her voice, as if she wasn't sure it was really me, but I didn't turn around. "Timmy and I became friends! He's doing well!" she yelled, but I didn't even react to that. I kept walking past the drugstore, then I rounded the corner and ran until my lungs felt like they would explode.

We moved to Harrisburg the next day.

Now I step into the living room, where Catherine is curled on the couch, her feet tucked beneath her. On the coffee table in front of her is the journal she bought for me. The page is open to my entry.

When she sees me, she reaches for the remote control and pauses her movie. "I'd love it if you kept writing in this. Or we could do it together."

Instead of answering, I drop a kiss on her head.

"Are you going out?" It feels like our roles have shifted. She sounds like the parent.

"Just for a bit," I reply lightly.

Her face shutters.

"With Melanie?"

I debate lying and saying yes like I usually do on nights like these, but something holds me back. Maybe it's because there seems to be a faint challenge in her tone.

"No, I need a little time to myself. I thought I'd take a walk and maybe stop somewhere for a beer. I won't be late."

Catherine doesn't like my answer. But given that she went out last night, she can hardly complain.

I follow her gaze as she glances down at my sandals—they're flat, but they're not exactly walking shoes.

"Fine." She stands up and tosses the remote control onto the coffee table, then she heads into her bedroom without another word.

I think about going after her, but I end up deciding a few hours of space would do us both good.

I wind my way down the stairs to the lobby, then step outside. It's nearly dusk now, but I keep on my sunglasses. I won't ever make the same mistake again.

When I'm two blocks away from home, I reach for my phone and set it to airplane mode.

After I've walked a half mile, I reach a little café with a red awning. Any customer who purchases food or drink can use the desktop computer set up at a table in the back. It's a convenient place to do my checking.

I come here every month or so because the café is never crowded and the beer is cheap. I tell Catherine I'm meeting Melanie for drinks, or I pretend to have the occasional date because it would seem strange for a forty-two-year-old woman who doesn't wear a nun's habit to be celibate for her entire adult life.

But I don't date. It's one more thing I deny myself, like food.

I can never forget that every single person I encounter is a potential threat.

Precautions rule my life.

If they aren't enough, I have one final plan in place to protect Catherine. I'm counting on the fact that I'll have time to make a quick phone call or send a text to Catherine. I'll tell her where to find my notebook and the fake ID I had made with her photo that's taped to the inside back cover. I'll instruct her to carry only what she can fit inside the gray duffle bag that's on the top shelf of my closet.

I'm not writing my journal simply to reveal my true story to my daughter.

It's also intended to teach her how to run.

When I get home, Catherine is dozing in front of the TV in the living room. Instead of waking her, I decide to write more in my notebook, even though my dyslexia worsens when I'm tired, forcing me to go more slowly than I'd like.

We've been in this apartment for almost four years now—the longest we've stayed at any address. I could be getting soft.

I need to remind myself how to run, too.

It was pitch-black outside when James pulled up outside my house, repeating his plan as I sat nearly catatonic next to him in the Corvette: I was to pack a few changes of clothes, grab whatever valuables I could find, and then drive to meet him at Pizza Piazzo at midnight.

We had one hour to disappear.

What would you take with you?

I stood in the middle of my bedroom, looking at the Polaroid photos tacked up on my bulletin board and the pink piggy bank I'd gotten for my eighth birthday and my trophy from when our Poms squad won regionals.

I only began to move when I realized how much time I was wasting.

I reached for the gray duffle bag on the top shelf of my closet and packed jeans, a sweatshirt, a couple of T-shirts, underpants, and an extra bra. I kept on the clothes I was wearing even though Coach's blood had stained them. James had instructed me to not leave any evidence behind.

I crept to the bathroom and collected my toothbrush, toothpaste, and hairbrush.

I knew my mother kept jewelry in a velvet box on her bureau—a pair of real diamond earrings she'd inherited and an opal ring. But I couldn't bring myself to sneak into my parents' bedroom. I felt cer-

tain they'd bolt upright in bed, somehow knowing what James and I had done.

I emptied my piggy bank of the bills and the two quarters it contained and put the money in my pocket, then carried my duffle downstairs, avoiding the creaky step. My limbs felt slow and heavy, as if I was moving underwater. It took every ounce of my will to keep going forward instead of falling to the ground and curling into a ball.

My mother's purse sat on the kitchen counter. I took all the cash she had, sixty-eight dollars. No credit cards, James had instructed me. Nothing that could lead the police to us.

My father's wallet was in a dish by the kitchen door, along with his car keys, but I couldn't bear to steal from him.

I looked at the gold watch James had put on my wrist. Fifteen minutes left. It would take me ten to get to our meeting spot.

It was so hard to think. My mind felt like it was shutting down.

What else might I need?

My school backpack was on the kitchen table. I reached into it and grabbed whatever my fingers touched: a pen. A green spiral notebook, the one I'm writing in now. A pack of tissues. An apple I hadn't eaten at lunch. I added it all to my duffle bag.

I looked at the phone on the wall. All I had to do was lift the receiver and dial 911. James wasn't here to stop me this time.

I took a step toward it. Then another.

Headlights cut through the darkness, briefly flashing into our kitchen as the driver turned the corner adjacent to our house.

Maybe James knew what I was thinking. Maybe he was coming for me.

I held my breath.

The car moved on. And I moved away from the phone.

Tick-tock, Coach's watch whispered.

My time was up.

Just as I opened the door to go outside, I saw a tube of cherry ChapStick next to Timmy's backpack. Timmy loved the sweet smell, so Dad bought him a tube at the drugstore every now and then. I couldn't bring any pictures with me or say goodbye to my little brother and dad. So I put the ChapStick in my pocket.

I walked out of my house for the final time and stood on the front walk in the soft night air.

Step two of James's plan: *You've taken what you can carry. Now it's time to disappear.*

Where would you go?

I slipped into my car, started the engine, and pulled away, praying the noise wouldn't wake anyone.

I reached the stop sign at the corner. A left turn would take me toward Pizza Piazzo. James would be there, waiting.

I twisted the wheel to the right.

My foot stayed steady on the gas pedal, but my hands trembled on the wheel. Two miles, five miles, ten . . . I kept going until I passed the city limits.

Logically I knew James could have no idea where I was going. I didn't even know where I was heading. But every time I saw another vehicle on the highway, I couldn't breathe until it passed.

I'm not sure how long I drove, but I think it was probably an hour or more. I'd seen enough crime shows on TV to know I couldn't stay in my car, with the license plate as connected to me as my fingerprints.

I might have been able to switch my plates with another car's, like I'd seen a bank robber do on one of those shows, if only I'd thought to bring a screwdriver instead of an apple.

Up ahead was a brightly lit twenty-four-hour Denny's, with several trucks and a few cars in the parking lot.

I pulled in at the last second and rolled to a stop as far away from the highway as possible, in a dark spot at the far end of the lot. My car might not be noticed for a day or two. In any case, leaving it here felt safer than continuing to drive.

I lifted my duffle bag off the front seat and walked toward the other vehicles. I reached an eighteen-wheeler first and crept around it in a slow circle, trying to figure out if there was a way to conceal myself inside. I climbed up on the running board and the steps above it and stood on *my tiptoes to peek in a window. There was a second row of seating—a long bench with some scrunched-up blankets where the driver must take naps. I could hide in the footwell behind the driver and cover myself with one of the blankets. When the trucker stopped for his next meal, I'd climb out. It wasn't a great plan, but I couldn't think of any other way to get out of the area fast.*

I tested the door. It was locked.

I stepped down and circled around the front of the truck and climbed up on the opposite side, stretching my hand toward the passenger's door handle.

Then a man's voice cut through the night. He asked why I was trying to break into his truck.

Fear and relief crashed through me in equal measures. The voice behind me—male, adult, annoyed—didn't belong to James.

I stepped down, keeping my head low, and mumbled that I wasn't going to steal anything, I just thought I could catch a ride. I started to hurry away, toward the highway.

But he called after me to stop.

I halted. I hadn't gotten a good look at the trucker, but I'd seen enough to know he was much bigger than me.

The trucker didn't say anything immediately. I waited, listening as the silence was briefly broken by the whoosh of a car speeding by. Maybe he'd let me continue on to the highway, where I could try to hitch a ride. Maybe he'd call the police.

It was almost a relief to have my fate rest in someone else's hands.

Finally he said that if I wanted a ride, all I had to do was ask.

I turned around. The trucker was standing there, gesturing for me to climb into the passenger's side. He looked to be in his late fifties, and he wore a red-and-blue plaid shirt. I couldn't read his expression.

I needed to be gone tonight. I had to get into that vehicle.

I slowly walked over, my head still hung low. He unlocked the door and I got into the cab. It smelled like French fries. There was an open can of Coke in the beverage holder and a half-empty roll of Rolaids in the console. And a decal stuck low on the front windshield of a young woman in a bikini, sitting with her arms behind her so that her boobs popped out.

The trucker walked around to the other side and began to hoist himself up and into the driver's seat. I knew this was it. If I wanted to jump out and run, now was my chance.

I stayed.

What could he do to me that was worse than what my mother or Coach or James had already done?

My fate still rested in the trucker's hands.

He settled into his seat and released a sigh, then reached for his leather belt and hiked it down, saying he'd eaten too much.

I watched him out of the corner of my eye as I waited for him to start the engine or put on his seat belt.

Instead, he turned toward me, his big arms reaching out.

I squeezed my eyes shut and tried to press myself in the other direction, but the door kept me pinned in place.

I couldn't breathe. All I could do was wait for his hands to land on me.

I heard his voice again, telling me he just needed to get a little something out of the back.

I opened my eyes. He was almost completely twisted around now, reaching toward the bench seat in the back of the cab.

The trucker lifted up a tiny, old Chihuahua from the nest of blankets. Her eyes seemed to look in opposite directions, and she had a vaguely annoyed air at being awoken.

He told me her name was Cookie, and that she usually sat right where I was.

Cookie stayed on my lap the whole drive.

CHAPTER NINETEEN

CATHERINE

The last time I came to work, every resident in the Memory Wing wore my mother's face.

Now my state of mind is completely altered.

The hours pass quickly as I conduct the monthly assessments we fill out for all our clients with Alzheimer's. Toward the end of my shift, a male nurse named Reggie and I take a small group of residents outside, into the fenced garden.

A small brown sparrow perched on a branch of a nearby tree begins to sing. Mr. Damon purses his lips and mimics the song, whistling note after pitch-perfect note.

Reggie nods at me, a silent acknowledgment to what we are witnessing. Reggie, who is about my mom's age and has twin boys, once told me he bought his sons special bars of soap with toy cars embedded inside. You could glimpse the perfectly formed cars, but they were buried under hazy layers of glycerin. "Working here feels like that sometimes," Reggie had said. I knew exactly what he meant.

Mr. Damon can't name the street he lived on during the two decades before he moved here, but he can hum along to every piece of music Beethoven ever wrote. His musical memory seems hardwired into the one place Alzheimer's can't touch: his soul.

Mr. Damon has a particularly difficult time at dusk. The Debussy CD I brought in last time is for him.

After forty-five minutes, we begin the slow process of helping residents back inside. We'd all like to stay out longer, but the sun will set soon.

We have to be in the locked ward before it does.

Once everyone is settled and finishing dinner, I slip away for my break. I typically leave the Memory Wing and take the elevator down to the kitchen on the main floor. Today, though, I need privacy.

I begin to walk toward the very end of the hallway, to the family quarters.

I look around to make sure no one is watching. Employees have been prohibited from using the space ever since a visiting family showed up and discovered a napping aide. Once I'm sure the hallway is clear, I step inside and quietly close the door behind me. The space is set up like an extended-stay hotel room, with a queen-sized bed and seating area, plus a half-fridge and microwave and sink. There's always a box of tissues on the table, alongside a book about grieving.

This room is used when one of our residents is near death, and family members don't want to leave the premises but need a place to nap or shower.

There's one other item in the room. A telephone.

I walk to it and dial the number I looked up last night. If I used my iPhone to make this inquiry, my name would appear on caller ID. This number is harder to link to me.

A woman answers after the first ring, "RJ's Steakhouse, this is Melissa, how may I help you?"

My mouth feels dry. I rehearsed my story last night, but maybe I should have written down my script.

"Hi, my name is Annie Nelson. I'd like to speak to the manager concerning an employee." I'm aiming for a tone that's just this side of gruff.

"Oh! Certainly. Hold on for a moment, please."

A man picks up quickly. "This is Curt Daniels. How may I help you?"

"Mr. Daniels, thank you for taking my call. I'm Anne Wilson"—I deliberately give a similar-sounding but not identical name than I first provided—"and I've been retained by the Sterling family. My law firm handles the financial trust created by Lucille Sterling."

I can almost feel his confusion seep through the line as I continue.

"We've been unsuccessful in our efforts to locate one of Lucille's nieces, and family members believe she was employed at your restaurant shortly before they lost touch with her."

"I'm sorry—what is this about?"

I throw more legalese at him.

"As trustee of Lucille Sterling's estate, it is my fiduciary duty to dispense assets to the parties named in the will. In other words, one of your employees will be receiving a nice sum of money. Just as soon as we can find her."

Mr. Daniels isn't foolish. He pauses for a moment, then comes back on the line. "It says you're calling from Sunrise Elder Care?"

"Correct. Lucille Sterling is a patient here. I've been working with her on codicils to her will since she cannot travel to me. We are nearly finished. Unfortunately, her time is very limited, which is why we are pulling out all the stops to locate her beneficiaries and tie up any loose ends. The last thing this family wants is an inheritance battle."

He takes this in.

"Mr. Daniels, can you give me any information about Ruth Sterling?"

My question is deliberately open-ended. He may not even be the same manager who fired my mother. This could be another dead end, like the panther mascot clue.

"I wish I knew where Ruth was, but I don't."

My stomach clenches.

Keep going, I mentally beg him.

"We owe her money, too. I've probably still got her final paycheck in her file. Our accountant makes us hang on to everything for years in case we get audited, and I doubt anyone has bothered to throw it out."

"Final paycheck?" I echo.

"Yeah, Ruth didn't show up one day and I haven't seen her since."

My legs weaken. I sink down onto the bed.

It's another catastrophic lie. We didn't have to leave my friends, my school, my Charlie. It seems like my mother wanted to wrench me away from anyone I felt close to—other than her.

One by one, I'm tearing down the layers of deception she built around us. What will I find when I get to the last one?

"You still there?"

I clear my throat to buy time while I try to remember what else I needed to get out of this call.

"I would appreciate it if you could forward any information you might have on Ruth to assist us in tracking her down."

"Um . . . I can look in her file. Probably nothing in there but that old paycheck and the application she filled out before she started here."

I feel my eyes widen.

"Her application?" My voice sounds a little strangled.

"Yeah, it should still be there."

"What's on it?"

"Where she worked before, her address, that kind of thing."

"Please fax it to me. Or you can scan it, whichever is easier."

"We've got a fax, but I'm not sure I can get to it tonight. We're fully booked for dinner, and honestly, the files aren't all that organized. That okay? Seeing as you're in such a rush."

"Tomorrow is better than never," I tell him.

I recite the fax number for Sunrise, grateful we still use one to send medical records back and forth to doctor's offices and insurance companies.

Then I hang up and fall back onto the bed.

I didn't locate just one stepping-stone. If that old work application comes through, I may be able to trace my mother back through all of them—perhaps even to the first place she landed after leaving her family's home.

I may finally be able to find out who she really is.

I'm still lying on the bed, stunned, when a man yells, "They're coming! They're coming!"

I leap up and run out of the room.

Mr. Damon is crouched by a window in the hallway, staring out intently, gesturing for everyone to keep back. Outside the panes of glass, the brilliant greens and blues of the trees and sky have been gray-washed. The night gloom is drawing up around us.

Sundowning is when Mr. Damon's muddled mind tricks him into believing it is 1971, and he is a young army draftee again.

"Do you see them?" Mr. Damon tilts his head at me. "They're sneaking in. Tell the men!"

Right now, Mr. Damon is back in Vietnam, and the enemy is just outside the window.

I move to his side, keeping down low.

"We're safe," I promise. "The men know."

Hurry, Tin, I think.

Mr. Damon is surprisingly strong for his age. He is preparing to fight.

His watery blue eyes narrow as he turns to look at me. "Who are you?"

I tell him the truth, keeping my words malleable enough to serve both his present and past worlds: "I'm a nurse."

"I don't know you. We don't have any nurses in our unit."

"My name is Catherine. I'm here to help you."

Mr. Damon leans closer to me, still keeping his head ducked beneath the window. "Are you trying to trick me?"

I shake my head. "I'm on your side."

He puts a finger to his lips. "They're getting closer," he whispers. "Can you see them? They found us."

At that moment, music fills the air. Tin found the CD.

The metamorphosis is astonishing. Music exerts such a powerful pull over Mr. Damon that it blots out his terrifying hallucination.

Mr. Damon's hands rise, as if pulled up by strings. His fingers perform a complex dance, in perfect time to Debussy's "Clair de Lune."

He stands up and begins to walk, still playing the graceful, gentle notes, drawn toward the source of the music.

I straighten up, too, and exhale a slow breath.

I need to talk to Tin about having the doctor do a meds check for Mr. Damon tomorrow. His hallucinations are getting worse. Someone could get hurt if the music ever loses its power.

I walk to the recreation room, following Mr. Damon's footsteps. The scene is peaceful. Several residents are reclining in chairs or on couches, listening to the music. Mrs. Jacobson is tenderly tucking in her baby dolls for the night. Mr. Damon is completely lost in the composition, his fingers sweeping up and down piano keys.

I'm watching him, but my mind is elsewhere. I'm wondering how long it will take for the fax to arrive.

My mother turned off her location on her phone last night, and I know it was deliberate. I have no idea where she went, but I'm certain it wasn't merely for a walk.

The words Mr. Damon whispered to me moments ago echo in my brain.

I don't know you.

CHAPTER TWENTY

RUTH

I peer out the window into the inky night, wrapping my arms around myself as I search the shadows.

I scan the parking lot four stories down as if I might actually see an old Corvette there, engine rumbling, James behind the wheel.

There's nothing amiss I can put my finger on, yet I feel deeply restless. It's the fourth time I've looked out the living room window in the past hour.

James isn't coming for us, I tell myself. Catherine and I are safe.

I draw the blinds closed and tell myself I'll keep them that way until morning.

I walk into the kitchen, the tiled floor cool against the soles of my bare feet, and fill the teakettle. I take my favorite chunky mug out of the cabinet—the one Catherine made for me in junior high school art class—and drop in a bag of chamomile.

The shriek of the kettle a couple of minutes later causes me to flinch, even though I've been anticipating the noise. I fill up my mug and inhale the fragrant steam, then carry it into the living room and set it down on a coaster on the coffee table.

I check the location of Catherine's phone, and once I confirm she is still at work, I walk over to the front door and engage the chain lock. No one else has a key to our place, other than the landlord, who isn't permitted to enter without advance notice. But I can't allow even a minuscule risk of anyone surprising me during the next hour.

I'm about to do the thing I've been dreading not just all night but for the past four years.

The one streaming channel we subscribe to offers reruns of a true-crime program. I watch a lot of those kinds of shows because you never know when something you learn might come in handy.

But there was one episode I couldn't bear to watch.

It's the segment about Coach's murder. It first aired four years ago, on the twentieth anniversary of the crime.

I can't afford to ignore it any longer.

I got rid of Coach Franklin's watch many years ago, but I swear I still hear it sometimes, like when I catch the clacking of a train moving down the tracks or notice someone rhythmically tapping their foot: *tick-tock, tick-tock.*

It's a warning. My time is almost up.

I use the remote control to bring up the program. I'm too agitated to sit, so I stand in front of the TV.

The first minute or so is an introduction. Eerie music plays while credits appear on the screen, along with sepia photographs. There's one I've never seen of James at around the age I knew him—nineteen. The background is blurred, so I can't identify where the picture was taken. Then my school picture from junior year slowly appears next to James's. In it, I'm smiling, and my waist-length hair is draped over one shoulder. Our photos drop off the screen and are replaced by several of Coach, including one of him standing in front of the Poms team while our squad posed in pyramid formation. I'm at the end of the middle row, and a red circle is drawn around my head so viewers can identify me.

My gut clenches so tight it's painful, but I force myself to keep watching.

It's only going to get worse.

The host begins in a deep, somber voice. "Ava Morales was a junior at Oak Hill High in Towson, Maryland—a good student, pretty and vivacious, from a family with deep ties to the community. James Bates was several years older, with a far more mysterious—and unsettling—background."

More photographs appear—one of our school sealed off with yellow police tape and several from Coach's funeral—as the host describes the crime scene and interviews the lead detective from the case.

I recoil a moment later when a familiar face pops onto the screen. It's Brittany. She must have had plastic surgery. Her lips were never that full when she was young. She looks almost exactly like her mother. *Apple from the tree,* I think, remembering the line I'd written in my journal.

The host lobs her a question—"Can you tell us about Ava Morales?"—and Brittany is off and running, talking about how we'd been besties since we were seven, and how she was present the night I met James at the restaurant where he worked.

"I knew something was wrong with him right away," Brittany confides. "All of us girls thought so."

"But not Ava?" prompts the host.

Brittany shakes her head vigorously, her big gold hoop earrings smacking her rosy cheeks. "I guess being in love can make people stupid."

My hands curl into fists. They don't relax until Brittany's vapid face is off the screen.

James's mother declined to be interviewed, the host somberly reports. So did my father and Timmy.

I begin to pace, keeping my eyes fixed on the screen. I know what is coming next. I read about it during one of my online searches long ago. It was a good thing the library had a little trash can by the computer station because I didn't make it to the bathroom in time to throw up.

"James Bates's stepfather could not be interviewed." A meaningful pause. "He was beaten to death six months before the Oak Hill High murder."

A photograph of James's stepfather appears on the screen. He was a medium-sized man with blond hair and a hard line for a mouth. "Troy Ganske was attacked with a blunt object one night as he worked alone in his garage, changing the tire on his car. Authorities suspect the murder weapon was a lug nut wrench found next to the body, but no one was ever charged in the crime."

Then: "The weapon was wiped clean of fingerprints."

I begin to hyperventilate. I blindly fumble for the pause button on the remote control.

My instincts are screaming at me to run, like I have so many times before.

I pinch the inside of my wrist as hard as I can. The sharp burst of pain distracts me enough to interrupt the surge of panic.

"We're safe." I say the words aloud.

But I don't believe it. I haven't believed it for one single day of the past twenty-four years.

I walk to the kitchen cupboard and pull out the bottle of Russian vodka I bought last year. I pour a shot and drink it down in one swallow, the burn racing down my throat. My heartbeat finally slows.

I pick up the remote again and force myself to press play.

There's more background on Coach Franklin's life. He receives accolades from our former school principal and from his brother, who talks about what a great guitar player Coach was. An old video of Coach strumming the Eric Clapton song "Bad Love" plays. *"Your love will keep me alive,"* Coach sings.

The video fades into blackness and is replaced by one of James.

He is seated in a courtroom, wearing a suit and tie I didn't know he possessed, beside a man who must be his lawyer.

"Daniel Franklin's battered body was found by a night janitor who arrived at the school shortly after the attack. He was barely clinging to life and was taken to Mercy Hospital by ambulance. A short while later, an officer on routine patrol spotted a black Corvette idling in front of a closed restaurant. Upon approaching the driver, the officer noticed blood on his sleeve that was later identified as belonging to Daniel Franklin. James Bates was captured at 12:15 a.m."

Fifteen minutes past our meeting time of midnight.

James was caught while waiting for me.

The video camera recording of the courtroom shows nineteen-year-old James standing up. The judge asks the jury if they have reached a verdict.

"We have, your honor." The jury forewoman says, her voice sounding far away and tinny.

The camera zooms in on James's face as the verdict is read. "We the jury find the defendant, James Andrew Bates, guilty on the charge of murder in the first degree."

James doesn't break down or say a word. He doesn't move a muscle.

A jump cut to a photograph of me alone on the front steps of Oak Hill High, holding a copy of *Romeo and Juliet*. I remember that day. I didn't want to eat in the lunchroom, so I took my Diet Coke and peanut butter sandwich and went outside to read a few pages. One of the student photographers who worked for our school paper must have snapped the shot without me noticing.

A voice-over with Coach singing the lyrics from another line in Clapton's song plays: *"No more bad love . . ."*

The host appears back on the screen. "Ava Morales's blue Dodge Dart was discovered in the parking lot of a Denny's restaurant the day after the attack. She has never been located."

Brittany is back. "I know, deep in my heart, that James killed Ava." Brittany's eyes well up. "And I swear to you, he killed my cat, too. A neighbor saw his car on my street the night Smokey disappeared."

She uses her fingertips to swipe beneath her eyes. "James is a psycho. Everyone knows he murdered his stepfather and Coach."

The host interjects: "Bates was never charged or convicted of killing his stepfather."

"Oh, come *on*. That's only because there wasn't enough evidence and James claimed he was asleep in the house. And why wouldn't Ava come home if she was alive? I'm telling you, James killed her and hid her body somewhere it could never be found."

"That's one theory. Another is that Ava was an accomplice."

The former lead detective on the case replaces Brittany on camera. The printed words below him identify him as a retired homicide detective.

"Ava Morales had a motive. She was angry. She was cut from the Poms squad that very afternoon. Daniel Franklin had humiliated her. He emailed the other members of the team to deliver the news just hours before he was attacked."

The host frowns. "It seems like a big leap to say a teenage girl would kill her coach over something like that."

"I'm not saying she didn't have help."

"Could someone as young as Ava really go into hiding for this long?"

The retired detective shrugs. "Sure. People do it all the time. Back then, it was a lot easier to evade. We didn't have facial recognition devices. Surveillance cameras were much rarer. Do you know how many people are missing in this country alone?"

"Hundreds?" the host guesses.

"Thousands."

The host nods somberly. "If Ava Morales is out there somewhere, here is what she might look like today."

An age-progression photo of me comes onto the screen. My hair is much longer than I currently wear it, and my face is fuller. It doesn't look too much like me, I tell myself.

The program ends with a close-up video of James back on the day he was found guilty of murder.

"James Bates has been behind bars in a maximum-security prison for two decades. But he will be up for parole in four years, shortly after his forty-third birthday, and legal experts we have consulted believe his chances for release are good."

James's face grows bigger as the camera moves in. I can see comb marks in his sandy hair and a tiny shaving cut near his Adam's apple.

"Bates pled not guilty at his trial, but he never spoke in his own defense. He has never granted a single interview, or apparently even uttered a word about the crime."

James turns his head slightly. It appears as if he is looking directly at me.

"His attorneys claim he has been a model prisoner. Bates has completed several college-level computer courses while in the Maryland Correctional Center in Baltimore. His attorneys will likely use this as evidence of how Bates is determined to lead a productive life and obtain gainful employment if he is allowed to reintegrate into society."

James's gentle, calm eyes are all I can see.

"Bates reportedly spends his free time in prison either in the weight room or using a pencil and scrap paper to draw. Most of his sketches, according to a prison source, look exactly like Ava Morales."

A shudder racks my body.

James waited for me that night. He has been waiting for me all these years.

I turn off the TV and stand in the void of sudden silence.

Four months ago, almost to this day, the parole board determined that James should be free. I learned about it during one of my library searches.

James wasn't immediately released, but he will be any minute now.

It's why I go to the library so often and search for news items about him. I need to know when he'll get out of jail.

The day when James will come for me is drawing closer.

I try to convince myself otherwise, and sometimes—especially when the sun rises over a fresh day—I almost manage to believe it won't happen. But in the darkest moments of night, I know the truth.

I didn't grow up in Virginia like Catherine believes. Johns Hopkins Hospital in Baltimore, where she wants to work, is a short drive from my family's home, from the neighborhood where my father and Timmy still live. It's close to the restaurant where James worked, and to my old high school.

I might have been able to accept that risk if I was merely weighing it against Catherine's excitement over her new job.

But Hopkins is less than four miles away from the prison where James is still incarcerated while he fulfils the conditions of parole, including establishing a housing plan and completing certain online courses all prisoners must take once they've won parole.

He could walk through the gates at any minute, with his new computer skills and the fury that has been mounting inside him ever since I left him alone to be caught.

What has nearly twenty-five years in a maximum-security prison done to a man who was already enchanted by violence?

It is almost unimaginable.

How far would you go to protect the person you love most in the world?

I have gone to a place so dark and bleak I barely recognize myself. But I know one thing for certain: I did it out of love.

Maybe I made the wrong choice. But I was desperate, and I couldn't find any other option.

I chose to lie to Catherine when I told her how my mother died many years ago. The real story is that my mother plowed into a tree while driving drunk. The obituary writer implied the accident was a result of her grief over her lost daughter and the questions lingering around my disappearance.

That's a tidy, tragic narrative, but it isn't anywhere close to the truth.

Here is *my* core truth, my reason for moving forward every single day. From the moment I learned I was pregnant, I burned with a purpose every bit as strong as the rage inside James.

I would do anything to protect my child.

Even fake Alzheimer's disease.

What I did is abhorrent. Unforgivable. There is nothing anyone could say that could make me feel worse than I already do.

But I swear on my life, I did it to save Catherine. If Catherine believes I am sick, I can keep her close. I can keep working to prevent

James from learning about her existence, and from coming after her—or at least be there to protect her if he does.

Telling Catherine the truth about my past is not an option. If she learns who her father is, her core sense of self will shatter. She will never be the same.

I've thought about this for more hours than I can count. And the conclusion I've come to is that this way will be brutal in the short term, but it will serve her best in the long run.

Alzheimer's is the perfect disguise for me. Unlike cancer or other illnesses I considered, it's challenging to diagnose.

I hope I won't need to keep up this charade for long.

I'm counting on the fact that James won't be able to reintegrate into society. He will either kill again or be killed. Violence is too seductive for him. He can't stay away from it.

When James is dead or back in prison, I will conjure a story about learning my Alzheimer's diagnosis was incorrect and say a serious hormone imbalance was to blame for my memory fog. I'll blame it on a mix-up at the lab, and Catherine and I will celebrate our new lease on life together. If she wants me to get tested to be absolutely certain I don't carry the familial gene for Alzheimer's, I will. Of course, the news will be good. I'll do whatever I can to restore her peace of mind.

I'll help Catherine reassemble her plans to move to Baltimore or wherever else she wants as quickly as possible, and even though I will miss her as deeply as if a piece of me has been torn away, I will celebrate the fact that she is on the right path.

But I also know, deep in my gut, our future will not be so simple. James is going to look for me as soon as he is released.

When he finds me, he will also find Catherine.

All he will need to do is look into her eyes to know she is his daughter.

CHAPTER TWENTY-ONE

CATHERINE

It's time to see if I can catch my mother in another lie.

There's something about her that has never quite added up, a loose thread I snagged a long time ago and kept tucked in my pocket. She claims to have been raised by strict Catholic parents. It's why she has a Biblical name—Ruth, with the middle name Mary—and also why her parents threw her out when she got pregnant. Her sin was too great for them to forgive.

But one night when I was about fifteen, my mother and I were flopped on the couch, watching *Jeopardy!* and shouting out answers. It was storming outside, a bad one. Rain rushed down from the sky and thunder shook our apartment.

I wasn't scared. I've always liked storms. The way the air turns thick and menacing, the static zag of lightning cracking across the sky—Mother Nature sure knows how to throw a tantrum.

When Alex Trebek asked for the source of the quote "Deliver us from evil," my mouth was too full of warm, buttery popcorn for me to speak. But my mother shouted, "Who is Shakespeare?"

A contestant buzzed in and gave the correct answer a second later. "What is the Lord's Prayer?"

Shakespeare didn't write those words, of course. They're in the Bible.

Not only that, but most Catholics repeat the Lord's Prayer during weekly mass. Even *I* knew how important a prayer it was. I'd learned it while watching a *Beverly Hills, 90210* rerun, during a scene in which Jennie Garth's character was trapped in a fire and began reciting it.

I'd said as much to my mother and she'd snapped at me.

"Give me a break, I'm tired."

I'd twirled a lock of hair around my finger, an unsettling feeling welling up inside me. "But it doesn't make sense. Just because you're tired—"

"Catherine, this conversation is ending now."

Her tone meant she was an inch away from losing her temper. So I let it go.

All these years later, I'm thinking about that conversation again.

I no longer trust it was a simple memory lapse.

In an ideal world, I'd find a way to get my mother to a Catholic mass and I'd watch her carefully. I'd see if she understood when to sit and stand and kneel. I'd gauge her familiarity with the ritual of Communion, and with the hymns. If she made a mistake, I'd be there to catch it.

But there's no way I'll be able to get my mother into a church. She told me once that I was welcome to pick a religion for myself, but she was an agnostic.

So I'm going to bring a bit of church to her.

My mother worked the early shift today and is due home from Sam's around 2:30 p.m. I have the day off. I already stopped by Sunrise at lunchtime, but no fax had come in from RJ's. I plan to check again toward the end of the day.

I'm freshly showered and on the couch with my hair drawn up in a loose, damp bun when my mother walks through the door. She's right on time.

I've made a bowl of buttered popcorn for us to share, for old time's sake.

"Hey." I turn down the volume on the TV show I've been pretending to watch. "How was your day?"

She pauses in the doorway. I can tell she's trying to gauge my mood.

"The usual." She slips off her shoes and sighs as she flexes and curls her toes against the carpet. "What're you watching?"

I turn off the TV. "Would you believe a dumb Christmas movie?"

My mother's forehead creases. "In May?"

"There's a channel that shows them year-round."

She rolls her eyes. "Tell me we're not paying extra for it."

I hold out the bowl of popcorn. "Want some?"

I need my mother close to carry out my plan. She's better than me at the art of subterfuge. I'll have a split second to read her expression before she creates a diversion or masks her true feelings.

"Yeah, let me just go change into sweats."

She heads into her bedroom, and I shift position, stretching out with my head against the armrest. She likes to put her feet up when she gets home from work, so it isn't unusual for us to lie head to toe on the couch, facing each other while we talk—or I study and she plays a game of solitaire on her phone.

She comes back out a few minutes later, her hair loosened from its headband. I catch a whiff of the clean, soapy scent of the Dove bar she uses to wash her face.

I start to hum as she enters the living room.

My mother pushes my legs over an inch, then climbs onto the couch and stretches out.

I keep humming, concentrating on making every note clear and distinct.

My mother reaches for the popcorn bowl and crunches a handful. "Pretty song."

"It's 'Ave Maria.' I've got it in my head from the movie I just saw. You know, it's the song they always play at Christmas . . . I think it's originally from that famous opera?"

I look into her eyes as I say the words. And it's what I don't see that gives me the confirmation I both need and fear.

My mother shrugs. There's no flash of recognition or knowledge, no effort to correct me.

"*Madame Butterfly,* that's it," I continue.

"Uh-huh." She nods and takes another handful of popcorn. "So how was *your* day?"

I feel my cheeks begin to burn.

"Ave Maria" is a prayer. I researched it just this morning. If you translate the lyrics, they begin, "Hail Mary, full of grace." Anyone who grew up in the Catholic Church would know the song is associated with their religion.

Still, I give my mother one final chance.

"My day was pretty interesting. I went into work for a bit."

My mother has a tiny piece of popcorn stuck to her chin. Normally I'd reach out and brush it off, but I don't want to touch her. I can barely stand to have her leg resting next to mine.

"Tin hired a new physical therapist," I lie. "He's about my age."

My mother raises an eyebrow. "Cute?"

"Yeah. Tin asked me to give him a tour, then we talked for a while. His name's Christopher."

I can't believe my mother doesn't sense the turbulent emotions that seem to be rolling off me in waves. Or maybe she does—she's a better actress than I am.

"I've always liked that name," she tells me, playing right into my hands. I couldn't have scripted a better response for her.

"Me too. He said his parents are religious, so all their kids are named after saints. He got St. Christopher, who was the patron saint of animals, which is pretty funny because he's allergic to dogs and cats."

My mother gives a little laugh, but it dies off when I don't join in.

"You feeling okay?" she asks. "You don't look that great all of a sudden."

Saint Francis of Assisi is the patron saint of animals. Saint Christopher is the patron saint of travel.

Three strikes. Wouldn't anyone raised in the Catholic Church know the identities of two of the most famous saints?

I cannot believe that of the few scanty facts she has told me about herself, at least one is a fabrication. Her parents weren't devout Catholics. So why did they throw her out when she got pregnant with me?

"Catherine? You okay?" she repeats.

I'm spared from having to answer when my iPhone rings. I reach for it and caller ID shows it's the cable provider for my new apartment in Baltimore, the company I've been trying to reach to cancel the service I'd arranged to begin next week.

The company made it easy to sign up for one of their viewing packages. Canceling has proved to be much harder. I was on hold for nearly thirty minutes earlier before I gave up and pressed the button on my phone to receive a callback.

My mother turns her attention to her own phone while I begin talking to the world's worst customer service representative. The line is a little staticky and he can't understand my name, so I have to repeat it twice, then spell it.

He tries to sell me an upgraded package, but I insist I need to cancel.

All the while, I can't help thinking about the stories I'd created about my mother in my mind. She didn't get confirmed at age thirteen, like I'd imagined. She never wore a little gold cross necklace. I wonder if she's ever set foot in a Catholic church in her life.

Does she even have Alzheimer's disease, or is that her biggest lie yet?

I want to shake her and demand to know the truth. I want to slap that popcorn kernel off her face.

The service guy wraps up his pitch. "So what do you think? It's just an additional four ninety-nine per month."

"No! I want to cancel my damn service agreement!"

My mother's head jerks up as I shout the words.

"Ohhhh, okay. Hang on one second and let me transfer you to our—"

"No!" I yell again, but it's too late. Canned music plays in my ears.

My phone flies across the room and smashes against the wall. I hear the crunch of breaking glass. Then I see my mother's face and I realize when I threw my phone, I barely missed her head.

Her arms are half-raised to protect herself, and her eyes are huge. "Catherine! What the—"

"What, you're the only one who's allowed to get mad? At least *I* didn't hit *you*."

I leave the rest of my sentence unsaid, but I can tell my mother knows what I'm thinking: *Like you used to hit me.*

She didn't do it a lot. Three, four times maybe in my entire life. And I could tell she felt horrible afterward, but I'm too mad to care right now.

I actually want her to hit me again because then I'll have the satisfaction of fighting back.

I leap to my feet, the bowl of popcorn falling to the floor and spilling everywhere. My mother cowers below me.

I'm surprised by how good it makes me feel.

I remain there for a breath, then walk away and pick up my phone. A needle-thin shard of broken glass snags my fingertip, drawing a dot of blood.

I don't trust myself to say a word, so I grab my purse and walk out without uttering one.

I arrive at Sunrise and drive through the parking lot, searching for a spot. The prime ones all require parking stickers, which are issued to residents who still drive and full-time employees. There's also a long row dedicated to visitors. Since I don't have a sticker—none of us part-timers get them—I have to bypass two empty permitted spots and leave my car near the very back of the crowded lot.

I exit the Bonneville and go through the ritual of flashing my ID and signing in, then I hurry up to the Memory Wing. I make my way to the small office connected to the nurses' station. There's a new fax on the machine. It feels slightly warm to the touch, like it arrived a second before I did.

I recognize the handwriting on the form immediately. I know it as well as I know my own.

It's the two-page work application my mother filled out years ago for RJ's, complete with a list of her prior jobs and a reference—a woman whose name I don't recognize, Diane Brown. It seems like a solid lead.

As I stare hungrily at the new information, I also come to a decision. I'm not just going to try to track down my mother's family. I'm going to devote myself to figuring out as much of the truth about her as I can.

If my mother is faking Alzheimer's—which I'm becoming more and more convinced of—I'll help her get whatever mental health services she needs, but I'm not going to destroy my life to enable her.

My lease is scheduled to start in seven days.

It's a good thing I didn't cancel my cable or find someone to sublet my apartment because I plan to arrive in Baltimore right on time.

CHAPTER TWENTY-TWO

RUTH

Here's a riddle: How long does it take to pick up every kernel from a spilled bowl of popcorn without using a vacuum cleaner?

Answer: The perfect amount of time for you to think about all the ways you've screwed up as a parent. Your shouts and threats. The bad choices and misguided advice and misunderstandings. The arm yanks and occasional spanks.

Compared to what my mother did, my few incidences of physical discipline were so minor they wouldn't even register on the same scale.

But our kids don't focus on the fact that we try as hard as we can to undo the mistakes of the previous generation. They don't know how difficult it is for us to break the patterns we were steeped in during our formative years.

They only see the errors we make. The ones taught to us, and the ones that are all our own.

Some of the worst incidents between me and Catherine are seared into my daughter's psyche. I could feel old resentments smoldering in her as she stood over me, her fists balling up.

Catherine scared me in that moment.

For a brief flash, it felt as if she was a stranger. As if I didn't know her at all.

It wasn't the first time I've experienced that eerie sensation.

The hairless patch of scar tissue on my right forearm is peeking out from beneath the edge of my shirt sleeve, like it sometimes does. I yank down my sleeve, but I can't blot out the accompanying memory.

It happened fifteen years ago, but sometimes I swear I can still smell the smoke that alerted me to the danger as I walked down the hallway toward our old apartment. I'd run out that afternoon to pick up laundry detergent because we were all out and my two uniforms were dirty. I'd only been gone fifteen minutes or so. Certainly long enough for a mature nine-year-old girl to be left alone.

At first, as the acrid smell filled my nostrils, I assumed someone was burning dinner. Then I heard the shriek of a smoke detector coming from inside an apartment on the right side of the hallway.

Our apartment.

I dropped the plastic bottle of detergent and flew the final few steps, banging my hand against our door and screaming: *"Catherine!"*

When she didn't answer I fumbled through my purse for my keys and burst inside. The smoke wasn't too heavy yet. I could still see clearly, but the smell was horrible.

Catherine hadn't responded to my cries, and she wasn't within sight. Instinct drove me to the kitchen first.

There I saw two things that stole my breath away. The first was orange-and-gold flames shooting up from our tall plastic trash can, greedily reaching out to devour the dish towel hanging from the stove handle.

I grabbed the dish towel, throwing it to the floor and stomping on it with my sneaker, hoping to stop the spread of the fire. It worked. The flames went out.

What I didn't realize was that I'd inadvertently provided another source of fuel for the fire to catch hold.

My pain didn't register for a few seconds.

Then the searing sensation of my left arm burning overpowered me.

"Get it off! Get it off!" I shrieked, slapping at the long sleeve of my cheap cotton shirt with my bare hand. I pulled my right arm out of my shirt and yanked it over my head, throwing it to the floor and stomping on it.

Catherine had been staring in horror, but now she leapt into action. "Cold water!" she yelled, turning on the sink tap.

I grabbed a pot that was sitting on a stove burner and filled it, letting the water course down over my forearm on its way into the pot. Then I dumped the water into the trash can, which was melting and warping in the intense heat. I had to do that twice more before the fire was completely out.

My arm still felt like it was being burned. The skin was raw and red. I slumped down onto the floor, next to a puddle of water seeping out of the bottom of the trash can. I felt dizzy and nauseated from the pain.

"Mama," Catherine said, her voice breaking. "We have to go to the hospital."

I nodded. I'd seen enough burns in kitchens at various restaurants where I'd worked to know mine was at least second-degree.

"What happened?" I asked.

"I'm sorry. I wanted to light a candle," she whispered.

I nodded again and managed to get to my feet. I soaked a clean dish towel in cold water and wrapped it around my forearm. Knowing our insurance wouldn't cover the cost of an ambulance, I collected my purse and Catherine's backpack and we took the bus to the hospital, where an ER doctor applied balm and dressed my wound.

I never again allowed candles in our apartment. Not even on birthday cakes.

Because the second thing I saw that stole my breath away when I burst into the kitchen and spotted the fire was Catherine. She was leaning against the refrigerator, staring at the flames.

She didn't look remorseful, concerned, or frightened.

She looked delighted.

Now I pluck the last piece of popcorn off the carpet, then straighten up and groan. I dig my knuckles into my lower back, which is protesting again from carrying too many trays today.

A vacuum would be an easier way to tidy up, but I haven't been able to use any device or appliance that makes a roaring sound since I was a teenager, when my hair dryer masked Timmy's cries for help. I guess it's like PTSD. I don't even own a blender.

I walk into the galley kitchen and see the silver popcorn pot and lid Catherine used sitting in the sink, coated by a sheen of oil. I wiggle off my topaz ring and stick it on its china holder, then squirt a few drops of dish soap onto a sponge and begin to clean.

I wish I had someone to confide in. But Catherine is my someone.

Maybe I should call a psychiatrist again. I found one in the yellow pages shortly after the fire and gave a fake name when I went in for a consultation. At first the balding guy with the horn-rimmed glasses sitting behind the fancy oak desk appeared bored. I swear he was sneaking looks at the document on his desktop instead of giving me his full attention as I described Catherine's occasional bed-wetting and the incident with the dead squirrel.

Toward the end of my free fifteen-minute consultation, I stood to leave and banged my injured arm against the hard arm of the chair.

It was excruciating, even with my wound wrapped in the layers of gauze the doctor had applied at the hospital. I couldn't help but cry out.

The shrink looked up and seemed to actually see me for the first time. "Are you okay?"

When I'd caught my breath, I nodded.

As I pulled up the sleeve of my loose sweater to make sure none of the protective bandaging had come off, he casually asked, "That looks like quite an injury. What happened?"

He was probably expecting me to say I'd fallen off a bike or something.

"I got burned putting out a fire."

He grew absolutely still. Then he leapt to his feet and walked around his desk to stare at my arm.

The shrink's voice was just above a whisper. "Did your daughter set it?"

I had his full attention now. And I knew why: I watch a lot of crime shows.

When certain traits bump up against each other in a person, they can collectively point to warning indicators of a tendency toward deep violence.

I'd gone to the shrink for reassurance. I wanted him to confirm what I'd already told myself: It isn't all that uncommon for an older kid to occasionally wet the bed—it certainly doesn't mean they'll grow up to do bad things. And what child isn't transfixed by the sight of burning candles that turn an ordinary cake into a birthday extravaganza? Catherine merely took it a few steps further, by finding matches and lighting one before holding it to the wick of a eucalyptus-scented candle I'd bought to mask the musty smell of our apartment. It wasn't Catherine's fault the match wasn't extinguished when she threw it into the trash. Or that when she saw the smoke coming from the plastic bin, she didn't think to pour water onto it.

It wasn't her fault, I told myself for the hundredth time. And I'm almost positive that fire was an accident.

The psychiatrist tried to keep me from leaving. He followed me all the way through the reception area. He said he wanted to get Catherine into a study one of his colleagues was conducting.

He wasn't truly interested in helping.

To him, my daughter was a lab rat. A thing to be tested and studied and used.

I finally got away by promising him I'd come back next week, but of course I never did. And when I saw his number flash on my phone, I handed it to the cook at work and asked him to speak in Portuguese until the shrink gave up.

Satisfied the popcorn pot is clean, I lay it on the drainboard to dry, then pull my sleeves back down, covering the hairless patch of skin.

I walk to the living room window and gaze down at the parking lot. The Bonneville is gone, and I don't know when Catherine will return.

I wonder if she has noticed that in all the years we've had the car, I have never once let the gas gauge dip below half full. No matter how tired or busy or broke I am, I always go directly to a gas station the moment the arrow nears that point.

It's one of my safety rules.

I gaze outside for a while longer, but the view doesn't change. Finally, I step away from the window and walk into my bedroom. I need to write more of my younger self's story while I wait for Catherine to come home.

When Mike the trucker pulled up at an Exxon station early the next morning to fill his vehicle with diesel fuel, I gave Cookie a final good-bye pat.

I'd been riding with Mike for six hours. It was time to branch off.

He asked if I was sure I was going to be okay. I told him my aunt lived outside of Youngstown and was going to come pick me up.

Youngstown, Ohio, was fourteen miles away. I'd seen a sign for it before we'd pulled off the highway to get gas.

Mike nodded, but his expression told me he saw through my lie.

I waved and walked away briskly, like I was confident I knew where I was heading. I could see a McDonald's a hundred or so yards away, so I went there, my duffle bag bumping against my leg with every other step.

I was grateful that even though the drive-through line was long, the fast-food restaurant was nearly empty when I stepped inside. I used the restroom, then washed up at the sink and tried to get the bloodstains out of my shorts. When I looked in the mirror, I saw a few tiny spots of Coach's blood on my neck and face, like angry red freckles. I frantically scrubbed at them with a soggy paper towel until my skin felt raw.

I waited until I was certain Mike had filled up his truck and left. I needed a map to figure out where I was and where I wanted to go, and I figured my best luck would be at the Exxon station.

I kept my head low as I hurried out the side exit of the McDonald's, then walked as quickly as I could back to the gas station, coughing as a rusty work van passed and spewed a thick puff of black exhaust in my face.

I wished I'd thought to pack a baseball cap or sunglasses, especially since the sun was rising. When I was little, I was afraid of the dark, but right now the shadows were my friends.

Inside the mini-mart, a tired-looking woman with permed blond hair was fitting boxes of cigarettes into the tall rows of a holder behind the cash register.

I cleared my throat and asked her if she knew where the nearest Greyhound station was.

She reached for a folded map next to the cash register and pushed it across the counter to me, saying she thought there was one in New Castle.

It took a minute to orient myself. We'd crossed the state line into Ohio, but just barely. Once I realized the small blue star drawn on the map represented the location of the Exxon station, I traced my finger to New Castle. It didn't look terribly far.

Too far to walk, though.

I folded the map up and returned it to the cashier.

I walked back outside and watched as a red Ford pickup truck pulled in and its owner, a man who looked about my father's age and who wore gray coveralls, began to gas up. There was an old brown chair with rips in the cushions in his truck bed.

I could ask him where he was going and see if I could catch a ride.

But I'd heard stories of what happened to girls who hitched. My luck might not hold the second time around.

I reached into the pocket of my shorts and felt my folded wad of money. One hundred and eighteen dollars, plus a few quarters. It wouldn't last very long. But I was running out of options.

I moved over to the payphone outside the mini-mart and reached for the heavy Yellow Pages directory dangling by a thick metal cord. I flipped to the Ts and saw ads for several taxicab companies. I slid one of my quarters into the slot and dialed the number to order the taxi. When the dispatcher asked for my address, I had to run inside the mini-mart again to get it from the cashier.

I felt like I was attracting too much attention. The duffle bag, the shell-shocked look I'd seen myself wearing in the mirror, my repeated questions . . . But by now the cashier was flipping through a Star magazine, and she barely looked up when she recited the address.

Once the taxi arrived and I slid into the back seat, some of the weight crushing my chest lightened.

I gave the driver my destination, then curled up and rested my head on the duffle bag on my lap. A deep wave of exhaustion rolled through me. I'd been awake for more than twenty-four hours straight, and the adrenaline fueling me was finally ebbing.

The driver seemed to pull into the Greyhound station moments after we left the gas station. I must've nodded off, even though I don't recall sleeping.

I paid him with one of my precious twenties, and he gave me back a ten and two singles in change. I wasn't sure if I was supposed to tip him. I'd only seen people take cabs in movies and on TV. I'd never actually ridden in one before. The wrong decision could make me stand out in his mind. If police traced me to the Exxon station and tracked down the driver, they could question him about the teenage girl with long, dark hair he'd picked up. Finally, I handed him back the two singles. When he casually thanked me, I felt like I'd done the right thing.

Several buses were parked outside the New Castle station, but I couldn't tell which one was going to depart first. When I went inside, I saw a few people in line at the ticket booth. There was a sign that read Schedules with an arrow pointing to a stack of flyers on a shelf, so I walked over and took one. The departure times were printed in a column of tiny numbers beside the destinations, but by now I'd tucked Coach's watch into my duffle bag and had no idea what time it was. I looked around and spotted a wall clock. I couldn't believe it was not even eight yet, or that yesterday at this hour I'd been walking through the front door of my school, alternately dreading the history quiz I was about to take and dreaming about James.

The next bus out was heading to Pittsburgh, about seventy minutes away. It would bring me closer to home. But the one after that would take me farther away in the other direction, to Cleveland. I got in line, and just as it was my turn to buy a ticket from the teller, I remembered something.

Once Timmy and I had been playing hide-and-seek in our yard, and after I searched for him for nearly ten minutes, I gave up and yelled Ollie-ollie-in-come-free. My little brother stepped out from his hiding place beneath a shrub a few feet from where I'd counted with my hands over my eyes before going to look for him.

Were you there the whole time? I'd asked.

He'd shaken his head, beaming, and said, I came back after you started looking for me.

I told the teller I wanted a ticket to Pittsburgh.

If someone came looking for me, they might not expect me to double back to Pennsylvania.

And part of me liked staying in a state I'd been to before, instead of a completely unfamiliar place.

When the teller asked if it was round trip, I swallowed hard and said no, one way.

I paid the twelve dollars, then accepted the ticket slip and my change and walked out to the line of buses. Their destinations were displayed in white blocky letters over the front windshields. I climbed aboard the first bus in line, gave my ticket to the driver, then slipped into a seat in the very last row. The bus was almost empty, and I prayed it would stay that way.

A few minutes after I boarded, the driver closed the doors and the bus lurched forward with a groan that sounded almost human.

I was safe, I told myself. I'd gotten a ride from a trucker who believed my name was Beth, I'd taken a taxicab, and now I was aboard a bus. No one would be able to find me.

My thumb twisted the topaz ring I wore on my right ring finger around and around. My father had given it to me for my sixteenth birthday. My mother had signed the card, too, but I knew it was my father who'd picked out the ring and wrapped its box in paper covered with bright red flowers.

A sob swelled up in my throat, but I forced it down.

Across the aisle, a woman with a dirty face and unlaced sneakers was muttering to herself and swaying back and forth. I figured she must be on drugs, but I didn't know what kind would make someone act that way. I'd never seen anyone smoke anything stronger than weed at a party. I averted my gaze and wished I was invisible.

After a while, the steady thrum of the bus's engine soothed me and my eyes grew heavy again. Just as I was nodding off, a shrieking sound erupted, jerking me awake. A police car was coming up behind us fast. I sank lower in my seat, breathing hard. The bus driver moved into the far-right lane and slowed down.

Nausea rose in my throat as I waited for the bus to pull over and for the officer to come on board. Instead, the police car shot past us, its red and blue lights twirling. A moment later, an ambulance followed, its siren drawn-out and mournful sounding.

A mile or so later, we passed the scene of an accident. Traffic was stop-and-go by then, and as we eased forward, I glimpsed two crumpled cars on the side of the road. A man was leaning against the guardrail, his head in his hands.

He'd probably been driving to work, his mind filled with the list of all the ordinary things he needed to do that day. Now he was caught in a vortex.

It wasn't until we'd passed him that I realized my hand had risen so my palm pressed against my glass window. The devastated stranger was the only person in the world I felt connected to at this moment.

I stayed wide awake for the rest of the ride.

When the bus arrived in Pittsburgh, I was the last one to get off. I felt like I'd put enough space and miles between me and James and the horrible crime we'd committed. But I had no idea where to go next. I'd have to sleep at some point, but I couldn't afford a hotel. Plus I didn't have any ID or a credit card to rent a room.

I looked around at all the people passing by: men and women walking rapidly with briefcases or BlackBerrys in their hands, a group of construction workers jackhammering up a section of the road, and a guy with a backpack slung over one shoulder jaywalking while a car horn bleated at him.

I began to walk, too.

I must've roamed the streets for a couple of hours before I passed a pretzel vendor. The yeasty aroma of bread made my stomach rumble. I was suddenly ravenous. I searched through my duffle until I found the red apple and devoured it, crunching all the way down to the core.

I wiped my mouth with the back of my hand and wondered if I could splurge on a pretzel. Then I mentally tallied what I'd already spent on the taxi and bus and kept walking.

I finally stopped when I came to a grand, gray building with arched windows and columns. Carnegie Library of Pittsburgh, the sign out front read.

I stared at it for a moment, then went inside.

The enormous, open space was beautiful, with soaring ceilings and intricate molding and rows of gleaming wood tables. I hadn't belonged to a church growing up—my father was Catholic and my mother disparaged his religion like she did everything else about him—but to me, this place felt like a sanctuary. It seemed like nothing bad could happen to a person here.

I found an empty seat at one of the wooden tables. Someone had left a few books there, so I reached for one and pretended to read. The subject was the Manhattan Project and the sentences were long and dense. I tried to focus on one, then reread it as the letters blurred and jumped around.

I woke up with a crick in my neck and a parched mouth. My face was pressed against the open book on the table. I lifted my head and rubbed my eyes. The library was more crowded now. A few other people were working at my table, but no one was paying me any attention.

I looked around for a clock, wincing as my tight neck muscles protested. It was a little after six.

I couldn't believe I'd slept for so long.

Outside, the light was waning. The sun would go down soon, and the library would close.

If I didn't find a place to stay tonight, I'd be in serious trouble.

I stood up and hurried out the door.

The streets were even more busy now. Car horns honked and brakes squealed and people wove around me on the sidewalk, bumping against my duffle bag. Everyone had somewhere to go.

I began walking, too, my fast pace eating up the blocks. At one point I passed someone in a sleeping bag curled up in front of a closed camera store. I averted my eyes and kept walking. A girl couldn't stay alone on the street like that, but maybe there was somewhere else I could camp for the night. There had to be a park nearby. I could find an isolated spot, maybe beneath a shrub where I wouldn't be noticed. I'd stay awake all night and sleep in the library again tomorrow.

I'd been walking for a long while and the sun was setting. I didn't have time to figure out a better plan.

I looked up to try to get a sense of my surroundings and spotted a giant red bull's-eye at the end of the block, marking the location of a Target store. I might find a cheap sleeping bag there, and I could buy a bottle of juice and a snack, too.

I walked to the entrance and stepped on the mat to trigger the sliding glass doors to open. I stepped into the brightly lit, clean space, featuring aisles stocked with everything from cereal to board games, and in the middle of the store, rack after rack of clothing.

I made my way to the camping supply aisle and stared at the two brands of sleeping bags that were for sale, one lightweight and one for cold weather. The lightweight one cost less. What else might I need?

I kept walking around the store, looking at all the things I'd buy if I had the money. Skippy peanut butter and saltine crackers. Clean socks. Hand lotion. Deodorant and a washcloth. A bottle of Snapple lemonade.

Then I stopped short. Beneath a glass display shelf by the camping section was a row of pocketknives.

Maybe I should get one, just in case.

But would I be able to use it to defend myself if I had to?

A vision of Coach's bloody, broken body swam before me and my legs buckled. I grabbed the edge of the counter to keep from falling.

I took a few deep breaths and forced myself to keep moving. My arm was aching from lugging around my duffle bag. I glanced at the backpacks, but everything was too expensive.

I passed by the big plate-glass window at the front entrance. It was completely dark outside now and the streets were quieter. The city was winding down.

I knew I should leave and find a place to stay. But I couldn't bring myself to walk out of this safe, tidy store.

I kept staring at things I'd taken for granted most of my life: paper towels and Pop-Tarts and emery boards and Tampax. How was I ever going to manage on my own?

A bell sounded, and a voice came over the loudspeaker announcing the store would close in fifteen minutes. A guy wearing a red vest and name tag passed me, heading toward the back. Maybe he was going to lock up. He'd probably loop back around this way again and tell me I needed to check out.

Tears filled my eyes as my chest constricted. I couldn't do this. There was no way I could live on the street, even for one night. I wasn't strong enough.

When the employee returned, I'd ask him to call my dad. My father would try to help me. He'd beg my mother's family to hire a lawyer, a good one. He and Timmy would write me letters when I had to go to jail or to a juvenile detention facility.

I wiped my eyes and when my line of vision cleared, I was still looking at the row of blue Tampax boxes.

It hit me like a bolt of lightning.

I hadn't thought to pack any Tampax in my duffle bag. I hadn't needed any in quite a while.

Over a month.

As I stood there dumbly, my mind so shocked it felt blank, the bell sounded again. This time the voice on the loudspeaker said the store was closing in five minutes. Any remaining customers should check out immediately.

I looked around wildly. There was a circular rack of clothing nearby.

I saw Timmy again, hiding almost in plain sight beneath the round shrub as I called, Ollie-ollie-in-come-free.

Without another thought, I bent down and crawled into the center of the ring of clothes, pulling in my duffle bag behind me.

All I could hear was my own breathing, ragged and too loud. I couldn't see anything but the pairs of pants hung together in front of me. I curled up as tightly as possible, hoping no part of me was sticking out.

Three simple words kept running through my head: I am pregnant. They didn't make sense yet. I didn't know that they would mean you.

A final announcement sounded. The store was now closed.

It was quiet for a moment. Then, in the distance, laughter broke out. I heard a man and woman conversing, his tone deep and slow and hers higher and crisper. Their words were muffled. I squeezed my eyes shut.

A few minutes later, someone walked past my hiding spot, their shoes squeaking against the linoleum floor. I held my breath until the footsteps receded. Then I couldn't hear anything at all for a little while. The silence was almost unbearable. I kept expecting someone to reach in and grab me.

I finally heard voices again, but they seemed farther away now. I couldn't tell how many people were talking. Two, maybe three?

The lights cut out, plunging me into complete darkness.

I felt a scream rise in my throat. I covered my mouth with my hand and rocked back and forth, like the woman on the Greyhound bus.

The store was utterly quiet.

After a few moments, though, something remarkable happened: My eyes adjusted. I couldn't see well, but I could make out the outline of my duffle bag, and the stripes on my sneakers, and when I glanced up, I could spot the demarcation line between the top of the circular rack and the space beyond it.

My racing heartbeat began to slow.

I forced myself to count slowly to one hundred, two hundred, five hundred. Then to a thousand.

I strained to listen, but I couldn't hear a thing to indicate a single employee remained in the store. If someone else were here, they would have kept on the lights, I told myself.

But it took a long time before I found the courage to unfold my aching limbs and crawl out of the clothing rack. I left my duffle bag behind in case I needed to jump back in quickly.

Target looked completely different at night. There were two red exit signs with glowing arrows overhead that provided a tiny bit of illumination, and a few dim safety lights near the front entrance of the store. I stood stock-still, my breath caught in my lungs, but I couldn't detect another presence. I seemed to be all alone in the giant store.

The first thing I did was stare down at my stomach. It didn't look any different.

Maybe I'd gotten the dates wrong, I told myself. But I knew I hadn't.

The thought was too huge for my mind to absorb. So I did what I always do when I get anxious: I moved into action.

I crept down the first aisle I came to. It was filled with toiletries and medicines. I turned the corner and saw what looked like an endless array of snack foods: potato chips and Goldfish crackers and pretzels and candy. My stomach felt hollow. It ached from hunger.

I forced myself to keep moving, tiptoeing down aisle after aisle, pausing every few moments to hold still and listen. I even lurked by the door to the men's room until I was satisfied it, too, was vacant. By the time I'd finished exploring, I'd familiarized myself with every corner and curve of the Target.

I didn't know how long it would be until a cleaning crew showed up, but for now the entire place was mine.

There was a movie starring Natalie Portman based on a novel about a young woman who'd stayed hidden for a time inside a Walmart before building a life for herself in a nearby town. I'd only seen a preview for it and didn't know how the story ended, but it made me wonder: Was it possible for me to actually stay here for a few nights?

I walked back to the snack aisle, leaning in close to see the packages because everything appeared gray and muted. When I spotted an

Almond Joy, my mouth watered. I reached out and felt the cool, crinkly wrapper. I could almost taste the creamy chocolate and coconut.

Then I put it back.

A baby needed nutrition.

There was a box of granola bars a few feet down. I carefully opened it and took one out, wincing at the rustle of the plastic wrapper coming off. But my luck held. The only noises in the store were the ones made by me.

At the first taste of the sweet, crunchy oats, I almost lost control and shoved the whole bar in my mouth. But I forced myself to take small bites and chew thoroughly. I finished it and tried to remember the location of the Snapple lemonade I'd been craving. I'd seen it in a refrigerated case near the front of the store, alongside individually sold iced teas and sodas. I couldn't risk being that close to the big window where anyone passing by might spot me, so I wandered deeper into the store, taking the granola bars with me, until I found a box of Capri Sun fruit juice pouches.

I would find a way to pay back the store someday, I promised myself as I opened one end of the box and pulled out a foil pouch and stabbed it with the attached little straw. I greedily drank three in a row, one after the other, the foil pouches collapsing as the sweet liquid emptied into my mouth.

My stomach made a gurgling sound, and my hand automatically moved to cover it.

I looked down, thinking about how I'd held my palm to the bus window earlier today, aching for a connection with someone—even a stranger who'd wrecked his car.

Now my hand was pressing toward you.

I stayed like that for a little while, thinking about you. Those were the moments in which you became real to me.

Because of you, Catherine, I was no longer alone.

Timmy was born when I was five, and I loved him from the moment I saw his red, crinkly little face. I took care of him as best I could because my mother wasn't exactly up to the job. I learned to support his neck while I held him and how to swaddle him in a blanket so he'd feel cozy. At night I rubbed his back and sang to him until he fell asleep.

I hadn't even met you, but I swear, I already loved you, too. You were the only thing good left in my life. If it hadn't been for you, I would have given up a hundred times that first week.

After a while I made my way back to the camping goods section and briefly thought about removing the sleeping bag from the box and using it, then putting it back in. But I didn't want someone else to buy a used bag, thinking they were getting a new one. I was about to move on when I spotted something right next to the sleeping bags. Flashlights.

The bigger ones were encased in hard plastic packaging, but a half-dozen small ones, the size of baby cucumbers, were just lined up on the shelf. I was pretty sure my dad had this identical flashlight in the glove compartment of his car. I'd seen him use it when he'd gone to help a group of college kids whose breaker had tripped in the basement of the house they were renting.

I reached for one and flicked it on. Nothing.

It probably needed batteries. I remember seeing Duracell packages over by the video cameras and VCRs. I retraced my steps there, guessing I'd need two double As.

It took me a minute to find and open the right package, and I almost lost one of the batteries when I dropped it and it rolled down the aisle, but I finally got the flashlight to work. And when I cupped my hand over it and flicked it on and saw a white-gold circle shining on the floor—that's the moment when I began to feel a bright spot of hope flicker within me, too.

I went back to my hiding place to tuck the remaining granola bars and juice pouches in my duffle bag and to grab a change of clothes and my toiletries. I could use the restroom to wash up and put on fresh underthings and clean jeans—and my sweatshirt because the store's air-conditioning was strong. Then I'd duck back into the rack of pants and make myself a little nest and treat myself to another granola bar and one more juice.

There was still so much to figure out. I didn't know when a cleaning crew might show up or if a night guard patrolled the premises. I would have to learn how to blend in with other shoppers tomorrow morning to get out of the store. I needed to find a place to throw away my blood-stained shorts and the shirt I'd been wearing for two days, too.

But for now, with my stomach full and my thirst slaked and a safe place to sleep, I felt for the first time as if I—as if the two of us—had a real chance.

CHAPTER TWENTY-THREE

CATHERINE

I fold the copy of the RJ's application my mother filled out and tuck it in my purse. I have what I came to Sunrise for, but I don't want to go home. I can't bear to be around my mom right now.

I exit the Memory Wing mindfully, aware that in my distraught state I'm more prone to making mistakes. I double-check that no residents are watching as I input the code—and after I step through the blue door, I test it to make sure the lock is engaged. I take these precautions even though it's daytime and so many staff members are on the premises that it's difficult for a wandering resident to go far.

Nighttime is a different story. There's only a skeleton crew of a few nurses, a handful of aides, and one security guard in the whole building.

I ride the elevator down to the lobby and wave to the receptionist, then step out onto the green lawn and breathe in the moist, late spring air. Several Daily Assisted and Extended Care residents are on the porch playing cards, while others work in the gardens. A few are sitting in Adirondack chairs in the yard, and even though it's seventy-five degrees, one has a blanket tucked over her lap. They're all women, with thinning hair and weakening bodies and limited time. They probably all have children.

I wonder if they, too, have betrayed their daughters.

As I head toward the parking lot, I spot a walnut-colored old Cadillac pulling into one of the spaces closest to the building. I wait until the couple exits the car, then walk over to greet them.

Of all the patients I've worked with, George and June Campbell have a special place in my heart. Even today, in the mood I'm in, I can't pass up a chance to say hello to them.

George and June moved to Sunrise after her stroke six years ago, shortly after I began working here. She needed access to physical and speech therapists to learn to walk again with a cane, and—in a bit of modesty I found sweet—she didn't want her husband of fifty-two years to be the one helping her bathe and use the toilet.

I was one of the aides who helped June with her daily needs, which is why they refuse to let me call them by anything other than their first names. As June once said to me as I bathed her, "Sweetie, now that you've seen me in my full glory, I think we've moved past the 'Mrs. Campbell' stage."

June is a type 1 diabetic, and she requires insulin injections several times a day, which I used to administer as part of her care. It's how I got so comfortable giving shots.

Despite the hardships life has thrown at the Campbells, they are two of the most positive people I've ever met. Even though I no longer work with them directly, we've stayed in touch, and occasionally they call or text and invite me over for lunch or a drink.

"Catherine!" June cries when she sees me. She's wearing a teal-blue dress and pearls, and George has on a button-down shirt and tan slacks. The two of them always dress elegantly, even when they're just running errands.

I give them each a big hug.

"How many more days until you leave?" June asks.

It takes me a moment to remember. "A week," I tell her. "But don't worry, I'll come by before I go."

"We're going to hold you to that," George replies.

We chat for a moment, but I can tell June is tired, so I excuse myself and promise to visit them soon.

The moment I bid the Campbells goodbye, the brief respite their presence provided evaporates.

I take my phone out of my bag and check the time. It's barely four o'clock, but that's usually when happy hour kicks off. I don't drink often, but right now there's nothing I want more than a strong gin and tonic. And someone to share it with.

My mother doesn't appear to be the person I believed she was. Maybe I was wrong about Ethan, too.

The truth is, ever since I learned my mom may have deliberately set him up, it has been hard to get Ethan out of my mind. I keep seeing him leaning over the bar, his biceps curving beneath his short-sleeved shirt.

My phone is already in my hand, so it takes only a few touches of the screen to dial his number.

He answers after the first ring. "Hey, you."

"What are you up to?" I ask.

I can hear the smile in his voice when he replies, "Waiting for you to come over."

A few hours later, I lazily roll over in bed and Ethan's body responds, echoing my movements as he spoons me. My body feels heavy and relaxed. The combination of a couple of drinks, sex for the first time in far too many months, and a nap have chased away some of my tension.

I stretch out my arm and reach for my phone on the nightstand to check my messages. Two texts and a missed call, all from my mother. The first text came in right after I arrived at Ethan's. How about we watch a movie tonight? You can pick which one. The second text arrived a few minutes ago, and the chime must have been what awoke me from my light sleep. Everything ok?

My mother probably knows where I am since I'm sure she has

checked my location. She must recognize this address from when I was dating Ethan.

Melanie's words float back to me. *Wow, you still share your location with your mom?*

My mother bought me my first cell phone. She's the one who set up the location-sharing system then. I never challenged it, just like I never really challenged anything else she did or told me.

The injustice of it all begins to boil inside me, erasing the fragile sense of peace brought on by cold gin and Ethan's warm body. I'm twenty-four years old, yet my mother tries to constantly watch over and control me. I don't know if I'm more upset with her for doing it or with myself for allowing it.

My anger fuels my resolve for what I need to do next. I slide out from beneath Ethan's heavy arm and put my bare feet on his not-too-clean bedroom floor.

"Where are you going?" His voice is raspy with sleep.

"I need to make a call. It's important. My phone is dead. Can I use yours?"

He sits up, rubbing his eyes and blinking. He reaches for the phone on the floor next to his side of the bed, and his fingers move across the screen for a few moments. My impatience grows as I wait. Ethan is probably covering up something he doesn't want me to see—maybe texts from girls he has been flirting with. He finally tosses it to me.

"Thanks." I walk across the room and reach for my purse, too intent on my task to be self-conscious about my nakedness. I pull out the folded piece of paper and dial the number for the reference my mother put down, a woman named Diane Brown. I've never heard of her, and I have no idea how she knows my mother well enough to be a reference, so I'm going to have to finesse my way through this. I'd rather Ethan not listen to the strange conversation I'm about to have, but his roommates are in the living room playing Xbox and razzing each other.

Ethan's arms are folded behind him on the pillow. He's watching me from beneath heavy-lidded eyes. I lift a finger to my lips, then dial the number.

It rings a few times, then goes to voicemail. The generic automated message tells me to leave my name and phone number, but I hang up before the beep.

Disappointment crashes through me. I can't use my own phone to call back. Caller ID will identify me, and there's no good explanation for why Ruth Sterling's daughter is calling a reference to inquire about Ruth Sterling.

I knew Ethan's phone would be far harder to link to me. The first time he called me on it, the name John Quinlan showed up, which was a little confusing until Ethan explained it was his father's name, and he was still on his parents' family phone plan.

It's like my mother is suddenly in the room with us, whispering questions about why a twenty-eight-year-old man is still on his parents' phone plan, and what else they pay for and take care of in his life.

"Everything okay?"

Ethan asks the exact same question my mother did in her text. I wonder why people always ask that, especially when their tone makes it clear they know the answer is no.

I give the answer everyone wants to hear. "Yeah, fine."

I wonder fleetingly how different the world would be if people asked instead, "What *isn't* okay?" and we responded with the truth.

Ethan's phone buzzes and I toss it back to him without looking at the screen. Ethan and I aren't a couple. It's none of my business who's texting him. I fold up my mother's work application again and put it back in my purse.

I spent a lot of time googling her this morning, but her name is common enough that there's both too little and too much on the internet to be of any help. I found plenty of Ruth Sterlings out there, but nothing that seems to fit her. Even when I added my mother's birthday—August second—to the search, none of the hits were a match.

I'm about to reach for my clothes and get dressed when Ethan lifts the covers. It's an invitation.

One drunken tryst I could write off as a mistake. But now I'm fully sober.

I hesitate, remembering Ethan's strong hands holding mine above my head as he slid apart my legs with one of his, murmuring, *I've missed this body.*

Then I think about my mother, worrying and waiting at home.

I make my choice easily. I climb back into bed.

The next time I wake up, sunlight is streaming through the window. I didn't come here intending to spend the night, but I'm glad I did. My mother is at work by now, so I can return to our apartment and avoid seeing her.

Ethan is still asleep, and so are his roommates, which means the bathroom is free. I pull on yesterday's clothes, then tiptoe down the hall. I use my finger and a dab of toothpaste to clean my teeth as best I can, then splash water on my face. I'm about to try to straighten a chunk of my hair that is sticking up when someone knocks on the door. I open it to see one of Ethan's roommates standing there in nothing but boxers, his eyes half-shut.

"Sorry, Kaitlin," he mutters. "Really need to take a leak."

"Be my guest, but I'm not Kaitlin."

His eyes widen. He looks at me, then back toward Ethan's bedroom. "My bad."

I wait while the roommate noisily pees for what seems like an inordinately long time. When he finally comes out, he brushes past me with a mumbled, "Thanks."

I step into the bathroom again, this time leaving the door open, and try to finger-comb my hair. It only makes things worse, so I look around for a brush. I don't see one on the vanity, so I pull open the drawer beneath the sink.

A fat pink cosmetics bag is in the drawer. I stare at it for a moment, wondering if I really want to know what it contains. Then I realize I already do know.

I unzip the bag and see a toothbrush, Secret deodorant, a pink disposable razor, a round brush, a tube of KUSH mascara, a travel-sized vial of perfume. . . .

The sorts of things that a woman who is in a serious relationship keeps at her boyfriend's place in case they end up sleeping there and she needs to put herself together the next morning.

I know because when Ethan and I were together, I kept a similar bag in this very drawer.

I zip up the pink bag and decide to give up on my hair. I walk back into Ethan's bedroom. He's hunched under the covers, whispering into his phone.

I quietly gather my things. By the time I'm slipping on my shoes, he has hung up.

"Was that Kaitlin?"

He flinches. "Look . . . I didn't plan on this, but when you called . . ."

"Don't worry about it. I didn't exactly expect us to get back together."

I did think about it for a few minutes, though. Ethan is far from dependable, but for a little while there he felt like the most solid thing in my life.

As I start to exit the bedroom, Ethan jumps out of bed and pulls on his boxers, scrambling to catch up with me.

I walk through the living room, seeing the beer bottles and the bong on the coffee table, the sofa cushions in disarray. I don't need to go into the kitchen to know the state it's in: pizza boxes piled on the counter, a carton of fermenting orange juice in the fridge alongside a few Gatorades for hangovers.

I haven't been here in a year, but not a single thing has changed.

His phone is ringing again. It's probably Kaitlin, wondering why he hung up so abruptly.

Maybe she is out of town, or perhaps she works a night job like Ethan. She could even be the blond waitress who always gave me cold looks when I came in to visit Ethan, even though he swore she was like that with everyone. Ethan never introduced me to her, but I heard other people at the bar mention her name—and I'm positive it began with a *K*.

"Better get that," I tell Ethan as he looks at me sheepishly. He blows his long hair out of his face, and his lightly tanned, beautifully tattooed body leans toward me for a goodbye kiss.

I turn around instead of giving him one.

As I walk away, his voice sounds faint, but I still catch how he greets his girlfriend. "Hey, you."

I can hear another voice, too, but this one is in my head. It belongs to my mother. *That could have been you,* she whispers.

CHAPTER TWENTY-FOUR

RUTH

Here are my vanishing rules: Keep cash in your wallet—a hundred dollars minimum. Never let your phone battery dip into the red zone. Store a granola bar and a bottle of water in your glove compartment.

And in the side pocket of your duffle bag, carry a flat-head screwdriver.

I'd never be able to sleep in a Target today, like I did the first time I ran. Security measures are more sophisticated now, with motion-activated cameras and invisible lasers.

But I'm better now, too. I'm more resourceful than I was as a teenager.

The lunch rush at Sam's is over. Just a handful of customers are lingering, reading the paper or skimming through their phones. I finish rolling a set of silverware into a white paper napkin and put the slim bundle atop the stack I've made by the coffee station.

"Miss?"

Two women at table five are summoning me. I reach for a pot of coffee and head their way. I learned long ago that carrying coffee saves me from making extra trips. Since I hold the pots with my right hand, the bicep on my right arm is always slightly bigger and more defined than the one on my left.

"Top you off?" I offer.

"Just the check, thanks."

I've already tallied their total, so I reach for the bill in my apron pocket and put it on the table.

I head back to the coffee station and take one of the white mugs stacked facedown on a tray and flip it right side up, pouring a cup for myself. It's my fourth so far today.

I'm tired because I tossed and turned all night. I couldn't sleep without Catherine at home. The strange thing is, I assumed we'd spend more time together after Dr. Chen told us he believed I had Alzheimer's.

Instead, the opposite is happening.

I'm stunned she went back to Ethan. After the night of their one-year anniversary, when I bought that bottle of Russian vodka and offered him a drink and watched him nod a little too eagerly, I figured we'd seen the last of him.

The two women at table five stand up and head for the cashier. I wait until they exit, then walk over and begin to clear their dirty plates. I notice someone approach out of the corner of my eye and my stomach drops. I have a feeling I know what's coming.

Melanie reaches for the empty juice and water glasses, stacking them up.

"Thanks," I tell her.

"Why should you have all the fun?"

I really do wish I'd been able to accept the invitations Melanie extended in the past. But alcohol leads to letting down one's guard, and women like to confide in each other. I would've slipped and made an unforgivable error. Maybe not the first time, or the second, but eventually.

Catherine is used to accepting what I say. Our dynamic was established when we were parent and child, and even though things are more equitable now, she still doesn't challenge me when I draw a line.

Melanie and I don't have that history.

Another rule for when you're always on the verge of disappearing: Don't get close to anyone or they might try to find you.

"It's dead in here. How about we take a break and grab a cup?"

Since I won't meet her out, Melanie is trying to get us to have a drink—in this case, coffee—right here.

"I wish." I give what I hope sounds like a regretful sigh. "I was going to try to duck out early. I've got a ton of errands."

Melanie is a smart cookie. She must sense how much I like her. My rebuffs have to feel confusing to her.

But all she does is say, "I'm here if you need anything." Then she reaches for the napkins crumpled on the table and clears them away. Other than the difference in our skin shade, her hands could be my hands. When you're a waitress, you keep your nails short and neat. And forget about wearing rings or bracelets to work—prongs or nooks can catch tiny bits of food. The last thing you want is to have to dig someone's sticky French toast crumb out of a crevice in your best piece of jewelry.

I wasn't really planning to leave early, but now I'm stuck. I go to the counter, where Sam is trying to fix a stool that is getting wobbly on its base, and ask if I can head out. His grunt seems to be in the affirmative, so I walk to the small employee room. I spin the dial on the locker, putting in my code, and when the door springs open, I pull out my bag. Then I look behind me.

Sometimes I keep things here that I don't want my daughter to see. When I learned Catherine had been offered the job at Johns Hopkins—shortly before James's parole hearing—I checked out a book and stored it here. *Understanding Alzheimer's.* It strengthened my decision to put on a charade to keep Catherine safe after James won parole. It even gave me specific ideas for symptoms to fake.

There's something else tucked in the back of my locker, too. A burner phone. It wouldn't be a catastrophe if Sam found it—there's nothing that links it to me, and I could always say a customer left it and I was holding on to it to return.

Still, I'd prefer it be kept a secret.

I've had this phone for a long time. Many years. I've never made a single call from it, though.

I didn't buy it because I intended to use it.

This phone is a trip wire.

If someone calls this number and starts asking questions about me, I'll know one of my last lines of defense is down.

I check the messages every time I come to work. Now I plug the burner into the wall socket, turn it on, and wait until the tiny screen activates.

Three words appear that fill me with terror: *One missed call.*

I frantically navigate to the call log to see where and when the number originated. It came in last night around 7 p.m. and caller ID shows it was from a guy named John Quinlan.

No message.

I stare down at the phone, half expecting it to ring again. That sound would feel like a bomb detonating in my hand.

It's silent.

Wrong number, I try to reassure myself. I occasionally receive them since the number for this phone is almost identical to that of a busy law firm in Philadelphia, with just the last two digits transposed. This John Quinlan was trying to reach the law firm and when he heard the computerized voice saying only, *"Leave a message at the tone,"* he realized his mistake and hung up. That's why he hasn't called back.

I start to put the burner back in my locker, then change my mind and secure it and the charger in my purse.

The risk of missing a call is far greater than the risk of Catherine discovering my secret phone.

I exit the restaurant, waving goodbye to Melanie and tamping down the flicker of guilt I feel when she cheerfully waves back.

I walk down the sidewalk and stand outside the bus shelter, shifting from foot to foot, my exhaustion erased. I'm acutely aware of the small black flip phone zipped inside the inner pocket of my purse.

If this phone rings and the caller asks for Diane Brown, I'll know they're seeking information about me.

Diane Brown doesn't exist. Her name is a snare I set in a few places. I wrote it down, along with the number for my burner phone, on rental apartments and job applications so I would be alerted if someone was digging into my past and trying to track me down.

Just another misdial, I repeat to myself as I compulsively check my surroundings.

Still, even after I board the bus, I'm too uneasy to sit. I hold on to the silver rail by the rear exit and keep my head on a swivel, searching the faces of everyone on board. A woman across from me is working the crossword puzzle, tapping her pencil eraser against her newspaper while she frowns down at the empty white squares.

The faint, rhythmic noise of the eraser hitting the page sounds like an echo from my past. *Tick-tock.*

I suck in a raggedy breath as the bus heaves forward. Catherine is safe, I remind myself. She is home—she left Ethan's around 9 a.m.—and I'll be with her soon. No one is hunting us.

I am seven stops away from getting off the bus. I'll walk down the familiar streets, my eyes alert behind my sunglasses. I'll scan every vehicle in the parking lot and take out my can of Mace before I climb the stairs to the fourth floor.

I will do all of this even though we are perfectly safe. It's just another precaution.

After I get home and change, I'll take the Bonneville and drive to the library to do my checking. Catherine and I will stay in tonight and make dinner—something fun like tacos—and we'll flop on the couch together and watch a show. Our relationship will ease back onto its warm, familiar track.

No one can find us. I've hidden our path well for twenty-four years.

I don't notice that it has begun to rain until I hear the bus's big, heavy wipers drag across the windshield.

Tick-tock. Tick-tock.

Dread infuses my body. I begin to tremble. Something is terribly wrong. I spin around, looking again at the faces on the bus.

The woman's pencil is still tapping. *Tick-tock,* it whispers, matching the rhythm of the wipers.

James is getting close. I know it not just because of these signs. I feel it deep in my core.

My body tenses as I inch toward the exit, my hand scrabbling in my purse for the Mace.

Then I break one of my cardinal rules.

I reach for my phone and google the name James Bates. The results pop up quickly. I click on the first hit, from *The Baltimore Sun* online newspaper.

It was published right around the time I started my shift this morning.

Then I see it, the news I've been dreading for most of my life.

The reckoning I've always known is coming.

A photo of James is staring at me below a headline that reads, "Oak Hill High Killer to Be Released Today."

CHAPTER TWENTY-FIVE

CATHERINE

I unlock the door to our apartment a little before 9 a.m. and kick off my shoes, then immediately head for the shower. I want to scrub Ethan's scent off me as quickly as possible.

I twist the knob to turn on the water, and because it always takes a few minutes to heat up, go back into my bedroom to toss my clothes in the hamper. My room is just as I left it yesterday. My cream-colored comforter is smoothed across my bed; the lights are off; and my clothes are hung according to color in the tiny closet, creating the rainbow effect my mother and I replicated after we saw it on *The Home Edit*.

I pause, looking around. Something feels off. It's the strangest thing, but I have the creepy sense someone was in here, running a hand through my clothes, scanning the titles of the books on my shelf, and picking up the picture on my nightstand to study the image of me as a baby with my young mother.

I'm being paranoid, I tell myself, and I walk directly to the shower.

I pull back the curtain and step in, relishing the feel of warm water beating down on me. I reach for the fancy shampoo my mother buys for a fraction of the retail price at a discount store and lather and rinse my hair. While my conditioner soaks in, I shave my legs.

I don't exactly feel like a new woman after I turban a towel around my hair and step out into the steamy air to rub lotion on my skin, but at least I'm ready to tackle the day.

I've got a good stretch of alone time in front of me, and I intend to make the most of it.

I pull on a T-shirt dress and decide to let my hair air-dry. The apartment feels stuffy, so I crack open the windows in my bedroom and the living room. Then I head to the kitchen to grab breakfast. Other than gin and the bag of tortilla chips Ethan offered me, I haven't eaten since the popcorn I made yesterday afternoon, and I'm starving.

There's a plate on the kitchen counter, covered in tin foil, with a sticky note atop it.

The sticky note has a simple heart on it, drawn in blue ink. I pull back the crinkly foil and see scrambled eggs, two of the vegetarian sausage links I like, and a toasted everything bagel. The Mr. Coffee pot is half full and set to the warming function. A bottle of ketchup is next to my plate because I love it on my eggs.

I thought we were out of those veggie links, but my mother must have made a special trip to the store to pick them up. The pan she used for the eggs is drying on the drainboard, so she must have taken the time to scrub it.

My mother doesn't eat breakfast. She got up with the sun to do all this for me, then she walked to the bus stop.

I look down at the heart she drew for me and burst into tears.

I didn't know it was possible to be so deeply angry with someone and simultaneously love them so much that you wanted to hug them until it hurt you both.

I cry until my throat feels raw, then I blow my nose on the paper napkin my mother left folded next to my plate.

I don't know what's going to happen between me and my mother, or whether our relationship will ever be the same. I can't know where we will go from here until I find out the truth about her.

I microwave my plate to warm everything, then I sit down at the little wooden table where we've shared so many meals. I eat alone, finishing every last morsel.

I wash and dry my plate and fork and pour a second cup of coffee, then retrieve my legal pad and open my laptop and begin to search again. I'm itching to phone Diane Brown, but I want to wait a few more hours to space out my calls. I can use the *67 trick to block my number, but if she doesn't answer and sees more hang-ups coming in, she may be suspicious when I do finally reach her using a blocked number.

I spent a lot of time yesterday morning searching for Ruth Sterling. It was like looking for a particular grain of sand when I didn't even know if I was on the right beach. Some of the hits I got were obituaries, while others didn't pan out because the women were all wrong in some fundamental way—their ages, photos, occupations, or marital status ruled them out. Today I try narrowing down possibilities by mixing in different details like my mother's birth month, Virginia, and even the word "waitress."

I find a few leads, but they lead me down rabbit holes.

I finally close my laptop a little too roughly and reach around with one hand to massage the back of my neck.

I'm grumpy and feel the threat of a headache, probably because I've been staring at a screen for so long and haven't hydrated adequately since last night's gin. I grab a glass out of the cabinet and reach into the refrigerator for the Brita pitcher. I chug down eight ounces of water, then refill my glass.

The water level in the pitcher is getting low, so I pop off the lid and hold it under the sink tap. Someday, I'm going to live in a place where pure, filtered water will be on tap, but right now that's a luxury I can only dream about.

My gaze drifts just beyond the stream of running water to the little china ring holder my mother has had for as long as I can remember.

On the pointy peak is her topaz ring, where it often sits when she is at work or doing dishes. When I was younger, I used to beg my mom to let me wear the ring. She never once said yes. She even used to yank away her hand when I touched the rectangular stone, telling me the setting was delicate.

She acts like that ring is worth a million bucks, which is silly because as jewels go, topaz is relatively inexpensive. I know because my old friend Aliyah got a pair of topaz earrings for her birthday when we were in tenth grade, shortly before we moved, and her parents could not have afforded anything extravagant.

The water overflows in the pitcher, running down my hand. But I can't move.

I was there when Aliyah's parents handed her the small square box, wrapped in shiny silver paper. We'd all eaten dinner at Aliyah's apartment and cheered as she had blown out the candles on her cake.

Aliyah put the earrings in right after she opened the box and beamed while her father snapped a picture.

Happy birthday, sweetheart, her mother had said. Aliyah had turned fifteen that day. It was early November.

I look at my mother's ring again. It's like I'm seeing it for the first time.

Sometimes the thing we've been searching for has been staring us in the face all along. Perhaps we miss the clue because subconsciously we don't want to acknowledge it.

Maybe my mother did bring along a talisman from her past, after all. The ring.

My mother claims her birthday is August second.

But topaz is the birthstone for November.

As if in a trance, I shut off the water, leaving the heavy pitcher in the sink, and dry my hand on a dish towel before walking back to my laptop.

I can no longer trust a single thing my mother has said.

Of course, she could have lied about her birth date, and I blindly believed her, never thinking to question such a seemingly fundamental fact about her. I assumed she loved the ring because it was pretty, not because it represented her secret truth. I created a story in my mind to support her deception, like an unconscious coconspirator.

All those years I drew balloons on construction paper cards and baked chocolate cupcakes to celebrate on August second. Was every bit of it a lie?

I feel the slow burn of deep anger welling up in me again. I clench and unclench my fists.

What else could she have fabricated?

For all I know, even her name might be—

I leap to my feet before my mind registers my movement, jumping back from the table like the thought is something poisonous that might strike me. My heartbeat races as I inch forward again to grab my legal pad. There was something I came across yesterday during my search, something I need to see again right now. A Google hit with a perfect match for my mother's name . . .

I flip back a page, my eyes scanning the scribbled notes, then I turn back one more page, impatience swelling inside me. I know it's here. I have to find it. I crossed it out, but when I see it again—

The words leap out at me, through the strikethrough black pen mark I made.

~~Ruth Mary Sterling, Wisconsin, same birth date. Died at 12.~~

I'm shaking so hard I drop the pad of paper.

Maybe my mother's real last name isn't Sterling.

Her skin is light brown. She claims to be white—I've seen her write that down more than once on forms—but she looks as if she might be partly Latina. I inherited her skin tone, too. My friends Chelsea and Aliyah and I once lined up our forearms—white, black, and brown—and I was the middle shade. Even Ethan, when we first met, expressed surprise when I told him I was white.

The floor beneath me feels like it's shuddering, trying to knock me off-balance.

I take a step toward the table and slowly ease back down in the chair.

Ruth Mary Sterling died a long time ago. So who is my mother?

The answer crashes down on me. She is the woman who stole Ruth Sterling's identity.

Identity theft happens after death. It's common enough that we've dealt with it at Sunrise more than once.

My mom told me she gave birth to me at eighteen.

But if she stole Ruth's identity, she would have also appropriated Ruth's exact age.

Name, birth date, age, race . . . these are typically among the first questions on paperwork people fill out in doctor's offices and on government forms, the core facts we use to define ourselves.

I have no idea who my mother truly is.

My mind begins shrieking at me to run, to get away as fast as I can. Adrenaline seizes control of my body, infusing me with the energy to move. I run to my bedroom and grab my backpack, dumping my old school notebooks and pens onto my bed. I shove a few changes of clothes into it and zip it up, then I remember my toothbrush and run to the bathroom.

I catch sight of myself in the mirror, and it pulls me up short. My eyes are big and wild looking.

Who is the woman who calls herself Ruth Sterling? Is she even my mother?

At least the mirror gives me a solid answer. I have her full lips and her high, flat cheekbones. She may have manipulated everything else about our lives, but there's no way she could have influenced the genes that dictated the shape of my features.

I slump onto the floor and wrap my arms around my knees, curling up tight.

When I was younger, I loved horror movies, and the best ones were when the monster was in the house. I'd yell at the screen, telling the oblivious heroine to get out of the basement, incredulous she couldn't sense the dark shadow creeping up behind her.

I watched those movies with my mother next to me, the two of us clutching each other at the jump scares.

"Nothing about her is real." I whisper the words aloud because I need to finally hear the truth, even if I'm the only one telling it to myself.

My mind is so overloaded I want to close my eyes right here on the blue bath mat and sleep.

But that's not the right escape. I have to summon the will to get out of here, but where can I go?

Then I hear a sound that sends a chill down my spine.

My mother isn't due home from work for a couple of hours. I thought I had more time.

A key is scraping into the lock on our front door.

CHAPTER TWENTY-SIX

RUTH

The moment I see James's grainy picture on my phone, I frantically yank the pull cord for the bus to stop. The doors aren't fully open when I leap down the steps and land on the sidewalk.

I look around wildly, scanning my surroundings. A woman in a blue-and-gold sari waits in the bus shelter, pushing a baby stroller back and forth and singing in a language I don't recognize. A couple of teenagers are sitting on the steps of a town house, exhaling wispy white clouds as they vape. A deliveryman with bags of Chinese food stacked in a plastic crate on the back of his scooter whips past me, the aroma of fried food drifting by a moment later.

Then I see a slender man walking directly toward me. He's wearing sunglasses and has sandy hair. I melt into the nearest storefront, my heart leaping into my throat.

As the man draws nearer, I see he can't be more than nineteen or so—the age James was when I last saw him. I step back onto the sidewalk, my legs shaking as I hurry toward home.

I have to get a grip. I need to battle back my panic with every ounce of my force of will.

"Protect Catherine." I say the words aloud as I begin to focus on the preparations I have made in anticipation of this day.

My emergency bank account, the one Catherine doesn't know about, holds seven hundred and forty dollars. It's running money, amassed through the years, mostly through deposits of five or ten dollars at a time. I keep the ATM card taped to the underside of the passenger seat in our car.

I'm going to need that cash now.

I didn't get off the bus early solely to change up my routine. I also need to talk to a lawyer. I already have the name of the person I intend to use. I began my research the day I learned James had been granted parole and added the contact to my phone.

I begin to walk briskly, constantly scanning my surroundings. When a car horn blares behind me, I flinch, but I don't miss a stride.

Protect Catherine.

Those two words form a mantra in my mind. Every action I'm about to take is designed to put another steel cage around my daughter and me.

I'm glad I followed my instincts and tucked my burner phone in my purse. Since it is untraceable, I need to use it for the first time ever for this conversation.

I dial the number for the lawyer, and after three rings he picks up the phone himself. It makes sense that the kind of attorney I can afford doesn't earn enough to pay for an assistant. Even so, my secret fund won't stretch far.

I launch into my cover story, explaining that I'm a relative of Coach Franklin, and that my family is devastated to learn James Bates is now a free man.

"You can't understand how hard this has been on us," I tell the lawyer, and I don't have to fake the emotion in my voice. "We'd just like to find out where James is living. I don't want my father to bump into James in the grocery store or something. Honestly, that might kill my dad. His health isn't so good."

I pass by a garbageman clanging down the lid on a metal trash can and shift closer to the curb to avoid a couple of laughing kids who are running down the sidewalk. The noises and movements don't pull away my focus now. My purpose is absolute.

I've been preparing for this day all of my daughter's life.

"Rough stuff," the lawyer replies, clicking his tongue against his teeth. "So listen, I might be talking myself out of a job here, but as the victim's family, you can reach out to the prosecutor's office. They should be able to keep you posted on the guy's movements. For free."

I already know this. But filing such a request would require me to provide information I cannot give to anyone. Those details would drop clues leading directly to me, and even if James never found them, I'm sure the police would.

"We'd rather keep this quiet."

The lawyer is silent for a moment. I wonder if he thinks I have another reason for trying to gather information on James's location without alerting the authorities.

Some families must do more than simply fantasize about revenge.

I know I would if James so much as breathed in Catherine's direction.

"They keep a tight leash on these guys. He'll be heading to a halfway house in Baltimore. He's going to have to check in with his parole officer. He won't be running around the streets bothering your family."

It's like the lawyer can hear the protest rising in my throat before I utter a word because he continues, "Okay, sure, I'll look into it. Give me his full name, and if you have his prisoner ID, that'd be helpful, too."

That information was easy to find on the state's website during one of my library checks, so I have it and more, stored in the notes section beneath the lawyer's name. It's disguised to look like someone's home address.

"I've got to take a deposition in—" the lawyer pauses and I imagine him looking at his watch—"thirty minutes so I won't be able to get to this till the morning. That okay?"

James may not even have been released yet. It isn't like giant gates will creak open at precisely 9 a.m. and he'll walk out alone, like in the movies. Prisons run on their own schedules; they don't revolve around any particular inmate's. Plus there will be paperwork to do, and they'll take a current photo of James, and then he'll need to be brought to wherever he's going to be living. Reporters might even be there to document all of it. I've researched this. I'm certain of it.

James has even less than I did when I ran. He'll get a little bit of gate money, but there's no way he can find me tonight.

"Tomorrow works," I tell the lawyer. "What's your fee?"

"For this, let's call it two-fifty."

I think of all the dollar bills and fives I squeezed out of an already impossibly tight budget and faithfully brought to the bank, week after week.

"Can I send it via PayPal?"

It's one of the easiest ways to pay someone anonymously. All you need is an email address, and I've already created a new one just for this. I'll buy a prepaid Visa card and use it for the transaction. I've had a long time to prepare for this day. I know exactly what to do.

"Yeah, but wait until I make sure I can find the info on Bates first. Just give me your number and I'll—"

I cut him off as I approach our apartment building. "I'll call you tomorrow morning."

James is in another state, I tell myself for the hundredth time. If he imagines me living anywhere, it's by the beach in California or in a small town outside Rome. He'd never expect me to be so close to home. No one would.

I pull open the door to the lobby and walk to the very back, where there is a row of gray metal mailboxes for tenants. I unlock ours, then dig the little white tag with the name *Sterling* written on it out of the slot at the top and flip it around to its blank side. I slip it back in, then lock up the mailbox and move on.

The mailman knows we live in 406. He probably never even checks the names on these boxes unless someone new moves in. He won't notice anything amiss.

But if James does somehow find out my name and learns I'm living in this building, I may have just made it a tiny bit harder for him to pinpoint the apartment.

I pull my Mace out of my bag and make sure the nozzle is facing away from me, then creep up the stairs, making wide turns instead of hugging the inside, like people normally do.

I reach our floor and crack open the door to glance down our hallway. It's completely empty. I walk quickly to our apartment, grateful I can hear the sound of the TV next door. It means someone is nearby.

I unlock the door and close it behind me, then twist the dead bolt and pull the chain home.

I know Catherine is here. My phone showed her location the last time I checked it, which was less than five minutes ago.

But I can't hear anything.

Usually it's easy for me to sense her presence in our apartment before I see her, and not just because our place is so small. Call it a mother's instinct, or maybe it's the invisible tie I've always felt connecting me to her, like a phantom umbilical cord.

I can't detect her at all right now, though.

I move slowly, my Mace held out in front of me, taking quiet steps as I scan the living room and kitchen area.

Empty. The breakfast plate I left on the counter for Catherine is gone.

Both bedroom doors are open. She could simply be asleep on her bed. That would explain the sense I have that she isn't present, even though she must be here.

I pass her bedroom first. Everything is just as it was last night, when she finally texted me to say she was staying over at a friend's and I felt so alienated from her that I went into her room simply to be near her things.

I step into the bathroom and gasp. Catherine is curled on the mat, her eyes closed. Her skin appears waxy and for a split second, I start to tip into a bottomless terror.

I drop to my knees. She's breathing.

"Catherine." My voice sounds odd. I clear my throat and try again. "Sweetheart?"

Her eyelids flutter. "I don't feel well."

I rest my hand on her forehead. It's cool. I wonder if she has a bad hangover from her night with Ethan, or whether she's coming down with the flu.

I tuck my Mace into my pocket as I ask, "Can I help you to bed?"

She nods and slowly gets up, holding on to the arm I offer. We shuffle down the hallway together and when we reach her room, I see she has been cleaning out her school backpack on her bed. I use my free hand to push aside her old notebooks and pens, then I pull back her covers.

She eases beneath them, moving like a very old woman.

It sounds awful, but I'm almost grateful she is sick. It means she won't be going anywhere.

I collect her school supplies from the foot of the bed and place them atop her bureau, then set her backpack on the floor of her closet. She still has some stuff in there, but I'll leave it for her to deal with when she's better.

Catherine's eyes are closed. She looks so vulnerable right now, like she's a little girl again.

"Do you want to change into your pj's?" I ask.

She doesn't reply.

As I bend over and smooth her soft hair, she startles. I withdraw my hand.

"I'll be right back," I promise.

In the kitchen, I make a mug of chamomile tea and sweeten it with a spoonful of honey, then find a few crackers. I bring this to Catherine along with two Advil I shake out of the jar in the medicine cabinet. I set everything down on her nightstand and move to the window. It's open a few inches, which makes me uncomfortable, even though we're four floors up. I close it and fasten the thumb lock.

When I turn around, I see Catherine's eyelids are cracked apart, like she's watching me. She closes them so fast, though, I might be wrong.

I watch her for a long moment. She's a still, silent form under the covers.

I finally step out of the room, but I leave her door wide open. My purse is still slung over my shoulder, so I put it on my dresser and take off my work clothes, sliding my Mace back into the pocket of my purse. I don't plan to go out again today, so I pull on sweats.

When I walk through the living room to make myself a late lunch in the kitchen, I see one of Catherine's legal pads on the floor by her computer. I pick it up and set it on her laptop.

I open a big can of Progresso vegetable soup, enough for two in case Catherine feels up to eating.

It's hard to swallow it, but I force myself to finish a small bowl. I cannot let myself weaken in any way.

After I return the full Brita pitcher Catherine left in the sink to the fridge and finish washing the dishes, I slip on my topaz ring and go check on her again. It looks like she hasn't moved a muscle.

I know I should elevate my sore feet, so I lie down on my own bed. I feel too agitated to focus deeply, but I force myself to pull out my journal.

Now that James is free, I need to write down everything for my daughter as quickly as I can. If something happens to me, I want her to at least know who I was, and why I did what I did.

By the time I'd been living in the Target for a week, the old me—Ava Morales—was morphing into someone else.

From the office supply aisle, I borrowed a pair of scissors and cut my waist-length hair to my jawline. In the accessories section, I tried on sunglasses until I decided the oversized rectangular ones provided the best camouflage.

I used to love makeup, but this version of me only wore Maybelline pressed powder, which I applied over my dark eyebrows to make them more subdued. A black-and-gold Pirates baseball cap completed my new look once I'd cut off the price tag and stomped on the brim so it didn't look brand new.

I considered trading in my sneakers for shoes that would add a few inches to my height, but I discarded that idea quickly. It's hard to run in heels.

I had a new routine, too. I ate breakfast before the store opened and packed a lunch to take with me to the library every day. I made sand-wiches from a jar of Skippy and a loaf of Wonder Bread, and culled single bananas from a larger bunch. I couldn't resist a pack of Life Sav-ers or a Milky Way bar every now and then, too.

From the health care shelf, I took a bottle of prenatal vitamins and swallowed one every night at bedtime.

By the end of that first week, I knew the store's rhythms well. Em-ployees closed up and exited a little after nine, extinguishing all but the two security lights at the front of the store just before they stepped out. From that moment until early the next morning, the entire Target be-longed to me. I wandered through the baby section, looking at the tiny outfits and bibs, and I studied contraptions like a co-sleeper and some-thing called a Jumperoo, trying to figure out what you'd need. Sometimes I tried on maternity clothes, stuffing a pillow into the billowy blouses. There was a beanbag chair in the kids' section that I'd curl up in with my flashlight and a crisp new People or US Weekly while I munched on Cheez-Its. For those few minutes, I could almost be a normal teenage girl, checking out the members of NSYNC and wondering if the cast members of Dawson's Creek were dating in real life.

Before I went to sleep, I used the bathroom sink to take sponge baths, and once I even washed my hair in it, filling a plastic cup with water and pouring it over my head again and again to rinse. It was a lot easier to manage with short hair.

Since I wasn't sure if the cleaners moved the rack of clothes I slept in to vacuum the carpet beneath it, I found a second hiding place. At six-fifteen, right before the cleaners showed up, I climbed onto a low shelf in the toy aisle and lay down behind a row of big boxes containing toy lawn mowers.

When the cleaners left, I slipped back into my usual hiding spot and waited for the doors to open. Only once did someone almost catch me. An early-bird shopper appeared just after I'd climbed out. I hadn't even had a chance to stand up. I was still crouched on the ground.

I ducked my head and pretended to be tying my shoe, praying she didn't notice the laces were already done. But nothing happened, so I guess I fooled her.

I knew I couldn't live in the Target forever, much as I wanted to. A baby wouldn't understand the need to be quiet.

So a week after I ran away, instead of going to the library to pass the day, I packed up my duffle bag and, fifteen minutes after the store opened, slipped out of my hiding place and headed toward the front door.

I bought a pack of gum from a cashier because it seemed less suspicious than exiting without buying anything. Even if I'd been stopped and my bag searched, they wouldn't find anything incriminating. The flashlight and alarm clock I used were back on the shelf, and the Pirates cap and sunglasses looked like I'd owned them for a while. The only clothes in the bag were my own, and I doubt anyone would think the loose granola bars and half-eaten jar of peanut butter with the missing label belonged to the store. I always made sure to get rid of any unnecessary packaging in case it had an electronic security device on it. My trash blended in with the other waste customers threw into the bins at the store.

The cashier barely even looked at me as he rang up my grape Bubble Yum and gave me a few coins in exchange for my dollar, and a moment later, I was out on the sunlit street.

I needed to do a couple of things. First, I had to get rid of Coach's watch. I'd thought about pawning it, but the initials DTF were engraved on the back. It was dangerously distinctive.

It also felt haunted. I slept with my head on my duffle bag and I swear I could hear its faint, relentless ticking through the thin fabric of my bag. I'd tucked the watch into one of my shirts and buried it beneath all the other clothes in my bag, but I still couldn't muffle the sound, even though I knew it existed only in my mind.

I pulled the brim of my cap a little lower and unwrapped a squishy purple piece of gum and popped it in my mouth as I headed to the Allegheny River. I walked through Market Square and passed by the Andy Warhol Bridge, then found my way to a path adjacent to the river. I walked along it for a half mile or so, passing joggers and people hurrying to work and the occasional mom pushing a baby stroller. All the while, I kept my eye out for a stone that was a little bigger in circumference than my wrist.

I found a smooth, white-gray one by the base of a tree.

I slid the watchband partway over the rock, until it fit snugly. I waited for a break in foot traffic, then I moved to the river's edge and hurled the rock as hard as I could.

The watch and stone sank together into the calm, murky water.

Rings of ripples spread out, small at first, then widening. They seemed to be reaching toward the shore. I took an involuntary step back.

I forced away the crazy idea that somehow the watch was crawling back toward me.

I began to walk quickly down the path. No one seemed to have paid any attention to what I'd done. I'd gotten rid of the only remaining physical link between me and Coach, which meant I'd wrapped another layer of security around myself. Plus, James had been arrested for Coach's murder, and he hadn't spoken a word about the crime or my involvement. I'd read about it a few days ago in a newspaper from the periodical racks in the library.

I had to keep my focus clear. Even without the watch reminding me of every passing second, I knew I had little time left to find a place for us both to live.

My next stop was going to be Pittsburgh University. The semester was well underway, and all the fraternities would be done with rush week. Frat houses were generally welcoming places to young females, and one thing I'd learned during all the years I'd accompanied my dad to fix up student housing was that there was always a guy on campus who knew how to make fake IDs. I'd seen the evidence plenty of times— some kids didn't even bother to put away their laminating machines and stacks of small passport photos when we came by to repair a leaking sink or board up a window that had gotten broken during a party.

Once I'd secured a passable-looking driver's license with a brand-new name—I'd picked Joan Smith—I'd apply for jobs. I'd walked by a lot of coffee shops and delis near my Target, and even though I didn't

have many skills, I figured I could manage waitressing. Once I'd saved
enough, I'd rent a cheap room from someone who wouldn't ask for refer-
ences or care about my age as long as I paid the rent on time.

I was finally feeling calm when I spotted a dad and his daughter
coming toward me. She was about five, and her little hand was tucked
in his big one while they walked.

As he bent down to lift her into his arms, I heard him say the words
te quiero. I knew what they meant—I love you—because they were the
same ones my dad used to say to me every single night.

All the air flew out of me, like I was a balloon someone stuck with a
sharp pin. I sank down on my knees in the middle of the path. I couldn't
stop crying for the rest of the morning.

I can't write any more.

I put my journal back and go check on Catherine again. She hasn't
touched the tea or crackers. She seems to be sleeping.

I take a quick, hot shower and try to watch a little television, but
I can't focus on anything. I end up puttering around, rearranging
kitchen drawers that are already tidy and watering the plants. At din-
nertime, I make myself a peanut butter sandwich, for old times' sake
and to remind myself I've gotten through seemingly impossible situations before.

Afterward, I stand in Catherine's doorway for a long time, looking
at her.

I have lost nearly every single person I ever cared about. My topaz
ring is all I have left of my father, and the tubes of cherry ChapStick I
buy every few months are my only connection to Timmy.

I can't lose my daughter, too.

I walk over to her bed and climb in next to her. Even though I
know James isn't nearby, I'd feel better sleeping here tonight. I want
to be between the front door and Catherine.

I don't feel the slightest bit tired, but somehow I eventually fall
asleep. Though I awaken several times during the night and do rounds

to make sure our apartment is still secure, hearing Catherine's feather-light breaths helps me doze off again. I don't rest deeply, though. It's more like I'm skimming the top, most superficial layer of sleep, alert for any noise or disturbance.

When I wake up for good the next morning, I see Catherine has inched away from me. She's practically hanging off the other side of the bed.

I lie next to her for a little while, thinking about all I need to do today. Finally, when the sun rises high enough to fill the room with light, I get up.

I make my rounds again, checking the front door and peering out the window into the parking lot. When I'm satisfied everything is as it should be, I get dressed and make a pot of strong coffee.

I slowly sip two cups while I sit on the couch, then I break my no-breakfast rule by eating a blueberry yogurt and a handful of walnuts. Something is telling me to marshal my strength.

After a while, I hear Catherine get up to use the bathroom, so I prepare toast for her. She must be starving since she hasn't eaten a thing since the breakfast plate I left for her yesterday.

I expect her to join me in our living area, but she returns to her room.

I walk down the hall and gently rap my knuckles against her open door.

"Mmm," she murmurs without opening her eyes. I know she can't possibly be asleep. She was up only a minute ago.

"Feel any better, Sleeping Beauty?" I ask.

"A little. Still tired though."

"Want breakfast?"

"Maybe later. Going back to sleep now."

She pulls her covers up to her neck and buries her head in the pillow. She didn't even look at me. At least she drank the tea I made for her yesterday.

I glance down at my phone, which I've been compulsively carrying around with me. It's 9 a.m. Too early for the lawyer to have done his checking, but I still feel compelled to call him. I can't do it from our apartment, though. The walls are so thin there's nowhere I can go that doesn't involve a risk of Catherine overhearing.

"I have to run out for a minute," I call out softly. "Be right back."

I follow the same precautions I took before—Mace out, hugging the far wall of the stairwell, moving slowly and listening hard for any unfamiliar noises. The only person I see on the stairs is a neighbor with fiery red hair who's heading down from the second floor to the lobby with his skateboard in one hand.

I almost make the call in the lobby. Then I decide to buy Catherine some flu medicine from the wizard hat shop down the street in case she gets worse. I'd rather be on the street now, in the light of day, than at night. I walk toward the corner, waiting until I'm about twenty yards away from the apartment before I dial the lawyer's number on my burner phone.

The lawyer answers midway through the first ring. He sounds breathless and amped up, saying, "Hello?" before I can get in a word.

Something is off in his tone.

I stop walking and instinctively shift to stand with my back against the nearest storefront wall.

"I'm calling about James—"

He cuts me off. "This is you, right? The family member? I hate to tell you this, but James Bates is gone."

My vision swims. The faces of people passing me are distorted, like I'm seeing them reflected in a fun-house mirror.

"When?" I manage to gasp. It's hard to talk. It feels like someone's hands are wrapped around my throat.

"He left the halfway house in the middle of the night. He's already in violation of parole. The cops and the U.S. Marshals are looking for him. They're going to find him. Don't you worry about—"

Catherine.

Her name explodes in my mind. I drop the phone into my purse and begin to run.

I need to lay eyes on her, now. I roughly elbow past a pair of men who are taking up most of the sidewalk and one of them shouts an expletive after me.

I'm less than ten yards away from our building now. Surely nothing has happened in the few minutes I've been gone. I don't care how sick Catherine is—she needs to get up and pack fast while I grab my journal and her fake ID and get us out.

I fly through the lobby and take the stairs two at a time, almost hoping I run into James. It's far better that he finds me alone than when I'm with Catherine.

The stairs are empty.

It takes me two tries to fit my key into the lock because my hand is shaking so violently. I burst through the door, yelling her name. I run down the hallway, into her room.

Her bed is empty, the covers thrown to one side.

I race to the bathroom, then check my room, and finally run back to the living room, screaming her name again.

She's gone.

I look out the window, toward the parking lot. That's when I see her, hurrying across the pavement toward the Bonneville.

She's alone. No one is chasing her. Catherine is wearing the same T-shirt dress she has had on since yesterday, and her backpack is slung over her shoulder.

Why is she moving so quickly, especially when she's sick?

I bang on the glass.

"Catherine!" I shout, even though I know she can't hear me.

She gets into the Bonneville and pulls out far too fast, her wheels screeching.

I stand there, stunned. She acted like it was painful to even move last night. She pretended to be too ill to eat. She must have leapt out of bed the moment I left the house and hurried down the stairs right after I did.

I stand there, breathing hard, in complete disbelief.

A text chimes on my phone and I instinctively look down. Things have been intense lately Mom. I guess I need a little break. I'm going away for a few days but I'll check in later. Please don't text or call me while I'm gone.

"No!" I shout.

I check her location on my iPhone, frantic to see where she is heading. I wait for the information to pop up as I begin to formulate a plan. I can take a cab and intercept her. Once I have my daughter in my sight again, I will not lose track of her.

The map is taking forever to load. I jab at it to refresh it.

But it refuses to reveal anything.

Catherine is hiding her location from me.

CHAPTER TWENTY-SEVEN

CATHERINE

When my mother locks my bedroom window, the hairs on the back of my neck stand up. When she settles down next to me to sleep, I feel like an animal caught in a trap.

I lie awake for most of the night, my body rigid, while she tosses and turns beside me. It's almost like she knows I'm planning to escape, and she's imprisoning me in my bedroom. My mother is a very light sleeper. If I so much as swing my legs over to the floor and stand up, the creaking of the bedspring will probably wake her up.

I can barely move.

My legal pad must still be on the living room floor where I dropped it. My mother has surely seen it by now. I have no idea whether she looked through it, but if she did, she'll know I've been investigating her.

This sounds crazy, but I'm scared of her.

I have no idea what she has done. Or what she is capable of doing.

At one point during the night, she rolled over and curled on her side, facing me, and I felt as if I couldn't breathe. Like she was suffocating me by stealing all the oxygen out of our shared air.

You're not Ruth Sterling, I'd thought as I'd watched her out of the corner of my eye, slowly inching as far away as I could on the mattress.

Then I'd thought, *So who does that make me?*

I've never been so grateful for the faint glow of the sunrise lightening my room.

When my mother finally got up, I kept up my charade of being sick. There was no way I could act normally in front of her, but I figured I could pull off being ill. If I outwaited her, I knew I'd eventually get a chance to escape.

I just had to be patient.

My chance comes sooner than I expect.

At around 9 a.m., she calls to me, "I have to run out for a minute. Be right back." Then the front door shuts behind her.

For a terrifying moment I worry it is a test and that she is waiting by the door to pounce when I leap out of bed. I push aside that fear and fling back the covers.

My backpack, my purse, my phone, my legal pad, my laptop, my sneakers.

I'm already dressed, and I just used the bathroom and brushed my teeth, so I'm ready to go in less than sixty seconds.

I open our front door and hold my breath as I peer down the hallway. It's empty. I creep to the stairwell and slowly pull the heavy door toward me, listening hard. I can hear someone several flights down, but I'm not sure if it's my mother or a neighbor. Whoever it is, they're moving slowly. I wait until the sound of footsteps recedes and finally disappears. Then I descend, holding myself back from running. If I trip and get hurt, it'll be a disaster.

I reach the lobby. My mother isn't anywhere to be seen.

I just pray she hasn't taken the car.

I hurry to the door that leads to the parking lot. My fingers are already scrabbling in my purse for my set of keys.

Just as I reach the side door and begin to pull it open, an elderly couple I vaguely recognize from the building approaches, each of them carrying a paper bag of groceries.

What kind of person would I be if I rushed through, letting the door close in their faces?

I hold open the heavy door and stand to the side and wait, my body clenching tighter with every passing second.

They seem to take forever to shuffle through, and once they're finally clear of the door, they thank me profusely.

"No problem!" I say, my voice shrill.

I force myself to walk slowly across the asphalt at first. But I'm not even halfway across the lot when my legs pick up speed, propelling me faster and faster.

The Bonneville is in sight now. No one is blocking me in.

I'm actually going to get away.

I slip behind the wheel and jab the key into the ignition and peel out, not bothering with my seat belt.

At the first stop sign, I turn off my location services and dictate a text to my mother, letting her know I'll be gone for a few days.

It isn't until I'm another few miles away, speeding down the highway, that I finally feel like I can breathe normally.

I have no idea where to go, or what I'm going to do next. But as long as there is distance between me and my mother, I feel safe.

I pull into a Wendy's parking lot and lean back, my heart rate finally beginning to slow.

Then a message chimes on my phone.

I flinch and instinctively look down. I don't know if I want to read whatever my mother has texted back.

But it isn't from her. The message comes from Tin: Please let me know ASAP.

I scroll up and see she texted me a little earlier this morning, writing that another aide called in sick today and the shift is mine if I want it.

I consider it for a moment, weighing the pros and cons. My mother doesn't expect me to be at work right now. No one does. There's a decent chance she might show up looking for me, but there's no way she'd be able to get into the Memory Wing. It's one of the most secure places I know.

On my way, I text Tin.

CHAPTER TWENTY-EIGHT

RUTH

Five minutes.

That's how long I allot myself to collect whatever I can carry. I need to be prepared to never see this apartment again.

I've planned for this moment for so long. I've even conducted drills through the years, tearing through our small rooms, rapidly considering and discarding different items, whittling down the seconds to lower my time.

I wish Catherine hadn't taken the car, but at least some of our supplies are already in it.

I reach up and grab my gray duffle bag from my closet shelf, leaving it splayed open on my bed. Moving fast, I pull two hats off the hook in my closet, then collect a few sets of clean clothes. I toss everything into the duffle and hurry to Catherine's dresser. I scoop up two changes of clothes and a sweatshirt for her. I take the photo from her nightstand, both for sentimental value and to keep us from being identified, and then grab our toothbrushes from the bathroom.

In the kitchen I take a flashlight, an extra pack of batteries, and a pair of scissors to cut Catherine's hair. All of these items are lined up, side by side, in one of the drawers I reorganized last night.

I drag a chair over the floor and climb on it to reach the top shelf of our food cabinet. I take down the box of stale Rice Krispies.

Catherine's laptop and the legal pad I'd put on top of it are gone from our dining table, and Catherine also has her phone and purse, so I don't need to bring those items. My topaz ring is on my finger, and my sunglasses are in my purse, along with my journal. I grab the folder of our important documents, including our birth certificates and Social Security cards, and remove the two framed pictures of her from the bookshelf in our living room. There's no photographic evidence of either of us left in the apartment now.

The last thing I take is a large knife in a protective sheath, one I've owned for many years.

By the time I step outside onto the sidewalk, I've got thirty seconds to spare and I've already called for an Uber.

I know exactly where I'm going.

Catherine may have turned off her location sharing, but for as long as she's carried a cell phone, I've always had a backup app tracking my daughter.

CHAPTER TWENTY-NINE

CATHERINE

By the time I reach Sunrise, I've arrived at a hard-fought decision. I'm going to confide in Tin. There's almost nothing she hasn't seen when it comes to a family crisis, and although we don't have a close relationship, I trust her.

I've got an ulterior motive, too. Tin lives alone in a small house she bought last year, and I hope that once she hears my story, she'll let me stay in her guest room for a few nights. I plan to pull her aside this afternoon when the residents are doing arts and crafts in the community room since we usually have a lull then. There's a fringe benefit in confiding in Tin. She won't think I'm completely nuts when I tell her I've decided to take the job in Baltimore, after all.

Coming to this decision lifts a weight off me. My mother's apparent deep mental illness, combined with all the disturbing questions I'm unearthing about her, is too much for me to carry alone. Tin is a helper. She'll do what she can.

I back the Bonneville into a parking spot at the far edge of the lot, where a row of trees will shield it from the main road. I lock up and hurry inside the building, going directly to the employees' locker room. I change into my salmon-colored scrubs and begin rounds on the Memory Wing, making sure everyone has taken their morning meds. I help Mrs. Abraham get dressed because she had a rough night and slept late. Then I reheat her breakfast and sit with her while she eats a little oatmeal. Mrs. Abraham rarely talks anymore, but just as I start to remove her bowl, she blinks and asks in a voice that is hoarse from disuse, "Are you one of my students?"

It's a glimmer of lucidity. Mrs. Abraham used to be a high school math teacher. When I ask what class she's teaching, clouds roll back across her eyes. Her fleeting reversion to her past self is already gone.

As the morning hours pass, the familiar, contained setting of my workplace and the interactions I have with my coworkers and our residents almost lull me into feeling as if part of the world makes sense again. Which is peculiar because on the Memory Wing people are locked in battles with their own minds, and the lines between past and present oscillate and blur.

The surreal has become the grounding force in my life.

At lunchtime, Tin lets us know that Mrs. Jacobson's family has sent a delivery of pizzas for the Memory Wing staff to thank us for the extra care we provided when Mrs. Jacobson came down with pneumonia last month.

I'm suddenly ravenous. It's been more than twenty-four hours since I've eaten.

I have to help one of our residents use the restroom and then wash her hands and mine afterward, so it takes me a few minutes to get to the little staff kitchenette on our floor.

Several of my coworkers are already there, standing around and gobbling down the warm, delicious-smelling pies. I walk into the middle of a friendly debate about pizza-eating styles. Tin is using a fork and knife to cut bites. Reggie, who was raised in the Bronx, has the edges of his piece bent up like a taco, New York style. Another of my colleagues is holding hers flat and biting off the tip of the triangle.

"C'mon, Catherine, tell us who's doing it right," Reggie jokes.

"None of you," I tell them as I reach for a slice of veggie. "Ever heard of lasagna pizza? You make it in a bread loaf pan. . . ."

I'm about to explain how it's cooked when Reggie nods. "Yeah,

I've had that before. It's pretty good. But nothing beats a street slice from Ray's."

I frown. "Wait, you've had lasagna pizza? I thought my mother invented it."

He shakes his head and swallows his mouthful before elaborating.

"I used to eat it at this place in Maryland back when I was in college. It was their signature dish."

It's as if a sheet of glass has dropped down, separating me from everyone else in the room. I'm acutely aware of Tin tossing her crust in the trash and heading back into the hallway, and of Reggie opening another box of pizza, and of the warmth of my untouched slice through the paper plate against my palm, but I'm not a part of this group anymore. I'm in the wings, watching characters play out a scene.

"Where'd you go to school again?" I manage to ask Reggie.

"Towson. It's near Baltimore."

He holds out the open box, offering it to the rest of us, then he grabs another piece for himself.

"Do you remember what that restaurant was called?"

Reggie frowns. "Pizza something . . . sorry, no."

"Be right back," I mumble. I edge out of the room, into the hallway. I desperately need a moment to think. I'm on the cusp of capturing something ephemeral. It feels like I'm chasing fireflies, watching them light up and disappear.

Reggie is around my mother's age. My mother claims to have grown up about an hour from D.C., on the Virginia side.

Towson is about an hour from D.C., but on the Maryland side.

Maybe all those hours I spent trying to locate her high school were fruitless because I was searching in the wrong state. She could have spun the geographical dial a hundred and eighty degrees, switching up one detail that changed everything. My mother appears to wholly be a fabrication. Why wouldn't this bit of her history be, too?

She lied about inventing lasagna pizza. She probably didn't want to tell me the truth because it would provide a clue to her background.

She probably ate it at the same place Reggie did.

The firefly flicker glows brighter, lighting up my brain. All I need now is my iPhone and a little privacy. I begin to hurry toward the visiting family room.

Mr. Damon is standing in the hallway, nodding his head in time to music only he can hear.

"Thank you," he says as I pass by, and I realize he's reaching for my paper plate. Like I'm a waitress bringing him his order.

I give him my untouched slice because he may have just provided me with another clue. My mother could have worked at that pizza place in high school. Maybe that's how she learned the recipe. She's a waitress. It could have been her first waitressing job.

I pause before the door to the family quarters, looking around to make sure no one is watching, then I slip inside. It's cool and dark and silent in here.

I don't have very long, but at least now I've finally got a few data points to narrow my search. I pull out my phone and begin.

It turns out I don't need long at all. Ninety seconds is all it takes for the lies my mother built for twenty-four years to come crashing down, like I've pulled out the final stabilizing wooden block from a game of Jenga we're playing.

I'm staring at the Facebook page for Pizza Piazzo, home of the famous "Lasagna Pizza."

We invented our signature dish more than 30 years ago. Try it! You'll never go back to eating pizza the old way again.

Beneath those words are photographs of lasagna pizza. They look identical to the dish my mother has made for me ever since I was a little girl. She even cuts them the same way: in squares rather than rectangular slices the width of the bread pan.

I quickly input Pizza Piazzo as a key word in a new Facebook search, select the option beneath it for "people," and then watch as hits begin pouring onto my screen. There's a wealth of information: photos of guests gathered in booths and around tables at the restaurant, and images of former and current managers and members of the waitstaff. There's an address, website, and phone number for Pizza Piazzo in Towson, Maryland.

I quickly start to type out a message to the first few people in my search who identified themselves as past or current employees.

Hi, I know this sounds a little crazy, but I'm trying to locate a woman who worked there about 25 years ago.

I pause, trying to think of what else to add. I can't give a name or even a physical description. My mother told me she had hair down to her waist in high school, but maybe that was another lie.

Finally I write,

If you worked at the restaurant back then, I'd be so grateful for your reply. It's really important.

I hit send, then copy and paste my message to a half-dozen other people connected to the restaurant. I skip over the woman who looks like she's in her teens and works there now. There's no way she could have intersected with my mother before I was born. But several could be possibilities, including a guy about my mom's age who looks brand-new to Facebook, and a woman who seems to be the current owner of the restaurant and might have owned it all along. There's no guarantee anyone will see my note because people are wary about opening messages from strangers on the Internet.

But for the first time, I feel like I'm truly onto something.

I don't catch a break for the rest of the afternoon. The usual lull during arts and crafts is eliminated when Mrs. Jacobson is walking toward a table and lurches to the side to avoid a deep pool of water. She trips and falls, hitting her jaw on the edge of a table.

Alzheimer's can affect vision as well as perception. The blue cardigan another resident dropped on the floor was transformed into a water hole in Mrs. Jacobson's mind.

It takes a while to assess her since she's understandably upset, but Tin examines Mrs. Jacobson's mouth and says she doesn't think the wound is serious. Our on-call doctor checks her out, and then we hold a FaceTime meeting with Mrs. Jacobson's family to let them know what happened. By the time we've finished dealing with the crisis, another resident has scattered the arts and crafts materials all over the table and floor, and it's time to clean up, serve dinner, and administer evening meds.

I don't make it back to the family quarters until close to 6 p.m., which is near the end of my shift.

But when I do, one new private Facebook message is waiting on my phone.

Hey there—yes, I worked at PP 25 years ago. I'm still in touch with some of my colleagues. It's a great group. Who are you looking for?

The little green dot by the guy's name indicates he's still online. I write back quickly, detailing the scant facts my mother can't alter.

I'm not certain of her name—she would have been about 18, with big hazel eyes and light brown skin. She's five foot two.

There's got to be something else distinctive about my mother that hasn't changed over the past quarter century. I think for a minute, then add,

Good dancer. She may have been on the Poms squad at her high school, but I'm not sure.

The guy writes back so quickly it's almost like he read my reply the moment I sent it.

Oh, I bet I know who you're talking about. Her name started with an A . . . shoot, can't think of it now but it'll come to me. Really long hair, great smile. She didn't work here but she hung out here a lot. She sure loved pizza! LOL.

I feel like I've stepped off a cliff and am free-falling.

It's her. I'm certain of it. My mother's real name started with an *A*, and she must have lived near the restaurant in Towson, Maryland.

I quickly scan the guy's profile information. We're not friends on Facebook, so what I can see of his page is limited—as is what he can view about mine—but his hometown is listed as Baltimore. He must live fairly close to Johns Hopkins Hospital.

I type back, using his nickname for the restaurant. Do you ever go back to PP?

Again, he writes back immediately.

Haven't been in a while, but now that you've got me thinking about lasagna pizza, I may just go tonight.

I think for a moment, then type,

I'm going tonight too. Maybe we can meet and chat a little more?

I could show him a picture of my mother. I've got some on my phone. Those images may jar loose his memories of her.

I look down at my response, then I slowly backspace through my words, deleting them one letter at a time.

My mother drilled into me that you can't trust anyone on the internet. She once clipped out a newspaper story about a girl who went to meet a new social media friend at the mall and was kidnapped by the middle-aged man who'd created the fake account. She left that story on my pillow for me to read when I begged her to let me join Instagram.

Even though I initiated contact with this guy, his profile photo is a picture of a sports car and he comes across as a little too eager.

Besides, if he remembers my mother, chances are other people who have connections to the restaurant do, too. And I bet I can find her old high school quickly now. I don't need this internet stranger to give me any more information at the moment. Still, I sign off politely in case I need to ask him questions in the future.

I write back, Have a great night and thanks again!

Then I log out of Facebook.

Pizza Piazzo is only about a seventy-minute drive from Sunrise. Even if I hit traffic, I can easily make it there while they're still serving dinner. Maybe I'll find a cheap hotel room in the area and spend the night in what may be my mother's actual hometown.

By this time tomorrow, I could finally know the truth about her.

My body is flooded with a mixture of dread and excitement. Part of me wants to abandon this quest now and go home and simply talk to my mom.

If I told her of my doubts, would she finally come clean?

But my trust in her is shattered.

Besides, I've come too far to stop now.

I peer out of the family quarters to make sure the hallway is clear, then step out and head to the community room, where I let Tin know I'm leaving. I start to walk to the blue door to input the code to exit.

I don't know what makes me stop, turn around, and go back to the big window in the hallway, the one Mr. Damon crouches beneath when he believes the Viet Cong are surrounding us.

Maybe it's the sixth sense that has always linked me to my mother, the one that sometimes has me lifting my head to listen for the sound of her key in the front door lock a minute or so before the noise actually occurs, or the way one of us will say something random, like *How about curry for dinner?* just as the other has the identical thought.

Whatever it is, it draws me to the window. I look out and see the Bonneville still in the far corner where I left it.

But someone is leaning against it, like they're waiting for me.

I lean closer to the window, squinting.

It's my mother.

I instinctively shrink back, even though she doesn't seem to be looking in my direction.

I cannot believe she has followed me here, especially since I turned off my location sharing. Did she somehow hack into my texts and see the exchange between me and Tin, or did she just take a lucky guess and show up?

Either way, it would have required an extraordinary effort since my mom doesn't have sophisticated computer skills and I took our only car. She must have taken an Uber here.

As I watch, she straightens up and begins to slowly walk around the parking lot, like she's on patrol. I wait, hoping she'll move far enough away that I can slip out and drive off.

But she's never out of sight of the Bonneville.

My mother is clearly prepared to outwait me.

What does she intend to do when I approach?

I think of her locking my bedroom window, then sliding beneath my comforter to sleep next to me. A chill runs through my body and I shudder.

Now that she knows how eager I am to get away, will she find new ways to tighten her hold on me? Perhaps she already knows I'm going to move to Baltimore, or maybe she suspects that I'm planning to tell Tin everything.

I can't let my mother see me. I need to find another way to Towson.

Then it comes to me as I stare down at the cars in the lot.

I already have another way.

CHAPTER THIRTY

RUTH

I so loved my birth name, *Ava Morales*. It felt graceful and ethereal, like it could belong to a ballerina.

Ruth Sterling sounded like a young woman who was Ava's opposite: a sturdy, stoic individual who worked hard and didn't complain. Those were qualities I desperately needed. I wanted to become Ruth Sterling in more ways than one.

I became Ruth shortly before Catherine was born, when I'd saved up enough money for a professional-grade ID—something better than the fake driver's license with the name Joan Smith I'd bought for forty bucks. That first ID had been good enough to get me a waitressing job and a rental room in an apartment sublet by another single mom. But I didn't go to a college boy to create Ruth's Social Security card and birth certificate.

I knew I had to pass for eighteen when I gave birth to Catherine for a few reasons. If I was an adult in the eyes of the authorities, no one would take my baby away from me. And as long as my ID held up and no one questioned it, I could give birth in a hospital and Catherine would receive her own Social Security card with a last name that matched mine.

It would be the first, vital step in building her identity.

One of the other waitresses at work knew someone who could do it. She gave me concise instructions: I was to wait on a certain street corner with five hundred dollars in cash in an envelope. I was to pass it to a man wearing an Eagles jersey. I could not ask a single question.

The next week, I stood on the same corner at the appointed time and almost before I knew what was happening, a different man walked past me and thrust a manila envelope into my hands, then continued down the street without missing a step.

My transformation was complete.

Sometimes I think about the real Ruth, who died at twelve, years before I took over her name. Our lives would never have intersected under ordinary circumstances. Ruth was born with a rare heart defect and lived with her big family in Wisconsin on a dairy farm. The names of all of her brothers and sisters and aunts and uncles were listed, along with Ruth's parents, in the obituary that ran in her local newspaper, the one I read on microfilm at the library when I was searching for a solid new identity, one I could permanently keep.

Being Ruth meant I could get food stamps and WIC vouchers for eggs and cereal during one terrible stretch when I was between jobs and Catherine was hungry. Because I'm Ruth in the eyes of the government, I can pay taxes, which means when I'm old enough I'll be able to collect Social Security.

Nowadays it's much harder to take an identity than it was twenty-five years ago. There's a slim chance I could be caught, but that risk seems to diminish with every passing year.

Sometimes I wish I could bring flowers to the real Ruth's grave in Kewaskum and ask for her forgiveness. If I could tell her anything, I would say I'm so sorry she lost her life far too soon, but I hope she knows she saved mine.

I lean back against the Bonneville, feeling the heat the metal has absorbed radiating against my back as I stare at the entrance of Sunrise. My hand rises in a salute to shade my eyes as the sun dips toward the horizon.

I've been here all day long, waiting and watching. Every thirty minutes or so, I patrol the parking lot, both to stretch my legs and to check my surroundings.

The low rumble of an engine catches my attention. I watch as a FedEx truck glides up in front of Sunrise and the driver jumps out. He opens the back of the truck and I glimpse rows of brown boxes with the familiar purple logo. He selects a small one and shuts the doors, then disappears into the building.

I push away from the Bonneville and begin to patrol the lot again. Catherine will emerge from the building soon. I'll be here when she does.

CHAPTER THIRTY-ONE

CATHERINE

I force myself to smile as I tap my knuckles against the door. George Campbell opens it a moment later, wearing jeans and a T-shirt that show off his still-fit physique. At seventy-six, he plays golf every Saturday, lifts light weights every other day, and drives wherever he needs to go.

That last bit is key.

"June! It's Catherine!"

He's delighted to see me, which makes me feel guilty.

I offer up the foil-wrapped plate I made from the leftovers in the break room.

"We had extra pizza, and I thought you might enjoy some."

George and June act like I'm offering them a three-course meal. They're so kind and gracious that it makes what I'm about to do even harder.

"Can you sit with us for a while?" George asks. "We just opened a bottle of Sauvignon Blanc."

I glance back toward the front door. I've already checked to make sure the little green bowl is still on their console, but I can't see what's inside it. If I take George up on his offer and sip a glass of wine, I'll have more time to check things out.

But I don't know when Pizza Piazzo closes, and it's far more important that I get there tonight.

People typically stick to their routines, I reassure myself. There's no reason George would have changed his.

"Thank you, but I need to run. Rain check?" As I say this, I let my purse strap slip down on my shoulder. My bag is unzipped, and a few small, loose objects are near the top.

George sees me to the door, as I knew he would, and as I go to hug him goodbye, I let my purse fall to the ground. The lipstick and cylinder of mascara and loose coins I've strategically positioned scatter across the wood floor.

George immediately bends down to pick everything up and I reach over him to feel around in the round bowl. I touch a sharp metal edge and pull out the keys to his Cadillac.

They're in my palm before George finishes picking the last coin up off the floor. He puts everything back in my purse and gives it to me.

"Thank you so much."

I keep my right fist clenched around his keys as I leave, promising to see them soon.

I intend to keep that promise. First thing tomorrow morning, I'll make up an excuse about missing something from my purse and wanting to check to see if it rolled under their entryway table. George's keys will be back in the bowl before he ever misses them, and I'll replace any gas I use.

I wish I could've asked George if I could borrow the Cadillac, but that car is his baby. I knew the request would make him uncomfortable, and I couldn't risk him saying no.

My hair is pinned up in a style I never wear, and I'm still in my scrubs. It isn't a great disguise, but my mother knows I never wear scrubs to and from work, so if she catches a glimpse of me from a distance, she may not immediately identify me.

Plus, the few residents who still drive get the parking spots closest to the building, which means all I have to do is walk about ten yards out in the open without my mother spotting me.

I wait inside the front door of Sunrise until a visiting middle-aged couple signs out at the front desk and departs.

I step outside a beat after they do, trying to position myself so that they provide a screen between me and the Bonneville.

Five yards to the Cadillac.

George's keys are pointed outward in my hand. I keep my head ducked low and move to the side of the vehicle, crouching down while I unlock the door and slide in. I start the engine, throw my backpack onto the passenger's seat, and back out of the spot.

In a few seconds, I'll know if my mother has seen me.

I drive to the exit and turn right onto the two-lane road, then glance in the rearview mirror. If the Bonneville roars up after me, I don't know what I'm going to do.

The road behind me is clear.

I step on the gas, exceeding the thirty-mile-an-hour speed limit, and coast through a traffic light just as it turns yellow.

The only vehicle in sight is a FedEx truck.

I'm free.

Dusk is leaching the color out of the sky. The highway is busy now, at the tail end of rush hour, but traffic moves steadily. I stay in the middle lane, keeping several cars' lengths behind the vehicle ahead of me. My full attention is on driving safely. I don't even look toward my phone when it buzzes with an incoming call. If I got in an accident and had to confess I'd taken the Campbells' car, I'd be fired—or worse, charged with theft.

The thought of those potential repercussions should have me turning around at the next exit, but all I do is grip the wheel a little more tightly and stare straight ahead. Twenty-four years of lies strengthen my resolve.

Her name begins with an A.

Tonight I'm determined to finally learn the truth about my mother.

I reach Pizza Piazzo a little before 7:30 p.m. The restaurant is located at the end of a strip mall, past a grocery store, beauty salon, and bank. Vehicles fill the parking area closest to the restaurant. It's clearly a popular place. I pull into a spot in the middle of the lot, near the grocery store. When I cut my headlights, I realize how dark it has become.

I check to make sure no one is nearby, then I climb into the back seat and quickly change into shorts and a fresh shirt I pull out of my backpack. I double-check that my legal pad is inside my purse in case I need to write anything down and then I step out, lock the doors, and walk toward the restaurant.

I might be retracing footsteps my mother left as a teenager, I think. When my fingers stretch out for the big metal door handle, I imagine the ghost of hers doing the same.

An electric pulse races through me. Something makes me turn around, but no one is there.

I step inside, and noise hits me like a slap. The place is packed. Dozens of animated conversations fill the room, with laughter cutting through it all. At rectangular tables in the middle of the floor, a family celebrates a child's birthday and a softball team in matching jerseys digs into a postgame meal. Wooden booths line the walls, each lit by a votive candle in a red glass holder.

A woman wearing a white button-down shirt and black slacks is behind the hostess stand. She looks about my age, which is a disappointment. She wouldn't have known my mother.

"Welcome to Pizza Piazzo. Table for . . . ?"

"Just one."

She nods and picks up a menu from the top of her stack. "This way, please."

I scan my surroundings as I follow her to a booth. Bread loaf pans filled with the restaurant's signature dish are atop trivets on many of the tables. I watch as a waiter eases out squares with a flat spatula, serving them to the couple at his table, and think of the many times my mother has done the same for me.

The hostess walks me across the restaurant to a tiny booth in the back, and I choose the side that affords me the best view of the other

diners. Directly behind me is the kitchen, where I can hear the clanking of dishes and loud voices behind the closed swinging door.

Instead of studying my menu, I pull out my phone.

The call I missed was from Ethan. He didn't leave a message. Perhaps he's already drinking and wanted company tonight. I flick away
the notice of his call from my screen, then navigate to my photos. I
search through them until I find a recent one of my mother. It isn't a
great shot—someone took it of us at my college graduation, and she's
wearing her big sunglasses—so I keep looking.

I scroll through an entire year's worth of photos, then work my way
even further back. I can't believe I never noticed it before. I only have
about two dozen pictures of my mom on my phone. In every one, she's
either wearing her oversized rectangular sunglasses or turning away
from the camera so it isn't a clear shot of her face.

It can't be a coincidence.

I return to the picture of us at my college graduation, enlarging it
on my screen so only she shows.

My waiter approaches, a guy of about thirty. I tell him I'd like a
Coke and I ask for his recommendation for my entrée.

"You've got to try the lasagna pizza," he says. "The smallest size
serves two, but I can pack up your leftovers."

I tell him that sounds perfect. He starts to turn away, but when I
say, "Can I ask you something?" he spins back around.

My waiter looks too young to be of any help, but it's possible he's
older than I think. I have to try.

"This might sound a little weird, but I'm trying to find a woman
who used to come here all the time." I slide my phone toward him,
pointing to the screen.

He looks down and frowns. "Sorry, I don't think I've ever seen
her. Hard to tell with the sunglasses."

"Yeah, it was years and years ago. . . . Is there anyone else I could
talk to who has worked here for a really long time?"

"Um, my manager has been here forever. I could ask him?"

"That would be great."

The waiter hurries off, returning a few minutes later with a Coke in a tall glass. He places it in front of me and tells me the manager will be over soon.

I already feel like I'm buzzing with energy and nerves, so I don't need the sugar and caffeine, but I swallow half of my beverage in one long gulp anyway. It's impossible to keep my hands still. I pull a napkin out of the holder on top of my table and begin to shred it into strips, then I roll each one up into a little ball.

I'm about to start on my second napkin when a man approaches my table. He's a genial-looking guy with silver-rimmed glasses and close-cropped graying hair, and his name tag identifies him as the manager.

"Hi, I'm Rich. Is there something I can help you with?"

I nod eagerly, my throat growing dry despite all the liquid I just swallowed.

"I'd really appreciate it. I'm trying to find someone who used to come here often. A young woman. It was a long time ago, though."

"How long?"

"Almost twenty-five years ago. She would have been in high school then."

His smile slides away. "What's her name?"

"It begins with an A . . ." I start to push the phone closer to him, but he doesn't look at it. His brow furrows.

When he doesn't immediately speak, my nerves take over and I start to babble. "She didn't work here but she came in here a lot. She had really long hair back then. . . . She may have been on the Poms squad at her high school."

The manager no longer appears angry. He's furious now.

"Almost twenty-five years ago?" His eyes narrow as he bites off each word. "And you're trying to find her now. Is this a joke?"

I shake my head. "What? No!"

He folds his arms. "Where are you from?"

"Me? Pennsylvania, but I—"

"What *newspaper* are you from? Who sent you?" He's almost shouting.

"I'm not—"

The waiter approaches with my meal, then stops short a few feet away.

"You can stay until you've finished your dinner, but if you bother any of my staff or any customers, I'm calling the police."

He storms off.

I stare after the manager in complete bewilderment as the waiter slips the pizza dish onto the table, then hurries away, too.

I watch as the manager talks to the waiter, gesturing and shooting a dirty look in my direction.

I stare back at them, blinking in confusion. My interaction with the manager was so bizarre it feels almost like a disjointed dream. I'm left trying to make sense of the pieces. He seemed to have known who I was talking about. But his reaction was so extreme, it's as if my mother personally hurt him.

What did she do?

The closer I get to her truth, the more alien and hostile the world seems.

My entire body is gripped by uncontrollable trembling. I want to call the manager back and explain I'm the daughter of the woman he's so angry with, but what if that only incites him more?

The waiter swings by my table and sets down my bill and walks away without a word. It's a clear message, especially considering I've yet to take a bite of food: I'm not welcome here.

I can't bring myself to leave, though. This restaurant is the closest connection I have to my mother's past.

The manager isn't trying to hide the fact that he's watching me from across the floor. I won't be able to talk to anyone else with him around. Maybe I can wait in the parking lot until other staff members leave and show them my mother's photo. *Someone* has to be able to tell me the truth.

Movement catches my eye. The hostess is leading another single diner, a man wearing a baseball cap, to a two-top table not far from mine. He's so chiseled he looks as if he is carved out of marble. I can see a tattoo on his arm, though it isn't a colorful, artistic symbol like Ethan wears. This man's tattoo is composed of a blue-black hue and it looks amateurish.

The man is acting appropriately. He sits down and toys with his silverware as he gazes around the restaurant. Yet I find myself edging away until I'm pressed against the far side of my booth, angling into a position where I'm shielded by a family sitting at a table between us so he can't see me.

When the man looks down at his menu, I peek out again and let my eyes travel over him. I feel helpless to stop looking at him. I take in the thick twin deltoids rising up in the space between the top of his shoulders and his tortoiseshell glasses, and his long, shaggy black hair flowing out from beneath his hat.

Then I stare more closely at the royal blue baseball cap he's wearing. There's a logo or something on it I can't quite see. It looks like a cartoon character, or maybe an animal.

I lift up my phone and pretend to be looking at my messages. In actuality, I navigate to the camera function and enlarge my view until it zeroes in on that blue baseball cap.

My hand is still trembling so hard it takes a moment to zero in on the image. When I do, I see it isn't a cartoon character. I was right the second time—it's an animal.

A panther.

I stare at the big golden cat, the skin around his mouth stretched back to reveal his fangs, his claws outstretched as if he's poised to attack.

A panther. Blue and gold.

My mouth goes dry. It can't be a coincidence.

That's the mascot for my mother's old high school.

This guy must have kids who currently attend it—or maybe he

graduated from there. He could have known my mother. He looks to be of her generation.

I'm still holding up my camera and gazing at the image on my screen when the man turns his head slightly and stares directly into my eyes through the camera lens, like he knows I'm watching him.

I immediately duck my head and drop my phone back into my purse and slip the strap over my shoulder, feeling a chill run through me.

I need to talk to this guy. But with the manager hovering nearby, I can't just walk right up to another customer and ask to join him at his table.

I'm so lost in my thoughts I almost miss the first sign that something is terribly wrong.

Then I hear a woman cry out, and I look up to see the family at the nearby table staring at me, their expressions wary.

For a wild, shaky moment I wonder if the manager has somehow spoken to them and turned them all against me.

It isn't until I smell smoke that I realize they aren't looking at me. They're staring at something behind me.

I whip around and see thick, black smoke curling around the edges of the kitchen door.

Then the swinging door bursts open, crashing against the wall, and the cooks come tearing out. The fire is impossibly swift. Red and orange flames leap out of the kitchen and climb up the dining room wall as if someone splashed around an accelerant.

The restaurant erupts into chaos.

Shouts and high-pitched screams fill the air as parents pick up their children and run toward the front door. Chairs are knocked over in the scramble as a loud voice yells in vain for everyone to keep calm. Black smoke rolls through the restaurant like a slow, suffocating wave. As I watch, it seems to swallow up the softball team in their matching jerseys.

I can't move. I'm mesmerized.

Fire has always transfixed me.

I watch the flames blaze higher, stretching out like a sheet billowing in the wind, covering one entire wall before reaching for the ceiling. Someone pulls the fire alarm and a siren blares.

I cough as tears leak from my stinging eyes. Smoke sears my lungs. In the distance, I hear sirens, but they sound far away.

I can't see anyone else right now—they've all disappeared. I've waited too long. I need to get out, right now.

The front door where I came in is all the way at the opposite end of the restaurant. I noticed a closer side exit earlier, but I can't see it anymore. There are big windows all around the restaurant, but I don't know if I'll be able to open any of them. Smoke keeps pouring into the room, obscuring my vision.

Terror chains me to my seat.

I don't know which way to go. I take another breath and cough harder, struggling to pull clean oxygen into my lungs. My throat is burning and smoke clouds my vision.

If I try to make it to the front door, I may not get there in time. I could crawl toward the side door, but what if I can't find it?

This is how people often die in burning buildings. Smoke inhalation kills them before flames ever touch them.

Before I can do anything to try to save myself, a figure bursts out of the kitchen, seeming to dart through a wall of fire, almost blending in with the smoke.

I can't tell if it's a man or a woman, but the person is heading directly for me in the booth.

Like I'm their target.

"Catherine!"

Dizziness engulfs me. This can't be happening. It's impossible.

My mother has a streak of black soot smearing her forehead and a small towel tied over her nose and mouth. Her eyes hold a wildness I've never before seen.

She grabs my arm and yanks me out of the booth. "Move!"

She half drags me to the side exit as my body is racked by uncontrollable coughing.

Nothing makes sense. Not my mother's presence here, not the lethal-looking knife she's clutching in her free hand, and not her words.

"He's here," she whispers urgently. "He's been watching you."

ACT
THREE

CHAPTER THIRTY-TWO

RUTH

The Bonneville is illegally parked by the curb in front of the side exit of Pizza Piazzo. My set of keys are in my hand. Our car is unlocked. The wheels are pointed toward the exit.

"Get in!" I command Catherine.

The crowd of shaken diners is gathered outside at the other end of the restaurant. Everyone who was in Pizza Piazzo fled in that direction because it meant running away from the kitchen fire.

That's what I counted on when I set it using a votive candle and a vat of cooking grease.

Catherine is moving too slowly. She's dead weight. I'm her polar opposite—electricity sparks through me, filling my limbs with an uncommon strength. I propel her to our car as sirens scream in the distance. The emergency dispatchers will send fire trucks and ambulances as well as police. It's impossible to tell which responders will arrive first.

Surely by now James has melted toward the edge of the crowd and is detaching himself as he prepares his own escape. The last thing he wants is to be here—the precise spot where he was arrested almost twenty-five years ago—when the cops show up, even if he is wearing a black wig and tortoiseshell glasses as a disguise.

James can't see us through all the chaos, I tell myself even as my panic soars to a level of near hysteria.

"Put on your seat belt!" I bark at Catherine, then I dart around the hood, sliding behind the wheel a few seconds later.

I yank the dish towel off my face and peel out of the parking lot, the rear of the car fishtailing as I stomp on the gas pedal. As we speed toward the highway, my eyes flick between the road in front of me and the one behind me. I don't know what kind of vehicle James is driving, but it's a safe bet he stole it.

Which means he could be in any of the cars or vans behind me, including the truck with a roofing company logo on the side.

I tap my brakes as another police car comes shrieking down the road in the opposite direction. The moment it passes, I accelerate.

It should be almost impossible for James to be tracking us right now, I tell myself. The parking lot was on the other side of the building, and the crowd would have blocked anyone from making a quick escape.

But James found our daughter the day after being released from prison. He must have lured her to the pizza place, and I got here just in time to interrupt whatever he'd planned for her.

James seems almost superhuman.

A chill races through me and I grip the wheel more tightly.

Seeing James again completely unnerved me, even though he had no idea I was watching him from the Bonneville as he entered the restaurant. At first, I didn't know it was him—his disguise worked— then something about the way he carried himself clicked.

During his time in jail, James shed his civilized veneer, like a creature crawling out of its exoskeleton. Now his surface matches his insides. He presents as a powerful, dangerous man, from his over-developed muscles to the way he picked up the serrated knife at his place setting and repeatedly ran his fingertip over the jagged edge as I watched from a side window.

As I approach a stoplight, it turns yellow. I press the gas pedal almost to the floor and run through the intersection a few seconds after the light flips to red.

I'm another five miles down the road before I briefly pull my eyes away from the road to look at Catherine.

She's curled up in her seat, her eyes vacant, still coughing occasionally.

I press the button to unroll her window a few inches, hoping clean air will cleanse the lingering smoke out of her lungs.

"What is happening?" Her voice sounds small and shaky.

"Listen to me. I need to know why you went to that restaurant. Who told you to go there?"

"What?" She doesn't seem to be processing my question. I want to shake her. We don't have time for her to be in shock right now. I need to know everything James knows, fast.

"There was a man sitting alone at a table near you. Were you supposed to meet him? How did he contact you?"

Catherine slowly shakes her head. She appears vague and unfocused, like someone who has had too much to drink and is on the verge of passing out.

"Answer me!"

Catherine flinches as the words roar out of me. They land on her like a slap. She sits up straighter, like she's coming back into her body.

"Answer *you*?"

Then my daughter says, in a voice so cold it's almost unrecognizable, "I don't even know who you are."

I don't react. I don't have that luxury. I keep checking the road behind me as I choose my words carefully.

"Right now, the only thing we're going to talk about is how to keep you safe."

It's like she doesn't hear me. "Did you set that fire? How did you even find me? Have you been *tracking* me?"

"Damn it!" I bang the heel of my hand against the steering wheel so hard it hurts. "You're in danger, Catherine! We both are now!"

Her blue eyes grow so huge they overpower the rest of her features. Did James glimpse them? Did he recognize the pieces of himself that Catherine carries?

I hear Catherine taking in measured breaths. She's trying to calm herself.

I do the same.

"What man are you talking about?" she finally asks.

"The guy with the long black hair. You must've gone there to meet him. How did he contact you?"

In my peripheral vision I see her shake her head.

"He didn't."

A dark sedan comes roaring up behind me. I'm going almost eighty miles an hour, so it's flying.

I press the gas down harder and feel our old car shake with effort. The sedan is practically on my bumper now.

There's nowhere for us to go on this four-lane highway. A concrete median separates us from the two lanes going in the other direction, and there aren't any exits within sight.

"Duck down!" I yell at Catherine, then I swerve into the right lane and slam on the brakes.

My body flies forward before being snapped back by the rigid seat belt. I gasp as some of the air is knocked out of me.

I keep my eyes fixed on the sedan, waiting for it to brake and reverse toward us.

But it doesn't. It keeps racing ahead and disappears over the next hill as I stare at it.

A blaring horn jerks me back to reality. A truck is coming up behind us, and I'm at a dead stop on a busy road.

I press down on the gas and begin moving forward just in time to avoid a collision.

"Mom! What are you doing?" Catherine screams.

The trucker honks at me again as he veers into another lane and passes us. I see him shaking his head.

Finally, I see an exit ahead. I take it at the last second, jerking my wheel to the right without signaling. It's only when I'm certain no one has followed us that I pull into a gas station and cut the engine.

Silence drops down on us heavily.

I lean back in my seat and exhale.

I reach to massage the area beneath my right shoulder where the seat belt strap bit into my skin, wincing.

It's hard to think clearly. My entire being is focused on getting Catherine to safety. But I have no idea what safety looks like when James seems to know so much more than he should.

"Why are you talking about that guy in the restaurant?" she asks. "How do you know him?"

I open my mouth, preparing to deflect her questions, like always. But the lie refuses to form on my lips.

I slump down lower in my seat, feeling completely defeated.

Nearly a quarter century of running. Three different names. Twelve jobs. Nine apartments.

I can't hide the truth from her any longer.

"That man is your father."

My words are spoken softly, but they land like an anvil between us.

Catherine gasps and turns her face away, like she can't bear to look at me.

Even now, with tension and lies and distrust choking our relationship, I still know my daughter better than I've ever known any other living soul.

I know her quick mind is working. She will also recognize that the tattoo imprinted on James's skin came from prison because she has watched crime shows with me and has seen felons with similar crude markings. Catherine must also have sensed the menace radiating from James.

I brace myself for her questions.

Instead, she gives me an answer.

"He didn't contact me." She shakes her head slightly to emphasize her words, still avoiding my eyes. "I think I may have contacted him, though."

I am both desperate and terrified to know more.

"How?"

"Through Facebook. I was looking for past employees of Pizza Piazzo and he listed it as his prior workplace."

I squeeze my eyes shut briefly. If Catherine knows about Pizza Piazzo, she must be dangerously close to learning the truth about my past.

I start to spiral, then yank my mind back into the present moment. Catherine is vulnerable out here in the open. Nothing else matters but keeping her hidden from James.

I ask two final questions.

"Does he know your real name?" Catherine nods, and my stomach free-falls.

I press on. "Does he know where you live or work?"

She peers up at the ceiling of the Bonneville, like she's thinking hard.

"No. He probably saw my Facebook profile, too, but all it shows is my name and that picture you took of me standing in front of the ocean. I keep all my other personal information hidden so only friends can see it."

I made Catherine promise to do that when she turned eighteen and opened social media accounts against my wishes.

"Does he know about me?" Catherine whispers.

"No," I say instantly, angry with myself for not having thought to reassure her sooner. "He never knew I was pregnant. No one did."

I see her absorb this information, then she turns her face away again.

I drop my forehead onto the steering wheel. I allot myself sixty seconds to work the problem. We can't go back to our apartment since James can easily find the address given that he knows Catherine's real name. Our savings will buy us some time at a hotel, but what will happen when it runs out? Or when James finds us again?

"Mom? What are you doing?"

I lift my head and reach over to squeeze her hand. My heart breaks when she jerks her arm away before I can touch her.

"Right now I'm going to get some gas. We have to keep moving."

"Where are we going?"

"We need a safe place to stay tonight. That man—James—is going to try to find us and we can't let him."

I jump out of the Bonneville and fill the tank to the brim. I'll drive another couple of hours and we can rest at a chain hotel tonight. It's not a great plan, but it's the best one I can come up with right now.

When I climb back in behind the wheel, though, Catherine surprises me again.

She says, "I know where we can hide."

CHAPTER THIRTY-THREE

CATHERINE

I hold my mother's arm, supporting her as she shuffles toward the front desk. Her affect is completely transformed. She's wearing the lavender-colored sweatshirt she packed for me, and her body is hunched.

She takes halting steps and hangs her head low, as if she is fully dependent on me to lead the way.

The night guard looks up as we draw closer to the reception desk.

"Paul! Wow, it's been a minute," I say, my tone cheerful.

His face breaks into a smile. "Catherine, good to see you again." His smile slips away. "You're out late tonight."

I feel my body begin to perspire, even though the lobby is pleasantly cool. I struggle to keep my tone casual as I say, "Yeah, I'll just sign Mrs. Jacobson in and bring her back to the fifth floor. She's pretty tired."

Paul watches as I begin to type on the keyboard of the computer next to his desk, signing myself in. I have the password, after all. We're at Sunrise.

"Big event tonight?" Paul asks.

He has seen me bring residents back to Sunrise in the evening many times since I used to drive the van for resident outings, but I don't think I've ever brought someone back this late. Plus, it has been a couple years since I've driven the van.

Paul has no reason to suspect anything is amiss, though. Since he works the overnight shift, he can't know I never signed out a resident earlier today. My mother is two decades younger than Mrs. Jacobson, but they both have short, dark hair. Paul probably has no idea what Mrs. Jacobson or any of the other Memory Wing residents look like since they are typically in bed by the time his shift begins.

Paul is prepared to spring into action if someone from the Memory Wing breaks out. He isn't expecting a healthy person to try to sneak in.

"There was a big birthday party for her son," I tell Paul. "The family really wanted her there, and she did very well. She even had a little cake."

My mother stands next to me, not saying a word, just as I instructed her. But she knows what to do in case Paul grows suspicious or tries to verify what I'm typing.

"All set," I say as I pull my hands away from the keyboard. All I've done is sign myself in, but Paul won't know that unless he checks the computer log.

This is it—our make-or-break moment. I can sense my mother's uneasy energy matching my own. I hold my breath, hoping Paul doesn't think it's strange that I'm carrying both a purse and my backpack, which contains my mother's purse along with my laptop and our toiletries.

Paul looks at me, then at my mother.

"I'm glad you had a good time, Mrs. Jacobson," he says softly. "Good evening, ladies."

I release my breath and bid him a good night.

My mother must also feel relieved that she doesn't need to moan and fidget, ratcheting up a display of agitation to deflect any attempt by Paul to verify the information I pretended to input into the system.

Perhaps I shouldn't have been so nervous, though. There's no reason for Paul to be distrustful of me or my mother. In his world, unlike mine, people are probably who they claim to be.

I guide my mother into the elevator and press the button for floor five. We remain in character, mindful of the camera recording all arrivals and departures on the Memory Wing.

Once we reach the fifth floor, I input my code and push the door open, then lead my mother through it.

It's imperative we avoid being spotted by anyone else. But the odds are on our side. All of the residents should be asleep, many with the help of medication. And while the lone nurse and aide who work the graveyard shift on this floor make rounds every hour, they tend to otherwise stay at the nursing station.

I put a finger to my lips, then gesture for my mother to follow. We tiptoe down the long hallway and pause, listening hard. I can hear the distant sound of conversation, but the voices are too far away for me to make out any words.

We glide past rooms belonging to a dozen clients, all dimly lit and quiet. The last door on the right is the one I'm seeking.

It should be empty. Staff members are always notified when family comes for an overnight visit, and when I subbed in for a shift earlier today, there was no mention of guests on the Memory Wing arriving tonight.

I twist the knob and peek inside. All clear.

I step aside so my mother can enter, then I pull the door closed behind us.

We're safe in the family quarters—for now.

I grab a towel from the rack by the shower, then roll it up and place it by the crack in the bottom of the door so no one will see light spilling out. If we avoid making loud noises, we should be able to evade detection. There's no reason for anyone to check this room, or even walk to the very end of the hallway.

My mother takes a step toward me, whispering, "Catherine, I—"

I lift my hand to stop her. "I need to use the restroom."

I go into the bathroom and flick on the lights, then lock the door. I close the toilet lid and sit down.

My mind is swimming and it's difficult to catch my breath, like I've just finished a long, punishing race.

In the past few days, I've learned my mother's identity is a fabrication. Now she tells me the person I always imagined my father to be—a selfish, immature boy—is a myth, too.

I drop my head into my hands.

Some of the pieces floating around in the puzzle that composes my mother are beginning to fit together. Maybe my father stalked her when she ended their relationship. She could have changed her identity to hide from him. All of our abrupt moves to different towns, her lack of connection to anyone from the first part of her life—it makes sense in that context.

But why wouldn't she have told me?

Now that I'm on the verge of learning about her past, it feels like I've hiked to the edge of a precipice. I'm gripped with the urge to back away.

But I can't. I am seconds from literally holding the truth in my hands.

I reach into my purse and pull out my iPhone.

I type new search terms into Google. Not *Virginia,* but *Maryland. Panthers. James. Pizza Piazzo.*

That's all it takes.

The first few hits are the website for the restaurant and Yelp reviews.

Then news stories flood my screen.

The first headline I read is, *Oak Hill High Killer Paroled.*

Nausea rises in my throat as I view the images attached to the story.

It's him, the man I saw in the restaurant just a few hours ago, minus the wig and glasses. His full name is James Bates. He's a murderer.

He's also my father.

I drop my head between my knees and suck in shaky, shallow breaths.

It isn't only my mother's entire identity that is a lie.

Mine is, too.

I force myself to begin reading the article. Midway through I have to close my eyes and wait for the dizziness to pass, but I press on.

I understand the words on my screen, but they are hard to comprehend, like I'm trying to translate a language I don't speak fluently. Nothing I'm reading computes with the tidy, quiet life I share with my mother.

James killed my mother's high school Poms coach. He went to prison. My mother disappeared the night of the murder. Her real name is Ava Morales.

The revelations slam into me, one after the other, like a flurry of punches.

When I'm close to the end of the second story—the one that says James skipped out on parole and there's a warrant for his arrest—a tap on the door startles me. "Catherine? Are you okay?"

No, I want to cry, but I say in a hushed voice, "I'll be out in a minute."

I slip my phone into my purse. There's a lot more information out there, but I've learned the basics. That's all I can handle for one night.

I sit motionless in the small, white-tiled bathroom. I have no idea how to feel, or what to do next.

I finally stand up and turn on the sink tap, letting cool, silvery water trickle into my cupped hands. I splash it onto my face and use the hand towel to dry my cheeks.

Then I open the door.

I can tell the moment my mother sees me that she knows I've discovered the truth.

She is sitting on the edge of the bed, her hands folded in her lap. The room is shadowy and the illusion we created together—that she is older and frail—seems real.

All the questions that have been bubbling inside me funnel into this one: "What happened the night you disappeared?"

My mother bows her head. "I didn't know what James had planned. I swear, Catherine, I thought we were only going to trash the office. Coach deserved that. He wasn't a good guy. . . ."

Her voice trails off, then she continues. "Afterward, when Coach was dying, I wanted to call 911, but James scared me so much. . . . One minute, he was this gentle, caring person and the next—he was completely different."

I nod for her to continue.

"We both went home to grab some clothes and valuables. I was supposed to meet James at the pizza place, but I drove in the other direction."

I can understand. If I saw James walking toward me, I'd turn and run as fast as I could, too.

"Did James ever hurt you?" I ask.

She shakes her head. "Never. But I believe he killed his stepfather. And if I hadn't pretended to agree to run away with him that night, I think he would have harmed me, too."

I take a few steps closer to her as I break through another lie. "Your family didn't disown you."

My mother's eyes are painful to behold. They're like shattered glass.

"No, they didn't. I sent my father a note a long time ago with no return address and a coded message to let him and my brother know I'm alive. I couldn't bear to think of them worrying, but . . ." Her voice breaks. "They didn't throw me out because I got pregnant. *I* didn't even know I was pregnant with you until after I started running."

My mother has a brother, which means . . . "I have an uncle?"

"Timmy." A tear rolls down her cheek, like it costs her everything to even say his name after so long.

"How old are you, really?" I ask.

"Forty-one." She swallows. "I was sixteen when I got pregnant and left home. Seventeen when I had you."

I try to picture my mother at sixteen, on her own, completely terrified. My heart begins to thaw, ever so slightly.

Then she says, "I stayed hidden for you. I researched what happens to children of killers. Do you know Ted Bundy has a daughter?

People think she's living under an assumed name in Europe. It was bad enough I had to be in hiding. I didn't want that to be your life, too."

Something in her words snags on me. My mother is a victim, yes, but it isn't that simple.

"You didn't stay hidden just for me. You might have been charged as an accomplice. You did it to protect yourself, too."

She nods. "Yes."

There's one final lie between us.

"You don't have Alzheimer's disease."

My mother's face collapses, then re-forms, this time with the steely expression I know too well.

"I'd do it all over again if I had to. James was getting out of prison, and if you were living alone, near him, and he found out about you—I wouldn't be able to protect you. I had to keep you with me, and I didn't know how else to do it."

I look at my mother for a long, steady moment. She perpetuated a horrific deception to keep me close, but it wasn't because of her neediness. It was to protect me. Still, that doesn't erase what she did, or the amount of pain and disruption I endured.

Her hands begin wringing themselves together, and her sleeve slips, revealing the old, slightly bumpy scar on her forearm.

My mother knows the agony of having fire sear her skin, yet she ran through flames tonight to save me.

She also made choices with momentous consequences for us both without ever once letting me know how much control she was exerting in shaping my life. She could have told me the man who impregnated her was dangerous. I deserved at least a small piece of the truth.

"Can you forgive me?" she whispers.

There have been enough lies between us, so I answer honestly. "I don't know."

We don't talk much more after that. We are both wrecked, physically and emotionally. We already changed into fresh clothes in the

Bonneville because the outfits we were wearing reeked of smoke. All that's left to do is brush our teeth and climb into bed.

The moment I lie down, though, a forgotten detail slides into my mind. I sit bolt upright.

The Cadillac I took from the Campbells is still in the parking lot of Pizza Piazzo.

CHAPTER THIRTY-FOUR

RUTH

I've gone over this in my mind a hundred times, and I keep landing on the same conclusion. There is only one safe path forward.

I'm sitting in an upholstered chair that I've dragged over to face the door of our hiding place while Catherine sleeps restlessly a few feet away. It's well past midnight. I should try to doze for a while too, but I can't bring myself to lie down.

"Mom?"

I whip around at the sound of Catherine's strained whisper. But she's only talking in her sleep.

I stand up and walk over and smooth her hair.

"Shhh," I whisper. Her face relaxes and she drifts into what I hope is a more peaceful dream.

I stare down at her, wishing Catherine had come to me to ask about my connection to the pizza restaurant rather than reach out to the worst person imaginable. But no, that isn't fair. I'm the one who built the wall of distrust between us. And I can tell by the way she is acting that it may be a permanent structure.

I stand in the darkened room, awash in the cruel self-judgment and what-ifs that accompany hindsight. After a moment, though, I banish those thoughts. If we are to get through this, I must look ahead, not backward.

There is *nothing* of her father in Catherine, I promise myself. Yet they found each other, as if by gravitational pull, both reaching out through the gray, misty ether until their fingertips touched.

By now, I am certain James is the man Catherine communicated with in private messages on Facebook. To begin with, he joined Facebook on the same day he was sprung from prison. He also filled his profile with just enough information to allow someone who knew him well to find him but not enough to alert the authorities to his new social media presence.

He listed Pizza Piazzo as his former place of employment. He chose a photo of a black Corvette as his profile picture. He identified himself as David James—his first and middle name reversed. And, in a sick nod to the past, he cited Eric Clapton as his favorite musician.

This information was freely available to me. I only had to log in to the fake Facebook account I'd made years ago to check in on Timmy.

At first, as my eyes skittered across the different clues on James's page, I felt completely bewildered. No one but me would know the significance of his background photo. It's the field in the middle of the woods behind my high school where we first had sex and often returned to together. It seemed as if James was leaving private clues on a very public forum for the express purpose of letting me know he was there.

Then it hit me. Maybe he was doing exactly that.

I tensed as a brand-new scenario, one I'd never before considered, exploded in my brain. If James was putting out gentle feelers to find a way to communicate with me, the assumption I'd been operating under for nearly twenty-five years was dead wrong.

I'd always thought James knew I deliberately left him waiting at our meeting place. I'd pictured him passing time in jail fantasizing about revenge.

But James was captured only fifteen minutes after we were due to meet. He had no way of knowing I was speeding down the highway in the opposite direction by then.

There could have been a dozen legitimate reasons for why I was late: I lost track of time in my state of shock. My father woke up when I came into the house to grab my things, and I had to wait to leave until he fell back asleep. I had car trouble. It took me longer to pack than the scant bit of time James had allotted me.

I was able to come up with all of those possibilities quickly. Of course, James would have considered them, too.

The fact that I never went to the police and gave a statement identifying James as Coach's murderer in an effort to save myself could support any inclination James might have to give me the benefit of the doubt.

Now I sink into a chair and lean forward, my elbows on my knees, my mind whirling.

Maybe all those pictures he drew of me in prison weren't a byproduct of his rage. Perhaps they were sourced in his twisted vision of love. He might have imagined we'd be a couple again once he was free.

All isn't lost. I have one more chance.

This is the only path forward: James must be captured today.

I know how to make it happen, too. After all these years of hiding from the police, I'm finally going to use them as an ally.

I reach for my phone and navigate to the private message function on Facebook and send a carefully thought-out one to James, sprinkling in a few clues of my own.

Meet me at our special spot under the stars at 9 a.m.? Love, your chocolate-chip cannoli girl.

I wait, but there's no immediate reply.

My eyes grow dry and itchy as minutes pass and I stare at the little screen, waiting for a response that doesn't come. It's the middle of the night. James must be asleep. There's no way he can be driving down the highway, retracing our path here.

Finally, I put down my phone. My mind can't be sluggish today. I have to get a bit of rest, too. I lie down beside Catherine, but I'm too uneasy to drift off. There's a flimsy lock on our door, nothing that would stop someone determined to get inside. Every distant footstep is James coming down the hall. Every creak or rustle of wind is him drawing closer to us.

I toss and turn for a long time. Finally, I get up and open the Rice Krispies I smuggled in here. I sprinkle the dry cereal over the tiled floor, in the space between the door and our bed.

Satisfied the crunching noise will alert me to anyone who tries to sneak up on us, I finally close my eyes with my Mace in my hand.

CHAPTER THIRTY-FIVE

CATHERINE

I roll over, my eyes adjusting to the thin light seeping in through the cracks in the blinds, and see my mother crouched on the floor, picking up Rice Krispies.

"I was hungry and spilled them," she whispers.

I watch her as memories of last night overpower my mind. *Your name is Ava Morales,* I think. *You've hidden from the world for most of your life. You've kept me hidden, too.*

I climb out of bed and jerk up the covers while my mother finishes clearing the last of the cereal off the floor.

"Did you sleep well?" she asks. It's such an ordinary question.

But nothing about today is normal.

I nod, feeling unable—or maybe unwilling—to talk to her.

I walk into the bathroom to brush my teeth and wash my face. When I come back out, my stomach growls loudly enough for my mother to hear it.

"Here." She reaches into her purse and pulls out a granola bar and a bottle of water.

"Where did you get these?"

She shrugs. "They were in the Bonneville."

I tear into the granola bar. It isn't until I've almost finished it that I realize my mother must be hungry, too. I offer her the last chunk, but she waves it away.

Just like she has always done when there isn't enough food for us both.

Something akin to guilt mingles with all the other emotions stewing inside me.

I tuck the empty wrapper in the pocket of my shorts and look around, making sure there is no trace of our presence.

Smuggling my mother into Sunrise was easy. Getting her out could be more complicated. Ideally, we'd wait until later this morning, when residents are milling around after breakfast.

But as I explained to my mother last night after I sat up in bed, I want the Cadillac back in its spot as early as possible. My hope is that George Campbell still follows the routine he used to. He swims in the lap pool or uses the weight room on alternate mornings, then showers and heads to the dining room for a late breakfast with June. Still, I can't risk the chance he might need his car early for some unforeseen reason.

I glance at the time on my iPhone. The security guard works the front desk from 9 p.m. until 5 a.m. He should be long gone. The receptionist covering the morning shift won't know who my mother is.

My mother could exit under the guise of a number of identities: resident, family member, visiting overnight nurse. I just have to figure out which persona will be the easiest one for the receptionist to accept.

But first we need to get out of the Memory Wing.

My mother and I do a final sweep through the family quarters, straightening the comforter on the bed and wiping a few drops of water from around the sink and removing the rolled-up towel from the bottom of the door. Once we're satisfied the space is exactly as we found it, I put the straps of my backpack over my shoulder and stand at the door, listening, for a long moment.

Then I slowly crack it open and peer out. The hallway is clear.

I look back at my mother and nod. I step out, my sneakers treading slowly and softly down the long linoleum hallway. My mother is directly behind me, mirroring my movements. I stop every few yards, listening hard.

It isn't quite 7 a.m. yet, which is when the early staff will start arriving. We've timed our exit for when the skeleton night crew is hopefully completing final paperwork. We shouldn't run into anyone, unless a resident awakens and draws the attention of the staff before we reach the exit.

We've almost made it to the turn that will put us within sight of the blue-painted exit door when I hear the noise I've been fearing: the light padding of footsteps.

Someone is heading our way.

I turn around and see my mother staring at me, wide-eyed.

There's no way I can explain our presence here. The night staff knows me, but I'm not on the work schedule. They'll also instantly know my mother isn't a resident.

I do the only thing I can think of. I open the door of the nearest room and slip inside. My mother follows and I ease the door shut behind her.

We step to either side of the window in the door and press our backs against the wall.

The footsteps are drawing closer now. The person coming our way must have turned the corner. If their destination is this room, we'll be caught.

I hold my breath.

The footsteps are rhythmic. Ten steps, then a pause. Ten more, then another pause. They draw closer, until they are just outside our hiding spot. There's another pause, then the footsteps continue on.

I exhale slowly. Someone peeked in as part of early morning rounds, but they obviously didn't see us.

Not ten feet away sleeps Mrs. Jacobson, the woman my mother impersonated last night. Mrs. Jacobson is curled up in the fetal position, with guardrails up on her bed.

I watch as my mother takes her in, then glances around the bedroom. There are no sharp edges here. The nightstand and dresser have rounded corners, as they do in all the other bedrooms. Contrasting colors for the furniture, walls, floor, and bed linens are designed to help Mrs. Jacobson differentiate between surfaces. Soft, pleasing hues fill the room rather than busy patterns. When Mrs. Jacobson first moved in, her son brought in her favorite easy chair. But the chair was covered in a chintz pattern, and one morning we discovered Mrs. Jacobson on her knees with a washcloth, trying to clean the "spots"— the rosebuds in the pattern. Now the chair is slipcovered in a solid green shade.

There's a row of family photographs on top of the dresser, including one of Mrs. Jacobson surrounded by her four children and eleven young grandchildren. It was taken before her disease progressed. In it, she's looking directly at the camera, her joy and vibrancy almost palpable. It's difficult to believe she is the same frail-looking, gray-skinned woman curled up in bed a few feet away.

I've told my mother lots of stories about my job, but this is the first time she's seen a piece of it close up.

This is what you did to me, I think. *You made me believe this would be you.*

I hope she takes a good, long look.

I wait until the footsteps come back around, moving more quickly with no pauses this time, and when they fade away, I crack open the door and make sure the hallway is empty before we continue.

We finally reach the blue exit door and I input the code, then push through. The clicking sound of the lock engaging behind us makes me flinch, but I doubt the noise will carry.

A moment later, my mother and I are inside the elevator.

We descend in silence.

When the doors open, we walk through the lobby together and as we approach the front desk, I wave casually to the receptionist, who I recognize. I've deliberately positioned myself between the front desk and my mother.

"Good morning," my mother calls cheerfully, and the receptionist returns the greeting.

My mother is wearing an item we picked up at CVS last night—a pair of glasses. Up close you can tell she's relatively young, but I don't plan to give the receptionist a chance to see her clearly.

My mother pauses briefly at a tall oval table that contains printed schedules of different activities being offered for today and scoops one up, as I instructed her to do. She moves assuredly, as if this is part of her regular routine.

"It's going to be a scorcher," I say. "Enjoy your walk, Mrs. Reed."

"I will!" My mother steps on the pad that triggers the automatic door to open, but I pause at the front desk.

The illusion is working. I can tell because the receptionist is looking at me, not my mother. Now I need to muddy her memory in case she tries to recall the name I just spoke.

"Do you know if Mrs. Williams got that package yet from FedEx?"

She frowns. "Package? I'm not sure."

I nod. "Yeah, I think it was delivered to Mrs. Davis—I mean, Mrs. Lee on floor two." I laugh. "Now I'm getting confused. Anyway, no worries. I'll be back in a bit and will check on it then."

She nods. I glimpse her phone screen and see she's playing a game of solitaire. There's also a large coffee from 7-Eleven on her desk along with a half-eaten SlimFast bar, and she looks a little bleary-eyed. Her brain isn't primed to be scanning and sorting and storing information right now.

With any luck, the details of this little encounter will slip away permanently, muscled out of place by all the other information— things like *the red eight goes on the black nine* and *I wish this bar was a chocolate donut* vying for attention in her crowded mind.

I silently will the message to her: *Forget us.*

CHAPTER THIRTY-SIX

RUTH

I step outside into a world that has no right to be so beautiful. The early morning sun lays down a golden filter as a gentle breeze ruffles the air. The gardens surrounding Sunrise are blooming, with cherry-colored and creamy white azaleas edging the front porch and clusters of rich purple and warm yellow petunias filling the beds.

I can't drink in my surroundings, as I might on any other morning.

A new Facebook message just came in for me.

I walk quickly to the Bonneville, scanning my surroundings with every step, and climb into the driver's seat. Only after I've locked the doors do I take off my glasses with the clear lenses and look down at my phone and read the reply sent by James.

9 a.m. it is. I can't wait to see you. But let's talk first.

He then lists a phone number for me to call.

My mouth goes dry. After so many years, I'm finally hearing from James.

I look up to see Catherine exiting Sunrise. I turn the key to start the car and drive to meet her a few feet from the door. She slips into the passenger's seat and clicks her seat belt into place without a word. Then she folds her arms and stares straight ahead.

Her edgy silence increases my agitation, but I can't do anything about that now. I need to focus on retrieving the Cadillac, making sure Catherine is safely out of range, and calling James.

James must want to verify it's really me before he heads to our meeting spot. It will be easy to establish my identity, and hopefully it won't be difficult to convince him I've been longing for him all these years.

I turn out of the parking lot onto a nearly empty, four-lane road. We're ahead of the rush-hour traffic, which means we'll make good time to Pizza Piazzo.

Inside the car it's warm and stuffy, and our temperamental air conditioner isn't helping. I lower my window a few inches and settle in for the drive.

I'm so focused on preparing myself I almost miss Catherine's question.

"What are we going to do?"

I frown. We've already gone over this.

"You made yourself memorable at the restaurant last night when you talked to the manager. So you can't be seen around there again. They may think you had something to do with the fire. I have to be the one to retrieve the Cadillac."

Luckily, Catherine parked it in the middle of the lot, far enough away from Pizza Piazzo that it might not have drawn any notice.

"I'll drive it back to Sunrise and meet you there," I remind her.

"*After* that." Catherine bites off the words. "Am I supposed to stay in hiding now, too?"

"Just until this afternoon," I promise. "Tomorrow at the latest. Then this is going to all be over. You can go back to your regular life, Catherine."

She gives a half laugh. "My regular life. Right."

She's silent for a long moment and my thoughts return to the phone call I'm going to have with James. He remembers me as a passionate, somewhat naive girl. I need to find a way to access that past version of myself, even though no part of her lives inside me now.

I brake at a stoplight and reach into my purse for my dark sunglasses.

"So what's your big plan?"

The hostile tone of Catherine's question jars me.

"I'm still figuring it out," I tell her. The less Catherine knows, the better for her. "Just trust me this one last time."

The light turns green and I press down on the gas.

Catherine shakes her head sharply. Her voice overflows with emotion as she says, "You've lied about everything. Now I'm supposed to trust you?"

I know Catherine needs to process this, but now isn't the time. I have to focus every bit of my mental energy on what lies ahead. So many things can go wrong today.

I feel my old nemesis, anger, rising up.

"Yes, Catherine. The only times I've ever lied to you have been to protect us!"

She puts her feet up on the dashboard, a habit I hate. I've told her before that if we're in even a minor accident, her legs could be seriously damaged by the airbag.

"Whatever you say, *Ava*."

I flinch at the sound of my real name, but I quash my desire to react. I keep driving, the speedometer steady at forty-five, both hands on the wheel, looking straight ahead.

An hour from now, I'll pull into a gas station or some other public place, and Catherine and I will switch spots in the Bonneville. She'll drop me off a few blocks away from the Cadillac and immediately drive back to the safety of the Memory Wing.

An hour after that, James will be arrested.

Then I can try to repair some of the damage I've done to my daughter.

I turn onto the highway and press down harder on the gas, the tires thrumming easily over the smooth pavement. The sun is a bit higher in the clear blue sky now. It's warming the left side of my face through the window.

We're drawing closer to my hometown.

I review my plan again in my mind. There are two calls I need to make, both from the burner tucked in my purse. The first will be to James. The second is the one I almost made years ago from my parents' kitchen, to 911.

Catherine moves her sneakers off the dashboard and sits up straighter.

"How did you end up with him—with James? You came from a normal family, and you were this popular girl in high school . . . what went wrong?"

As hurt and angry as she is, her curiosity is winning out. And I know I have to finally start answering her questions or I may lose her forever.

"None of that is true. The media likes to paint certain pictures because it makes a better story. But my family wasn't normal. . . . My mother was an alcoholic, and she abused us."

"You and your brother?"

I nod. "And my father, at least emotionally. She screamed at him a lot, but I never saw her hit him. I wasn't all that popular in high school, either. I guess when I met James, I felt like he really saw me and cared about me."

Catherine digests this.

"Maybe he saw you, but you didn't see who he was."

She has no idea how right she is. James knew me far better than I knew him.

"Yeah." I exhale. "Now that I look back on it, there were little hints. But I didn't know what he was capable of until that night with Coach."

She reaches up to rub her temples. I have the beginnings of a headache, too. We could both use a cup of coffee right about now, but I can't afford to stop. I need Catherine to be as far away as possible by the time James ventures out to our meeting spot.

We ride the rest of the way in silence, other than Catherine giving me the occasional direction from her Waze app.

It's strange being back on these familiar roads, traveling into my past. Last night I drove here in a blind frenzy after I checked my phone and saw the little blue dot representing Catherine speeding down the highway. I tore along the roads, weaving around trucks, and cutting in and out of the far left lane, already intuiting that it was James who'd lured my daughter to that precise spot.

We're driving the same route this morning, but it feels like a very different journey.

"Take the next exit," Catherine instructs me, reading the map on the screen of her phone.

"I know the way now," I tell her.

I weave through the streets, guided by memory. I drive past a big, grassy park with a playground and sports fields. Timmy's Little League games were held here, and the first time he got a hit my dad and I stood up on the bleachers and cheered as Timmy turned to look at us, a smile splitting his face, before he dropped his bat and ran with everything he had for first base. Another time, my dad made Timmy and me kites with spare scraps of wood from his job, and we brought them here to test them out.

The details of that Saturday afternoon come back to me as if they've been preserved all these years, tucked away between layers of protective wrap like a glass ornament.

Timmy's kite got stuck in a tall oak tree, so before he could start crying, I gave him mine. My father squeezed my shoulder in a silent thank-you and left his hand there for a moment. We ran up and down the fields, the red-and-white-striped kite soaring above us, until we were breathless and sweaty. Just as we flopped down on the soft grass, we heard the jingle of an ice-cream truck. We looked at each other, then got up and sprinted after the truck, waving and yelling for it to stop until it pulled over to the curb. Timmy chose an ice cream shaped like a cartoon character, with bubble gum balls for eyes. I got a chocolate eclair, and my dad picked a strawberry shortcake. When we'd eaten them down to their little wooden sticks, my father put an arm around each of us as we walked back to the car.

That was the spring before I disappeared.

I turn left again, putting the park in my rearview mirror. We're less than a half mile to the pizza restaurant. I need to find a place to pull over, somewhere with enough cars and people so we won't attract attention, but not a location that's too busy.

I choose the parking lot of a Rite Aid drugstore. I coast to a spot toward the middle of the lot and cut the engine of the Bonneville. My fingers ache when I take them off the wheel. I must've been clutching it more tightly than I'd realized.

I pull out the key and give it to Catherine. She reaches into her purse and gets out the keys to the Cadillac. I already know the car is a walnut color and Catherine described its location, so all that's left for me to do is walk there.

I'm seized with the urge to hug Catherine, but I know she won't welcome it, so I merely say, "See you soon," as I open the door of the Bonneville.

"Mom?"

I look back.

Catherine seems to be struggling to figure out what to say. She finally chooses "Good luck."

"I'll be right behind you," I promise.

Ten minutes later, the Cadillac is almost within my reach. All I have to do is cross the street, walk down a block, and enter the parking lot.

I stand by the curb next to a traffic light, waiting for it to turn.

Cars and vans and trucks whiz past me. I try not to think about the fact that any of them could contain someone who knew me as a teenager—or who saw me last night when I was sneaking into the employee entrance of Pizza Piazzo, the one that leads directly to the kitchen. I didn't encounter anyone during the few seconds it took me to set the fire and I'd tied a dish towel around my lower face, I remind myself.

I feel completely exposed, even with my big sunglasses. This place brings me nothing but terrible luck. I can't help feeling like I'm tempting the darkest of fates by returning here.

The light turns.

I cross the street, noticing as I draw closer to the strip mall that ribbons of yellow police tape cordon off Pizza Piazzo. The fire department got there in time to save the building. From the outside, other than the broken windows some workers are boarding up, you can't even tell there's anything wrong.

I take a deep breath and look down at my burner phone. I've already tapped in the number James gave me. All I need to do is press enter.

But my fingers refuse to move.

I briefly close my eyes and do what I've done for the past twenty-four years whenever terror or despair or grief overtake me: I visualize Catherine. I see her as a little girl, reaching up to hold my hand as we walk to the bus stop. I see her as she is right now, her long hair blowing in the wind streaming in through the open car window.

I hold the images of her in my mind as I press the green button to connect the call.

James answers midway through the first ring.

"Ava?"

His voice is lower and deeper than I remember. Hearing it sends a shock wave through me.

"Hi, James." My voice sounds different, too. It's higher and tighter than usual. Hopefully James will mistake the fear threading through it for excitement.

I hear James exhale. "I had to be sure it was really you."

I've reached the parking lot. The Cadillac is twenty yards away. I move toward it as I launch into the lines I've rehearsed in my mind.

"I've been waiting so long, James. Every single day I thought about you. Every night I fell asleep dreaming about you."

My words are completely truthful but not in the way James will interpret them.

"That night we were supposed to meet—I got held up at home," I continue. I'm on the verge of tears now, but I don't quash the emotion in my voice. It should work to my advantage. "I'm so sorry. I still can't believe you were caught because I was late."

"What happened?"

I can't sound too rehearsed.

"My mom—she was awake when I went back to pack. She started yelling at me—you know how she used to get. . . . I finally had to lock myself in my bedroom and climb out the window. I was coming to meet you when I saw the cop car at the restaurant and I just—I guess I freaked out. I didn't know what to do—I just kept driving. I'm so sorry."

There's a long pause. My hands tremble while I await James's response.

Then James says, "I knew something like that happened."

He believes me. This is actually going to work.

I try to imagine where James is right now. He might be in a no-name motel, or maybe he's in a car already parked near the spot where we're supposed to meet.

"Where do you live now?" James asks, like we're acquaintances getting caught up at a reunion.

I give the answer I've crafted in the hopes of pleasing him. "California, but the moment I heard you'd been granted parole, I caught a plane to Maryland."

If James asks for more details, I can provide them. I've created a complete backstory for myself that's fully fictional.

"I've rented a car and I just checked out of a Holiday Inn near Annapolis," I say.

The city I've named is about an hour south of our meeting place in Towson. I deliberately cited a location in the opposite direction that Catherine is traveling.

I unlock the Cadillac and climb in and slam the door, hoping James recognizes the sound for what it is. "I'm getting in my car to come to you now."

"God, Ava . . . I can't believe I'm going see you after all these years."

"This time nothing will keep us apart. I better go, James. I don't want to get pulled over for using a cell phone while I'm driving."

I start the engine. The more details James can confirm that corroborate my story, the less likely he'll be able to question things he can't confirm.

"Of course . . . just one more thing?"

James's voice is calm and warm, but ice runs through my veins.

"Who was that girl who contacted me on Facebook? I saw her in the restaurant. Did you send her to meet me?"

Of all the things I've told James, this is the one he must believe without question. I cannot waver. I must give the performance of my life.

"Oh, she's just someone I hired on TaskRabbit after I was trying to find you and I saw your profile on Facebook. I wasn't sure how secure Facebook is, so I had her get in touch with you . . . I paid her to go to the restaurant to give you a letter from me, but that stupid fire happened before she could deliver it."

"How did she recognize me?" James asks.

"She didn't," I tell him. "She didn't know anything other than to look for a forty-three-year-old guy who was there alone and put the letter on his table. I kept it vague enough that it wouldn't alert anybody in case she got the wrong guy or if someone was setting me up."

The story I've spun is a little convoluted. But if I were as obsessed with James as I'm pretending to be, it might be plausible that I'd be so desperate to reach him that I'd try every possible avenue, including social media, which is a great connector for long-lost friends and lovers. I wish I could see James's face to gauge how my story is landing. But it probably wouldn't matter even if I could since James's eyes always lie.

"Okay, Ava," he says.

I think he bought it.

"I love you." Nausea fills my throat as I speak the words.

"I love you, too."

I expect James to hang up, but he doesn't. Something compels me to stay on the line, too.

The hair on the back of my neck rises as the silence stretches on.

Finally, James says, "See you."

Then the line goes dead.

CHAPTER THIRTY-SEVEN

CATHERINE

Secrets slip out when people are at the end of their lives.

Working in a nursing home means I'm always in close proximity to death. Sometimes I'm by a patient's side when they take their final breath. Most of the confessions I hear from our more lucid Extended Care residents have been relatively minor: *I wish I hadn't fought with my sister and cut her off . . . I should have spent more time with my kids when they were growing up . . . I didn't say "I love you" enough.*

But sometimes, huge deceptions emerge, as if their owner wanted to enter the afterlife with a clean slate: *I gave up a baby for adoption and never told anyone . . . I was in love with another woman for most of my marriage . . . The man everyone thinks is my younger brother is really my son.*

I've wondered what it would feel like to carry such an enormous secret for so long. If it would always feel heavy and alien, or if in time it would integrate like just another limb.

I'm walking around the grounds of Sunrise because I'm too restless to sit in the Bonneville and wait for my mother to bring back the Cadillac.

I can't help wondering what I would do, given the chance. Would I go back to being blissfully unaware of my origins and true family history?

I don't have the answer, but I do know this: My life was far easier when I believed the lies my mother fed me.

Those thoughts are running through my mind when I see Tin and an aide bringing a few Memory Wing residents outside. I turn my head and quicken my pace, hoping they won't spot me. Then I hear Tin calling my name.

I wave, hoping that will be the end of it. But Tin motions me over.

My mother should be arriving any moment now. She texted a little while ago to say she'd pulled off the highway at our exit to get a few gallons of gas. As I walk toward Tin, my mind races, trying to recall what I've told Tin about my mother. The two have never met, and I don't think Tin has any idea what my mother looks like. All she knows is that my mother is ill.

"Hey, Catherine. You're not working today, are you?" Tin frowns.

"I just can't stay away from the place," I joke. "No, I forgot something here yesterday and came back to get it."

Tin begins telling me about a folder she has for me with some forms to fill out and a parking sticker for the permit-only spots, now that I'm going to be a full-time employee.

I smile and nod, but in my mind I'm calculating time and risk. It's only about 9 a.m. now, so Tin will be gone by late afternoon or early evening. Tin won't be on the Memory Wing after dark if I need to sneak my mother in again tonight.

I'm perspiring, and not because of the heat. This must be a taste of what life has been like for my mother—constant calculations and conversational parrying.

I realize Tin is waiting for me to say something.

"Sounds good, I'll go upstairs and grab the folder in a few minutes," I tell her. "I might just soak in the sun a bit longer."

She looks at me a little more closely, her brown eyes filled with kindness. "Are you okay?"

I force a smile. "I didn't sleep well, but I'm fine."

Tin briefly squeezes my arm and I know it's a silent message of sympathy. She still believes my mother is so ill that I canceled my plans to move to Baltimore.

"I'm heading up myself, so I'll leave your folder on my desk," she tells me.

Out of the corner of my eye, I see the shiny brown Cadillac turn into the parking lot.

"Perfect," I tell Tin. The car stops. My mother doesn't know where to park. And I can't gesture her toward the spot where Mr. Campbell last left his car while I'm talking to Tin.

Thankfully, Tin begins to walk back into Sunrise. The moment she disappears through the doors, I start to point to the correct spot.

But was it the fourth spot from the front door, or the fifth?

I stare at the two spots, willing my mind to pick the right one. The Cadillac is idling in the middle of the parking lot. The longer it remains, the more likely it will draw attention.

I point to the fourth spot and my mother eases the car into it. By the time I've walked over to meet her, she has slipped out of the car and locked the doors.

I palm the keys she hands me.

"I adjusted the seat back," she told me. "I figured George is taller than five-foot-two."

"Good thinking."

Now I need to do two things, fast: figure out what to do with my mother—and get these keys back into George and June's bowl.

It will probably be safe for my mother to take on the guise of a Daily Assisted resident. Nearly two hundred people live at Sunrise, and no staff member knows all of them well enough to identify my mother as an imposter.

"Keep strolling around, and I'll be back as soon as I can," I say as we begin to walk together toward the entrance of Sunrise. I fall quiet as we approach Mr. Damon, who sits on a bench, staring off into the distance. The aide who brought him down is a dozen yards away, holding the arm of a woman who is in the late stages of Alzheimer's.

"Good morning, Mr. Damon," I say, and he looks up.

His face transforms.

"Are you my daughter?" He's looking directly at my mother.

She blinks rapidly a few times, clearly at a loss for words.

"Sorry," she finally says, and continues walking. But she only makes it another step or two before Mr. Damon cries, "Sheila! Stop!"

My mother freezes, and I do the same.

Mr. Damon does have a daughter named Sheila—I've met her once—but she lives in San Francisco and rarely visits.

"Why are you walking away from me?" Mr. Damon's voice is loud, and if we keep moving, he's certain to grow more agitated. He might even run after my mom. Instead of blending in, she will become the center of attention. A dozen or so residents and staff members are nearby. There's no way a scene will go unnoticed.

The Cadillac keys are pressing into my palm. I have to get them back, now. My mind whirls, trying to find the least risky path.

"Sit with him," I whisper. "Play along. He used to play piano in an orchestra, and he loves classical music. Mention Bach and Beethoven. It'll calm him down."

My mother walks back to Mr. Damon and eases down onto the wooden bench beside him. Before I move away, I hear her begin to speak to him in a soft, soothing voice.

I hurry into the building, wave to the desk clerk, and go directly to George and June's apartment.

I hold my breath as I knock on the door.

It takes June only a minute to answer, but it feels like a lifetime. She's already dressed in a lime-green pantsuit and has on rosy lipstick. At least I haven't awoken her.

When I see her genuinely warm smile, some of the crushing weight on my shoulders falls away. If she and George had noticed their car was missing, she wouldn't appear so carefree.

"Twice in two days!" she exclaims. "What a treat!"

"I'm so sorry to bother you," I tell her. "I can't seem to find my phone, and I'm wondering if I left it here last night."

"Oh, dear, I didn't see it, but you're welcome to look around."

It's as simple as that. As June begins to lead me into the living room, I slip the keys back into the bowl.

They make a clanking sound as they land.

Thinking quickly, I put my hand in the bowl as June turns around.

"Not here," I say, feigning disappointment.

I step into the living room. Since I didn't even sit down, there aren't many logical places to check.

The only items on the coffee table are a stack of magazines and a device that looks like a computer mouse, which is the blood sugar monitor June uses to manage her diabetes. Still, I pretend to search, even ducking down to check under the coffee table.

"I don't see it," I finally say.

"Oh, I'm sorry. There's nothing more frustrating than losing your phone, is there?"

The kindness in June's voice intensifies my guilt. She and George are the closest thing I have to grandparents. They even gave me a card and a generous check when I graduated college.

I look down to avoid her eyes and see there's a pristine white test strip in the end of the blood sugar monitor. June must have been about to check her glucose levels when I interrupted her.

"Can I help you with this?" I ask, wanting both to do something for her and to change the subject.

I take the monitor and reach for June's index finger, pricking it with the lancet before touching the drop of blood to the white test strip, like I've done hundreds of times before. Like most diabetics, June keeps her insulin pens in her refrigerator, but I don't need to get her a dose right now. Her levels are good.

I hope the distraction will change the course of our conversation, but the next thing June says is, "Do you want me to call you and we can listen for the ring?"

I suck in a breath. My phone is in my purse, and I don't know if it's set to vibrate.

"You know what? I just remembered—I'm pretty sure I left it charging upstairs in the break room last night." I back away.

"Okay, sweetie. And remember, you promised us that glass of wine. Want to come by tonight?"

I'm at the door now.

Her question throws me. If James isn't caught, my mother and I will have to sleep at Sunrise again. I can't tell June I have other plans because she could easily spot me on the grounds this evening.

"Um, I-I may have to work through dinner. . . ." I hedge. Before June can reply, I quickly hug her and slip out.

I'm so rattled I have to stand in the hallway for several moments to compose myself.

As my anxiety recedes, anger rushes in to take its place. My mother did all of this to me. Because of her choices, my work situation and the relationships I've built here are so tangled up that I might not ever be able to straighten them out. Surely Tin will be perplexed—maybe highly annoyed, too—when I tell her I'm moving to Baltimore after all.

I think of the other relationships my mother has destroyed on my behalf. With Ethan, for one. He wasn't the right guy for me, but shouldn't *I* have been the one to decide that?

My anger mounts.

I haven't been eating much or sleeping well, and my body feels simultaneously jittery and heavy. I desperately want a shower and a hot meal and to rest in my own bed, but I can't do that either.

If my mother's big plan to keep James away from us fails, I may never be able to go back to the apartment again. I may have to leave everything behind and go into hiding, just like her.

I storm down the hallway, determined to confront her. I'm going to tell her to get into the Bonneville so we can drive somewhere private to have it out. The words I have for her aren't ones I want anyone to overhear.

I stalk through the lobby of Sunrise and burst through the front door, squinting as the sun hits my eyes.

My mother is exactly where I left her, sitting next to Mr. Damon on the wooden bench. Their backs are to me.

But something has changed. It draws me up short.

Mr. Damon's arm is around my mother's shoulders now.

They look exactly like a father and daughter. It's as if Mr. Damon's addled mind has spun magic, creating the very relationship he believed he saw.

I begin to walk toward them again, more slowly now.

Another part-time aide, a woman I don't know terribly well because our schedules rarely overlap, smiles at me, then nods toward Mr. Damon and my mother.

"Isn't that sweet?" she whispers. "I've never seen him so happy."

Mr. Damon is talking softly as I draw nearer to them, but I can't make out his words. My sneakers land silently in the thick grass. Neither my mother nor Mr. Damon notices my approach.

I'm about to circle around them to make my presence known when I catch the words composing their conversation.

"Will you come see me tomorrow?" Mr. Damon asks.

"If I can," my mother replies.

My mother's head slowly tilts down until it is resting on his broad shoulder.

An aura of love surrounds them. They're both filling in for the people they must miss with their whole hearts. I can't move. I don't want to break the spell.

"You've always been such a good daughter," Mr. Damon tells her. "I'm lucky to have you."

I told my mother to play along, but I think she's doing more than that. She's allowing herself to pretend, for these few moments, that she is with a father who loves her.

It's the first time I've ever seen her as a daughter.

I never truly thought about what it must have cost my mother to run at the age of sixteen, leaving everyone she loved behind.

Now I can hear the almost unfathomable price of it in her raw, ragged voice.

"I've missed you so much, Dad," she whispers.

CHAPTER THIRTY-EIGHT

RUTH

The sun feels hotter now that it is directly overhead.

It's almost noon, and Catherine is somewhere inside Sunrise, rustling up a bite for us to eat. Mr. Damon is back in the Memory Wing, where residents are being served lunch.

Everyone who was outside earlier has escaped into the comfort of air-conditioning.

Surely by now James has been arrested. When I called 911 at five minutes to nine from my burner phone, I told the operator I'd just seen escaped convict James Bates walking in the field behind Oak Hill High, carrying something that looked like a black wig. The operator asked if he was armed, and I said I didn't know. I hung up when she asked for my name.

I would have loved to have seen James being arrested with my own eyes, but it was too dangerous for me to be anywhere near that field.

Now I reach for my iPhone and refresh my Google search on James. There's no update, but that's probably because the media hasn't gotten ahold of the story of his capture yet.

Tension roils my body, so I force myself to lean back against the wooden bench I shared with Mr. Damon and think about something pleasant.

What comes to mind is an image of my father, laughing as he chased after the kite we flew on that long-ago summer day.

When I was with Mr. Damon, it felt as if my dad was sending love across space and time, channeling it through a stranger, surrounding me with it during one of my darkest days.

This has happened before.

Such as on the night when the trucker with the sleepy old chihuahua let me ride in his cab. As we drove farther away from everything and everyone I knew, a panic attack tore through me. At the precise moment I began to hyperventilate, the trucker reached for the radio knob and a song my father used to sing to us—Cat Stevens's "Wild World"—came across the radio. It soothed me.

There was another time when Catherine was four years old, a few nights before Christmas on a bitterly cold evening. I had no money to buy food for us, let alone presents for my little girl. I was desperate enough to go into a restaurant that set down free bread baskets on the tables, hoping to fill our tummies and flee.

The restaurant was busy that night, but the hot bread still arrived via a busboy a moment after the waiter handed me an adult menu and Catherine a kiddie one. I set the menus on the table and quickly grabbed the basket and buttered the thickest slice of bread for Catherine, then I shoved a piece into my own mouth and washed it down with ice water.

I tried to get us out of there before the waiter approached to take our order, but I was too slow.

The waiter caught me just as I was standing up and walking around the table to grab Catherine. He knew exactly what we were doing. We hadn't even taken off our coats. Even though it wasn't a fancy place, I guess we looked like we didn't belong. Catherine was in a jacket two sizes too big for her because it was a hand-me-down I'd gotten from a former neighbor, and my outfit was a little ragged.

The waiter pointed toward the door and told us to get out as my cheeks flushed hot with shame. But we'd only taken a few steps when a man at the next table drew himself up. His black mustache matched his glossy hair, and his accent reminded me of my father's.

"These ladies are my guests," the man told the waiter. He wasn't wearing expensive clothes, and he didn't have a commanding voice, but something in his tone left no room for argument.

The man with the mustache came over to our table and pulled out Catherine's chair, treating her like she was somebody important.

She sat back down, and so did I.

"Order anything you wish," the man said before he returned to his seat.

I got Catherine chicken tenders with a side of green beans and another of roasted potato wedges with extra ketchup and a glass of apple juice, trying to get as much nutrition into her as possible. I ordered minestrone soup for myself because I didn't want the man to think I was trying to take advantage of him.

The whole time we were eating the hot, delicious food, I kept ducking my head and pretending to wipe my mouth, hoping no one could tell I was really wiping my eyes.

The stranger stood to leave before we'd finished, and when he passed our table he put down forty dollars. Enough to cover our meal, with some left over to buy food for the next few days.

When I saw all that money, I wanted to drop my head onto the table and sob.

I walked by that restaurant many times afterward, but I never saw the man again.

A sharp cry jars me from my reverie, making me look up. A crow is sitting on a nearby branch, staring at me and cawing.

Some people believe crows are bad omens, but I refuse to buy into that. Crows are intelligent, playful creatures who get a bad rap.

Still, as another shrill cry cuts through the air, goose bumps rise on my skin.

By now James is sitting in a jail cell with his hands cuffed, I promise myself.

Which also means that by now he realizes how completely I've betrayed him.

I force my mind away from the horrifying thought.

Because Catherine hasn't returned with our food yet, I pull out my journal and a pen. There's a particular entry I want to write down, one that reminds me of my father's love.

For one amazing evening when you were two-and-a-half years old, we were wildly rich.

It was one of the best and most terrifying nights of my life.

We'd just been evicted from the small room I'd rented in a rundown town house that was owned by another single mother. I didn't blame her. Even though the rent was cheap, I couldn't keep up with it. I'd already had to move twice by that point, and I'd burned through several jobs— first as a nanny for a little boy (I got fired when the parents decided they didn't like me bringing you along, after all), then as an overnight front-desk clerk at a cheap hotel. Even though you quietly slept on the floor beneath my desk, cozily rolled up in a blanket, my manager came by unexpectedly once and saw you and that was it.

The single mom wanted to help me, but she had bills of her own to pay. We both had tears in our eyes when she told me I needed to move out.

Since I'd rented the room furnished, I didn't have much to take: my gray duffle bag with my clothes and toiletries, and a backpack filled with your clothes and supplies.

I didn't have a car or any friends whose couch we could crash on until I got myself together. So I went back to Target.

You were a very quiet kid. I wasn't too worried you'd cry when the lights turned off. But I bought insurance—one of those Ring Pops that are shaped like pacifiers. You'd never tasted candy before, and the moment I popped it into your mouth, your eyes lit up.

I followed my old routine, waiting until a minute or two before closing time to climb into the circular rack with you in my arms. I whispered into your ear, telling you the lights were going to turn off but that mama would keep you safe. You looked up at me with your round blue eyes, your mouth working that cherry Ring Pop like you were scared someone was going to take it away before you could finish it.

Thirty minutes later, we were climbing out of the clothes rack. We had the whole store to ourselves.

I wanted to make it fun for you—a kind of adventure. So the first thing we did after getting a flashlight was grab a red plastic shopping basket and wander through the aisles, choosing anything we wanted for a picnic. I picked Fruit Roll-Ups and pretzels and lemonade juice boxes. You added a package of Oreos. There was a little table and chairs set up in the kids' section, so we sat there and ate until we were full.

Then the real fun began.

We walked through the clothing section, picking things we wanted to try on. You looked so cute in everything that I wanted to get it all for you, but in the end we settled on tiny red corduroy pants with a soft cream-colored shirt and little sneakers with Velcro instead of laces. I got new jeans and a hoodie, and we both put on clean socks and underwear.

I'd saved the best for last. We went to the toy section next.

Oh, Catherine—the look on your face when I told you that you could pick any toy you wanted. It was as if you couldn't quite believe it, as if nothing this good had ever happened to you before.

You walked up and down the aisle for what felt like an hour, staring at different items as I shone the flashlight on them: A doll with long red hair. A set of mini pots and pans with plastic food. Puzzles and marble mazes and brightly colored blocks.

You finally chose a soft, stuffed brown-and-white puppy with floppy ears.

It was easy to cut away the packaging and security tag. The scissors were still available in the office supply section.

Next, I picked some chunky Sandra Boynton books and we settled into the big beanbag chair together. I read to you until you fell asleep, your warm body nestled next to mine.

I meant to carry you back to our hiding spot, but my eyes were so heavy and we were so cozy. I shut them just for a moment.

Heavy footsteps woke me.

I opened my eyes and a sharp light blinded me. I winced as I strained to see what was happening. The overhead lights were on in the store, and someone was walking toward us.

Sheer panic turned my legs to liquid. I wrapped my arms around you more tightly, trying to sink deeper into the beanbag chair.

A tall shape loomed over us.

We were completely helpless. Terror paralyzed me. I couldn't even cry out.

A man in blue coveralls was staring down at us.

I croaked out the word please.

The man kept looking at us, not saying anything.

I thought he must have broken in, too. Maybe he was planning to rob the place.

He pressed his index finger to his lips.

I nodded vigorously, trying to convey that we'd be quiet, that we'd never say a word. I didn't care if he stole everything in the store and both of our bags with all of our belongings. As long as he didn't hurt us, nothing else mattered.

Then I heard more voices. I could tell they belonged to another man and a woman.

My eyes had adjusted by now. I could see a cleaning cart next to the man. He was young—probably just a few years older than me. He was just trying to make a living.

I exhaled and my body relaxed a fraction, but we still weren't safe. If this man called the police, I could be arrested and you could be taken from me. And that would only be the beginning of it. The police might be able to learn my real identity.

I'd counted on everything in Target staying the same. I didn't realize the cleaning crew had switched hours from early morning to late at night.

I'd made a terrible mistake.

The man in the coveralls began to gesture frantically. It took me a beat to understand he wanted me to get up, to follow him. I climbed out of the beanbag chair, with you still sleeping in my arms. The puppy you'd named Brownie fell to the floor.

The man scooped up the stuffed animal and rushed toward a corner *of the store where the fitting rooms were located. He used a key on his chain to unlock one of them and gestured for us to get inside.*

I could hear a woman calling for him in the background.

The man closed the door and locked us safely inside until the end of the shift. The woman called his name again and he replied, Estoy aquí, which means I'm here.

I sat on the floor of the dressing room, you still asleep in my arms, unable to believe my ears.

The name of the cleaner, the one I'd heard the woman calling out, was very familiar to me.

Mateo. It was also my father's name.

It felt like another sign that my dad was somehow still protecting me.

I close the journal and look toward the front door of Sunrise. Catherine is coming out, holding a cardboard tray with two white Styrofoam cups nestled in its holders and, in her other hand, a brown paper bag.

I check my phone again. A police reporter should hear the news about James's capture soon. The cops won't want to keep this quiet. They'll be proud of the arrest.

Any moment now, I'll be able to breathe easy.

But there's no update on my phone.

Catherine offers me the tray and I pull out a cup of coffee, gratefully breathing in the rich aroma.

All that's left to do is wait.

CHAPTER THIRTY-NINE

CATHERINE

There is so much I need to untangle with my mother.

After we sip our coffee and devour the hummus and veggie wraps a cook in the kitchen slipped me, we begin to talk. Hours later, I've barely scratched the surface of what I want to know.

For the first time, my mother is opening up to me.

I can tell it's excruciating for her to dismantle the walls she spent more than two decades fortifying, the ones she wanted to keep me contained within.

But she clearly understands the only way we can go forward is for her to invite me into her past.

We've been sitting on Adirondack chairs beneath the shade of a big, sprawling tree, but even though it has grown uncomfortably warm, I don't want to move and rupture this strange new intimacy.

The stories my mom is weaving—of how vicious her mother was to her and Timmy, and how James plotted to punish the Poms coach for his sexual abuse, and how she hid in a Target until a month before I was born, saving every penny she'd earned as a waitress until she had enough to rent a tiny room for us—are jaw-dropping.

It's hard to reconcile those tales with the image I have of my mother as a hardworking woman with a vanilla sort of life.

I guess I've never really looked at my mother as an individual. She has always felt more like a planet that orbits around me. Maybe that's true for most daughters, at least until we reach a certain point in adulthood. We define our mothers through the lens of how they relate to us.

By now, my mother has explained how she lured James to their old meeting spot and alerted the police. As soon as we confirm his arrest, she tells me, we can go back to our apartment.

My mother sighs and leans back in her chair, looking drained. Her skin has a yellowish tint, and she is so thin her cheekbones are even more prominent than usual. She runs the back of her hand across her brow, wiping away the light perspiration that has accumulated.

"I'll help you figure everything out," she says. "You can still move to Baltimore. We can pack up the car and drive you there next week."

I crumple the thin Styrofoam coffee cup in my hand.

"I think I should figure things out for myself," I finally say.

Hurt briefly flashes across her face. "Fair enough."

Because I don't want to look at her right now, I reach into my backpack for the folder Tin left me. I picked it up from her desk before getting lunch for me and my mom.

I pull out the contents. There are a few forms Tin wants me to fill out, and a dental plan pamphlet, and a blue-and-white parking sticker for Sunrise with its name and logo and the current year.

I stare down at the parking pass, thinking that I'll never get to use it since I'll be giving Tin my resignation for a second time.

"There's one more thing I want to ask you about," I say.

My mother's eyes are closed, but she opens them at the sound of my voice.

"Ethan. The night of our anniversary . . ."

My mom sighs and sits up a little straighter.

Whatever she is going to tell me carries the feel of vital importance. It will reveal not only how honest she is committed to being now but will also help me gauge if her deceptions were not solely to protect me but also to keep me close and exert control over my life.

"You drugged him."

"*What?*"

Her shock appears genuine. But it isn't enough to convince me.

"He said you poured him a drink and then he passed out."

My mother shakes her head.

"Here's what really happened. He left his phone at our apartment the night before." This computes with what I know, so I nod for her to continue.

"It got wedged into one of the cracks between the couch cushions. I didn't even know it was there until I got off work that afternoon and was watching something on TV and felt it vibrating beneath me."

My mother's eyes are steady on mine.

"I'm sorry, Catherine. It was vibrating because someone was texting him. When I pulled out the phone, I could see the first line of the message on the screen."

My stomach twists. I feel a little nauseated. I know what my mother is going to say before she utters her next sentence.

"It was another woman." Her voice is gentle, but even after all this time—and with everything else going on that should make Ethan's betrayal as inconsequential as the bee buzzing around me—it hurts badly enough that I fold my arms across my stomach.

It feels like no one in my life was who they pretended to be.

I take a shaky breath before asking, "What did the message say?"

"I could only read the first bit since his screen was locked. But it was enough for me to know they'd slept together the afternoon before."

The afternoon before, when Ethan told me he was busy with preparations for our anniversary. I'd imagined him buying roses and washing his sheets and writing me a love note on a card, not screwing another woman.

"So you set Ethan up?"

My mother shakes her head. "I went out and bought a bottle of vodka. I offered him a drink when he came by. He made his own choices."

I drop my head into my hands.

"I poured him his first drink, but he poured his second one. And the ones after that. This was sipping vodka, but he wasn't sipping it. That's the only reason why he passed out."

I don't know what to think. Everything is muddy.

"Why didn't you tell me the truth?" I cry. "Why can't you *ever* tell me the truth?"

My mother's hand lands on my shoulder but instead of soothing me, it burns. I shake it off.

"I thought it would be easier for you this way. Ethan was your first big love—I was worried about what it would do to your self-confidence if you knew he was cheating. I thought it would be better if you were in control of the way you broke up."

"But I wasn't in control." I tell her. "*You* were."

A thought tickles the back of my brain: She could be lying again. I need proof.

"The girl who texted him," I begin. "What was her—"

It's like my mother knows what I'm thinking before I even say it.

"Kaitlin," she replies. "I've never forgotten it."

That's the name of the woman Ethan is with now. The same one I'm almost certain is the blond waitress who seemed to send poison in my direction whenever I came in to see Ethan.

I never once mentioned her to my mother. She must be telling the truth.

So Ethan deceived me, too. I must be pretty gullible.

Exhaustion falls over me like a weighted blanket. My brain feels completely overloaded. It's shutting down.

My head is too heavy to hold up, so I tilt it back against the hard wooden slats of the chair.

My last vision before I close my eyes is of my mother getting up from her chair and beginning to patrol the grounds.

When I open my eyes again, there's a throbbing in my temples, and the sun is lower in the sky. I check my phone and see it's after 5 p.m.

My mother is sitting next to me, but she isn't sleeping. She's writing something in a green spiral notebook that looks a thousand years old. She notices me watching and she closes it and slips it into her big purse.

"Did I miss anything?"

"Someone came out and drove off in the Cadillac a few minutes ago," she says. "A couple—he had white hair and she was wearing a pink dress and used a cane."

"George and June. They're probably going out to dinner."

She nods.

"No word on anything else," I say.

It's a statement, not a question. I only have to look at my mother's face to know the story of James's arrest hasn't broken.

We just have to wait a little bit longer, my mother keeps saying. I stand up and stretch, then go into Sunrise to use the bathroom. I walk into the main-floor break room and take a few cookies off a giant plastic tray that someone set out for the staff, then fill up two cups of water from the dispenser.

When I return to my mother, she puts down her phone. She bites into one of the oatmeal raisin cookies and washes it down with a big sip of water. "Thanks."

Time ticks forward. My mother's face grows a little tighter. Her posture stiffens.

The sun is sinking lower in the sky. A few floors above us, the Memory Wing residents must be growing agitated.

Something about this phase of night triggers their sense of danger.

I'd hoped to be home by now, taking a long, hot shower. I'd like to close the door of my bedroom and be alone with my thoughts.

But twilight is falling, and we're trapped in limbo.

"We should walk around back," I finally say. We've been sitting out here a long time, and by now most of the residents are inside, finishing dinner and settling in for the night. The grounds are nearly deserted. I don't want to attract attention.

My mother gets up and we circle around the building. It's far less attractive back here. Instead of manicured flower beds, the trash and recycling are stored in huge metal containers. There aren't any chairs or benches, so we stand.

I try to pass the time thinking about what I'll do once this is all over. I'm scheduled to work tomorrow, so I need to have a difficult conversation with Tin and come up with a reason for my reversal. I can't tell her the truth, but neither do I want to lie to her.

I'm fed up with lies.

The last wisps of gray in the sky are being overtaken by black when my phone buzzes. I flinch.

If Ethan is texting me again, I'm going to tell him off, then block him.

But it isn't Ethan.

The incoming text is from George Campbell. Catherine, I noticed your car is still here. Could you come see me and June as soon as possible? There's something important we need to discuss with you.

My heart sinks as I read the words.

I thought I did everything right—telling my mom to fill the tank to the three-quarters mark and making sure I didn't leave anything in the Cadillac. What could have tripped me up? Perhaps George noticed something off about his vehicle, and June mentioned I'd been rummaging around in the bowl that held their keys just this morning.

Now they suspect what I've done.

"What is it?" my mother asks.

I turn around my phone screen so she can read the message.

Her face falls. "Oh, no."

CHAPTER FORTY

RUTH

I don't like not having eyes on Catherine.

Logically I know she's just a few dozen yards away, sealed in the safety of the Campbells' apartment.

Still, my breathing has grown shallow and my chest feels tight. I pace relentlessly: ten steps forward, swivel, then ten steps back.

Catherine's plan is to throw herself at the Campbells' mercy. She's going to tell them the truth—that she desperately needed to borrow a car last night and made a split-second, foolish decision—and hope they forgive her.

She says George and June are very kind people. She thinks they'll be understanding.

I watched as Catherine walked away from me to face the Campbells, every slow step like a stab to my gut. She rounded her shoulders, preparing to face judgment. It was the same way she walked into all the schools she attended on her first day as a new kid.

Head up, shoulders back. I willed her the message, just as I did on all those first school days.

Then she turned the corner and disappeared.

She has been gone nearly fifteen minutes.

I can't help myself. I look down at my iPhone and check her location.

She's still in Sunrise.

I don't know how long a conversation like the one she's having with George and June should take. Surely not too much longer, though.

A breeze cuts through the air and I wrap my arms around myself, shivering. The temperature is plummeting now that the sun has sunk below the horizon.

I packed a sweatshirt in my duffle bag, but it's on the other side of the building, in the Bonneville, in the back of the lot. There's no way I'm leaving this spot. I don't want Catherine to return and not see me.

I refresh my Google search on James. No new results.

I try again with different keywords: *Oak Hill* and *field* and *escape*. But there's nothing.

I move a little closer to the building. The front of Sunrise is very well lit, with wide, paved walking paths and yellow light spilling out from every window. Back here, where residents never come, it's a different story. It's so shadowy I can't see more than ten or fifteen feet in front of me, and there's an unpleasant smell coming from the big trash dumpster.

I wish I could tell which window belongs to the Campbells. I should have asked Catherine what floor they live on, but I didn't think of it in time. I'd just feel better if I knew exactly where she was.

I sense movement out of the corner of my eye and whip around, but it's only a squirrel darting up the base of a tree.

I put a hand over my pounding heart and exhale.

My mind and body are growing increasingly jittery. My need to be near Catherine is so intense it feels like I'm undergoing a chemical withdrawal from her.

I count to a hundred, then two hundred, just as I did on that long-ago night at Target when I was alone in the darkness.

By now she's been gone nearly twenty minutes.

No one is around. It's completely dark. The grounds are deserted.

Something is terribly wrong. I feel it deep in my core.

My gaze jerks down toward my iPhone again, but there's nothing amiss.

Then my eyes widen.

Without being consciously aware of why I'm doing it, I reach into my big shoulder bag and pull out my burner phone. I haven't looked at it since I made the call to the police just before 9 a.m.

I power on the phone as my pulse gallops faster.

It's a cheap device. The screen flickers for a moment, then goes black. Then it comes on for good.

My mouth is completely dry.

I have one new text message, from an unknown number. It came in less than an hour ago.

Terror rips through me. My hands are shaking so violently I nearly drop the phone as I frantically navigate to the message and bring it up.

At first, I blink at the screen in bewilderment.

There are no words at all. There's an image, though. A small, grainy photograph.

I can't see it in this dim light, so I fumble for my iPhone with my free hand and turn on the flashlight. I aim it at the burner phone's screen.

It takes me a moment to understand what I'm looking at.

Then I drop the burner phone onto the ground and run toward the entrance of Sunrise, my arms churning, my feet barely touching the ground as I fly across the grass.

The photograph was taken as I climbed into the Cadillac in the parking lot by Pizza Piazzo at 9 a.m. today. From the angle, I can tell the photographer was standing up on the retaining wall toward the back of the lot, by the cover of trees and bushes.

Breath tears at my lungs as I force myself to run even faster.

I'd told James I was an hour away, at a hotel in Annapolis. I never asked where he was during our phone call. I'd assumed he was lying low in a cheap hotel.

But he was in the same parking lot, matching my lies with ones of his own. He was watching me during our whole conversation. He even told me so during our phone call.

See you, James had said, moments after he snapped the picture of me.

CHAPTER FORTY-ONE

CATHERINE

My heart is hammering in my chest as I tap my knuckles on the door of George and June's apartment. They live on the first floor, in a two-bedroom corner unit. I can't count the number of times I've knocked on this door before. The Campbells have always opened it with a welcoming smile.

That's not going to happen tonight.

It takes them an unusually long time to answer. Finally, the door eases open and I see June.

Her expression shocks me. I take an involuntary step back.

She doesn't appear the slightest bit angry. Instead, her face is full of barely suppressed mirth.

"Catherine!" She leans her cane against the wall and throws her arms around me, like it has been months since she has seen me instead of just hours.

I'm completely disoriented. My speech is all prepared. I'm ready to grovel, to cry—to do whatever it takes to keep the Campbells from reporting me.

George joins us in the narrow entryway, standing next to the little table with the green bowl holding his car keys.

"Hello, sweetheart." He hugs me, too.

"You—you wanted to see me?" I stutter. Almost against my will, my eyes are drawn toward the Cadillac keys.

"Come into the living room," June urges me. "There's a surprise waiting for you!"

I have no idea what is happening, but I force a smile that feels wooden.

"Close your eyes first," George commands in a playful tone. "No peeking!"

I obey, and feel June's cool, bony hand slip into mine. She leads me several steps forward, her cane tapping with each one. I don't need my vision to tell me where we're going. I've spent so much time here that I know every inch of this place. We're standing in the opening to the living room. When I open my eyes, I'll see their beige sofa and two oversized chairs encircling a shiny wooden coffee table.

The Campbells know I'm planning to move to Baltimore. Could this be a going-away party?

The air seems to thicken with an eerie pressure.

"Open your eyes!" June cries.

At first glance, the scene before me is anticlimactic. The only guest is a man quietly sitting on the couch.

For a split second, I'm even more confused than I was when I arrived. I have no idea who this man is, or why the Campbells summoned me.

Then my eyes drift past his deeply muscled arms and overdeveloped shoulders to his face. He's bald now—he must have shaved his head—and his glasses are gone but I recognize his features.

All the breath rushes out of me, like I've taken a punch to the solar plexus.

James stands and walks to my side as a wave of terror engulfs me. This can't be happening, not here in George and June's cozy apartment, with the two of them thinking this is a joyful moment.

James stretches his arms out and I flinch, but all he does is trap me in a hug. Being pressed to his chest is like being squeezed against a cement block.

"Call me David." His whisper snakes into my ear.

June clasps her hands together.

"Can you believe the coincidence?" she says. "George and I were out to dinner tonight, and your cousin came in a minute later and sat at the next table over and we all started chatting. And it turns out he was in town to surprise you!"

I'm dizzy. I've stepped into a surreal scene, one James is directing. He has dressed the stage and arranged the players. He's pretending to be a man who doesn't exist: my cousin David.

The Campbells believe we're having a family reunion. Which, of course, we are—but I'm the only one here who knows the truth about my relationship to James.

"How long has it been since you last saw each other?" George asks.

James stares directly at me and I feel the blood drain out of my face. His tone is warm and light. "It seems like forever, but at the same time it feels like I just saw you last night, doesn't it, Catherine?"

Every word is a needle driving into my skin. James is enjoying this. He's feasting on my fear.

How did James find the Campbells, or even have any idea of their connection to me?

Then I see the answer as clearly as if I'm reaching into the folder Tin left for me and pulling out the clue James used to track me down: the parking sticker for Sunrise.

The Campbells have one on the back window of their Cadillac.

When I went to Pizza Piazzo last night, James entered the restaurant after me. But that doesn't mean I got there first. He could have been surveying the crowded lot, watching as I stepped out of the Cadillac. He would have recognized me from my Facebook photo.

All he had to do to notice the Sunrise sticker was walk over to check out the car I drove up in.

June seems to be picking up on my distress. Her smile slips away, and a crease forms between her eyebrows.

"Catherine? Is everything okay, honey?"

James walks back over to the couch as the silence stretches out, and

George turns to look at me, too. They can't see James clearly from their vantage point.

Which is why James is able to reach down and pinch a piece of his jeans between his fingers, pulling up the hem, without anyone else noticing.

I've never seen a real gun before.

James's expression carries a menace equal to the gleaming black weapon in his ankle holster.

If I don't play along, will he kill us all?

Tears spill out of my eyes. "I'm just—I'm so happy I can barely talk." I choke out the words.

June smiles. She bought it.

James lets his hem drop. His face morphs back into that of a genial, ordinary man.

"George, let's get some drinks going and give these two a moment alone."

June reaches for her cane, and she and George head to their kitchen. The silence they leave behind feels like a gaping void.

I stare at James, still unable to comprehend how he found me so quickly. Somehow, he eluded the trap my mother set for him and tracked me here.

"Sit with me, Catherine." James taps the cushion next to him.

I'm terrified to obey. I'm even more scared to refuse.

I walk over on shaky legs and sink down next to him, keeping as much distance between us as possible.

James takes my iPhone out of my hand and places it on the coffee table, closer to him than me. Any hope I had of secretly texting my mother evaporates.

"We have a friend in common," James says softly. "I need to know where she is."

"A friend?" I'm playing catch-up—I have no idea how much James knows.

I shift away and James inches closer to me, a smile playing at the corner of his mouth. He's deliberately pinning me against the arm of the couch. "She hired you to find me. Now you're going to find her for me."

James wants to know where my mother is, but he doesn't know she's *my* mother.

A loud pop explodes in the kitchen and I recoil, instinctively curling my head down toward my knees.

James doesn't even flinch. He laughs as I slowly lift my head. It was only a champagne cork coming out. June and George truly believe this is a celebratory night.

"You drove the Cadillac to the restaurant last night," James says, confirming my suspicion that he watched me exit the car and walk into Pizza Piazzo. Then he continues, "But Ava picked up the Cadillac this morning. So you must have seen her and given her the keys. That means you know how to reach her. You probably even know where she lives. I threw out her name to the Campbells, but they didn't react. But when I brought up *your* name, they kept raving about what a wonderful young woman you were."

I shake my head, but James keeps talking.

"We're going to sit here for ten minutes and have a drink, and you're going to act delighted to be reunited with your long-lost cousin. Then we're going to get in your car and you're going to take me to Ava."

James's voice is calm and steady. His jeans and the long-sleeved navy polo shirt that covers his prison tattoo are neat and clean. His breath, so close to my face, smells minty. The juxtaposition is dizzying. He's a monster draped in the façade of a man.

"If you try to signal George and June, or if you run, I will kill them both before you get halfway to the door."

I have no doubt he means it.

George and June come back into the room. George is carrying a tray with four champagne flutes, and June has a silver bowl of mixed nuts in her free hand.

June sets the dish on the coffee table as George passes out the drinks.

My fingers are trembling so badly I nearly slosh the golden liquid over the rim of the glass.

George raises his glass. "To family."

We clink flutes, and I tip my glass and let the champagne touch my lips, but my throat feels too tight for me to swallow any.

"I hope our little prank didn't shock you too much, Catherine," June says. "We gave David a ride here from the Thai restaurant to make sure your Bonneville was still in the lot. Then we signed him in as our guest so you'd truly be surprised!"

"You got me," I say. George has an interest in cars. He knows mine because I once asked him for advice when I thought a mechanic was overcharging us for a new carburetor.

"I'll need to catch a ride back with Catherine to pick up my car," James laughs, and I pretend to laugh along with him as my mind whirls.

I have to do something soon. Once James gets me alone in a vehicle, it'll be too late.

There's an emergency pull cord in the bathroom. If I can get to it, someone from the nursing staff will be at the door quickly.

But then what? James might just decide to shoot his way out of the apartment.

I can't risk antagonizing him until we're away from George and June. "Catherine?"

Everyone is staring at me. I must've missed a question.

"I'm sorry," I say. James reaches over and takes my hand in his while revulsion curls my stomach.

"I was just wondering if you and David are related through your mother's side?" June inquires.

James shakes his head. "I'm on her father's side."

June's brow creases. I frantically try to recall what I've told her of my family history. Probably not much, other than I live with my mother and have no siblings. Certainly I've never mentioned a cousin to her.

If June follows up her line of questioning, she might unravel enough to grow suspicious. She could unearth enough holes in James's story to worry her—maybe even make her concerned enough to call the police after James and I leave.

June's face clears. "How nice." She's too polite to dig.

I try to pull my hand away from James's. He grips it tighter, until my bones grind painfully together.

"June told me how wonderful you were in taking care of her after her stroke and managing her diabetes medication," James says easily. "I always knew you'd be a good nurse, Catherine."

James looks every bit the proud older cousin.

He's a chameleon, adapting to his circumstances. No wonder he fooled the Campbells. He must have been parked somewhere on the road outside of Sunrise, waiting for the distinctive Cadillac to exit. Once he recognized it, he followed George and June to the restaurant and snagged the next table and began a conversation. James already had my true name and knew I had a relationship with the Campbells because of the car. He could have laid down any number of conversational tracks to get them to pinpoint their connection to me.

Then he set the trap I walked into.

"When Catherine was a little girl, I used to babysit her. One Halloween, she even dressed up as a nurse. Remember that plastic stethoscope and blood pressure cuff you had?" James laughs.

I force myself to smile again. I feel as stiff as a marionette, waiting for James to pull my strings and direct my movements.

"How many years older are you, David?" George asks.

"Well let's see, Catherine, you're . . . remind me again?" James prompts. "I know I sent a card for your last birthday, but in my mind you're still a little girl with pigtails."

"Twenty-seven," I lie, hoping to muddy as many details about myself as I can.

The moment I utter that number, though, I wish I could snatch it back.

"And I'm forty-three," James says. "Since I was sixteen when Catherine was born, everyone figured I was old enough to babysit when we got together."

"I must be getting forgetful in my old age," June jokes. "Catherine, I could've sworn you were twenty-four."

James moves his head slowly to stare at me as his grip on my hand intensifies. I nearly whimper from the pain.

He has cataloged the discrepancy. Now I've highlighted the information in his mind as something significant.

It feels as if a noose is tightening around my neck.

My mind whirls as I try to envision what will come next. My mother is outside, around the back of Sunrise. If James takes me out the front, she'll never even notice I've left the building.

"How long have the three of you known each other?" James asks, releasing my aching hand and leaning back and putting an arm around the sofa behind me. I instinctively lean forward, as if we're counter-balancing. I can't stand the thought of him touching me again.

"Six years," June replies. Her brow creases briefly, and I suspect she is remembering that I came to work at Sunrise and met her right after I graduated from high school, which means the age I just pretended to be is incorrect.

Please don't say anything else. I will her the message.

"Anyone need a refill?" George offers.

My drink is still untouched, and James's and George's are half full. If June nods, I can jump up and run to the kitchen under the guise of bringing back the bottle of champagne. Maybe I can find something to defend myself with there.

But before she can answer, James stands up.

"This was lovely, but we shouldn't keep you any longer. I'm sure you both have things to do. And Catherine and I are going to meet up with an old friend."

My time is running out.

"Let me get a picture of you two together before you go," George offers.

"Oh, that isn't—" I begin.

"Trust me, you'll be glad you have it later," June chimes in.

The last thing I want is to stand pressed up next to James.

"Sure, let me just help you clean up first," I say, scooping up my glass and James's before anyone can protest.

I linger in the small kitchen as long as I dare, glancing at the butcher block of knives on the counter. I left my backpack with my mom, and the pockets of my shorts are too shallow to conceal a long knife. My iPhone is still on the coffee table, and there's no landline in the kitchen. And I'm positive the Campbells don't keep a gun in their apartment—plus I don't know how to use one.

I'm hoping by the time I come back out, the photograph will be forgotten. But when James sees me emerge, he says, "Catherine?" and lifts up his right arm, the gesture an invitation. I have no choice. George scoops up my iPhone as I walk to James's side. James wraps his arm around me, drawing me close again as George tells us to smile.

"Let me just make sure this came out okay." George frowns and uses two fingers to enlarge the picture on the screen. "Wow, I didn't see it before, but you can really tell in this photo that you two are related!"

A shrieking noise erupts in my head. Adrenaline floods my body. I'm seized by the desperate urge to run, but I'm trapped as James's steely arm tightens around me.

George tilts his screen to show the picture to June.

"Oh yes, I see it, too. You have the same beautiful blue eyes. They must run in the family."

James turns to me slowly and reaches with his free hand to tip up my chin. I'm completely helpless as his unblinking eyes bore into mine.

I can see the precise moment the realization clicks into his mind.

James knows I'm his daughter.

CHAPTER FORTY-TWO

RUTH

My lungs burn as I tear around the corner of Sunrise. I'm within sight of the entrance now. It's less than fifty yards away.

Then the world tilts beneath my feet. I skid to a stop.

James is stepping out of the front doors, very close to Catherine, his arm pressing against her back.

Time shudders to a halt. I can't breathe.

I watch as they move together down the paved walkway, into the parking lot.

My deepest fear has arisen.

A silent scream fills my throat as my vision tunnels to focus only on my daughter and the man with her.

How did he find us?

James is far too close to Catherine, and he seems to be holding something against her back. I can't tell for sure, but from the angle of his hand I suspect it's a gun.

My legs begin to move, propelling me toward them. I walk slowly, as soundlessly as possible, using cars as shields.

Catherine stumbles, and James grabs her arm with his free hand, roughly jerking her upright. She releases a small, high-pitched sound.

Fury mingles with my terror. I want to claw off James's face. I slide my hand into my purse and pull out my knife and car keys, then ease my purse to the ground and leave it there. I don't want anything to encumber my movements.

I cannot let James get her into a vehicle. If he does, she may be gone forever.

It's too late to call the police. Even if they arrived in time, sirens blaring, Catherine could be caught in the cross fire if James starts shooting.

James has nothing to lose right now. If the thought of him and me being together sustained him during his prison sentence, he knows now his fantasy was no more substantial than a fever dream.

The parking lot is well lit close to the Sunrise entrance, but shadows nibble at its corners. At this time of night, no one else is around.

I ease nearer to James and Catherine, ducking my head low as they move toward the far end of the lot. I watch through the clear window of the Sunrise van as James turns around and checks behind him, then resumes walking.

I look back, too. No one is coming. The three of us are alone in the parking lot, but James hasn't seen me yet.

Strength is pouring into my body in equal proportion to every ounce of love I have for my daughter. My senses are sharpening, and my vision is expanding. I'm aware of the flickering bulb in an overhead light, the sliver of moon in the sky, and the faint chirping of crickets. Through it all, my gaze never leaves Catherine.

Catherine and James are nearing the Bonneville, but James may not know it's our car.

If I could slip inside and drive toward them, and Catherine manages to dive out of the way, I could run James over.

I can't risk it, though. A bullet is faster than a speeding car.

They've stopped moving.

I draw as close as I dare, aided by darkness, until I can hear their voices. I'm concealed behind a Buick now, less than ten feet away.

"Call her," James orders.

"What do you want me to say?" Catherine asks.

"Whatever it takes to get her here."

A plan forms in my mind: My phone is inside my purse, which I dropped. I can't remember if it's on vibrate or not. If Catherine calls and it rings, will the sound carry and distract James long enough to give me a chance?

I unsheathe my knife as Catherine takes her phone out of her pocket and dials a number. I crouch lower, like a sprinter getting into a starting line stance. I tighten my grip on the handle of my knife.

But there's no ringing sound from across the parking lot. My phone must be on vibrate or the noise is too muffled from within my purse for us to hear it.

I desperately want to answer Catherine's call, but I'd have to move too quickly to get there in time, which would almost certainly attract James's attention.

Then James says something that makes my stomach plummet.

"Mom isn't picking up?"

He knows Catherine is my daughter. She must be far more valuable to him as a pawn now.

What else has he discovered?

I can't risk what might happen to Catherine next.

I hold my knife down, pressing it against the outside of my right thigh in an effort to conceal it, as I step out of the shadows.

"James, I'm here."

James half turns to look at me but doesn't otherwise react. If I've shocked him by suddenly appearing, he doesn't reveal it.

Catherine is staring at me with a blank expression. I can feel the waves of fear rolling off her.

Anger bubbles deep inside me. It's the primal rage of a woman whose child is being threatened.

"Let her go, James."

"Let her go?" he echoes. His voice is mocking. "When we're finally having a family reunion?"

Shock whips through me. He knows everything.

"I waited for you, Ava."

I know he means not just on that long-ago night when he was arrested, but for the past twenty-four years.

"She has nothing to do with this," I tell James. "She had no idea you were her father until last night."

James blinks, the only sign I've caught him off guard. "Is that true?"

Catherine looks toward me, unsure of what to do.

"Tell him the truth, Catherine," I urge.

"She told me that my—that her boyfriend got her pregnant and denied I was his," Catherine says.

"Stop looking at her!" James commands Catherine. He moves slightly away so he can face her. Now I can clearly see the gleaming black gun he has trained on her.

Catherine obeys, shifting her eyes to James.

"Why did you reach out to me on Facebook?" he asks.

The truth, Catherine, I think. For her to have a chance of surviving this, James must blame me and me alone. I built up lies like a wall of bricks to protect her from James, but the only way to keep her safe now is to smash them down.

"I was trying to learn more about my mom. . . . She never talked about her past. I didn't know where she grew up or what her real name was or—or anything, really."

"So she kept us apart all these years. Did you ever miss having a father?"

Catherine is torn—I can see it. She doesn't want to spark James's anger toward me.

"Answer my question." James's voice is dangerously calm.

"Sometimes."

James stares at Catherine intently. Then he slowly begins to lower his gun.

He must sense she isn't lying.

"Everything was my fault, James," I whisper. "Please let her go."

I take a slow step toward them. James twists his head to look at me and his eyes widen.

He sees the knife I'm pressing to the side of my leg.

His reaction unnerves me. He throws back his head and laughs.

"I'll give you credit, Ava. You're tough as hell. You always looked as sweet as candy, but I saw what you were hiding inside. It's why we belong together."

James does something to his gun—I can't tell if he's taking the safety off or putting it on—then flicks his wrist sideways like he's skipping a stone across the water. His weapon goes skittering beneath a car.

I don't relax for a millisecond.

James is most dangerous when he seems peaceful. Violence centers him in a way nothing else can.

He lifts his arms and spreads them wide, like he's surrendering.

"Go ahead, Ava. Come at me. Catherine must think I'm the bad guy. Let our daughter see you're a killer."

He's goading me.

"How will you feel after you stab me, Ava? Will you regret it once you see my blood? Will you change your mind and try to call an ambulance to save me?"

I know exactly what he's doing. He's trying to push inside my head to throw me off-balance.

I take a step closer, the knife steady in my hand.

Catherine is frozen in place.

Run! I will the command to her with every fiber of my being.

She begins to edge away.

"Catherine?"

She halts at the sound of James's voice. "Your mother is right about one thing. None of this was your fault. You *did* have a father, one who loved your mother very much. He would have loved you, too."

James is speaking in the past tense, as if he is already dead. I lift the knife an inch higher.

"To tell you the truth, I kind of like the thought of having a part of me continue on."

Then James does something that curdles my blood. He walks over and puts his hands on either side of Catherine's face and tenderly touches his lips to her forehead, like he is a loving father kissing his daughter good night.

We both watch as Catherine turns and walks toward the entrance of Sunrise. When she's almost to the front door—to safety—I lunge at James, my knife slashing, hoping to seize the element of surprise.

He rears back and lifts his forearms to protect his throat, his reflexes lightning quick. My blade cuts through his skin, but not deeply enough to do any real damage.

James skips backward as I jab at him with the knife, like this is some lighthearted game.

Blood drips from his arm. He's smiling.

"This is who you are, Ava. This is who you've always been."

I shake off his words. I cannot let him overpower me psychologically.

I lunge at him again. But this time, my knife meets air as he feints to the side and grabs my wrist with one hand. His grip is so powerful that my hand feels immobilized. I hold on to the knife as long as I can, but when he shakes my wrist, it slips from my fingers and clatters to the pavement.

James kicks it away as he draws me to him, his wounded arm snaking around me. He crushes me against his body.

Then he leans down and kisses me, his mouth greedily covering mine.

I bite down hard on his lip. He pulls back his head and smiles.

"That's my girl," he whispers.

Then he headbutts me.

My legs give way and I fall back on the pavement, my ears ringing. Pain crescendos through my body. James straddles me, his knees on either side of my rib cage, his hands tightening around my throat.

"Look up at the stars, Ava. They're still our stars."

I twist and thrash, trying to knock him off, but I'm no match for his weight and power. My lungs are burning.

I see a blue vein bulging in James's neck as he increases the pressure. White bursts of light explode in front of my eyes.

I stretch out my arms and feel around on the cold asphalt, trying in vain to touch the gun or knife. Then I arch up desperately, putting all of my strength into my back, but I can't even shift James off-balance.

My lungs scream for air. Strength ebbs out of my body. I have almost no fight left.

James is staring deeply into my eyes. He must want to watch the life drain out of them.

But I no longer see James.

Instead, I see Catherine as a baby, sleeping in my arms, her dark lashes resting on her cheeks, her pudgy hand wrapped trustingly around my pinky. I see her as a five-year-old, sitting on a stool and coloring while I close up at work. I see her as a ten-year-old, running through a grassy park, the red-and-white-striped kite I bought at the Dollar Store sailing through the air behind her.

Then I see Catherine rise up like a dark shadow behind James.

She's clenching a thick white pen in her fist. She jabs it into the vein in James's neck, then silently dances backward and disappears from view.

James jerks his head to the side in an annoyed gesture, as if he has been bitten by a mosquito.

He reaches up with one hand to touch the spot but keeps his other hand pressing down on my neck.

I frantically suck in a sip of air.

James shakes his head and wraps his hand back around my neck. But now the pressure he exerts is weaker.

Catherine appears out of the darkness a second later, jabbing at James's neck again. This time he swings an arm back as she makes contact, catching her in the side, sending her flying onto the hard pavement.

James shakes his head again.

"What did you do to me?" he whispers.

He winces, then slowly blinks a few times.

I claw at James's arm, digging my nails into the cut I inflicted with the knife.

His upper half slumps to the side, as if he's lost control over his limbs. His hands fall away from my neck.

I desperately suck in oxygen, hyperventilating. The blackness slowly recedes from the corners of my vision.

I'm too weak to move yet, and James seems to be, too. He is still sitting on me, but it's like he's made out of putty.

Catherine rises to her feet, rubbing her elbow, and walks over to him.

As if he is no more substantial than a mannequin, she lifts her foot and pushes him over.

He topples onto the pavement beside me, his eyes open. He's alive but seems unable to control his body. He reaches out toward me, then his arm flops down.

Catherine stretches out a hand and I take it. She helps me sit up.

I immediately retch and she rubs my back. "Easy," she says.

"What did you do to him?" I croak, echoing James's question. My throat is so raw it hurts to talk.

"Insulin. I injected almost two months' worth of doses directly into his bloodstream."

A thin line of drool oozes out of James's mouth. His eyes are half-closed, but they are still watching us. His mouth twitches, as if he is trying to speak.

"What's going to happen to him?" I ask.

"If he doesn't get help now, he'll die."

I stare at Catherine. She looks steadily back at me.

Neither of us moves.

CHAPTER FORTY-THREE

CATHERINE

No one was with me in the Campbells' kitchen when I opened their refrigerator and tucked June's insulin pens into the waistband of my shorts. Most people know insulin tilts the scales of life and death for diabetics. Fewer are aware of how lethal it can be when injected into a nondiabetic.

When people have low body fat and high muscle mass, like James, their veins tend to be more prominent. Even before we left the Campbells' apartment, I'd identified the one that would be my target.

As I help my mother into the passenger's seat of the Bonneville, I assess her vitals. Her heart rate has slowed, but her skin still feels cool and clammy. The whites of her eyes are stained red with burst blood vessels, and her forehead is swelling up.

"I'll be right back," I tell her as I close the car door.

I know it may be disconcerting for her to be alone with James's body, which we lifted into our trunk. My job means I often brush up against death, but she has never witnessed it up close.

But I need to retrieve my mother's purse, her knife, and James's gun before we drive off.

After I've collected the items and returned to the car, I slip into the driver's seat. The only sign James was in the parking lot is the small, reddish-brown stain from the blood that spilled from his arm. As it dries and its hemoglobin breaks down, it'll darken and eventually disappear.

I start the engine and ease our car out of the lot.

My mother seems to be in shock, but I'm functioning well.

The only sound in our car is the low growl of our wheels moving across the pavement. My mind is spinning, too, as I probe every corner and seam of my plans, making sure they are airtight.

I already took James's phone out of his pocket and made sure he wasn't carrying anything else that could identify him. The only thing I discovered was a single car key. It must belong to the vehicle he used to get to the Thai restaurant before he caught a ride with the Campbells.

When I'm a few miles down the road and no other headlights are in sight, I wipe down the key on the hem of my T-shirt and toss it out my open window, aiming toward the grass on the side of the road. A mile or so later, I wipe down James's phone. I press the brakes of the Bonneville before I hurl James's phone onto the road ahead of us. Then I drive over it, pulverizing it beneath a tire.

The crunch it makes is satisfying.

Disposing of James's body will be more challenging.

Insulin overdoses are very difficult to trace forensically. Even autopsies can't pinpoint them most of the time, which means it would be hard to ever prove James was murdered.

George and June are the only witnesses who saw the two of us together, other than Paul the guard, who waved when James and I walked out. But James ducked his head and pretended to scratch an itch by his eyebrow, so I doubt Paul even glimpsed his face.

As for George and June, they would never in a million years believe an escaped convict sat in their apartment drinking champagne. Even if they saw a TV clip with James's photo, their conscious minds would override that instinctual snap of recognition, reminding them James is my cousin. Their polite, socially groomed brains would create acceptable explanations. Lots of people look alike, they'd tell each other.

They'd decide they could be misremembering James's features—what with the champagne and my surprise, there was a lot going on during our brief visit.

Our minds do this all the time. They talk us out of things we don't want to know.

Still, it would be better if James's body was never found.

I've been thinking through the problem, and I believe burying it in a remote location is the solution. It will be safe to keep James's body in our trunk tonight.

Before I know it, we're turning in to the parking lot of our apartment building.

I've been so lost in thought I don't even remember driving here.

I cut the engine.

There's one more thing I need to do before we go inside. I unbuckle my seat belt and twist to face my mother. I think of how furious and bewildered and scared I've been and say, "Everything you did—I still don't understand it."

Then I release those emotions and allow myself to remember the bone-deep fear and rage I felt when I saw James atop her limp body and thought I might have gotten there too late. "But I will always love you."

She exhales and closes her eyes.

Then she opens them and tells me she loves me, too.

CHAPTER FORTY-FOUR

RUTH

I lie in bed, feeling strangely immobile.

Catherine has diagnosed me with a mild concussion, which may account for the condition I'm in. I'm not experiencing any pain, though. I don't feel much of anything. I'm suspended in an eerie, detached state.

James is dead.

Catherine killed him.

These two staggering facts overload my brain. It feels like every time I try to comprehend them, my mind short-circuits and brings me back to the safety of numbness.

Catherine is behaving the opposite way. She seems acutely focused and energetic. She has even taken over the planning necessary to keep us safe, seamlessly stepping into the role I held for so long.

She knocks on my door, then opens it without waiting for me to invite her in.

"I found a good place to bury him." She walks over to my bed and shows me a map on her phone. "We'll need to drive to West Virginia tomorrow. We should leave as early as we can. It'll take us all day."

She has everything planned, down to the shovels we'll buy at Home Depot with cash, the old sheet we'll need to drag James through the woods, and the gloves we'll wear to prevent any transfer of DNA.

She sets two white pills down on my nightstand next to a glass of water. "Here's some more Tylenol. You can take it now. Do you need another ice pack?"

"I'm fine. I'm going to try to sleep."

"I'll wake you up in a few hours. Standard concussion protocol."

I'm glad she warned me. I would not want to wake up abruptly and see a figure looming over me in the night.

Catherine turns out the light, plunging my room into darkness, then closes my door.

I don't believe in ghosts.

But as I lie there, my body feeling boneless and weak, I swear I sense a vapory presence.

It's my imagination, I tell myself.

Or maybe it's my conscience.

How will you feel after you stab me, Ava? Will you regret it once you see my blood? Will you try to call an ambulance to save me? James had asked as I'd pointed my knife, preparing to stab him.

He was referring to Coach, of course. James knew I wanted to call 911 that night while Coach was still clinging to life.

No, I answer James in my mind now. *I had a chance to save you, but I wanted you to die.*

They are both gone now, Coach and James.

It is finally over.

I sleep for what feels like only a few minutes, but when I check the time on my phone I see I've been out for a couple of hours. My headache has abated—the Tylenol is doing its job.

I lie in bed for a while as my mind begins to drift, dipping in and out of memories, skimming as lightly over the years as fingers moving up and down the keys of a piano.

I remember James handing me a glass of water with a slice of lemon in it that first night at the restaurant. I see myself holding Timmy on our front steps, promising to take him to Italy and eat gelato every day. I see Coach staring at my body, his eyes roaming over it like he owned me.

Then one memory rises above the rest and takes hold.

I find myself homing in on it as the sights and smells and feelings drift back to me.

My purse is on the floor beside my bed, so all I have to do is turn on my nightstand lamp and lean over to extract my notebook and a pen. Then I begin reliving that long-ago day.

I'd been missing for several months when I took a Greyhound bus to Baltimore.

I crossed back into Maryland for a single morning because I had two letters to mail, and I didn't want the postmarks to reveal I was living in Pittsburgh.

I felt nervous about traveling so close to my hometown, but I desperately needed to convey those two messages.

Plus, my pregnancy was aiding my disguise. Now that I was entering my second trimester, I'd put on a few pounds and my face looked a little rounder. My shorter hair helped with the illusion that I was older, too, but I suspect the real reason people thought I was an adult was because I was so different on the inside. I felt like I'd aged more in three months than I had in the previous three years.

On that crisp late November day, I splurged on a locker at the bus station to store my duffle bag. I brought nothing with me other than the letters I'd handwritten one night in my Target, using sheets of blank white paper from the office supply section and a blue Bic pen I'd borrowed from a cup by the cash register.

I'd bought two first-class stamps at the post office and sealed each letter in an ordinary white envelope. I used my left hand to print the addresses so the handwriting wouldn't resemble my own.

I stared out the window as we rolled past the border of Pennsylvania and the sun crept higher in the bluebird sky. My hand rested on my stomach—on you—for most of the ride. Whenever I felt fear or despair, your presence always steadied me.

When I arrived in Baltimore, I stepped off the bus and walked down the sidewalk, aimlessly choosing a direction. I'd only gone a few blocks when I spotted a mailbox.

I slipped the first letter into the wide mouth of the mailbox and watched as it was swallowed up. My father was smart and detail oriented. He would notice the date on the postmark matched my birthday.

My note to my dad contained two words, a kind of code to let him know I was alive: Te Quiero.

My second letter wasn't to Timmy, or to anyone else I knew well.

I wrote it to Rosie from my Poms squad.

I'd only had one real conversation with Rosie. It occurred on the afternoon I came out of Coach's office and found her waiting by my car with my backpack and water bottle.

She frowned as she peered at my face and asked if I was okay.

Sure, I replied. I may have even smiled.

But Rosie kept staring at me.

She started to say, It's just that you look like . . .

But her words trailed off, and I took my backpack from her and tossed it into my car.

I stretched out my hand for my water bottle, but she didn't let go of it immediately. We stood there, our hands linked by the plastic bottle, her gaze searching my face.

I desperately wanted to get away. I was on the verge of splintering into a million pieces, and her kindness felt like a mallet bearing down on me.

Something was changing in Rosie's expression as she stared at me, like she was working out a problem, teetering on the cusp of the solution. I kept smiling, even though my lips felt strange and rubbery.

I finally asked her what I looked like because I couldn't stand the overpowering silence.

Rosie let go of my water bottle. Her hand flew up to cover her mouth.

She told me I looked like her sister did when Coach came to their house to visit.

My hands began to shake. Violent trembling spread through my body until I felt as if it would tear me apart, as if shards of me would go flying in a thousand different directions.

Rosie's sister Marie was a year ahead of me in school, but she'd dropped out at the beginning of her junior year after she almost killed herself by overdosing on pain medicine.

Everyone at school knew Marie's story. She'd been a good student and guitar player, but all at once she seemed to self-implode. She started cutting herself—people could see the wounds on her arms—and she quit playing guitar and began using drugs.

My voice sounded alien, even to my own ears, when I asked why Coach came to the house to visit Marie.

Rosie told me it had been happening even before Marie quit school. Coach took a special interest in Marie because she was so musical. Their mom was grateful and said he was like a father figure.

A sob tore itself free from my throat. Tears began to stream down my face.

I cried out to Rosie that she couldn't ever let Coach in their house again.

Then I climbed into my car, slammed the door, and sped away. In my rearview mirror I could see Rosie still standing there.

Of course I wasn't the only girl Coach abused.

There's always more than one.

My note to Rosie was brief, too: Timmy Morales's mother hurts him. Help him.

That long-ago day when I saw Rosie on the street in Lancaster, she told me she'd heeded my plea.

She'd helped protect my brother.

When I think about the brutal way Coach died, I remind myself of this: He will never again touch Marie, or any other girl.

It helps.

CHAPTER FORTY-FIVE

CATHERINE

One week later

I pull the final drinking glass out of the packing box labeled "kitchen" and unwrap the sheet of newspaper cushioning it. I set the glass on the lowest shelf of the cabinet next to the refrigerator and close the cabinet door.

That's my last box. I break it down, then lean the flattened cardboard against a wall with the half-dozen others to bring down for recycling.

I blow a strand of hair that has escaped from my ponytail off my face, then put my hands on my hips as I glance around my studio apartment.

It's a quirky, pleasing blend of old and new. Tall, double-hung windows welcome the sunshine and late-afternoon breeze, and a tiny balcony has just enough room for the wrought-iron table and two café chairs I found at a secondhand store. In the wintertime, my place will be snug and cozy with its small gas fireplace and steel-gray, elegant radiators.

I used my last paycheck from Sunrise to splurge on a deep, impossibly soft, dusky rose love seat that I put in front of the fireplace. I also assembled a tall Ikea bookshelf and moved in my bed and dresser from my mother's apartment.

There's plenty of time to add more photos and knickknacks and books to my new shelf, and to pick up a funky lamp or two at a flea market.

There's room for me to grow in this apartment.

I open the double French doors to my balcony and step out.

It's a balmy, beautiful Saturday afternoon. Below me, people mill about on the cobblestone street, and happy notes of reggae music play in the distance.

My new place is in Fells Point, only a block from the water. Cafés, funky little stores, and bars are all within a stone's throw. There's a raw vegan restaurant around the corner and a coffee shop called The Daily Grind I know I'll be frequenting often. My apartment isn't far from Hopkins, where I start work on Monday at 8 a.m. sharp.

Tonight, I decide, I'll venture out and explore my new city. Maybe I'll head to the Inner Harbor and find a restaurant with outdoor seating. There's also Little Italy if I decide I'm in the mood for a bowl of homemade pasta. Or I could just find a neighborhood place, somewhere with beer on tap and crispy French fries and a good veggie burger.

I guess I'll see where my feet take me.

As I pass my bookshelf on the way to my closet, I pause. The old picture of my mother as a teenager and me as a baby, the one she framed more than twenty years ago and gave to me, is off-center. I move it an inch to the left, balancing it, then step back.

Better, I think.

I love my mother, but I'm still angry with her. It isn't the kind of quick, hot anger that boils away with a speed equal to its formation, either. I understand my mom was faced with impossible situations and choices. I also believe she could have done things differently.

But now I've broken free from the old secrets that ruled both of our lives. I intend to call my mom once or twice a week, but I'm going to wait awhile before I invite her up for lunch or dinner. I need distance from her.

It's time for me to get acquainted with myself as an individual. To finally chart my own course.

I walk to my closet and open the door and pick out a black sundress that leaves my shoulders bare. I pull off my sweaty T-shirt and unbutton and step out of my cutoffs, deciding to take a cool shower before I head out for the evening.

I'm twenty-four years old, and my life is opening up before me.

Maybe I shouldn't feel so carefree right now. Four days ago, I took a man's life—and not just any man. I killed my biological father. My mother and I buried the body in a remote wooded area in West Virginia. My mother was still pretty weak, so I dragged it away from where we parked off the highway using an old sheet as a sled, taking frequent stops to catch my breath, while she followed.

My mother got physically sick when I dumped the first shovelful of dirt onto James, even though I'd covered his face with the sheet. I guess she'd hit her emotional limit. Burying him was too much.

I told her to go back to the car. I could handle it alone.

Afterward, she was quiet the whole drive home.

Those final few days in our apartment, I kept catching her staring at me, as if she was trying to gauge how I was affected. She asked me lots of questions. She wanted to know if I was experiencing any PTSD. If I wanted to find a therapist. If I had nightmares.

It's almost like she's worried because I'm not more upset—like she wants me to cry or stop eating or wake up in the middle of the night screaming. Maybe she thinks I'm suppressing my emotions.

But I'm not upset or traumatized.

Quite the opposite. There's a new sensation thrumming through me, a high-pitched kind of thrill that makes me want to leap out of bed every morning. Maybe every young woman who moves to a new city and embarks on a fresh, wide-open life feels this way.

My conscience is sparkling clean. James would have killed my mother if I hadn't stopped him.

I did what needed to be done.

I sleep well at night.

CHAPTER FORTY-SIX

RUTH

The field where I once flew a kite with my dad and Timmy is nearly empty at dusk. But I swear I can almost hear the jingle of that ice-cream truck from long ago.

In the distance, I see a man walking his dog and a group of women jogging on the paved trail that cuts through the wooded area bordering the park.

I stand alone beneath the branches of a giant oak tree in the center of an expanse of emerald grass. It's the same tree where Timmy got his kite caught long ago.

I look up high into the branches, searching for an old scrap of red-and-white-striped fabric. But even though I crane my neck until its muscles grow tired, all I discover is a chattering squirrel.

When I lower my head, I see the man with the dog walking toward me. The animal, a cute mixed breed with black spots on its white fur, is pulling at the leash, like he knows the man's destination and wants to hurry him along.

They draw closer. I straighten up and remove my sunglasses with a hand that has begun to shake.

My heart is pounding so hard it's almost painful.

Just say hi. That's what Catherine suggested when I told her I was going to have this meeting. I thought about not mentioning it because she moved a couple of days ago and I didn't want to layer one more thing on top of all she has dealt with recently, but I don't want to keep amassing secrets between us.

The man is very close now. I can see the sprinkling of freckles across the bridge of his nose.

He's staring at me intently, his eyes searching my face.

Then his face breaks into a smile.

I have always loved Timmy's smile.

"Hi," I say.

He stops a couple of feet away. "It's really you."

His smile slips away. He keeps staring at me, and now I can't tell if he's angry or numb or if he has truly put me in the past.

My throat thickens as unshed tears prick my eyes. I have so much to say to my little brother, but this is the most important part.

"I am so sorry I left you."

He looks down and rubs the toe of his sneaker in the dirt, back and forth. "I cried every night at first. Then Dad told me you were okay. Where did you go?"

"Not far from here. I got a job and then I rented a room and eventually I got an apartment . . . things worked out, in a way."

He nods slowly. "Things worked out for me, too. I'm married now. Her name is Jeanine. We have two kids."

He touches the gold wedding band on his left hand, then he stretches out his hand to me. "Want to go for a walk?"

His hand used to be so soft and little when I held it as we crossed the street. Now my fingers are swallowed up in his strong grasp, and I can feel the calluses on his palm.

My heart is full and aching, at the same time.

We walk in silence across the grass. Sometimes there is so much to say that words aren't enough.

The evening air is soft and mild, and in the distance a bird is singing. I know this moment may be all I'll ever have with my brother, and I want it to last forever. But all too soon Timmy says, "I'm parked over this way," and points toward a silver Honda minivan that's in the back of the deserted lot.

Maybe this is overwhelming for Timmy, I think. After all, I was able to glimpse bits of his life throughout the years, but he has no idea what became of me or who I became. He doesn't even know I have a daughter.

We pause at the edge of the parking lot. Even though I have on a hat and it's growing dark, I'd rather stay away from the lights ringing the space.

Timmy lets go of my hand and turns to face me.

"If you'd ever like to get together again . . . or just talk on the phone . . . I mean, I don't want to pressure you or anything," I say haltingly.

My heart sinks as Timmy's forehead creases into a frown.

"I know it's a lot, me showing up after all this time . . . ," I continue. "I don't want to intrude . . . That's why I reached out to you first, instead of Dad, because I thought maybe you could ask him if he wants me to call. But I don't want either of you to feel like you owe me anything. And we can't tell anyone about this . . . I have to stay hidden because the police will still want to question me if they find me, so I get it. I mean, you have a family now, so you probably don't want to risk anything. . . ."

I can't stop babbling until Timmy brings me up short by saying, "Ava."

The words dry up in my mouth.

Timmy is shaking his head and my body clenches as I await his verdict.

"My son's middle name is Mateo."

I smile because that was the middle name I would have picked if Catherine had been a boy.

"Good choice."

"And my daughter's middle name is Ava."

A sob wrenches free from my throat. Tears pour down my cheeks as Timmy wraps his arms around me, hugging me so tightly it's hard to breathe. I'm hugging him back just as hard, feeling my brother's body shake as he cries.

"I'm sorry, Timmy. . . . I'm so sorry . . ."

Then I hear a car door slam shut. My head jerks up and I look toward the parking lot.

A man has exited from the passenger side of Timmy's minivan and is running toward us.

I am rooted to the ground as I stare at him in disbelief.

His once-broad shoulders are slightly slumped with age, and white is woven through his black hair. But when my father throws his arms around me, I can still smell his Old Spice.

"I told Dad I was coming to see you and I couldn't keep him away," Timmy says.

Time collapses. I'm a girl again, back with my family.

My father is whispering my name over and over, like he can't believe it's me.

"I love you," I tell them, and they repeat those sweetest of words back to me.

My father finally leans back and studies me, like he's engraving a picture of my face in his mind. I do the same.

New lines crease my dad's skin, and he has a little scar on his chin now, but he is gazing at me as if I am still the daughter he loves. As if he never stopped loving me.

He reaches out and gently wipes the tears from my cheeks.

"I sent you prayers every single night," my dad tells me.

I think of "Wild World" playing on the trucker's radio, and the night cleaner at Target who concealed us, and the man who bought Catherine and me dinner on that cold December evening when we were so hungry.

I whisper, "They worked."

EPILOGUE

RUTH

I will always be grateful to Rosie for protecting Timmy.

He told me that after I disappeared, she began to pick him up from school, taking him for ice cream or to the library to study until my father got home from work.

Sometimes I wonder if Rosie did it because she knew I'd helped protect her sister Marie.

For nearly twenty-five years, I've tried to avoid remembering what happened after James slammed the bat into Coach's stomach.

But the memory has pushed back, asserting itself at odd times, like when I've skimmed past a TV channel airing a baseball game, or spotted a man wearing a Bruce Springsteen T-shirt.

Now that James is dead, I can no longer repress the truth about that long-ago night.

After Coach collapsed on the floor of his office, moaning but still conscious, James lifted the Louisville Slugger a second time, preparing to strike again.

But he didn't.

Instead, James lowered the bat and held it out to me.

It was an offering. I had a choice.

Coach was still wearing the same clothes he'd had on when he'd molested me. I was standing in the same spot, too.

But this time he was at my mercy, not the other way around.

I didn't hesitate. I took the bat and raised it over my head.

I brought it down on Coach again and again as a roaring noise filled my ears. I know now it was the sound of my rage.

When I was spent and sweaty, I handed the bat back to James. He took it from me and set it down on the floor.

Coach was no longer moving.

Every word I wrote in my journal was truthful. But I didn't write the entire truth.

When I described the night of Coach's attack in my green spiral notebook, I skipped over the details of my involvement. I picked up the story by detailing what happened after James took the bat from me, after I'd released my blind rage and come back into my own body.

> *Of all the images of the night of the attack that I keep replaying, the one I go back to the most often is this: James setting the bat down on the floor, then looking at me as he grabbed Coach's limp arms and dragged Coach deeper into his office, leaving a trail of smeared blood.*
>
> *James's eyes were as gentle and untroubled as if we'd just finished making love.*

When James saw what I was capable of, he knew he'd found his soul mate.

After my rage passed, I regretted what I'd done. I wanted to call for an ambulance.

But in the moment, when I was hearing the thud of the bat slam onto Coach's body?

It felt right. More than that, it felt good.

James never told a soul that I was the real murderer of Coach Franklin—except for Catherine.

Let our daughter see you're a killer, James taunted me while I pointed my knife at him in the parking lot of Sunrise.

Catherine missed the clue.

And now the truth will go with me to my grave. I will never share it with a soul.

Not even Catherine.

Especially not Catherine.

I think about this on my drive from Harrisburg to Baltimore.

Even with rush-hour traffic, I make it to Catherine's new city in just under ninety minutes.

I find a spot near the entrance of Hopkins on the corner of Broadway and Fayette—but not too close—and cut the Bonneville's engine. It sputters a few times, as if in protest, before settling into silence.

Catherine should be arriving soon. When she telephoned last night, she told me she planned to walk through the main entrance as a way of marking the occasion.

"My energy level has been through the roof lately," she'd said, laughing.

It was the sound of her bubbling laughter that made me grow very still, my sponge halting midway through its arc across the kitchen counter.

Should Catherine be this joyous, this lit up, given what happened less than a week ago?

Now that our apartment is so empty at night, I can hear all my old fears crashing around within its walls. That's why I've been over-thinking things, I tell myself as I unclip my seat belt and step out.

I stare up at the redbrick buildings that compose different parts of the hospital. A young nurse walks out of one of the doors, pushing the wheelchair of a boy whose leg is in a cast.

A question I've asked Catherine pops into my mind again. I've never received a satisfying answer from her. She may not even have one.

Why did she choose geriatrics as her specialty? Unlike obstetrics, or pediatrics, or any number of other departments, she was drawn to a field with an intimate proximity to decay, to death. Because Catherine worked in a nursing home when she graduated from high school, she has watched many people take their final breaths. This was fully her choice, an unusual one for a girl of eighteen.

Evidence of her compassionate heart, or something else?

Last week, while I was helping Catherine pack up the things she needed for her new apartment, scenes from her childhood played in my mind, like a reel from a home movie.

But not the bittersweet, tender scenes mothers usually reach for when their child leaves the nest.

I didn't envision Catherine's first day of kindergarten, or the stuffed dog named Brownie she carried around for two solid years.

I thought about the fire she created that left me with a permanent scar and could have burned down our kitchen.

And her bed-wetting that persisted far beyond the appropriate developmental age.

And the mangled body of the squirrel that so intrigued her. The dead mouse under her bed. The cat that went missing from the home of our next-door neighbor with the wind chimes.

James once asked me this question about the little cat named Smokey, but now I imagine Catherine's voice chiming in, entwining with his: *Do you think I'd hurt an animal?*

I didn't want to know the answer. It's why I never let her have a pet, not even a gerbil or fish, no matter how much she begged.

At night, when sleep refuses to descend and grant me peace, I tell myself these data points don't prove anything. They are individual stars, not a constellation.

Still, what I would give to be able to peek inside my daughter's mind.

I don't kid myself that I know Catherine through and through. I hid big pieces of myself from her. She may not even know yet that certain parts of herself exist.

During my good moments, I almost convince myself I have nothing to worry about. I tell myself my tendency to catastrophize is sharpening my fears to an unrealistic point. Catherine's life will unspool gently—she'll marry and have a few kids. I'll go to every school recital and birthday party.

I try to picture this brightly colored reel of the future, to will it into existence: Catherine and her husband heading out to celebrate an anniversary while I wave at them from the couch, a baby in my arms. *Go have fun,* I'll say. *I've got this.*

Life will be easier from here on out. The worst is behind me.

There's just one thing I can't get out of my mind.

When Catherine looked at me after she plunged the lethal doses of insulin into James's neck, I didn't see fear or remorse or doubt in her denim-blue eyes.

They were utterly serene. They were her father's eyes.

The old adage rattles around in my brain, taunting me: *Apple from the tree.*

This weekend, I visited the McCormick Riverfront Library again. I'm accustomed to planning for every eventuality, to calculating all possible risks. It's how I kept us safe for so many years.

But now my research takes me in a different direction. I try to distill the information I have into a prediction of what it may mean when a daughter is born to two murderers. There seems to be a genetic component to violence, but whose genes will prove dominant in Catherine?

I tell myself Catherine doesn't have an addiction to violence, like her father.

She's like me. Catherine killed in the heat of the moment, and only because it felt justifiable.

Now I drop my car keys into the side pocket of my purse and suddenly I see Catherine on the night she killed James, wiping down the car key from James's pocket before tossing it away, as if guided by something stronger than instinct.

Never leave fingerprints, James whispers in my mind.

I've learned enough about murderers to understand that for some, the taste of their first kill whets an appetite. It's as if a switch has been flicked.

For some, it ignites possibilities.

A breeze ruffles the air, which is already warm at 7:45 a.m. on this June morning. Catherine should come into view any second now. She'll want to be here early for her first day.

The mournful wail of an ambulance splits through the air as the vehicle turns the corner, approaching the ER entrance. And in its wake comes Catherine, striding down the sidewalk, excitement blooming on her lovely face.

My hand rises to cover my heart.

A moment later, she disappears through the hospital doors.

She never even noticed me, which was my intention. I'm used to traveling through life as a ghost. I'm very good at disappearing. Women do it all the time.

It's much harder to make a man vanish. But we did it, my daughter and me.

I walk back to the Bonneville and climb into the driver's seat. I have the day off, which means I can spend time wandering around Catherine's new neighborhood, getting to know it. I like the idea of being able to picture her as she moves about her days. It will help me put new safeguards into place.

For the rest of my life I will continue to watch over Catherine, in ways she knows about and in ways she does not.

Because there is one thing we women do even better than disappearing: We protect our children.

Even if that means protecting my daughter from the darkness inside her.

I reach into my purse for my keys, but my fingers brush the metal spiral of my old notebook.

I pull it out. I need to add one final line.

I would do anything to keep you safe, Catherine, anything at all.

ACKNOWLEDGMENTS

The first person I need to thank is the woman who loosely inspired elements of my book: my grandmother, Lucille Pekkanen. She dropped out of high school to help support her family and worked as a waitress all her life, like Ruth Sterling. She was a fiercely protective mother, too—but I should make clear that's where the similarities end.

Jennifer Enderlin, my extraordinary editor, continues to awe and inspire me with her brilliance, creativity, enthusiasm, and unfailing editorial instincts. My deep gratitude to the magnificent team alongside Jen at St. Martin's Press, including super publicist Katie Bassel; marketing gurus Erica Martirano and Brant Janeway; and the spectacular audio team of Guy Oldfield, Mary Beth Roche, Emily Dyer, and Drew Kilman. I am very thankful to Robert Allen, Jeff Dodes, Marta Fleming, Olga Grlic, Tracey Guest, Sara LaCotti, Christina Lopez, Kim Ludlam, Kerry Nordling, Erik Platt, Gisela Ramos, Sally Richardson, Lisa Senz, Michael Storrings, Tom Thompson, and Dori Weintraub.

My agent, Margaret Riley King, had unwavering faith I could write this book. I am so lucky to work with her and the rest of the fantastic team at William Morris Endeavor: film agents Hilary Zaitz Michael and Sylvie Rabineau; foreign rights director Tracy Fisher; and the indefatigable Sophie Cudd, Celia Rogers, Kate Whitman, and Victoria Nunez. My thanks also to entertainment lawyer Darren Trattner.

Laurie Prinz, thank you for talking through these chapters with me, for reading every single page and offering valuable suggestions, and for being such an all-around awesome human being. My gratitude to the sharp-eyed early readers who improved my first draft: Napheesa Collier, Rachel Baker, Jamie des Jardins, Dana Shell Smith, John Pekkanen, Lynn Pekkanen, Ben Pekkanen, Tammi Hogan, and Stephanie Hockersmith. And to the friends and family who buoyed me while I wrote it, especially Laura Hillenbrand, Amy and Chris Smith, Cathy Hines, Lucinda Eagle, and Robert and Saadia Pekkanen. My thanks also to Greer Hendricks for our many wonderful years of friendship and working on books together.

The very smart Suzy Wagner made several vital suggestions—including one that improved my final page. Alex Finlay, I cherish our authorly walks and talks and the way we cheer each other on. Kathy Nolan, my website and social media guru, you are a gem. And, as always, to Holly Bario at Amblin Partners, for being so wonderfully supportive through the years.

I acknowledge the excellent book *Still Alice* by Lisa Genova, which helped inform my research, and my friend Laurie Strongin, who provided valuable insight. To Politics and Prose in D.C., for being a terrific hometown bookstore, and to my favorite mayor, Jud Ashman, and his team at the Gaithersburg Book Festival.

On the home front, Roger Aarons read every single draft of *Gone Tonight*, pointed out my typos and helped me brainstorm twists, and loved and supported me in countless other ways while I wrote.

To my sons, Jackson, Will, and Dylan—thank you for being proud of what your mom does for a living. I'm even more proud of the creative, kind, and funny young men you've become.

And finally, to all the bookstagrammers, social media friends, librarians, booksellers, and readers—a high point of my day is interacting with you on Instagram and Facebook. I would so love to hear what you think about *Gone Tonight*. Please tag me and let me know!

Reading
Group
Gold

GONE TONIGHT
by Sarah Pekkanen

About the Author
• A Conversation with Sarah Pekkanen

Behind the Novel

Keep On Reading
• Recommended Reading
• Reading Group Questions

Also available as an audiobook
from Macmillan Audio

For more reading group suggestions
visit www.readinggroupgold.com.

🦁 ST. MARTIN'S GRIFFIN

A
Reading
Group Gold
Selection

A Conversation with Sarah Pekkanen

What was the inspiration for this novel?

Although my plot sprang solely from my imagination, the best elements of Ruth's character are inspired by my grandmother, who was forced to drop out of high school to help support her family. Like Ruth, she worked as a waitress all her life. When she gave birth to my father and was told he had a hole in his heart and wouldn't live into his twenties, my grandmother's whole purpose became to save him. She single-handedly channeled her intelligence and drive into locating a surgeon and convincing him to take a chance on my father by performing one of the first open-heart surgeries in this country in 1961. My father is still alive today at eighty-three years old. When it comes to protecting children, women are warriors.

How did you become a writer?

Writing is all I've ever wanted to do, and it's hard for me to imagine being anything else. I don't feel fully myself unless I'm immersed in a manuscript, crafting an alternate world. Writing has been there for me since childhood, and I've leaned into it during the roughest times in my life. I'm not sure who I would be without it. As a kid, I'd mail off manuscripts to top publishers in New York and breathlessly await a reply. A few years back, I opened one of my old Nancy Drew books and discovered a letter I'd written on Raggedy Ann stationery to a publisher, asking when the masterpiece entitled *Miscellaneous Tales and Poems* would be hitting bookstores. Another time I wrote a book called *The Lost Gold* on three-ring binder paper and bound it by weaving red knitting yarn through the holes. It was a Nancy Drew–style mystery, complete with my illustrations.

I sometimes wonder if writing is hardwired into
my DNA. My grandma was absolutely ruthless in
games of Scrabble, and she enjoyed reading, and
I've wondered if she secretly wanted to be a writer.
My father also knew very early on that he was a
writer, and he became a nonfiction medical writer.
As for me, I worked as a newspaper journalist
and magazine writer before I finally gathered my
courage and chased my dream of writing novels.

Would you care to share any writing tips?

To become a writer, all you need is the same
toolbox that's open to anyone, consisting of
twenty-six letters and a blank page. As for tips,
my bedrock rule is consistency: I rarely skip a day
of writing. My personal theory is that learning to
write is like learning a foreign language: It takes a
while to gain fluency. It helps to immerse myself
into the landscape. So when I'm not writing or
reading, I often listen to podcasts and read books
about the craft of writing. I try to share some of
the knowledge I've gained on my Instagram page.
Here's another deceptively simple-sounding tip: If
you write one page a day, you'll have a draft of a
book in a year.

*Can you tell us about what research, if any, you did
before writing this novel? Do you have firsthand
experience with its subject? What is the most
interesting or surprising thing you learned as you
set out to tell your story?*

I spent a fair amount of time researching
Alzheimer's disease, interviewing people whose
parents were afflicted with it, and learning some of
the basics of how the disease strikes. I also highly

recommend the excellent novel *Still Alice* by Lisa Genova for a view into what patients experience. For sections of *Gone Tonight*, I also researched everything from when cameras first became common in gas stations to what year Target stores began opening. I did take a few liberties in my flashback sections that described a Target, since most of the stores didn't sell a lot of food back then—but luckily, I write fiction, so those liberties are permissible. One of the big surprises that came about through my research was how many people go missing every year in the US. I was shocked to learn it is close to 600,000—though most people are found quickly.

Are you currently working on another book? And if so, can you tell us what it's about?

Yes, I'm excited to say I'm writing another thriller for St. Martin's Press that will be published in 2024. It's about a woman with a fascinating—and highly unusual—job, whose life is completely upended when she begins working with a child who witnessed a murder.

Behind the Novel

The spark of the idea for *Gone Tonight* came from a woman I never knew very well: my grandmother.

Like Ruth, my grandmother had to drop out of high school and work as a waitress her entire life. She flew under the radar. The one thing that defined my grandma was this: She would do anything at all to protect her children. Just like Ruth.

In *Gone Tonight*, Ruth has created a fortress around herself and her daughter, Catherine, that no one can penetrate. She insists they move frequently. She has a tracking app on Catherine's phone. But now, Catherine is twenty-four and is finally ready to fly the nest and begin a life that isn't intertwined with her mother's.

From Catherine's point of view, there have always been things about her mother that don't add up. Ruth is cagey about her past, and she refuses to tell Catherine anything about her family or Catherine's biological father. So Catherine decides to find out for herself.

Catherine and Ruth alternate between cat and mouse. They are compressed in a small apartment with thin walls, both wary of what the other knows—and what the other is capable of. Their relationship is threaded through not just with love, but with secrecy and suspicion and the danger that's drawing closer to engulfing them.

This book utterly consumed me during the four months it flew out of my fingertips onto the page. At night I would dream I was inside scenes of the novel, talking to Ruth and Catherine. Every morning, I couldn't wait to run to my keyboard to write. I hope you love reading it as much as I loved writing it.

Sincerely,
Sarah Pekkanen

Behind the Novel

📖 Recommended Reading

Romantic Comedy by Curtis Sittenfeld
Thrillers are my usual go-to when I read for
pleasure, but I also love to switch up my genres
sometimes, and Curtis Sittenfeld is always a sure
bet. This smart, laugh-out-loud story is about Sally,
a comedy writer for a *Saturday Night Live*–style
show who has sworn off love—until she meets
a hunky, charming pop star. But while funny,
average-looking men are often linked to gorgeous
female stars, can the reverse be true? Sally doesn't
think so. Finding out whether she's right makes for
an emotionally insightful ride.

Bright Young Women by Jessica Knoll
This is such an important book, and not just
because of the powerful storytelling. Knoll flips an
old, established narrative on its head by focusing
on the stories of the victims of a real-life famous
serial killer rather than the murderer (who she
never names in the book). A riveting read.

The Push by Ashley Audrain
This utterly consuming novel weaves together
themes of generational trauma and motherhood.
When Blythe gives birth to a child she can't
emotionally connect with, she doubts herself. But
she also fears her daughter may harbor something
dark and chilling. The last few lines of this novel
rocked me to my core.

Lessons in Chemistry by Bonnie Garmus
If you haven't read this gem yet, what are you
waiting for? Sure, you can catch the television
version starring Brie Larson, but don't let that
keep you from opening this novel, too. Set in the
1960s, it centers around a brilliant woman named

Elizabeth Zott who finds herself the unlikely star of a cooking show. But this is no typical cooking show. The proverbial icing on the cake? This book features an awesome dog, too.

***Friends, Lovers, and the Big Terrible Thing* by Matthew Perry**
He gave us the gift of laughter, even when he was in pain. And, shortly before he died, he gave us his story, writing unflinchingly about his struggles with substance abuse. I've long been a fan of the show *Friends*, and while reading Perry's autobiography, I grew to respect and appreciate him not just as an actor but as a person.

***The Poet* by Michael Connelly**
This was the first Connelly novel I ever read, and I became an instant fan. Recently, I reread it, and it held up beautifully. A journalist is mourning his brother, a police officer who seemingly committed suicide. Then he grows convinced there is more to the story. The author's background as a police reporter imbues his scenes with authenticity, and the twists are served up perfectly.

📖 *Reading Group Questions*

1. How did the multiple perspectives affect your reading of the story? How would the story be different if it were told from only one perspective?

2. What was the turning point in Ruth and Catherine's relationship? Why did you select this moment?

3. How did Ruth's flashbacks to her high school relationship with James enhance your reading experience? What did you learn about her that you might not have otherwise?

4. Do you support Ruth's decision to keep the truth from Catherine? Why or why not?

5. In chapter 30, Ruth says:

    I so loved my birth name, Ava Morales. It felt graceful and ethereal, like it could belong to a ballerina.
    Ruth Sterling sounded like a young woman who was Ava's opposite: a sturdy, stoic individual who worked hard and didn't complain. Those were qualities I desperately needed. I wanted to become Ruth Sterling in more ways than one.

    How did Ruth's identity change when she took on her new name? How does a name impact one's identity? Why do you think Timmy named his daughter after Ava?

6. In chapter 2, Ruth says, "I'm good at disappearing. We women do it all the time." What do you think this statement means? Explain how this statement is expressed throughout the novel.

7. A line Ruth writes to Catherine in the journal is, "I would do anything to keep you safe, Catherine, anything at all." How did that line make you feel? Were you surprised by how Catherine handled the situation with James? Why or why not?

8. The book explores the theme of keeping secrets from someone to protect them. What is a time in your life when you experienced this? Why did you feel like you had to keep that secret? Do you still feel the same way?

9. Did you expect the ending? What moment surprised you the most? Did you suspect that Ruth was more involved in Coach's death than she let on? What parts led you to your suspicion?

10. Explore the concept of family as portrayed in this novel. What defines family? How did Ruth's reunion with her family make you feel? How does it contribute to this novel's definition of family?

*Keep On
Reading*

Turn the page for a sneak peek at
Sarah Pekkanen's new novel

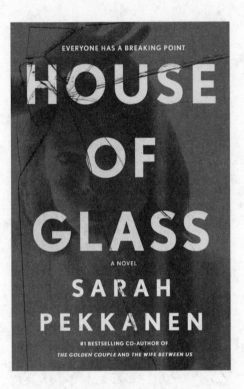

EVERYONE HAS A BREAKING POINT

HOUSE OF GLASS

A NOVEL

SARAH PEKKANEN

#1 BESTSELLING CO-AUTHOR OF
THE GOLDEN COUPLE AND *THE WIFE BETWEEN US*

Available Summer 2024

CHAPTER ONE

Tuesdays at 4:30 p.m. That's her routine.

I stand on a grimy square of sidewalk near the busy intersection of 16th and K Streets, scanning the approaching pedestrians.

My new client will arrive in seven minutes.

I don't even need to meet her today. All I have to do is visually assess her to see if I'll be able to work with her. The thought makes my shoulders curl forward, as if I'm instinctively forming a version of the fetal position.

I could refuse to take on this client. I could claim it's impossible for me to be neutral because the media frenzy surrounding the suspicious death of her family's nanny has already shaped my perceptions.

But that would mean lying to Charles, who is the closest thing I have to a father.

"You know I hate asking for favors, Stella," Charles said last week from across the booth in his favorite Italian restaurant. He unfolded his heavy white napkin with a flick of his wrist, the crisp snap punctuating his words.

Perhaps a reminder that in all the years I've known him, he has never asked me for a single one?

"I'm not sure if I can help her," I'd told Charles.

"You're the only one who can. She needs you to be her voice, Stella."

Saying no to the man who gave me my career, walked me down

the aisle, and has provided a shoulder during the dissolution of my marriage isn't an option. So here I wait.

My new client won't take any notice of me, a thirty-eight-year-old brunette in a black dress and knee-high boots, seemingly distracted by her phone, just like half the people in this power corridor of DC.

Two minutes until she's due to arrive.

As the weak October sun ducks behind a cloud, stealing the warmth from the air, a nasal-sounding horn blares behind me. I nearly jump out of my skin.

I whip around to glare at the driver, and when I refocus my attention, my client is rounding the corner a dozen yards away, her blue sweater buttoned up to her neck and her curly red hair spilling over her shoulders. Her expression is wooden.

She's tiny, even smaller than I expected. She appears to be closer to seven years old than nine.

Her mother—tall, brittle-looking, and carrying a purse that costs more than some cars—holds my client's hand as they approach their destination: a gray stone building with its address discreetly displayed on a brass plaque. Inside is the office of DC's top child psychiatrist.

In another few moments, they'll disappear through the doors and be swallowed up by the building.

She's just a kid, I remind myself. One who has been through more in the past month than some people endure in a lifetime.

I'm good at my job. Maybe the systems and strategies I've developed will carry me through. I can put a favor in Charles's bank for a change.

A few steps away from the entrance of her therapist's building, little Rose Barclay stops. She pulls her hand out of her mother's and points down to her shoe. Mrs. Barclay nods, busying herself by removing her oversized sunglasses and placing them in a case while Rose bends down.

I squint and crane my head forward.

People stream past Rose like water around a rock, but no one seems to notice what she's doing.

Rose isn't adjusting the buckle on her shiny black Mary Janes, as I'd assumed.

Her left hand is stretching out to the side. Seeking something.

I'm drawn forward. Closer to her.

It happens so quickly it's almost over before I realize what she has done. If my angle had been off—if I'd been watching from across the street or inside the building—I never would have noticed.

Rose straightens up, her left hand slipping into the pocket of her sweater as her right hand reaches up for her mother's.

The evidence is gone now, tucked away.

But I saw it. I know what this shy-looking girl collected off the sidewalk and concealed to keep.

A shard of broken glass, shaped like a dagger, its end tapering to an evil-looking point.

CHAPTER TWO

My first rule for meeting a new client: It's always on their turf.

Sometimes that means at a skateboard park, or in side-by-side chairs at a nail salon, or in their backyard while they throw a tennis ball for their golden retriever. Food is typically involved. My clients rarely want to confide in me early in the process, and eating pizza or nachos provides space for silence.

I never press hard during the first meeting. It's all about establishing trust.

By the time I see them, any trust my clients once held in adults has been shattered.

When divorce court judges are presented with the most brutal, complicated custody cases—ones in which no resolution seems possible— they appoint someone like me: a best interest attorney, or guardian ad litem. We represent the children.

My particular area of expertise is teenagers. I never take on clients younger than twelve. But Charles—or Judge Huxley, as he's more widely known—wants me to break that rule. One of his colleagues is the presiding judge on the Barclay case, and she is having trouble finding the right attorney for Rose.

I take a last glance up at the gray building Rose disappeared into only moments ago. She's in a safe space, being tended to by a highly trained professional. Her mother is present.

So who does the girl think she needs to protect herself from with a shard of glass that could double as a knife?

My Uber pulls up to the curb. "Stella?" the driver asks as I slide into the back seat, and I nod.

He turns up the radio, and an NPR reporter's modulated voice pours out of the speakers. I'm relieved the driver doesn't want to make conversation. I need to gather myself before reaching my next destination, another office building close to the National Cathedral. This appointment is a personal one.

I stare out the window as the driver winds his way north through clogged streets, muttering under his breath when he gets stuck behind an illegally parked Tesla.

My mind feels overly full, a dozen discordant thoughts buzzing through it. I reach for my phone to send a text to Marco, my soon-to-be ex-husband, then discard the idea. He knows I'm coming, and he won't be late. Like all the partners in his prestigious law firm, he parcels out his days in six-minute billing increments, which makes him acutely aware of time.

I step out of the Uber at the stroke of five o'clock, heading for a nondescript brick building that holds more than its share of heartbreak.

I bypass the elevator and climb the stairs to the fourth floor, then walk into the small reception area of suite 402. Marco is waiting, leaning back in a chair as he smiles at something on his phone.

The sight of him still takes my breath away. His Italian roots show in his glossy dark hair, tan skin, and eyes that turn to amber when the sun hits them. Our coloring is so similar we've been asked more than once if we're related.

"Just one of those old married couples who start to look alike," Marco used to joke.

He rises now, placing a hand on my shoulder as he leans in to brush a kiss across my cheek. I start to wrap my arms around him, but he pulls back before I can embrace him in a real hug.

We both speak at the same time, our words entwining instead of our bodies.

I aim for a joke: "Fancy meeting you here."

Marco pulls out a DC cliché: "How was traffic?"

He gestures to the coffee table where two sets of documents topped by identical blue pens await. "Lakshmi already brought out the paper-work."

I blink hard. This is happening fast. "So all we have to do is sign?"

He nods and hands me one of the slim stacks of paper.

Unlike the divorces I encounter through work, the one Marco and I are going through is as amicable as it gets. Our biggest disagreement came when Marco insisted on giving me the little row house we'd bought together near the DC line. We both know why: He makes twenty times as much as I do now. I accepted the house. But I insisted he take our fancy espresso maker. It was a bigger sacrifice than it sounds; I love a good cup of coffee.

I hesitate, then scrawl my name across the bottom of the final page of our divorce agreement. When I look up, Marco is recapping his pen.

Lakshmi steps into the waiting room. "Hey, Stella. You guys all set?"

I nod, my eyes skittering away from her sympathetic ones. This is the final step in the dissolution of our marriage. After Lakshmi files the papers, I'll get a letter in the mail notifying me our uncontested divorce has been granted.

My gaze roams across the box of tissues on the coffee table. Next to it is a sculpture of an eagle in flight, its wings outstretched. I recognize the symbolism: tissues for grief at an ending, the bird an image of hope for the future.

Marco and I wed on a crystalline winter day nearly ten years ago, just as the first snow of the season began to fall. Even before I said the vows I meant with my whole heart, I knew we'd end up here.

It was only a question of when.

ABOUT THE AUTHOR

Kristina Sherk

Sarah Pekkanen is the number-one *New York Times* bestselling coauthor of four novels of suspense, including *The Golden Couple,* and the solo author of the thrillers *Gone Tonight* and *House of Glass.* She is also the solo author of eight international bestselling women's fiction books and is an award-winning former journalist. She serves as US ambassador for RRSA India and works hands-on in India to rescue street dogs. She lives just outside of Washington, DC, with her family.